I

As soon as Romany opened the door, she knew she wasn't alone. Someone waited for her. Somewhere in the apartment.

She had never carried a gun. There had never been a need. Except that one time . . . Now, she allowed her eyes to become adjusted to the gloom, and easing herself against the wall, moved to the edge of the living room. She searched the shadows. Nothing. She crouched lower and inched closer to the door opening into her bedroom.

Whoever was in the apartment had switched on the ceiling fan and the small lamp that sat on a dressing table in the adjoining bath. The soft light cast the room in semidarkness, and she could make out the large solid shape of a man. He reclined easily upon her bed, a marshmallowy heap of pillows propped against his back. He hadn't bothered to draw back the covers, and he lay on top of the spread completely naked.

She should have run, gotten out of her apartment as quickly as possible. Except she recognized the hard muscles under the deeply tanned skin, the black curling hair, the famous smirk that passed for a smile. Recognized the man who was a cold-blooded killer—and her lover . . .

SACRED LIES

"Literately written, a pleasure . . . exciting reading at its best."
—*Baton Rouge Advocate*

Bantam Books by
Dianne Edouard and Sandra Ware

MORTAL SINS
SACRED LIES

SACRED LIES

*Dianne Edouard
& Sandra Ware*

BANTAM BOOKS
NEW YORK · TORONTO · LONDON
SYDNEY · AUCKLAND

SACRED LIES

A Bantam Book / June 1993

PUBLISHING HISTORY
Doubleday edition published / February 1993

All rights reserved.
Copyright © 1993 by Bluestocking, Inc.
Cover art copyright © 1993 by Alan Ayers.
Library of Congress Catalog Card Number: 92-24607.

ISBN 0-553-29063-0

Published simultaneously in the United States and Canada

Bantam Books are published by Bantam Books, a division of Bantam
Doubleday Dell Publishing Group, Inc. Its trademark, consisting of the
words "Bantam Books" and the portrayal of a rooster, is Registered in
U.S. Patent and Trademark Office and in other countries. Marca Regis-
trada. Bantam Books, 1540 Broadway, New York, New York 10036.

For our parents:
Edward and Mary,
Harold and Annabelle

SACRED LIES

JUDEAN DESERT, 1072

Allah had sent the storm. Had made the winds to blow hot and thick and sharp, so that Abu's eyes oozed water and his mouth and throat became caked with sand and felt like the dried bottom of an emptied bowl. If he were older and wiser, he might have pulled down the hood of his robe, wrapped a swathe of white cotton over his nostrils and mouth, and hidden in a cave without complaint or wonder. Age brought consolations, one of which was surely a peaceful resignation to the will of Allah.

But he was yet a young man even by the harsh standards of Bedouin life, and Abu questioned Allah's wisdom in sending the storm. It was spring, when the weather should have been kinder, as kind as ever the weather turned in the desolation that was the Judean desert.

The shepherd bit hard on his lip and twisted his dark brows into a scowl. The ways of Allah were unknowable and simply had to be borne. This was how the universe worked. He had been made to understand that from the beginning. It was the single thread that tied together the tiny beads of his narrow, circumscribed life.

Abu lowered the cotton batting from his handsome, tanned thirteen-year-old face and spit into the grit of the desert. At once he prayed for deliverance. Deliverance from the storm, and deliverance from Allah's judgment that was certain to punish him for his pitiful lack

1

of faith. He looked about, straining to see through the whirling sand that plucked at his exposed face like the wicked beak of a vulture.

The goats were scattered. Of that he had little doubt. Unless Boulos had managed to gather some of them before the winds had grown too strong. Perhaps even now his companion waited with the anxious little flock inside one of the caves. Boulos was smart and knew the desert like the features of his own face. But the goats, the hairy black devils that they were, were a stubborn lot, and not easy to handle once they became frightened. All could be lost, Abu lamented, wondering what it was they had done to bring this calamity down upon their heads. Then his heart stopped, crushed by the weight of his monumental sin. For today had not been the first time Abu the shepherd had taken it upon himself to question the will of Allah.

The goat kicked its spindly limbs into Abu's stomach, causing a sharp pain to run its hot fingers all the way up the column of his spine. He tugged tighter around the beast's neck, his hands struggling to pin the four legs into one manageable knot. He would have to find a place for them. He had not Boulos's instincts for navigation or geography, but he knew that the great wasteland stretched westward far beyond to the bosom of Jehoshaphet in the Valley of the Kidron, almost to the foot of Jerusalem itself. The Dead Sea was just below, the mountains of Moab in the distance to the east. And everywhere, cut deep into the limestone cliffs, like marks upon a papyrus, were the caves.

For centuries his people had used the caves, as had the Jewish monks who had once walked among the chalky white hills. But the holy men were long gone, driven away for a thousand years by the soldiers. He was all alone now, alone in the storm with a small kid pressed against his belly, fighting him and the stinging merciless sand. Yet he knew he was not stupid, that he was strong and agile and tireless. If he kept his head down, breathed not too deeply, he could with Allah's help find shelter in one of the caves.

He plodded through the pitting sand, dreaming that he was elsewhere, that he was with Boulos near a cool wadi eating goat's cheese, watching the heat quiver above the land, tending the herd as it grazed upon the soft downy carpet of green grasses that came but once a year in the spring. But his dreams were useless, and worse, they were dangerous. Dangerous because they made him wish for what was not to be, made him lose sight of what he must do if he were to save himself.

He could barely see it at first, but Abu finally made out the single dark eye of an opening inside one of the cliffs. Just a few more paces, he whispered words of encouragement to the young goat, cooing the soft Arabic behind the gauzy pleats of his mask. And then he was there. At the mouth of a wide fissure, running it seemed for miles through the limestone shelf.

Abu set the animal down, unwrapping himself like a mummy come back to life. He arched backward and breathed deeply of the cooler air inside the cave. He had made it. He was not going to die. He bent down and ran his rough clay-colored hand across the goat's back. The small animal turned at his master's touch and cast its soft brown eyes up at him, a glance so purely full of thanksgiving that for an instant Abu wanted to weep.

Abu squatted, drawing his caftan up around his bare legs, spreading his wide burnoose out behind him. He could yet hear the shrieking voice of the storm just beyond. As always, that sound was for him a remembrance, a memory of the cries of the black-robed old women who'd descended like buzzards to make mourning for his father the day he'd died. He had grown up on that sound, that awful wailing that held nothing in it of hope or promise.

He closed his eyes, eyes that were darker than the ripest olives his sisters set out in bowls, and sighed inside himself. He was becoming a man, and certain things were expected of a man. Losing a prized herd of goats was not one of them. But he could not control the weather. That was Allah's province. And thus without realizing it, Abu had come full circle, come back to where he'd begun, back to blaming Allah for his misfortune.

Then a noise, nearer, clearer than the voice that raged outside the cave. Abu opened his eyes. The foolish goat had become restless in its confinement and had climbed upon a small ledge, disturbing a nest of rocks that seemed to have been set by some design against the far wall.

Abu moved closer, lifting the animal from its perch. Strange he hadn't noticed the symmetry of the stones before. His hand reached up and dislodged one of the rocks. Small pebbles rumbled softly and fell in a tiny heap at his feet. A puff of chalk made him cough.

He stepped back, turning his head to one side, examining the wall. The whole of the structure was a fastidious work, each stone wedged and wedded to another. He moved forward and lifted another rock. Then another and another after that. Several fell easily without his intervention. Soon Abu had cleared a fairly large portion out of the wall, and he bent over and peered into the dark hole.

It was some moments before his eyes adjusted to the gloom, and a watery illumination from outside found its way into the clearing he'd made. Yet even as the stream of light seeped slowly into the darkness, Abu refused at first to believe what his eyes beheld, refused to acknowledge what lay upon the smooth limestone shelf.

Why at that moment he did not feel fear, Abu would never understand. But his heart grew suddenly quiet, and a kind of peace settled like wings upon him as he beheld the wonder behind the wall, its delicate web of fingers clasping an earthen jar, its face now no more than a small naked skull. Yet it seemed that even in death that ancient fleshless face favored Abu with the sweetest, the most gentle of smiles.

CHAPTER 1

She had been a child of mystery. A self-created little girl nurtured by her own fantasies and the deliciousness of her father's imagination.

It had always been a game with her, this discovery of self. Never quite knowing who Romany Chase would be on any given day. She'd wrap herself in sheets and slither around like an exotic Hindu, or anchor flowers in her curling dark auburn hair so that she'd become Guinevere "a-Maying." A Guinevere who knew Arthur and Lancelot as brothers, and so had happily managed to keep the both of them content.

Most often she would slink around the corners of her home, her bright gray-green eyes alert, trying to glimpse the evil assassin who lurked menacingly in the shadows. She loved the warm flutter of butterflies inside her stomach, the icy fingers gripping round her heart. In any moment she might be caught and tortured and forced to tell.

Sometimes Papa would say, "Okay, Romany, today you are the Empress of China, and inside a peach you discover an emerald of rare beauty. . . ." She loved these times best of all, when her wonderful father would draw the magic out of her.

Yet despite all of the joy of make-believing, there was in Romany that which had always said there was a real mystery at the heart of her peaceful and easy existence, a mystery about which her young and innocent life was wound.

Romany Chase confronted a mystery now as she shifted her feet on the hard marble floor. She stood inside the Pinacoteca, the Vatican Museum gallery of paintings, the muffled sounds of voices and shuffling shoes registering somewhere in her subconscious. But she was oblivious to it all, as her eyes were riveted to a single canvas—Caravaggio's *The Deposition*.

She was remembering the description in a textbook she had written several years ago. *Absorbed with the dramatic potential of light, the artist presents us with a composition that is at the same time both classically theatrical and starkly naturalistic.* The words were true enough. But they were only words. They conveyed nothing of what had always been her private response to this painting. Her favorite Caravaggio.

She studied the familiar figures on the canvas in front of her now—the three Marys hovering like protective graces as John and Nicodemus prepared to lower the moonlit body of Christ into the absolute blackness of the grave. There was something in the staging, the cascading of those six heads, a frozen but liquid movement that had always suggested to her the arrangement of scored notes, as if the painting itself possessed an inherent music.

Masterpiece was a word much overused, but the term was correctly applied to *The Deposition*. She stepped forward, getting as close to the canvas as her role as a tourist would allow. Composition, brush stroke, the complex mastery of dark and light—it was all still there. And not. Her eyes closed on the certainty of sadness beneath her anger. The painting in front of her was worthless. The masterpiece was a fake.

CHAPTER 2

It was only twelve-forty, Romany noted, checking her watch against the centuries-old clock tower that stood in the nearby piazza. Still a good twenty minutes before Elliot would arrive for their lunch date. Twenty minutes more to pretend that life was simple.

The umbrellas sprouting from the café tables stood unfurled against the flat blue sky—bright stripes swirling about their central poles like the colors in a peppermint. She leaned back deliberately in the little bistro chair and listened to the music of the fountain, to the cooing of the strutting pigeons, like the soft lazy cadences of noontime Italian. It was wonderful being in Rome again. ·

She'd allowed more time than was necessary for the walk from her apartment, and the trattoria had seemed all but deserted when she'd arrived, one o'clock being the earliest that most of the city's restaurants began serving lunch. But an apple-cheeked cameriere with the thick black hair of a Genoese had come out and accepted her order of a mineral water while she waited. Romany poured out the last of it now, squeezing the thick circle of lime against the rim of her glass. A citrusy fizz tickled her nose as she raised the drink, and she smiled.

Several tables away the trattoria's only other customer smiled back, a young man in black pants and long-sleeved white shirt—the unofficial uniform of the Roman male on the prowl. Unbuttoned almost to his waist with his cuffs rolled casually back, he sat with a cup of coffee and the remains of a late breakfast. Even from this distance she could see the calculation in the liquid brown eyes, sense him sizing her up as some rich American tourist. Her smile turned inward. Sorry, Mario, but she wasn't what she seemed.

She finished her drink and reached for the shoulder bag that rested on the chair beside her. Shopping was always her response to too much second-guessing, and yesterday afternoon she'd hit the Via Condotti with a vengeance. The Falchi, a huge butter-soft pouch large enough for all the junk she toted, was her latest acquisition. She fished around in its cluttered interior and, finding her cosmetics bag, she tossed back her hair and began to reapply her lipstick. The gesture was entirely innocent, but the forgotten Italian had taken it as a deliberate provocation. From the corner of her eye she sensed him rising and turned on him with her *look*.

She didn't know exactly what the particular arrangement of muscles did to her face. She'd never tried it out on a mirror. But whatever it did, it always worked. The Italian, only halfway out of his chair, stopped dead in midair. And sat down.

"Romany."

She flipped the lipstick back into her purse and turned smiling toward the familiar voice. "Hi, boss."

Elliot Peters, the Director of the Arte per Pace International Exhibit was standing next to her table looking three weeks tanner than when she'd seen him last in New York. Elliot was roughly the same age as her father, and moved in most of the same Washington circles as her parents. He had known her since her early childhood, and over the years had somehow managed the trick of an almost fatherly concern that wasn't in the least bit patronizing.

"Sorry I couldn't meet you at the airport Sunday." He bent to give her a light kiss before he sat down.

"No problem," she said. "I remember my way around." Then, still smiling across at him, she tilted her head to take in the blazing sun, the umbrellas, the splash of the nearby fountain. "It's great being in Rome again, Elliot."

"And the apartment?"

"Even better than you made it sound. I love it."

"I'm glad, Romany. The big shots in New York expect me to keep everybody happy here in Rome, but especially their Acquisitions Coordinator. You're the one they're paying to juggle the pride and tender feelings of all the countries who've signed on for this three-ring circus. Sweetness and light are part of your job description."

She laughed. Elliot's gentle cynicism served him well, trapped as he was at the top of the administrative ladder, smack dab in the center of the inevitable tug-of-war among Arte per Pace's three major players. A consortium of five big U.S. corporate sponsors. An international board of directors headquartered in New York. And here in Rome, the Vatican.

The clock in the piazza chimed one, and the tables began to fill as waiters in white ankle-length aprons launched themselves from the kitchen.

"So when do you want me to come in?" she asked when their drinks had been brought to the table.

Elliot glanced up from his menu to look owlishly at her over the rims of his reading glasses. "Monday's soon enough for the office," he said. "I do have something set up for you tomorrow afternoon, though."

"Oh?"

"Two-thirty at the Vatican. Nothing formal. Just a short meeting to let you get acquainted with the papal liaison over there. A Father Julian Morrow."

Morrow? It wasn't the name she'd expected. "Morrow?" she said it aloud. "I thought I was going to be working with the Vatican Curator."

"Monsignor Brisi. So did I. But the Pope surprised us all. Got himself a Jesuit. An American who speaks half a dozen languages. Almost as many as you."

She smiled, picking up her menu.

"The exhibit was up to twenty-six countries at last count," Elliot went on. "How many languages *do* you speak, Romany?"

"Not twenty-six, Elliot . . . but enough."

"Enough? Don't go modest on me, Ms. Chase. On you it's not becoming."

It was Elliot's kind of compliment. "It's all in the genes. A gift," she said, "from Dad."

"How is Theodor? And your mother?"

"Mother's okay, I think, except that her leg is giving her a little more trouble than usual. Dad's fine. Says he's planning on flying over here sometime next month. Supposedly it's research for a new book. I think he's coming for the food."

"The food, huh? That sounds like a hint." Elliot's eyes were back on the menu. "What do you say we share an antipasto? . . . And I think I'll have the *abbachio al' cacciatore.*"

"The lamb sounds good to me too, as long as I can have raspberries for dessert."

"Done." Elliot motioned to the waiter and placed their order. Their wine came and a basket of hot baked bread.

"So what have you been doing with yourself these last few days, Ms. Chase?"

"Shopping . . ." She broke off a piece of bread from the loaf, the crust crumbling tiny brown flakes onto the cloth as she buttered it. ". . . eating."

"What, no museums?" Elliot was watching her crookedly. "Or would that have been too much like the busman's holiday?"

Her hesitation was brief. "Actually I did go to the Vatican Museum yesterday. It's changed a bit since I was there." She put the bread down, uneaten, on her plate. ". . . I was wondering, Elliot, since His Holiness is playing host to this whole show, has it already been decided what pieces the Vatican itself is going to put in the exhibit?"

"No, but I was hoping you could bring that up to-morrow at your meeting with Father Morrow."

"This Father Morrow—what's he like?" she asked.

"I don't know. I've been dealing with one of the Pope's secretaries these last three weeks. Morrow's appointment is brand new. Actually I should go with you and meet him, but I'm hung up at least through the end of the week with the architects."

Romany nodded, breathing an inward sigh. Tomorrow the game would begin. A deadly earnest game with winners and losers. And rules.

And now there was this last-minute change in the roster. Julian Morrow wearing Umberto Brisi's number. Somehow they had all gotten the wrong information, let Pope Gregory throw them a curve. Surely there were adjustments being made in Washington, but that didn't help her now.

She wished Sully were already in Rome. This was only Thursday, and she knew he wasn't due in till late on Sunday. In the meantime she would just have to wing it. Trust her instincts and try to get a line on this Jesuit who seemed to be a mystery to everyone.

The antipasto arrived, huge and perfectly presented. But the mood was gone in spite of the wine, and the fountain sang less brightly. She picked up a tight little roll of spicy prosciutto and popped it into her mouth. She'd play hell saving room for the raspberries.

He was a murderer, a liar, and a thief. Yet measured against the primary evidence of the man's official identity, these descriptions were essentially inconsequential. He was Cardinal Bishop Vittorio Marchese DeLario, a Prince of the Holy Roman Catholic Church. And for anyone with the slightest interest in human nature, it might have been an extremely arresting argument, debating whether the man had fashioned the priest, or the priest had fashioned the man.

Vittorio smoothed back imaginary wisps of his still surprisingly dark hair from his high forehead. It was a habit he'd acquired during his early days in the seminary, and one he'd never felt the need to justify. Any more than his habit of tidying the scarlet sash that spanned his now spreading girth, or toying with the heavy Byzantine cross that hung around his neck. These last affectations had come much later, but were as characteristic of Vittorio as the inevitable fussing with his hair.

Short and bluntly muscular with a flamboyance of movement more practiced than natural, Vittorio had never been considered a handsome man. In his mideighties he still resembled a della Robbia cherub. Rosy-cheeked with plump rosebud lips, the Cardinal could have almost been accused of unabashed cuteness, had it not been for a single remarkable feature—his dark and flirting eyes. Eyes keen, it seemed, with something more akin to perception than intelligence.

He had grown almost fat these last years, attributable to his love of *la dolce vita*. But his mind was still spartan. Razor-thin, sharp. And as life would have it, he had grown more comfortable with himself as time passed, openly acknowledging his middle-class roots, his aristocratic bent, and with great good humor, hands and feet that more nearly resembled those of an Italian peasant.

Though some adored His Eminence, his congenial ways, his insinuating childlike charm, it was surely the case that most feared Vittorio DeLario. And that was most gratifying of all. For it had been fear that had allowed the Cardinal to succeed over these many years, would yet permit him to accomplish whatever remained in such time as God, or more likely the Devil, granted him.

And Vittorio had been remarkably successful, had gained everything he'd set his mark upon. Every thing save one. The ring of Peter had exceeded his grasp. He had, he supposed, come to terms with never having been elected Pope. It was an old wound, and one that he was less likely to nurse these days. After all, his meteoric rise from priest to Prince of the Church, and his subsequent service as Papal Secretary of State to three popes, added a fine patina to his mounting years. His Eminence Cardinal Vittorio DeLario was still one of the most powerful men in the Vatican.

And none of this even included his most daring adventure. An adventure for which he had most especially his long-dead friend, Eugenio Pacelli, to thank. Vittorio could still hear, even after all these years, Pius XII's frail voice as the two of them had walked the Vatican grounds, not even the gardeners permitted about. They'd spoken in German during those private times, safe from other Italian ears.

From the first it had been their mutual love of Germany that had brought them together. A Germany that had nothing to do with Hitler, or with the Third Reich. And though the war years produced particular anguish for Pius XII, they were to prove for Vittorio DeLario an unexpectedly fertile time, a time when seeds of incomprehensible proportion were sown.

Vittorio smiled now, thinking of the past. Thinking too that retirement had come as a kind of liberation. Freeing him to pursue the greatest passion of his life, to continue on that path upon which Pius XII had unwittingly set his foot.

It had not been difficult ten years ago, upon his seventy-fifth birthday, convincing his old friend Niccolo Fratelli, Pope Gregory XVII, not to turn him completely out to pasture. Not to let him wither away like so many of the old cardinals who walked the marble halls of the Palatine, stumbling about in their long red robes, mumbling prayers or, more likely, bitter curses. No, dear simple Niccolo had said he understood, understood Vittorio's need yet to serve, serve in some small way.

So the Pope of the Holy Roman Catholic Church had given him his way. Not that there had ever been any doubt. The tiny bumbling man still deferred to his former Secretary of State, the cardinal who'd delivered the votes that had put him over the top, won for him the chair of St. Peter. Well, deferred until recently. Because lately Vittorio had begun to wonder if perhaps Gregory was not without his own will after all.

Still, Gregory's little retirement gift had been precisely what he wanted—absolute control of the Vatican museums and archives. Almost immediately he'd made himself a kind of ex officio prefect and began a process of centralization and desecularization of the two institutions. Weeding out members of the old regime, systematically replacing them with men he could trust, he eventually appointed Monsignor Umberto Brisi Director General and Chief Curator.

Of course the transition had not been without its headaches. Director General Francesco Scotti in particular had proved troublesome. And though murder might have been considered a bit extreme, there was no doubt in Vittorio's mind that what he'd done was entirely in keeping with the spirit of the very hierarchy he served.

He pulled now on the heavy chain about his neck, then patted down his hair. He had been only half listening to Monsignor Brisi for the last twenty minutes. The priest had raised his voice, which had finally jarred him out of his reverie. The Curator really did have an ungovernable Italian temper. Yet taking everything into consideration, Brisi had been the best he'd been able to do. And Vittorio was inclined to forgive the monsignor all his shortcomings, intrigued as he was by the priest's performances.

He watched now as Brisi drove his arms up in exasperation, then as quickly let them fall to his sides in a kind of elegant futility. Then the monsignor shook his head, tossing about his curling black hair. And for an instant Vittorio imagined that what passed across the straight uncompromising mouth was a smile. But the handsome face went blank, except for the very dark brown eyes, which shifted slightly, taking in their audience. The priest had asked him another question.

"*Scusi*, Umberto, my mind wanders. Forgive an old man, what was it you asked?"

Brisi waited a few seconds before repeating the question. The man had such a wonderful flair for drama.

"This Jesuit, this stupid American, is he not going to be a problem for us, Vittorio?"

"Umberto, you must learn to calm yourself. If one is to reach great heights in the Church, one's ambition must be as a Trojan horse."

Brisi's tanned skin blanched and the cords of muscle in his long neck constricted. His mouth opened as though he were going to say something, but in an instant his jaws snapped closed.

"Umberto, Umberto." The Cardinal walked up to the priest and placed one of his hands on his shoulder. "I too am distressed that it is not you who will represent the Vatican to Arte per Pace. Surely you must know that I was surprised by His Holiness's appointment of Father Morrow."

Brisi had turned his head so that his eyes watched him like a specimen. The monsignor moved out from under his hand.

"But I was the logical choice, Vittorio. I do not understand any of this. First Arte per Pace, now this Jesuit. What is Gregory up to?"

"My dear Umberto, can you not see that our Holy Father has at last begun to worry what it is that history will say of him? Arte per Pace is his big chance to play the grand and glorious role of peacemaker. And as for this little matter of Julian Morrow, it is but Gregory's way of proving to the world that the Italians aren't going to run the whole show."

"This little matter of Julian Morrow!" Brisi exploded. "If I do not understand His Holiness, I understand you less, Vittorio. I do not see how you can take this whole matter so lightly."

This time it was his turn at high drama, and he paused a long moment before offering the young monsignor his most adorable smile. "I assure you, Umberto, I do not take the matter lightly. But are you of so little faith that you refuse to believe that I can handle a single American priest?"

Brisi continued to watch him. The anger in his eyes

seemed less certain now, yet his answer was another question.

"But what about the Caravaggio, Vittorio? Is it not showing our balls off a bit too much in letting them have it for the exhibit?"

He laughed. "Monsignore Brisi, I did not get where I am today because I was afraid of showing off my balls."

CHAPTER 3

No one knew how many rooms there were in the Apostolic Palace, and Romany felt much like Alice going down the rabbit hole. It was a labyrinth of halls and chambers, corridors and passages. Narrow vacant stairways that led to God only knew where.

She had entered St. Peter's on the north side, via the service entrance through St. Anne's gate, and had at last managed to arrive by some miracle precisely where she was supposed to be. Following now in the silent wake of a diminutive nun, dressed in a habit the color of which could only be described as Virgin Mary white.

A sudden sharp turn, and through a half-opened door she spied a wedge of vaulted loggia overlooking a fragment of green garden. Hastily the nun reached out and closed the door. "The wind," she mumbled in Italian without looking up, then her tiny feet in the chalky polished shoes of a nurse were moving again.

That Romany was regarded as a kind of pesky interloper to be suspiciously though politely tolerated was obvious. She had the distinct feeling that everyone in the Vatican had something to hide, and that anyone outside the establishment somehow posed a very real threat. It was all a curious mixture of condescension and paranoia.

The little sister turned to see now if she was still

following, and Romany started to speak but forced a
smile instead. She watched the nun glance quickly down
the length of her short skirt to the shiny toes of her
spiked heels. It was a kind of cursory assessment and
obviously she hadn't passed muster.

Perhaps it was just the time of day that was to blame
for this double dose of Vatican sanctimoniousness. No
sane Roman was up and about from two to four in the
afternoon. But then, she wasn't a Roman. She was a
stupid American, invading the sanctum sanctorum of
the Apostolic Palace at two-thirty in the afternoon.
Which of course didn't say much for the other crazy
American who'd scheduled the appointment in the first
place. And that led her back to where she'd been since
her meeting with Elliot—trying to get a handle on who
Father Julian Morrow was.

Jesuit priest. *That* should tell her something. But it
didn't really.

Gregory's personal liaison to Arte per Pace. Now
that was a real bone to chew. Not the Vatican's representative, or a papal representative. But Pope Gregory's
handpicked boy. And that was strange indeed, that Pope
Gregory had sprung Julian Morrow on all of them, like
a rabbit out of a hat. For in spite of his recent stab at
political assertiveness, it was still a most extraordinary
tack for a pope viewed almost universally as something
of a weak sister. And a pope reduced by her own
sources to little more than a pawn in the game afoot,
the instrument of one particular Roman cardinal.

Was that it? That despite appearances, Morrow was
really Cardinal DeLario's choice? That would certainly
make more sense, considering everything they suspected
about His Eminence, the Cardinal. But why not appoint
Brisi? Or someone else from inside the Vatican ranks?
An outsider wouldn't seem to fit the bill. Unless Morrow wasn't an outsider?

Of course, it could all be as simple as what Elliot had
said—Morrow was selected because he was an American fluent in half a dozen languages. But that seemed a

little lame. So what was the deal with the Jesuit? She
didn't think he could have any sort of credentials in art;
she would probably have heard if he had. Maybe he was
just a good politician. God knew, being able to kiss ass
while saving face was an asset of incalculable proportions.

The sister finally halted, opening a pair of impressive
double doors. "Father Julian," she said, as though she
were introducing the priest himself.

For a moment Romany just stood there, looking
around the large reception room, gawking at all the
gilded excess. Who could possibly feel comfortable in
such a place? she wondered.

"He is not here." It was sister speaking again. "He is
away. I was told to tell you to make yourself comfortable, please." Then there was what passed for a kind of
bow, and the nun swept shut the double doors, leaving
her standing alone in the middle of the room.

He is not here. He is away. What in the hell did that
mean? They had a two-thirty appointment, didn't they?
She fumbled inside her purse and found Elliot's memo.
Father Julian Morrow. 2:30 Friday. She checked her
watch. Two-fifty. Well, you're off to a grand start, Father
Morrow. And a fine time to tell me, Sister. What's *your*
little game? Why in the hell did you wait until you
brought me all the way up . . . And what in the hell
did you bring me up to? She had no idea how clerics
inside the Vatican lived. But she had imagined something a little more in keeping with the vow of poverty.

Didn't this guy have an office of some kind? She
knew he could have space over at the Arte per Pace
building if he wanted it. And what was this invitation to
make herself comfortable? Certainly not the good sister's sentiments. She looked down at her straight skirt.
So what if it was a good two inches above her knees? It
wasn't as though she were meeting the Pope.

Voices. Out in the hall. Then the double doors
swung open again and he was standing there.

He was tall, well over six feet. And blond and

tanned. California blond and tanned. With clear blue eyes staring out from beneath a wide terry-cloth headband. He was sweating and shirtless, and she could count the twin ridges of muscle running up from his navel across his stomach. He carried a tennis bag in one hand and a racket in the other. He seemed totally unaware that he was half-naked, and he smiled an impossibly handsome smile.

"Sorry I'm late. Romany Chase, isn't it? Julian Morrow." And he ran his palm across the side of his shorts and reached out to take her hand.

"Yes." She shook his hand. It was still moist, but surprisingly cool.

"Sister Clemensia . . ." He'd turned to find the nun. "How about something cold to drink, Romany?" He was looking back at her. "I know I could use something. My boys gave me a real run for my money this afternoon."

"Boys, Father?" Why did she sound so mealy-mouthed?

"Please, Julian will do fine." He was smiling that Pepsodent smile again. "The boys are street kids. They've had a rough time of it. The tennis keeps them out of trouble and gives the old bod a good workout."

She watched him draw a hand across his shoulders, kneading the muscles. Who was this man kidding? He was built like a Greek god. And what was this "old" bod crap? He looked as if he were all of twenty-five. Shit, no one was supposed to look that good. And virtuous too, helping the poor street kids stay out of trouble. A regular Father Flanagan. It was enough to make her sick.

"Something to drink, Romany?" He was repeating his earlier question.

"Yes, that would be fine." Now her voice sounded a bit on the bitchy side.

"Orangina, Sister Clemensia." He smiled, but received only the customary nod. It was apparent that Sister Clemensia was trying very hard not to look at Father Morrow's naked chest. The woman was clearly having a difficult time coming to terms with this handsome and altogether too American Jesuit.

For a moment she watched Julian stare after the retreating nun, then she heard him laugh. A deep rich sound. Was he actually enjoying scandalizing the poor sister? He was still smiling when he closed the doors and bent to unzip his bag. He pulled out a towel and began patting some of the perspiration off his face and neck.

"Listen, I'm really sorry about being so late. And . . ." He looked down at himself, then up again at her. Was he actually embarrassed, or was she only imagining it? "God, I'm a mess. If you don't mind, I'd like to grab a quick shower, then we can talk. That okay with you?"

"Of course." Damn, he really was uncomfortable.

"Back in a sec." Another of his boyishly handsome smiles, and he left the room.

In a few minutes she heard the sound of water slapping against a shower stall. Well, Romany Chase? *Well what?* she snapped back. God, he was cheerful. And what was with him anyway—was he just naive, or outright stupid? A stupid Jesuit. Now that would be one for the books.

A knock, and the door opened slowly. Sister Clemensia stood in the threshold for a moment, casting furtive eyes around the room. Then her thick brows shot up into deliberate arches at the sound of the running water. She glanced at Romany. Whatever she felt, she wasn't afraid of letting this outsider see it. Chalk up another black mark for the American Jesuit. Taking a shower with a woman sitting right in the next room.

Romany watched the sister place a tray, with two bottles of orangeade and two glasses filled to the rim with ice, on a table. The ice sparkled in the crystal. Yes, things were definitely nicer inside the Vatican than on the outside.

"*Grazie, grazie mille.*" She thanked the nun but received only the now familiar nod as she backed out of the room, shutting the doors behind her.

". . . And who is Romany Chase?"

She looked up, startled at the sound of his voice, which sounded huskier than she'd remembered. He'd put on a pair of faded jeans with an oxford cloth shirt rolled up at the sleeves. His hair was slicked straight back, looking much darker now that it was wet. She could still see the tracks of a comb. There were fine wrinkles channeled across his high forehead, and laugh lines at the corners of his eyes. He looked much older now, and he didn't smile at her as he had before.

"Who am I?" she repeated his question. Like the sound of his voice, his words had startled her.

"Yes, you, Romany Chase." He'd somehow made her name sound sexy, and she watched his long legs in the tight faded jeans move toward her.

"I'm what I want to be."

"I like that," he said, sitting down next to her, drawing up one leg over the other. He didn't wear socks. "And just what is it that you are, Romany Chase?" His eyes were serious, and she imagined that her answer held some kind of real significance for him.

"I guess I'm what you'd call an art expert." She laughed, trying to make what she'd said sound less pompous.

"So you discriminate good art from bad?"

"Now that's a loaded question, Julian Morrow."

He laughed then too, his eyes crinkling like paper at the corners. "Well, I'll try to be more objective, Romany. Can you tell a fake from the original?"

"That depends." She was trying not to read anything into the question.

"Depends on what?"

"On how good the fake is," she said. "Afraid one of the countries is going to slip a fake by us?"

"No, of course not. That would be foolish. But I wouldn't want anything to happen to embarrass the Vatican, or upset His Holiness."

"This Art for Peace exhibit is very important to Pope Gregory, isn't it?"

"Yes, it is." His words seemed very solid and sincere. She watched as he raked his fingers through his hair. "It is the hope of His Holiness that Arte per Pace serve as an example of unity and harmony for the world." Then, smiling, he asked, "Was art your major in college?"

He had again made her the focus of the conversation.

"No . . . no, my undergraduate degree was in languages." She forced herself to change gears. "It seemed I inherited this language thing from my father."

"Your father . . . ?"

"Yes, he chairs the language department at Georgetown."

"How interesting, a language gene. How many do you speak?"

"Oh, about a half dozen. Like yourself."

"So when did the art come in?" He had ignored her opening.

"The art . . . my doctorate is in art history. My first practical experience was as an assistant curator. At the National. But until Arte per Pace, I've spent most of my time teaching."

He smiled, but didn't say anything more.

". . . Turnabout fair play?" she finally asked directly, reaching for a glass.

"Please forgive me. Here, let me." He took the glass from her hand and emptied the bottle. "Yes, of course, turnabout is fair play." He passed her the drink and began pouring himself one. "I usually start off by saying I'm a Jesuit. That, I'm told, is supposed to give one some kind of orientation. However, I've never been convinced."

"And just what is it you do for the Jesuits, Father Morrow . . . Julian?"

"I do public relations here in Rome. For the American delegation to the General Congregation. At least I did until the Holy Father asked that I come to work for him."

"An offer you couldn't refuse?"

He didn't seem to mind the overworked humor and gave her another of his smiles. "Definitely an offer I couldn't refuse."

"And so you have some background in art? I mean since His Holiness asked you to come on board?"

He really laughed. Like that first time. At Sister Clemensia. "No, Romany, actually I'm a canonical lawyer." He was still laughing, but softer now, through his words. "Your name, *Romany,* means gypsy girl, doesn't it?"

And then before she could answer, he was touching her hair, rubbing strands of it between his fingers. "That name suits you. You have gypsy hair, Romany Chase."

The Villa Bassano was a huge marble palace in the Alban Hills outside of Rome. Within its vast echoing hallways one always felt transported, not so much to an Italian past, but to an Imperial world that never was, a fantasy of what might once have existed before the First World War.

Vittorio sat waiting today in one of the many drawing rooms. Smaller than most of the salons there, it was still large even by the standards of the Papal palace, and like all of the other rooms in the Villa Bassano, it was filled with art. The Cardinal had been in this particular room only once before, and that time only briefly. It was all part of the game, never letting any ground become too familiar. And he had always to wait for the Baron. That too was part of it, the waiting.

He was glad it was to be this room today. He wanted this time to be able to study the paintings here, in particular the one he was looking at now. The panel was large and depicted the god Pan instructing an odd assortment of classical figures in the magical art of the flute. There was something hauntingly beautiful about the piece, which had made it an especially tragic loss when the painting had burned in the mysterious fire that had swept through the Berlin museum.

The Cardinal smiled as he looked about. He saw it now. A variation on a theme. Renaissance or modern, all of the paintings in this room, all except for Arno Breker's portrait of the Baron, had disappeared in one way or another from the great European museums.

He stared at the portrait of the Baron. Vittorio had no more illusions. He had denied his God in deed if not in word. And he would laugh at the Devil, if Devil there was, when the time came. He was afraid of nothing but the loss of that worldly influence and power that his whole life had been given to gain. And if the Baron was the dominant one in their friendship, it was only because of this. That of all the men Vittorio knew, the Baron stood alone, inviolable. A creature to inspire fear. Because the man, in his own turn, feared nothing.

The Black Baron had been an integral part of the occult circle that had moved like a shadow within the Third Reich. And the Baron, most shadowy of all. The only one to ride Hitler's tiger who had known how, and precisely when, to get off. In spite of their long association, Vittorio knew little even now beyond the rumors, for there were questions he would never dare to ask. The Baron was a singular figure, eccentric perhaps, though in no way ridiculous, despite his consuming attachment to a Europe that had died before he was born. And for all his courtly manners, there yet clung to him an air of almost preternatural menace, an aura of immense power he but barely held in check.

As Vittorio stood, still staring at the portrait, Friedrich appeared in the doorway. Two barons confronting him. The young, and the old. The tall trim body still ramrod straight. The clothes, tailored and perfectly modern, gave somehow the impression of a military uniform, or even a kind of costume. And the eyes, icy blue, twinkled with an implied smile that was nevertheless a warning.

With himself, Vittorio thought, the years had brought a diffusion, had spread him out in more ways than the simply corporeal. But with Friedrich there had been only a refining. The blond hair was now a snowy white, but in everything essential the Baron remained exactly as Breker had painted him. Hitler's perfect man. Except that the Baron had never been anyone's man but his own.

Friedrich was watching him now with his predatory smile, as if his guest's thoughts had been easily readable. *"Guten Abend,* Vittorio. I am sorry to have kept you waiting." The same words always. The false security of an inflexible opening gambit.

"It's nothing," he answered with his own smile. "I have been admiring the paintings"—his eyes returned to the Breker—"and remembering where I first saw your portrait."

Vittorio had been only a monsignor that summer after the fall of France, when as Pius's secret envoy he had traveled by request to Hitler's Alpine retreat. It was there at the Berghof that he'd been presented by the Führer himself with documents from the Vatican's own archives. Documents stolen away by Napoleon more than a century before. To be returned now in a gesture of goodwill by Germany's conquering Führer.

He had spoken with the Führer each afternoon at the small teahouse, but it was the Baron who had been his main contact at the Berghof. The Baron, who had so diplomatically explained that it was Pius's silence that the Führer expected. Silence in return for this gift of the documents. Silence for Pius's very freedom within the Vatican, only an island after all, surrounded on all sides by Mussolini's Italy.

Most of what was knowable of Friedrich he had learned in those few days at the Berghof. That he was the heir of one of Germany's oldest and wealthiest families. And that he shared with Vittorio an all-consuming passion for the glories of Western art.

It was Friedrich himself, Vittorio discovered, who

had found in Paris the documents stolen by Napoleon. The Baron's mission was to follow Hitler's armies, looting for the Reich the treasure troves of Europe. Centuries of Western art flowed into the warehouses in Munich, with the crème de la crème set secretly aside for the Baron's own growing collection. It was at the Berghof they had each begun to glimpse the first vague outlines of what, by the end of the war, would become their private alliance.

They sat now on facing brocaded sofas with Mozart drifting softly on the air. Over the years the Cardinal had examined carefully several of the rooms, looking in vain for the source of the music. Even as they sat listening to the concerto, he was searching over the high ceiling and walls for the venting of concealed speakers. But his gaze was soon lost in the baroque intricacies of the molding, and he gave up gratefully when the serving men appeared with cheese and fruit and a perfect bottle of Piesporter.

When the wine was poured, and they were left alone, he asked the obvious question.

"The auction, Friedrich, was it a success?"

"A great success, dear Vittorio. In fact, among our greatest."

He fingered the Byzantine cross that hung around his neck. "How much?" he asked.

"Twenty-three million deutsche marks. About what I expected."

The Cardinal nodded heavily, leaning forward to slice a piece of the cheese. He was thinking of his commission, the marks converted to gold certificates piling up in his account. It was virtually automatic, he never touched it at all. There were only the yearly statements sent to an anonymous box in Rome. And the occasional trip to Switzerland when it was warranted.

"It's good we obtained so much," he said, washing the cheese down with a sip of his wine. "The Caravaggio will have to be the last for a while."

"Because of Arte per Pace." It was a calm statement of fact.

"Yes." He poured himself more of the wine. "Their people will be everywhere poking around," he said. "You know what these Americans are."

"Americans," the Baron repeated the word. "Like Romany Chase?"

Vittorio felt himself frown. He had never mentioned the woman by name. But it was typical. The Baron, no doubt, had his own spy at the exhibition offices.

He set down his glass. "I don't think there'll be any real problem handling the Acquisitions Coordinator," he said, wiping his fingers on a napkin and smoothing back his hair. "She got the job, it appears, because of her father's friendship with the Exhibition Director."

"Nepotism doesn't of itself imply incompetence, Vittorio. You're not perhaps underestimating her danger to us simply because she's a woman?"

"That's ridiculous."

"Is it?" The eyes were gently quizzical. "It's not the first time, surely, that a Roman priest has been accused of that particular sin."

He smiled in spite of himself. "Perhaps," he said. "But I don't think I'm underestimating anything. This new situation is delicate, but entirely manageable."

"And Julian Morrow . . . ?"

"Monsignor Brisi is not happy." The Cardinal bent toward the table again and paused to toss a perfect grape into his mouth. "No, Monsignor Brisi is not happy," he repeated the words in the sweet aftertaste of the fruit. "His vanity has been wounded. But His Holiness obviously wanted somebody who would please the Americans." He smiled.

The Baron smiled back, and for a time nothing else was said. They drank the wine and listened to the music.

"Vittorio." It was Friedrich who interrupted their silence. "I wish to ask a question."

A question. The Baron wished to ask him a personal question. The signal that business was indeed finished, and a more interesting game was at hand. They had played at it since the beginning of their friendship. But sparingly, because the game was dangerous.

"Very well, Friedrich," he replied ritually. "What do you want to know?" If he answered, the Baron had to answer a question in return.

"I have watched carefully, Vittorio"—the words were heavy with irony—"the seriousness with which you have observed your other vows. And so, when contemplating your pledge of chastity, I have wondered over the years, was it boys that you preferred? Or girls?"

He laughed. The question was such an easy one. "Why do you put it in the past tense, dear Friedrich?" He chuckled again. "But you are right. These"—and he indicated the food and drink on the table—"are the only pleasures that are left to me since my mistress died nearly twenty years ago. A rich and respectable widow in Orvieto. I was faithful to her for thirty years, more or less. . . . And you?" It was his turn now. "Men or women?"

The Baron looked strange, as if he were actually hesitating. But what had he expected? That he, Vittorio, would ask something else entirely? Not turn the question around?

And indeed, he almost had not. It was not a question that seemed to fit the Baron at all. He had never thought his friend's sexual preferences to be anything but normal, if he thought of it at all. In truth the question did not even seem to fit. Friedrich had always appeared to him somehow removed from the sins of the flesh. A stoic and an aesthete.

The seconds passed. He was beginning to be afraid. Why had Friedrich begun this?

"Women." The word when it came out was almost a whisper. And for once the blue eyes had lost their transparency.

For a moment Vittorio sat transfixed. He had seen something just now, something that it was better not in any way to acknowledge. He put down his wineglass, and made much to do of the slicing of a melon.

A servant came in to announce that dinner was being served in the dining room. His host's Cheshire-cat smile was again in place, as if nothing at all had happened. But for only once in fifty years Friedrich's control had been shaken. And Vittorio knew he could not forget. Knew the unaskable question would plague him through dinner. Would now forever plague him. Exactly what, or exactly *whom*, had the Baron been remembering?

As soon as Romany opened the door, she knew she wasn't alone. Someone waited for her. Somewhere in the apartment.

She had never carried a gun. There had never been a need. Even though Sully could have gotten her easy clearance, and had more than once urged her to take along some insurance. But her assignments never warranted it. Except that one time, in Geneva, and that situation had come totally out of left field.

She allowed her eyes to become adjusted to the gloom and, easing herself against the wall, moved to the edge of the living room. She searched the shadows. Strained to see something behind the thick lumps and bumps of furniture. Nothing. She crouched lower and inched closer to the door opening into her bedroom.

She peered around the corner. Whoever was in the apartment had switched on the ceiling fan and the small lamp that sat on a dressing table in the adjoining bath. The soft light cast the room in semidarkness, and she could make out the large solid shape of a man. He reclined easily upon her bed, a marshmallowy heap of pillows propped against his back. He hadn't bothered to draw back the covers, and he lay on top of the spread completely naked.

She should have run, gotten out of her apartment as quickly as possible. Except she recognized the hard muscles under the deeply tanned skin, the black curling hair, the famous smirk that passed for a smile. Recognized the man who was a cold-blooded killer—and her lover.

Romany moved through the doorway and smiled. "I'm not even going to ask how you got in here, David."

She heard his dark laugh. "Is that any way to greet an old friend?"

She walked farther into the room and stood by the side of the bed. She stared into the bright green eyes, still a surprise after all this time. But then everything about David ben Haar was a surprise. "Why don't you make yourself comfortable?"

"I am . . . almost." He reached for her hand and ran it slowly down his chest, stopping just short of the black hair at his groin.

She glanced down, focusing on her hand, pale and thin clasped inside his. She could hear her breath catch inside her throat. And as if that sound had been meant as some sort of signal, he pulled her down beside him.

She rested with her back against him, letting him work the muscles at her shoulders, brush his lips against her hair. She didn't turn when she finally decided to speak. "What are you doing here, David?"

"I came to see you." The words didn't sound like a complete lie.

She twisted herself round to look up at him. "That's terribly flattering, David, but it won't work."

She watched the smirk almost stretch into a real smile. "Okay, I came to make sure that Sully is taking good care of my girl."

"I'm not your girl, David." She tried not to sound mean, or hurt, or anything. But she could feel the muscles of his stomach tighten against her back.

"You know Sully's a fucking asshole," he said finally. "What's he waiting on, those jerks to open up a concentration camp and gas a few thousand Jews?"

"David, Sully's not an asshole. . . . Hey, what in

the hell do you mean?" She jerked around, waiting for an answer, watching his eyes turn cold.

"Gimme a break, Romany."

"Dammit, David, I don't have the slightest idea what you're talking about. Besides, what in the hell have concentration camps got to do with . . . ?" She stopped short, not willing to play her hand, even though David probably knew all the cards she was holding.

"Well, Romany, I can save you, and Sully, and all your little friends over at the CIA a whole helluva lotta trouble. Somebody—and I think you're deaf, dumb, and blind if you haven't pegged who that is—is stealing the Church blind, swiping paintings right off the museum walls, then slipping by some pretty goddamn good fakes."

She watched him stare at her from inside the darkness of her bed, waiting with that flirting smirk on his mouth for her to say something. But she didn't answer.

". . . And the SOB at the other end of this operation"—he was finishing what he'd started—"whether your CIA geniuses want to admit it or not, is blackmarketing the genuine articles, funneling the profits to a group of neo-Nazis who aren't going to settle for German reunification."

"Neo-Nazis?"

She could hear him grit his teeth. "Yeah, neo-Nazis. Getting East and West Germany together was just the first stage of their nasty little operation. They've got big plans, Romany. But they're the same old fuckers. Just a little slicker."

"David, I can't believe—"

"Shit, you people never want to believe—"

"Stop it, David."

He dropped his head and took in a deep staccatoed breath. She felt his hands move up her arms to her shoulders and force her body close to his. "Sorry, Romany." He sounded hoarse. Then suddenly she felt him laughing against her. "You know something"—he was drawing back—"you're on the wrong side, Romany. We wouldn't have these stupid fights if you'd come and work with me. With the Mossad."

"Yeah? Work with you, huh? And just what inducement can you offer, David ben Haar?" She pulled away from him and stood up.

Her feelings about David were a tangled mess—which, after she'd watched him board the plane for Tel Aviv thirteen months ago, she'd thought she could safely leave unwound. But here he was again, still looking at her with that quizzical twist to his lips that she couldn't help but read as a challenge.

She wanted his hands on her. That was the thought that kept repeating itself, blotting out everything else in her mind. Her own hands trembled as she pushed the hair away from her neck and began to undo the buttons at her back. Undressing for him slowly, the way he liked it.

She hadn't let herself know how much she'd missed this, until she was beneath the covers naked beside him, and his hands were really on her again, taking control, his mouth moving everywhere on her body. The pulse of the ceiling fan blended suddenly with the rush of blood in her ears, and David's heat was under her skin like fire.

She pressed herself closer against him, her need for him blocking out her doubts. She wanted his solidness, his back under her hands, the hardness of him along the length of her body. David ben Haar, the perfect sexual fantasy. But real. Flesh and blood with eyes green as the sea. She looked into his eyes as he pulled her beneath him. There was no lightness in them now, only the same intensity of passion as when he killed. He came into her hard, and she shut her eyes, matching her rhythm to his. To dream was all right, as long as you didn't let it go beyond the borders of your bed.

CHAPTER 4

Romany slowly cracked open her eyes, first one, then the other. Through a gritty haze she could just make out the perfect circular motion of the ceiling fan overhead. The visual effect was slightly nauseating. She swallowed hard. Perhaps her sense of touch could better be trusted. She reached out and felt the empty rumple of pillow next to her. How like David to leave before she woke. Leave without a sound. Hit and run. A thief in the night.

Just what in the hell was David up to anyway? God, she couldn't wait for Sully to get here. This shit about neo-Nazis had come out of nowhere. But if David said neo-Nazis were involved in the art scam, you could take it to the bank.

But she could just hear Sully now, warning her that neo-Nazis were none of her business. Her assignment in Rome was clear. Substantiate that Vatican art was being forged. The *who* and the *how*. Period.

There was little doubt in her mind that the Caravaggio was a forgery. An incredible one. But a fake nevertheless. Which of course gave real muscle to the rumors that the original had been recently auctioned on the black market. What she needed now was a cross section of paint from the fake. Nothing like proof positive.

But that still left her with the who and the how. Her best information pointed in one direction and one direction only—His Eminence Cardinal Vittorio DeLario. But what about the Pope? Was His Holiness involved? If he was, why would he have been so eager to make Arte per Pace his baby? Invite the spotlight? But innocent or guilty, Pope Gregory's baby was at risk, and Art for Peace was a lot more than a simple art show.

And where did the Jesuit fit in? The joker in the deck? The wild card? And by whose draw? She twisted one end of her pillow into a tight pig's tail. Morrow was certainly not what she'd expected. In the very brief time they'd met, she'd seen the priest wear two entirely different faces. Yet her instincts told her that Morrow was the key that unlocked the door.

Yesterday after she'd left him at the Vatican, she'd made trips to the American Express office and the bank. Necessary errands she'd been putting off, which had suddenly become welcome distractions. And then there'd been David. But David was gone now, and nothing was left as a barrier to her thoughts. The truth was undeniable. Her meeting with Julian Morrow had been an unqualified disaster.

She'd let him control the situation from start to finish, dictating through Elliot where and when they would meet. Two-thirty at the Vatican. Foreign territory. She should have known she was in trouble from the beginning.

And where had her mind been? Letting him get the best of the questions, and certainly the best of the answers. She cringed mentally hearing herself telling him about getting her doctorate, working at the museum, teaching. Even talking about her father.

And what had she learned about him? That he had been in Rome, a canonical lawyer working in public relations for the Jesuits. Who, in spite of the fact he apparently knew next to nothing about art, had been chosen by his Pope as Vatican liaison to Arte per Pace.

It didn't exactly add up. And yet she hadn't pressed him. Not about his inexcusable lateness, or his whole dizzying "now you see me, now you don't" routine. Oh no, not Romany Chase, Girl Superspy. She'd just sat there in that confusing jumble of plasterwork and gilt, drinking in his smile and his Orangina, while he dazzled her with his footwork, teased her with questions about fake art, and played with her "gypsy" hair.

She groaned out loud, turning away from the brightening square of the window, dragging the pillow over her head. She had blown it. Blown it totally. And for the first time she was actually glad that Sully wasn't already in Rome.

She was meeting Julian Morrow again on Monday at his new office in the Pinacoteca, where he'd promised to have the list of Vatican submissions ready for her. Thank God, she was going to have another shot at the Jesuit. She tried to console herself with the thought and get back to sleep, but the Roman sun seemed to seep even through the thickness of the pillow.

At seven she gave in and got up. There was only one surefire way to clear her mind. She'd take a long hot soak, then walk down to the neighborhood trattoria. A cup of coffee and a newspaper. By the time they opened, she'd be ready to hit the shops.

Switzerland looked like a postcard. It was a thought he couldn't help thinking, no matter how often he saw it. No matter how tired the cliché. Julian Morrow was thinking it now as he drove south in the rented Audi through the Fribourg Alps. But even the beauties of the Swiss countryside could not divert his mind for long, and he was soon replaying the uglier scene he'd just left behind moments ago in the convent infirmary.

Her hair was just the same, fiery, full of life. It was the first thing he'd noticed when he'd walked into the bright clean room—her wonderful red hair falling across the back of the comfortable modern chair that faced the uncurtained window. He'd stood silent behind her for a long time, staring through the glass to the river Sarine below, on its quicksilver path through the mountains.

There'd been no change. Sister Lucienne had warned him of that when he'd called the week before to arrange the visit. After almost six years it was hardly a surprise. Colleen wouldn't be here in this room at all, if the doctors had held out any real hope. Still *he* had hoped, had let himself imagine that the nuns, the serenity, the sheer beauty of this place, might somehow make a difference. The chance to bring Colleen to Switzerland was a large part of his reason for getting involved in this whole thing in Rome.

He had touched her hair, curling a lock of it round and round his finger. Perhaps it was only selfishness, his insistence that Colleen be brought here to the convent, as everything he had ever done concerning her was selfish. He knelt and looked into her face. The blue eyes were wide open. The trauma of the accident hadn't aged her at all. She looked perfect, healthy. Her expression was not blank, but intent, as if she were concentrating very hard on something that only she could see.

"Hello, Colleen, it's . . . me." He couldn't make himself say his name. The false name, the only one she had had for him. "Please, Colleen. Come back. There's someone here who needs you. . . ."

He had come now to the junction of the Warme and Kalte Sense, the valleys of the warm and the cold springs. He let the image of her fade and took the road to the right, ascending the Warme Sense toward Schwarzee. The sky was cloudless above the white peaked mountains. A postcard.

In a little while he turned off the highway that led to the lake, and drove higher up into the hills. A storybook farmhouse with boxes of red geraniums underscoring its neat windows stood at the top of a long wooded driveway. He stopped the car and turned off the ignition, pausing a moment to let a smile take over his face. He was only halfway out of the seat when the red-haired boy burst like a bright pinwheel out of the painted door. Five-year-old Patrick Shaunessy running laughing down the path toward him. Calling him.

"Mon oncle. Mon oncle Julian."

Signora Agostina never spoke to Herr Anton Arendt. Never acknowledged his presence. Not once in all the many months he'd been coming to her pensione. He came and went like a ghost, moving through the door, down the long hallway to descend the cellar stairs. And then back again, retracing his steps once he'd completed his business.

But then that was exactly as he wanted it. The less conspicuous the better. Besides, he couldn't bear the thought of talking to that Italian cow. God, Italians were a crude and stupid lot. In his estimation the last Italian of any estimable worth had died in the Renaissance.

Dressed in a dove-gray suit, Anton Arendt suited the part. His steel-colored hair combed into oiled, even tracks fit like a cap on his small cadaverous-looking head. A hawkish nose had grown years ago above an unforgiving slit of a mouth, and the only evidence of life in the masklike face was a pair of dark ratlike little eyes.

The form beneath the clothes appeared brittle, as though the bones could be snapped like so many matchsticks. Yet the body worked with a kind of feverish energy, the muscles and tendons seemingly attached to long endless strings and literally jerked into action.

Anton's pale kid glove touched the wormy tip of the banister, marking the end of another leg in his long journey. The bother of these never-ending precautions. Yet he was not so stupid as to fail to see the absolute necessity of it all.

He opened the cellar trapdoor and looked down. Neon-orange light zigzagged against the walls. Like the belly of a large pumpkin, the tunnel seemed ready to eat him alive. He lowered himself in jerky little motions, one rung at a time down the narrow ladder. He hated the tricky descent, and there were shadows he did not like where the light could not reach. But the air was strangely pleasant. Cool and lichen-scented, it made him think of a particular variety of mushroom he was fond of eating.

He stepped down onto solid packed earth and followed the metal spine of railway tracks until he reached a small motorized car. As always Gustav was waiting. A polite nod, and he settled himself inside the car on his way to this, his final destination. The Villa Bassano.

The car clunked from side to side down the winding track. How many times? How many times this same route? He had lost count, since he had grown to hate everything about these trips now. But it was not forever, he reminded himself often enough. And the victory would be sweet.

He fidgeted on the hard seat, already anticipating the long wait ahead. As always the Baron would be late. God, he hated kissing the man's boots. Yet it meant nothing, just another necessary part of the process. But there was no use for it, he was only deceiving himself. For there lay in all his self-assurances, something dark and ugly. A secret that caused him no end of great personal shame. A pain for which there was no cure. Anton Arendt was afraid of the Black Baron.

And to make matters worse, he was certain the Baron knew of his fear. Fed on it like a vampire. They were, all of them, fools in his eyes. So why did the Baron do it? Do what he, Anton, and the others asked of him? The answer was simple. Because it amused him. They were but another act in his circus. That was the beginning and that was the end of it.

Once he'd arrived, Gustav had shown him into one of the reception rooms. And now he had been pacing for the last twenty-five minutes. Walking up and down, anticipating the Baron's grand entrance. The son of a bitch had no regard for anyone.

"Herr Arendt."

The Baron's even voice. Always the same meager greeting. Never an apology. He'd been kept waiting almost half an hour in this mausoleum and nothing more than *Herr Arendt*.

Anton walked forward and bowed. He hadn't offered his hand. He'd made that mistake once, and it was one he'd not likely make again. The Baron did not like to be touched.

"Baron, you are in good health?" He forced his thin lips into a smile.

"I am well, Herr Arendt." The Baron walked farther into the room and seated himself. His clear eyes looked up. "The elections are very close now."

"Less than a year, Baron. And I think it will go very well. Our people have worked hard. There is every good reason to believe that our candidates will be elected."

A small nod from the Baron. His fingers were stroking the brocaded upholstery of the chair, petting the padded arm like the back of a cat.

"This is a piece of history, mein Herr Baron," Anton was used to doing most of the talking, "first a united Germany, now our people but waiting in the wings to restore the Fatherland to its rightful place."

"How fortunate for you that the Soviets managed to prove themselves as stupid as I have always suspected."

Anton was able to produce a genuine smile this time. "Indeed, Baron, the fools in the Politburo committed political suicide. But we knew it was but a matter of time before the Communists, if you will pardon the expression, chewed off their own asses."

The Baron's blue eyes seemed to twinkle. The old bastard was in a good mood. Arendt was sure of it. He felt himself begin to swell with new confidence. "With the Soviet state having lost its grip on Eastern Europe and literally caving in on itself, and with the West slowly abdicating its power . . ."—he paused for dramatic effect—"the stage is set for us, Baron, the bearers of the true German national spirit to take up the mantle and lead the peoples of Europe, the peoples of the world."

He looked for approval in the Baron's face, but all he saw was that the eyes were no longer happy. He'd gone too far. He had to be more careful. He'd gotten carried away. And never again could they get carried away. Not like before. The most important thing was to appear rational. No one goose-stepping in the streets, no troops *sieg heil*-ing like a bunch of trained seals.

"But of course we understand that we must allow

those others who helped us win reunification to have their place. We cannot make enemies now. Indeed, mein Herr Baron, these others give our efforts, shall we say, a clean new face. Oh, there are ways, mein Herr Baron, to keep everybody happy."

The Baron was standing now, and Arendt marveled at how well the man kept himself. If it weren't for the snow-white hair, he would have appeared almost middle-aged.

". . . keep everybody happy." The Baron had repeated his last words.

"Oh yes, Baron," he jumped in like a gypsy's monkey, "we have learned many lessons since that other unfortunate time. Modern technology gives us many tools that we did not before have. Tools that will help us, shall we say, manage the people. They shall have their democracy."

"Democracy," the Baron spat the word out as though he'd ingested something distasteful.

"A fiction, mein Herr, a fiction." He brushed the reference off. He had to get to the matter of more money. "Mein Herr, the last sale, the Caravaggio." He put on an appropriately grateful smile. "Who would have thought anyone would pay such a price for some paint and canvas? Twenty-three million deutsche marks."

A small muscle twitched in the Baron's jaw. Nothing that anyone could really notice. But there was in the clear eyes a look one less familiar might have mistaken for pain. But Anton knew it for what it was. He'd seen it before. That look of complete and utter revulsion.

He coughed nervously. "This arrangement with the art has worked out very well, mein Herr."

"This arrangement, as you call it, has met most recently with certain difficulty." The look had disappeared and now the Baron seemed only vaguely bored.

"Difficulty, mein Herr?"

"Arte per Pace."

"But that is only temporary. Arte per Pace will not

go on forever. Besides, this whole sideshow has worked well for us. The Pope has from the first put his stamp of approval on our reunification efforts. Given us his papal blessing." He snickered audibly, congratulating himself on his sense of humor.

"Mein Herr Baron?" He felt brave again as his eyes shifted around the room. "Villa Bassano's walls are covered with art. Surely one or two paintings could be spared for the cause."

For a long time the Black Baron just stared at him. But this time the blue eyes told Anton nothing. Then without the slightest warning, the Baron began to laugh. Not a polite chuckle of amusement. Not the kind of sound one might have expected. But a vulgar, belly-deep laugh that shook his whole body.

"Mein Herr . . . ?"

"You . . . you must forgive me, Anton." The Baron was attempting a recovery.

Forgive me, Anton. Was he going mad? Like the laugh, he'd never expected to hear such a thing from the Baron's mouth. He waited for the old fear to rise up like bile into his throat. But there was only confusion, and just the slightest twinge of discomfort that the fear did not come at all.

"Did I make a joke, mein Herr? I mean about the paintings?"

"No, no. Not a joke." The Baron was still smiling. "Just a bit of irony."

"Irony, mein Herr?"

"Yes, irony. For you see, it would be impossible to sell any of these paintings." And the Baron waved his hand around the room to take in the four walls. "For these paintings, my dear Anton, are fakes."

And in the very instant he said it, staring into those cold, unfriendly eyes, Anton knew the Baron lied.

. . . *And you, Baron, is it men or women you prefer?* It was perhaps not so strange for Vittorio to have turned the question on him the other evening. Though it was entirely unexpected. He'd have thought his friend might have been a bit more original. Yet if he now wished to ponder overlong the reasons for the Cardinal's asking it, he did not. For bubbling within his mind was not the question, but the answer.

For thirteen days he'd made the necessary preparations. It was instinctive now. Thirteen days consecrated to this ritual. A small portion of each day spent alone, set aside to concentrate his energy, to purify himself, separate himself from this mortal plane and all its distractions. Often, time seemed to move not in months at all, but in absolute cycles of thirteen days. Yet this obsession should never be construed as any loss of control on his part. Rather the whole of it was a direct consequence of his own will.

He removed the dark cloth veiling the small faded photograph. At first his eyes fixed only on the point of candlelight shining on the glass covering the young girl's features. He did not see the burnished auburn waves cascading in loose tendrils about the pretty face. Nor the eyes, glowing green and wide and innocent, staring at him for all the years between as though it were only yesterday. Then suddenly there was nothing but her image. And her name—the secret mantra that would once again begin it all.

"Lise, my beloved," he whispered, "come and sup with me. From out of the darkness come, from out of the womb of night, come and break with me thy eternal fast."

And because he traveled along the paths of the dead, he moved backward toward the small table. The wood still gave off a pleasant scent of beeswax, though the table was draped and fitted like an altar with starched white linen. There were sweet-smelling flowers in a silver bowl, and dozens of thin tapers flickered and danced in the cooled silent air. Dinner steamed hot on fine china plates, and wine sparkled deep red in crystals. And the chairs, only two now, had been placed one to the east and one to the west. He took up his knife and fork.

He ate a small bit of this and a small bite of that, concentrating on the portions, never once looking up at the empty chair across from him. Slowly, meticulously chewing the food. When he'd swallowed the last of it, he took a large swill of wine down smoothly. Then he lifted his head. It was always the same physical reaction; his body never betrayed him. The fine hairs on the backs of his hands stood on end; the insides of his nostrils prickled.

The air in the room had shifted.

She sat across from him. A ruffle encircling her white throat looked excessively constraining. Instantly he wanted to reach out and undo the tiny pearl buttons. She smiled, as though she'd read his thoughts. Yet she did nothing to loosen the blouse, and he watched as her hand instead took hold of the wine. He stared in fascination as she drained the glass, the tiny buttons bobbling as the wine slipped past her mouth down into the slender column of her throat. He heard just the barest clink of teeth on the lip of the crystal as she finished. Then her eyes found his.

He could feel the anticipated vibration starting, the electricity moving from his scalp along the muscles of his neck into the walls of his chest. If he were a fearful man, a less instinctive one, he would have believed that his heart was giving way. But he understood what was happening, and he scratched his tongue across the sharp edges of his front teeth and closed his eyes.

Time and the walls of Villa Bassano had fallen away. And he found himself with her in that season they'd shared in the Berlin woods before the war. The two of them in their secret place, under the cover of sheltering trees, lying on the broad cape he'd worn because there was yet a chill in the air.

He pressed her against him, tucking his hand beneath her blouse, under the thin chemise she wore. Feeling her tiny ribs beneath the soft goose-pimpled flesh, the warm secret hollow at the small of her back. She smelled of lavender behind her ear and he flinched as a lock of her hair tickled his face. He snapped like a wolf at the strand, clamping it between his teeth. She pulled away, tugging on the curl, laughing at this wild madness in him. It was a perfectly girlish giggle that parted her lips, and he bent without warning and closed his mouth over hers. He felt her sigh against him as though her heart might break. Then her arms tightened.

"Love me, Friedrich," she whispered in what seemed a desperate little voice, "love me. It is what I want . . . truly." And she looked at him with eyes that shone too brightly.

He placed his hands about her small pale face, marveling that anything alive could be so beautiful. Always before he'd believed that only a painting, or a piece of sculpture, could be this perfect. Never had he dared to hope that a thing made of flesh and blood and bone could stir him to such heights. And for this he loved her beyond all imagining.

His arm jerked now in a kind of palsied movement, causing him to spill his half-emptied glass. The wine spread quickly against the bleached white linen like a stain of fresh blood. For an instant he thought he'd cut his hand. But he knew the absurdity of such an idea, and he lifted the overturned glass, twirling the stem between his long fingers, observing how the crystal split and spread the light from the candles. He set the glass down and glanced at the empty chair across from him.

What had happened those long years past, what particular role he had played, were of no consequence. Not then, not now. He still had her memory left to him. And like all of the exquisite art hanging upon his walls, like all of the beauty surrounding him, he would yet allow it to give him pleasure.

CHAPTER 5

Monday morning and Romany looked around her brightly lit office. The money men in New York had wasted no expense; everything was first-class. She reached out and ran a hand over the sleek surface of her desk, then sank back into the spine-hugging curve of her chair. It was a completely fascinating irony that a country overrun with the ghosts and haunts of an ancient past could also produce the world's finest contemporary furniture.

She listened for a moment to the soft sounds of Italian easing its way through her half-opened door. Elliot was going over a press release with one of the secretaries. The level hum from the belly of a computer filled up a short lapse in their conversation. Then as if on cue the staccatoed clicking of keys, the high-tech buzz of a phone.

She sighed and sat up, touching again the bare surface of her desk. She certainly couldn't be accused of being a pack rat. No, Romany Chase was a woman who traveled light. She needed few reminders. Most of what was worth keeping, she'd stored away in her memory. She popped open her briefcase and reached in for one of her few attachments—a 5 × 7 color photograph of her parents.

She smiled back at their smiling faces. God, she missed both of them. Yet with the way things were here, she didn't know when she'd see them again, unless her father was really serious about coming over. She frowned. Her mother hadn't been at all well lately. But that wasn't the real truth. The real truth was that Marthe Chase had never been well. She closed her eyes and let the silent mantra come. *Please God, don't let anything happen to Mother.* Always the same prayer. The same fear. And it never seemed to get any easier.

But Papa would take care of her. Dear sweet Papa. He always took care of everything. She looked at his broad cheerful face. Even in the picture the clear intelligent eyes seemed to read her mind. Did he know about what she was doing? She imagined that he did. But he'd never say anything, no matter how he felt. That wasn't his way. Theodor Chase had always given his daughter the freedom to live her own life.

But hadn't he in a way been responsible for this particular turn her life had taken? After all, Andrew was his good friend. Friends since their days together at Harvard. She looked down and wrapped her fingers around the small paperweight still resting at the bottom of her open briefcase. She removed the protective covering, cradling the delicately painted lid from an ancient Chinese temple jar. Its finely wrought brass base felt cool and smooth against the flat of her palm. The second of her attachments.

Uncle Drew, she'd always called him. She never did know what dignified and handsome Uncle Drew did for a living. But whatever it was, it must surely be something important, something that took on all the seductiveness of a murder mystery in her curious young mind. Especially when he and Papa would go into the study after dinner and close the doors to have one of their talks.

She'd been teaching full-time at the university only a few months, still trying to fit in some hours at the museum, when Uncle Drew had paid her a surprise visit. She hadn't seen him in over a year. Called away to Europe on some kind of business, he'd said. At first, she remembered, Papa had received almost weekly letters, then nothing. And now here he was, as handsome as ever, waiting for her in her office.

She would never quite be able to describe the expression on Uncle Drew's face that day. There was a concentrated intensity in those cool gray eyes she'd never seen before. Yet it was a look that told her instantly, he wanted something.

It seemed a dream now, that whole episode in her office that late fall afternoon. The way Uncle Drew had smiled and told her how much he'd missed her. Then the beautifully wrapped package. The paperweight. Handed to her almost shyly, as though she might think later that the gift had been offered as some kind of ridiculous bribe. Then his back had seemed to straighten and his voice took on a strange texture. Almost like a recording. But warmer, more human. And gone was the reticence of a few minutes before. The mystery of who he was, what he did, came out like the quiet recitation of a poem. And what those talks with her father had been about. Then, at the end, the question he'd been working up to all along. Would she help them?

She hadn't given him an answer that afternoon. He hadn't expected her to. She could have all the time she needed. Time to adjust to everything he'd told her. Time to adjust to the idea that her Uncle Drew was a high-ranking member of the CIA. That for years her father had helped him whenever there was an especially tricky code to decipher. No, her father was not an agent. And no, Theodor never asked why or for whom the work was being done. The truth was that it had become something of a game between the two of them—Andrew challenging Theodor to solve a real linguistic brain teaser every now and then, "just to keep his old friend on his toes." And no, her father didn't know he was asking her to become an operative.

She could call her own shots, he had said. Pick and choose her assignments as she wished. Be sort of a "free-lancer." And there would never be any real danger. She wasn't really being recruited for the James Bond kind of stuff. And if by a long shot something did happen, there would always be backup close by. The work would actually be kind of fun. Of course, Andrew hadn't really needed to tempt her by saying that. But he had.

Yet for the most part he'd played it straight. There

was never any kind of foolish appeal made to a sense of patriotism. He knew she was too smart to fall for that. She didn't have any more illusions about the CIA than he did. No, the only route to go was the one he'd taken —appeal to her need to be a player. And though he knew she was above having her ego stroked, surely she couldn't deny her suitability for what they were asking her to do. Her language skills, her art expertise, made her absolutely perfect for certain assignments.

Two months passed before she was able to make the call to Andrew. She'd never been able to call him Uncle Drew after that day in her office. That had been three years ago. And everything had been just as he'd said. Except for that one incident in Geneva. And David ben Haar.

She touched the last of her attachments. A strange thing for a Catholic-reared girl, who now thought of herself as something of an agnostic, to tote around. But David had given it to her, and she was never without it. She twisted the small cap off the mezuzah and read The Prayer of the Martyr. It had become a daily ritual since Geneva.

Geneva had started off as a very simple operation. But she'd never been asked to get this close to "the enemy" before, not face-to-face. And of course this was her first assignment outside the states. And there was the collaboration with Mossad.

Dance with Hakim, that was all she had to do. And smile pretty, make the old bastard forget he's a good Moslem with a dozen wives. Just a simple little diversion. Just for thirty minutes, Romany. Just long enough for Mossad to do what they had to do in his room. But she'd somehow overplayed her part, and Hakim wasn't such a good Moslem after all. What was she supposed to do when he suddenly insisted they go to his suite upstairs for some especially good French champagne? She could still feel his hot breath as he'd whispered the invitation in her ear, then his strong thick fingers locking around her wrist as he'd literally pulled her off the dance floor.

The key in the lock. And then a hurried noise on the other side. The Arab shot her a quick glance. She tried a smile, but what he read on her face at that moment caused him to lash out and grab her. Shove the business end of a revolver against her back. Then a swift lunge with his foot and the door came crashing open.

Silence in the darkness. He edged her into the room, using her as a kind of shield. One careful step after another. Then before she knew what was happening, a muffled burst from behind. And slowly the barrel of Hakim's gun slid down the ridges of her spine, and the Arab loosened his grip on her arms. A small click, and the room was flooded with light. When she turned, she was staring into the hard green eyes of David ben Haar.

She replaced the tiny piece of parchment inside the mezuzah and walked around her desk. Through the blinds she had a beautiful view of the small piazza below. It was not yet noon, but the pigeons were already looking for handouts from a few pedestrians making their way into the square. The birds had become so tamed, they were a nuisance.

She turned and glanced back at her desk as though she half expected to see herself sitting there. Out of the corner of her eye she caught a glimpse of Elliot ushering a group of VIPs into his office. Elliot and Andrew, her father's two closest friends. She'd come to Rome because both of these men in turn had asked for her help.

She looked back down into the piazza again. A few of the pigeons had given up on the pedestrians and were taking a bath in the fountain. She smiled. Rome was her home now. At least for a while. And for better or worse, she'd been dealt a strange hand. A pope, a cardinal, and a priest.

She had a two-thirty meeting with Julian Morrow this afternoon. If he remembered. Okay, Romany old girl, no more fancy footwork from Father Julian Morrow. This time she was going to lead.

She took in a deep breath. She knew it shouldn't make a bit of difference. That she'd gotten past all that crap long ago. That she was a mature, focused, inner-directed woman with a job to do. But why, oh why in God's name, did Father Julian Morrow have to be so damn good-looking?

It was barely two o'clock when Romany arrived at the staff entrance of the Pinacoteca flashing a smile and her special Arte per Pace pass to the uniformed guard at the door. Her meeting with Father Morrow wasn't for another thirty minutes, but she wanted the extra time.

The ladies' room on the office floor was surprisingly large and well lighted, and as empty as the elevator that had brought her up. The museum downstairs had closed at one o'clock, and the administrative staff obviously insisted on the traditional Italian siesta.

She dried her hands with a paper towel and took a step backward from the mirror. She looked pretty damn good today, and when she looked good, she could tackle anything. It was stupid, she knew, linking her abilities with her looks, but it was still the way she felt. Even if she would never admit it.

If her brains had come from her father, it was to her mother that she owed her peaches-and-cream complexion and the natural slimness that let her forgo dieting. The eyes that changed color with her mood, and the mane of dark auburn curls, she liked to think of as her own.

She straightened the waistband of her skirt and smoothed the hipline of the Armani jacket she had purchased on Saturday. The suit was perfect. Tailored yet completely feminine. For one short second she had considered telling the store's seamstress to lower the hem. But her legs were too good to hide just to please the Vatican. She freshened her lipstick and checked her watch. She was ready for Father Julian Morrow.

She had expected a fairly elaborate office, perhaps

with a secretary-receptionist, but there wasn't even a
title on the door. And only the one room, a small efficient space in sharp contrast to the opulence of his
apartment. Predictably he wasn't there. But that was
good, it was the reason she'd come early.

She let the door swing closed behind her and walked
quickly around to the back of the wooden desk. There
was not much on top except for a brand-new blotter and
some of the official literature sent out by Arte per Pace.
Father Morrow, it appeared, traveled even lighter than
she did.

An appointment calendar, open to the preceding
Friday, was free of any notations. She flipped backward.
Then forward to today. Nothing. Did Julian Morrow
keep all of his appointments in his head? Maybe that's
why he was chronically late. Well, not late today, she
reminded herself. At least not yet.

She had just sat down in the black leatherette desk
chair, and was reaching to try the middle drawer, when
she heard the clear march of footsteps approaching in
the marble hallway. There was plenty of time to walk
back around and arrange herself sitting patiently in
front of the desk.

"Scusi. Scusi, signorina."

She recognized the handsome man immediately
from the photos Sully had shown her weeks ago in
Washington. Monsignor Umberto Brisi looked at her
from the door with a strange combination of genuine
and mock surprise.

"Father Morrow . . ." He came farther into the
room, his black eyebrows shooting upward to the dark
sweep of his widow's peak. ". . . He is not here?"

"No." She smiled at this dramatic statement of the
obvious and reached out to offer him her hand. "I'm
Romany Chase." She spoke to him in Italian. "Acquisitions Director for Arte per Pace. I'm a little early for my
appointment."

He had taken her hand at once, was still holding
lightly to her fingers. "Monsignor Umberto Brisi," he

introduced himself with a kind of bow, "Director General and Chief Curator. I am, of course, speaking for our Prefect, Cardinal DeLario, as well as for myself, when I say that we are eager to help you with your work here in any way that is possible."

"That's very kind . . ."

"Not at all." He straightened with a gesture that brushed her words away. Monsignor Brisi was a man obviously in love with the sound of his own voice, and eager to clear the way for it. "I cannot tell you how happy His Eminence and I were when His Holiness took our little suggestion to heart."

"Your suggestion?"

"The sponsorship of Arte per Pace." His smile was at once sly and defensive, daring her to contradict. "It is very important in these troubled times that the Holy Father take a moral and political lead. Be the Good Shepherd. Our dear Pope Gregory"—and here the monsignor made a point to smile most affectionately—"is a very holy man, but sometimes the Cardinal and I, we have to . . . how do you say it in English . . . put an insect into his ear?"

It was an entirely extraordinary performance, and so broad that she was at a complete loss trying to come to some conclusion as to its purpose. It was almost an anticlimax when the door opened again to Julian Morrow in full cassock and sneakers. A kind of clerical David Letterman, she decided.

"*Buon giorno.*" The American's accent was perfect, and Brisi bristled at the sound of it. The two men exchanged a look.

"Good afternoon," she said in English.

But it was Brisi who turned to her, again taking her hand. "Do not forget what I have said, Signorina Chase. If I can be of any help . . ." He left in a slow-motion exit with a poisonous smile for Julian Morrow.

The priest was apparently too busy with seating himself at his desk to have noted the Curator's exit, but she saw his mouth twist slightly at the corner. "Monsignor

Brisi doesn't like me," he said. "He thinks he should have had this job."

She stared at him. That he'd said it surprised her.

"This is the list you asked for on Friday." He took a paper out of his briefcase, pushing it across the desk toward her.

He still hadn't really smiled, or even made eye contact. She had told herself she was prepared for anything, but not for this aloofness.

Finally he glanced up. "What do you think?" he said.

Great. She hadn't even looked at the damn list. She pulled the paper closer. There were works from each of the ten Vatican museums. Coins and manuscripts from the Library. Historical documents from the Secret Archives.

"His Holiness has tried to select things that have a historical as well as aesthetic relevance to the Church," Julian Morrow spoke again. "He doesn't want it to seem as if the Vatican is in some kind of artistic competition with the Italian pavilion."

She had skipped quickly to the paintings while he was talking. The Caravaggio was on the list.

"I . . . I don't see da Vinci's *St. Jerome,*" she finally managed to say. "I was hoping we'd get something from each of the 'big three.' Raphael. Leonardo. Michelangelo." She looked up. Tried smiling.

He smiled back. *"The Transfiguration*'s there. Which takes care of your Raphael. Michelangelo is tough. Most of his stuff is on walls, as you know. And after that hammer attack a few years ago on the *Pieta* . . ."

"So no Michelangelo?" She let disappointment color her voice, but her mind was busy speeding over the possibilities. Who had approved the Caravaggio? If DeLario was truly behind the forgeries, why hadn't he stopped it from being exhibited?

"I'm sure there must be some of Michelangelo's sketches you could have. Maybe some preliminary studies for the Sistine," Julian was going on. "And I'll speak to His Holiness about the *St. Jerome.*"

He gave her a half smile this time, but his eyes had glanced away. Her mind gearshifted back to the puzzle that was Julian Morrow. On Friday he had waltzed into their interview half-naked, and then hadn't thought twice about playing with her hair. Now this apparent coolness. Well at least Father Morrow had done exactly what she asked, gotten the list of Vatican submissions ready. What she needed now was an excuse to stick around here. Observe the activity in this place. Observe him.

"I'm not familiar with some of these things from the Library or the Archives," she said innocently.

"We're having pictures made." He had picked up a pencil from somewhere on the desk and was marking up the once clean surface of the blotter with X's. Or maybe they were crosses.

"I'll have a set of proofs sent to you as soon as they're available," he went on. "And of course you'll have full access to our inventory descriptions."

"That's good," she said. "But we'll need to get some commercial shots made somewhere down the line. For the souvenir catalog."

He didn't say anything now, and she watched him go carefully over the marks he'd made.

"I really need to get a better feel for this stuff, Julian"—she waved the papers he'd given her in front of him—"before the submission lists from the other countries start coming in. I'd like to have a look at some of these things right now if I could. Especially the paintings."

"Sure." He stood up, the pencil hitting the green blotter with a tiny thud. Amazingly it didn't roll. He opened his top drawer and pulled out some keys.

There were more people about now as they walked toward the elevator, the clerks and secretaries trickling in from lunch. The two of them got their share of second looks, not that she couldn't guess why. *Harper's Ba-*

zaar meets Nike priest. They had to make a pretty peculiar couple.

Julian seemed to warm a bit as they went through the Pinacoteca and she took notes. He was loosening up, and she was congratulating herself by the time they'd reached the room with the works from the seventeenth century. When they finally stopped in front of the Caravaggio, she didn't say anything, but continued scribbling in her notebook.

She hoped when she gazed up that he'd be looking at the canvas and she'd get a chance to catch his unguarded reaction. But when she did glance up, he was looking back at her. Not in any way priestly, but with a man's frank appraisal. And he was smiling too. That all-American-boy smile that had made him seem so young and candid the first time they had met. She looked away.

Stop it, Romany. She shook herself mentally. Julian Morrow wasn't a man. He was a priest, and dealing with him was a major part of her job. Both of her jobs. She made herself look up, and smile back. But now he was turned toward the Caravaggio. His face registered nothing. He was playing with the ring of keys he still held in his hand.

"May I see that?" She hadn't paid much attention when he'd locked his office, but now she was startled to recognize the figure that hung from the chain.

"This?" He held it out to her. "It's just something somebody gave me once as a joke. It's supposed to be some kind of demon."

She had taken it into her hand. "It's a baphomet. The legend is that Baphomet was worshiped by the Knights Templar. But figures like this only started showing up hundreds of years after the Templars were disbanded." She handed the keys back. "I'm afraid you're toting around a fake, Julian. The Knights probably never even had such an idol. Most historians think they were framed."

He was turning the figure over in his hand. "A forgery of an original that never existed. That's an interesting concept."

"A Jesuitical concept?" She had said it only half-mockingly.

"Yes." He turned to her. He was smiling again, but this time it was totally different. This time her feeling of nakedness had nothing to do with her body. And only now did there seem something that was vulnerable in him too. It passed almost as quickly as she'd glimpsed it, so that afterward she knew she would question whether she had ever seen it at all. But now she was certain. If ever a man hid a secret, that man was surely Julian Morrow.

Intermission. Romany got up quickly from her seat in the last row and walked up the gravel pathway toward the black outline of the trees. It was a perfect Roman night. In front of her were the moonlit ruins of Caracalla, behind her the brightly lighted stage with all the gilt and fantastical glamour of an outdoor *Aïda.*

It was just like Sully to pick this place to meet, a performance of *Aïda* at the Baths. In one of their more inflammatory discussions he'd told her how much he hated opera. A charter member of the "I don't know art but I know what I like" school of aesthetics, Sully hadn't flinched when she'd lost her cool and told him he was too much the Philistine for a career-diplomat cover. He'd simply laughed and launched into a perfect parody of a *Times* Met review. Grudgingly, very grudgingly, she'd had to laugh too.

Sully was already waiting for her when she arrived. He was standing in a corner of a ruined building, out of reach of the moonlight, but she could see the burning dot of the ever-present cigarette in his hand.

He stepped forward. "It's about time."

"This is Rome, remember. *Aïda*'s running late. And it would've been too conspicuous, getting up before the intermission."

"If your goal is not to be noticed, you should stop wearing that kind of dress."

His face was mostly in shadow still, but she could sense his eyes on her, feel his appraisal of the décolletage of her emerald-silk chemise. It was their first face-to-face in Rome, and already the man was trying to pick a fight. David was right, Sully could be an asshole.

"Is that an order?" she asked. "About the dress?"

"I can't *order* you to do anything, Romany. Not technically. You know you weren't my choice for this. It was your friend Andrew who insisted."

She ignored the impulse to be angry. There was plenty of time to get mad later.

"Look, Romany." Sully was getting to the point in the face of her silence. "I won't tell you that this isn't a game. It *is* a game. But it's a game where you *don't* play fair. You do everything and anything to get the job done."

"I'm not exactly an amateur," she said coolly. "And Andrew wanted me because I was the logical choice."

"Nothing personal, Romany." He said it with a mild reasonableness that made her want to hit him. "I just think you're in over your head. Like you were in Geneva. And no David ben Haar this time to cover your ass."

"David's here," she answered him flatly. "He turned up at my apartment Friday night."

"Shit." Sully threw down the cigarette, grinding it out in the centuries-old dust. "I should've known Mossad couldn't play straight with us."

The last thing she wanted was to get into the CIA/Mossad relationship with Sully. "David said that neo-Nazis are behind all this. *I* didn't say anything. Just played at playing dumb. Don't you think it would be good if you filled me in on everything, Sully?"

"Why? It sounds like ben Haar's doing a pretty good job."

"Because I just might need to know."

"I doubt that. The German thing doesn't really affect anything on your end."

"Maybe. Maybe not."

"Okay . . . okay." He fished in his pocket for the cigarettes. "Our friends the Israelis have convinced themselves that most of the art money is being spent to finance a neo-Nazi takeover of Europe."

"Are they right?"

"Looks like it." Sully got busy lighting another cigarette. "The point is, we've got agents close to finding out for sure, if Mossad doesn't jump the gun and screw it." The lighter flared, illuminating his face. Sully wasn't that bad looking if you could get past all his bullshit.

A sharp metallic click. Sully had stoked up the cigarette and was putting the lighter away in his pocket. "This whole Arte per Pace circus has become a political football with the Pope as quarterback," he said. "What we've got to know is if he's on the home team."

"So now you think Pope Gregory might be directly involved?"

"That's what you've got to find out, Romany. Because if his hands are dirty, it's going to make things a lot more complicated. And either way, we've got to move our asses quick and control the damage."

"Pretty serious, huh, Sully?"

"You got it," he said. "So what have you been doing, besides shopping the Via Condotti?"

The line was a jibe, a throwaway. Still she wondered. Did Sully really have a man on her? She shrugged the question away.

"I met with the Vatican liaison today," she said. "I guess you know it's not Umberto Brisi."

"Yeah, we took too much for granted on that one. The American Jesuit was a real surprise." He took a long drag on the cigarette. "So what did you find out, what's Morrow like?" he asked her.

"I don't know yet."

"Come on, Romany. You can do better than that."

"He changes. I've met with him twice now, and I still

can't get a fix. This morning when I went to see him, he wasn't in his office. Brisi showed up while I was trying to get into his desk."

"Was Brisi there to check you out?"

"Possibly. I had the feeling he knew who I was. The guard could have notified him when I entered the building." There was a rustling movement in the weeds. A lean gray cat was stalking something in the shadows. "What about you?" she asked, turning the tables. "What's Washington been able to come up with on Morrow?"

"It's tough with the Church. Especially the Jesuits. On the surface Morrow checks out. But there are gaps in the record. A lot of times when he just seems to drop out of sight. The last six months he's been in Rome."

"Yeah," she said, "he told me. Public relations."

"What you probably don't know is that for the two years before that he was hiding out in a Cistercian monastery in Switzerland."

"A monastery?"

"Does that surprise you, Romany?" Again he was watching her closely.

"I don't know, but I'm having trouble pegging Julian Morrow for a monk."

"Oh . . . ?"

Sully's teeth shone whitely for a moment. She followed his gaze to the revealing neckline of her dress. "That's not exactly what I meant, Sully."

"Too bad."

She ignored the implications of his remark. "Listen, Sully," she said instead, "I've checked out the Caravaggio. I'm sure it's a fake. And it's on the Vatican's list for Arte per Pace. What I can't figure out is, if DeLario's our man, then why in the hell did he let that happen?"

"Ballsy son of a bitch. But maybe that'll work in our favor."

"I still want to get you the paint samples from the Caravaggio," she said. "And Brisi's my key to DeLario.

I'm going to take the monsignor up on his offer to help." She smiled.

"That's fine. But Morrow's the nut we've got to crack. If the Pope *is* playing footsie with DeLario, this Father Morrow would have to know. Think you can get to him, Romany?"

"Get to him? Let me make sure I'm reading you right, Sully. You're telling me you want me to seduce a Roman Catholic priest?"

"If that's what it takes."

So that's what this little talk was all about. He'd been working up to it from the beginning.

"I can do my job, Sully."

"I know, Romany." The bastard didn't have the good grace to keep his grin to himself.

CHAPTER 6

Romany sat forward in the black leather chair in her office. A thick square of pizza from the little *pizzerie* around the corner lay half-eaten on her desk. Elliot had invited her to lunch along with some official from the city's planning office. But she'd passed, preferring to snack at her desk instead. She had real work ahead of her today, and she liked the early-afternoon quiet.

It was one-thirty now, and she was virtually alone on the floor. The APP staff might be overloaded with Americans, but the office ran on Roman time. Lunch was roughly from noon to four, after which people returned to their desks to stay till eight. Her own hours were completely flexible, especially now with everything just beginning. And no one looking over her shoulder. Elliot simply trusted her to get the job done.

She rewrapped the unfinished pizza carefully in its waxed paper and put it in the white paper sack. Maybe she'd be hungrier later. Her crumpled napkin was stained liberally with tomato sauce, and she tossed it into the waste can, then took a pack of tissues out of her purse. She wiped her fingers completely clean and reached for the invitation that was sitting still unopened on the corner of her desk. It was for the cocktail party being held on Friday night for the Arte per Pace elite—everyone who was anyone with a vested interest in the success of the exhibition. It was a list that was getting longer as the political and social importance of Arte per Pace grew.

She took the cream-colored square out of the envelope and turned it in her hands. Nothing here but paper and ink, and yet the outdated copperplate handwriting seemed to offer an air of promise, the magic almost of a past age. And with a sudden eerie force she was remembering her childhood fancies—the Cinderella balls and parties that a grown-up Romany would someday attend.

She made a face. The sad fact was that Romany grown-up had long ago tired of these kinds of affairs. They were usually boring and she ate too much. The parties she attended were showcases, not celebrations. Sometimes, not often, she met someone who was genuinely interesting, but long conversations, one-on-one, were a no-no. The imperative was to circulate, circulate. With a watery drink in her hand and a practiced smile on her face.

And still I always hope. The little voice in her mind took over, and she shook her head as if to be rid of it. But it was the truth and she knew it. The grown-up Romany was still waiting, still expecting to find the kind of party she had imagined as a child. *And still waiting for the Prince, no doubt.* The voice had turned ironic.

No, she told herself. There would be no princes Friday night anyway. Only a count. Count Klaus Sebastiano, the man who would be their host. Apparently he'd made the offer through Giuseppi Aldano, the Director General of the Italian pavilion, a gesture that Arte per Pace's board of directors had summarily approved.

"Very rich. A patron of the arts," was Elliot's bare

description when she'd asked him about Sebastiano. Something about the puckish twist of his mouth when he said it made her think there was a lot he wasn't telling. But Elliot only smiled when she pressed him. "Wait and see," was all he'd say.

She had questioned Linda, but Elliot's secretary hadn't been able to tell her much else. Just that the Count was some kind of eccentric, and a staple, apparently, of *la dolce vita* society. She tossed the invitation down onto the desk. Compared to what else was going on, it was a very minor mystery.

She drank a sip of her bottled water and picked up her copies of the materials that had arrived this morning from the printer—an artist's rendering of the exhibition center, and a schematic of the floor plan with the name of each country printed in its designated space.

The building, to be erected near the Borghese Gardens, was in the form of a huge domed circle. Combining elements both classical and modern, the design was meant to echo the goals of Arte per Pace itself, harmony and balance, the many within the one. Inside, the exhibits were arranged within concentric colonnades radiating outward from the central Vatican Pavilion—the smaller countries closest in, the larger and wealthier countries assigned to the periphery where they would have the most space. It was a good plan. Aesthetic, fair, and practical.

A bulletin had already gone out, she knew, requesting a preliminary submission list from each of the participating nations. Now that copies of the floor plan were available, her immediate task was an accompanying letter for each exhibitor specifying in detail that nation's individual space assignment within the hall, and setting the deadline for both the finalized submission list and a scale rendering of the exhibit's physical design.

Arte per Pace's official language was English, as it was for most international projects these days, but she had decided her letters should be written in the language of each country. For a lot of reasons she wanted it all to go as smoothly as possible, and communicating in each nation's native tongue would, she had decided, be the best way of preventing any confusion. Elliot's exaggerations aside, she couldn't personally handle all the translations. But with the resources available to Arte per Pace, she ought to be able to locate the right personnel.

What she should do, and right now, was call Julian Morrow. The Vatican had some of the best translators around, and that was, after all, what the Acquisitions Director and the Pope's liaison were supposed to be doing, working closely on this project together.

"What's he like?" had been the first thing Elliot asked her yesterday morning. And she'd sure as hell painted a rosier picture than she had for Sully last night. Having Elliot doubt her ability to get along with Father Julian Morrow was a complication she couldn't afford.

Today when Elliot had popped in bright and early to ask about yesterday's meeting with the priest, she'd been able to produce for him the Vatican's preliminary submission list. He'd been delighted. More delighted still to know she was in there pitching for Michelangelo and Leonardo. "Excellent, Romany," he had said, beaming at her, and gone off to keep his lunch date. Ready again to do battle with the bureaucrats.

Sully was not going to be so easy to please. She'd had on her game face last night, had played it disgustingly close to cocksure. The same defensive attitude Sully usually managed to provoke. The fact was, she was feeling more doubt now than at any time since she'd agreed to the assignment. She'd been confident, in fact, before this. But seducing a Catholic priest wasn't exactly what she'd signed on for.

Seduce Julian Morrow. She'd been awake most of the night thinking about it. Trying to form a plan. Wondering how good she would be at seduction. Wondering how Julian Morrow would respond.

She'd rarely taken the lead with men since Alan. She'd planned that seduction all right. But that was nearly a decade ago. Every man she'd dated after that disaster had pursued *her,* and behind her stretched a string of unsatisfying relationships that she'd been the one to end. Control was what she wanted. She believed that of herself. And she'd been in control . . . until David. She still was, but at a price. She'd let him get on that plane over a year ago without a whimper. But what would Sully think of Romany Chase, seductress, if he knew she hadn't taken a man to her bed since? At least not until last Friday night.

She pushed away all thoughts of David. Sully was right. She wasn't qualified. She was an amateur. She pushed away that thought too. She'd be damned if she was going to fail Andrew.

She forced her mind instead to Julian Morrow. Concentrate, Romany. Put this in perspective. The man, and he was just a man in the end, was very possibly a crook. An accomplice to forgery and worse. She remembered the way he had looked at her yesterday in front of the Caravaggio. *That* Julian Morrow could be had.

Hold on to that thought, she told herself. Take it one step at a time. A last flicker of doubt darted up her spine and knotted itself in her chest. She ignored it. Turned to the phone. She would make herself call him. Now.

The phone buzzed a warning as she reached for it. Her hand jerked convulsively, and the knot coiled up to her throat. Shit. She took a breath, angry at herself. "Romany Chase," she said calmly into the receiver.

"Good, I caught you." The voice was Julian Morrow's. "I'm looking at the floor plan," he said. "It came by messenger this morning. Looks good. Outside looks good too. . . . Romany?"

She realized he'd been waiting for something from her. "Yes," she finally answered.

"Have you been out to the site yet?"

"No. But I've heard it's nice." *God!* She had the good grace to cringe. What a really dumb answer.

"I've been out there once," he was saying. "I

thought I might run out again this evening. Just to get a feel. Can you go?"

"Yes, of course. There are some things I need to talk to you about."

"Good. Is seven okay? It won't be so hot. I can pick you up there at the office."

"Fine . . . I'll see you then."

"Ciao." She heard his breezy laughter.

"Ciao," she answered and heard the click. She stared for a long time at the phone.

Skyscraperless, the great dome of St. Peter's dominating, Rome was ever changeless. The Eternal City. So that in this grand and glorious place of the Caesars one had no need to unearth a crypt of ancient memories to discover the city's soul, for everywhere the city that was, remained truly the city that is.

And because of the feeling that it had all somehow happened before, that everyone had trod in the same well-worn ruts left by ancestors who existed one-half millennium before Christ, there was always a kind of harmless cynicism in everything that Romans did. A sense that there was truly nothing new under the sun, an essential certitude that life was as it had always been.

Romany looked up at the Roman sky, at the failing light of sunset, and wondered at the destiny that had brought her here, here to this moment, to stand in a street off the Via Condotti next to this mysterious, enigmatic Jesuit priest. Looking tall and handsome and somewhat indistinct in the early shadows, Julian was saying something about the restaurant being named for the one-time chef of Queen Victoria.

". . . of course he didn't come to Rome until Empress Carlotta's husband lost his head to a firing squad."

". . . Empress Carlotta?" She hadn't moved, but stood watching him as he paused stock-still in front of the doorway. He was wearing civilian clothes. Spare but expensive civilian clothes, which seemed more natural than the heavy dark cassock.

"Romany Chase, I don't believe you've heard a word I've said. And I thought I was impressing you with my little history lesson."

"I'm sorry, I was just looking at . . ."

". . . the Roman sky." He hadn't allowed her to finish, and his eyes shifted from her upward to where she'd been staring. "I know. It does give you a kind of feeling." After a moment he glanced back down and smiled. "Ready?" And he pushed open the door.

The interior was small and intimate, and she thought Julian was about to say something about the peace and quiet in contrast to most noisy Italian restaurants when . . .

"Julian, Julian." The name was spoken enthusiastically, and she saw a man almost as short as Julian was tall rush over and embrace him. The two were obviously glad to see one another. And as the older man scolded the priest for staying away so long, Romany watched Julian's face take on that same innocence she'd seen the day they'd met. Suddenly the man became aware of her and quickly whispered something to Julian.

"Ask her yourself." Julian turned to face her. "She speaks perfect Italian. Paolo, may I present Ms. Romany Chase."

The unexpected revelation that she could speak the language seemed to embarrass the maître d', but he quickly recovered with all the continental grace one would expect.

"So pleased that you have joined us for dinner, Signorina Chase. We are honored by the presence of such a beautiful lady."

"Grazie, grazie mille, Paolo." She extended her hand, giving him one of her brightest smiles.

"Go ahead, Romany. Tell Paolo about our secret liaison." Julian was staring at her, the soft light in the restaurant playing favorites with his blond hair and tanned skin. For an instant his words sounded odd, but there was nothing in his expression except that he was having a little fun, if slightly at her expense.

"There is no secret liaison, Paolo," she said at last. "I am working with Father Morrow on Arte per Pace."

"Ahh, Arte per Pace, it will bring all the world to Rome."

"*Sì*, Paolo, all the world. Just what Rome needs, more traffic." Julian laughed.

"Traffic?" The maître d' seemed momentarily stumped. Then he laughed too. "You are a very funny man, Father Julian Morrow. But let me show you to your table. The best in the house."

The table was in a small corner, and Romany somehow sensed that it was one Julian had occupied before. He was talking about the house specialty when he lifted a menu and placed it in her hands.

"I know it by heart," he said without any smugness.

She looked up. "You do seem to know your way around." It sounded like an indictment. Damn, what was wrong with her? This certainly wasn't the script she'd written.

He stared at her for a moment, as though trying to figure out the sharp edge he'd heard in her voice. "I studied in Rome after I was ordained," he said finally. "Over the years I've made time to come back. It's not a city easy to ignore." He smiled again.

"No, I guess not." This time she tried to make her voice friendlier, but with little luck. No, this was definitely not going to be easy. Damn you, Sully.

She glimpsed another couple at a nearby table. The man was handsome as only Italian men can be handsome, and she watched as he took his companion's fingers and brushed them slowly against his lips. *Wonderful,* she groaned to herself. She glanced back down at her menu.

"I'm in your hands, Julian Morrow," she said at last, meeting his eyes across the table. "Order for me." And for the first time she smiled at him.

"Oh, I don't know if I like the way that sounded,

Romany Chase." He seemed satisfied now that whatever had been wrong with her, the worst was over. "But if you insist." He called over the waiter and ordered wine and antipasto.

"What did you think of the site?" he asked finally, settling himself more comfortably into his chair.

"The construction site? I think it's incredible. But I can't believe ground hasn't even been broken."

"Don't forget you're in Rome, Romany. Things are rather slow to get started here. But they'll pick up. There's too much American money involved to allow the Romans to get too lazy."

"Not to mention Elliot's nerves."

"He sounds like a nice man, Romany. Perhaps too nice for this job."

"Oh, Elliot can handle himself. He's tougher than you think. I sometimes believe the nerves are a show to keep everyone off guard."

"And you?"

"Me?"

"Yes, do you have any tricks to keep everyone off guard?"

It was an unexpected question. But she'd come to expect the unexpected from Julian Morrow. What she didn't like was being on the wrong end of the question. "I don't know. I've never really thought about it. I guess I would have to say I go the other route from Elliot."

"High indifference?"

"No, no . . . detached is more the word, I think. Indifference would mean you didn't care. Being detached just gives you some distance." Go ahead, Romany, tell him your whole life story. Yet if she'd expected a response, she was wrong. He simply continued to stare at her as though he hadn't actually heard what she'd said.

"And what do you do, Julian . . . to keep everyone off guard?" She'd at last gotten her foot into the door.

"I'm not very good at camouflage." He shrugged, but even in the low light she could see his eyes harden.

She would never know if he'd been going to say more, because the waiter arrived then, and Julian kept himself busy joking with the young Italian as he poured the wine.

"To the success of APP"—he lifted his glass—". . . and a new friendship."

She clinked her glass against his and felt the bridge of his fingers brush against hers. When she brought her glass to her mouth, she could see that he was watching her.

She set her glass down. "When I was a little girl, my father would always let me have a sip of his wine at dinner. Mother would make such a fuss. I can't imagine what she thought a little taste of wine would do."

"At least you didn't try to sneak into a wine cellar and sample everything in sight." He was shaking his head, and she was noticing again what wonderful things his smile did to the corners of his eyes. "I don't know how Jeremy and I survived that one."

"Jeremy?"

"My twin brother. We were only fourteen, and Mom and Dad had gone away . . . a bar convention. Jeremy and I decided that it was high time we sampled the famous Morrow wines. I don't know how much we consumed, but it was enough. I passed out, and poor Jeremy was left to face Dad when he finally discovered our bodies in the cellar."

His laugh was contagious.

"What happened . . . afterward?" She took another sip of her wine.

"Well, Dad, being the paragon of justice he is, decided that we'd probably suffered enough with the hangovers we had the next morning, and settled on a nice lawyerly lecture on prudence in conduct."

"So your father's a lawyer?"

"In Philadelphia. Morrow and Phillips."

"No Morrow and Morrow then?"

"No Morrow and Morrow. There's little room for a canonical lawyer on staff." There was just the barest tinge of something in his voice. Bitterness or regret, she couldn't tell.

"And Jeremy?"

"Jeremy?" His voice was harsh.

"He didn't follow in your father's footsteps?"

"No, no, he didn't." He was staring down into his wineglass, sloshing its contents around.

"Another rebel?"

"Jeremy's dead." He stopped worrying the wine, and glanced up. "It was a long time ago." The words had a finality to them.

"Oh . . . I . . . I'm sorry, Julian." Damn, she didn't want to know this. Didn't want to know about his dead twin brother.

"That's all right. As I said, it happened a long time ago. Listen"—his voice sounded slightly false—"have you seen much of Rome since you've been here?"

"Some, but I must make a confession . . ." She stopped, considering her last words, and laughed. "I am in the right company for a confession, aren't I, Father?"

For an instant he seemed embarrassed. Then he made a kind of waving motion with one of his hands as though wiping clean some kind of slate. "Dispensing absolution is not one of my strong suits."

"Hopefully, Father Morrow, my penance will be small. Well, the truth is, that I've spent most of my free time shopping."

"Oh, one of those women." He smiled, angling his head to the side as if assessing the Valentino blouse and leather trousers she wore.

"Yes, one of those. Am I forgiven?" She could hear the musical sound at last come into her voice. She was flirting with him.

"Forgiven," he said. "So what have you seen?"

"Actually I've been to Rome a couple of times. Done most of the sites. But I've never made it to Tivoli."

"You haven't seen the Villa d'Este?"

"No," she was confessing again.

"Well, Romany Chase, if you're free Thursday evening, I'm going to drive you to Villa d'Este."

"It's a date, Julian," she said smiling. Yes, she was definitely flirting with Father Julian Morrow, and the most amazing thing was that he didn't seem to mind one damn bit.

CHAPTER 7

Romany sat at her desk, reviewing the letter that was to be sent to the exhibitor countries and fiddling with her hair. She scrolled the computer screen and reworked one of the combs that was meant to control the thick waves that had a mind of their own when the weather got too humid. Damn, the letter sounded stale, and her hair was driving her crazy. Like most women with long hair, Romany wrestled with occasional bouts of wanting to cut it all off. One of those nice no-frills styles. She was on the verge now, and the Roman heat wasn't helping.

She leaned back in her chair and pushed up the thick length of hair at her neckline so that a mass of shiny auburn curls spread across the top of her head like a fan. The air hitting the back of her neck felt good. Yes, she was definitely at the critical stage with her hair.

She dropped her hands when the phone rang.

"Hello, Romany Chase speaking."

"So it is."

"Dad?" She could hear his dark rich laugh coming through the line. "I can't believe it." But of course she could. She'd gotten used to his "surprise" calls long ago.

"What's my girl up to? Not working too hard, I hope."

"Not very. Elliot's really got things pretty well organized around here."

"Yes, I know all about Elliot, and you better watch

out for him. He expects everybody to keep the same long hours he does."

"What time is it there?"

"Two-thirty."

"Two-thirty in the morning and my father is still up. And what's this about Elliot keeping long hours?"

"You know me, Romany, I get my best work done when everyone else is asleep."

"Yes, I know. Remember the times I used to sneak down when I couldn't sleep, and curl up in the big chair, and watch you work until I couldn't keep my eyes open?"

"And I had to carry you off to bed."

"You never did tell Mother about those little visits, did you? How's she doing?"

There was just the smallest hesitation. "Actually your mother's doing fine. Better than she's been for months. In fact, that's part of the reason I'm calling."

"So there is an ulterior motive." Romany kept her voice light, ignoring the knot of anxiety in the pit of her stomach that was inevitable at the mention of her mother. "Go on, out with it."

"Well, you know I was planning on visiting you later on this summer."

"Yes, can't stay away from the pasta or the Etruscans."

"Such abuse, and from my own daughter. Actually, Miss Chase, I've lost a few pounds. You'd be proud of me. Anyway, your mother's decided to come along."

"What? She's feeling that well?"

"Apparently so. In fact, she became really angry when I first tried to discourage her."

"What do the doctors say?"

"They think it'll do her some good."

"This is unbelievable." Her voice rose with excitement.

"Yes, I know. At any rate we're hoping to leave in the next few weeks, as soon as I can work out a few

things here. I'll get back with all the details later. I'm
sure Elliot can find a house for us."

"Great. I don't think Mother'd like staying in a hotel."

"No, not for as long as we'll be there."

"How long are you planning to stay, Dad?"

"Not sure yet. But it looks close to six weeks."

"Dad, that's perfect. God, I can't wait to see you.
Please tell Mom how excited I am she's coming."

"I will, Gypsy. . . . And Romany, take care of yourself."

She was still his little girl. "Always, Dad. I love you."

The last person Romany wanted to run into was Julian Morrow, and Monsignor Umberto Brisi was not
making things any easier. The Director General was giving her the grand tour of the Pinacoteca, stopping inter-
mittently, making what she thought sounded for all the
world like rehearsed speeches. The man was an absolute
ham, and she couldn't help but believe that his heavily
accented English was somehow calculated.

She breathed a sigh of relief when at last they moved
out of the building, away from any possible danger of
meeting up with Morrow. Next stop, the Sistine Chapel.

"But what a profusion of criticism we had to arm
ourselves against, Signorina Chase." Brisi had resumed
his defense of the Vatican's restoration of the Michelangelo masterpiece, stopping now just outside the Chapel.
His face wore the expression of a martyr. "So many
were unjustly censorious, afraid we were damaging the
great master's work. It was a time of trial for us all.
Many crosses we had to bear." The man rolled his dark
eyes, showing off to best advantage their almond shape,
the thick fringes of eyelash.

"But of course, Signorina Chase, you understand
how wrong our accusers were." It was meant as a compliment, in deference no doubt to her reputation as an

art expert, and she watched Brisi's face light up. The "martyr" switch had been turned off.

"Yes, Monsignor Brisi, the restoration was entirely justified, and from all accounts impeccable." Although her words were targeted more as a sop for Brisi's ego, she'd spoken the truth. Lies would come later.

It was after five o'clock in the evening, and though museum personnel were still presumably hard at work in their offices, the Vatican Museum itself was closed to the public. Romany could sense the emptiness beyond as Brisi opened the doors to the Chapel.

The genius of Michelangelo always came as a revelation, no matter how many times she saw his work. And the revelation came to her now, gazing up at his masterpiece, executed as it was from but pigment and plaster, one man's startling vision of life and time.

"True, we made our mistakes." Brisi was speaking again, and though his admission was meant to sound sincere, it had missed the mark. "The lights." He swept one long arm upward and pointed. "We left the same lights. They were too strong. They drained away the color. Like blood drawn from the vein." She saw him smile at the supposed cleverness of his simile.

"It seemed to everyone we had cleaned too much," he was taking up his narrative again. "But that was not so. It was the light. But it is better now. Much better." The last words were almost whispered, and for the first time Monsignor Brisi seemed not to be putting on any kind of performance. Romany watched as the priest gazed up at the ceiling, his face suddenly not a man's face, but a small boy's. Full of wonder and awe.

Quickly she glanced away. She didn't want to contemplate what she'd just seen in Umberto Brisi's face. That was too much like knowing about Julian Morrow's dead brother.

When she turned back, the priest was studying her. His face was wiped clean of the innocence she'd glimpsed a moment before. In its place was the handsome, patronizing smile he wore most of the time. "It is beautiful, is it not, Romany Chase?" He waved his hand to take in the whole of the Sistine Chapel.

"Yes, Monsignor Brisi, it is very beautiful. The Vatican Restoration Department has much to be proud of."

"We are the best in the world, Signorina Chase." He was still beaming his smile like a kind of radar.

"If I could, I would very much like to visit the Restoration Department, Monsignor Brisi."

In an instant she saw the handsome smile evaporate. "The Restoration Department?" Brisi stumbled over the words.

"Yes, I would like to visit the restoration facility . . . the place where individual canvases are taken to be worked on." She had hit a nerve, and she enjoyed watching the pompous priest squirm.

"That, Signorina Chase, will require approval." The muscles of his face formed a serious expression. "The work there is very delicate. Visitors might . . . well, we must not put any of our great works at risk." He finished with a smile of considerably less wattage.

"But I am surely not just any visitor, Monsignor Brisi, and surely you, as Director General, could secure permission for me to visit the department." In contrast she gave him a smile to rival his earlier ones.

"I . . ."

They both turned at the same moment, as though the presence were somehow felt more than seen. And Romany watched as the intruder moved like a broad sailing ship toward them, his long scarlet robes furling and unfurling about the floor. He was rather obsessively fingering a jeweled cross that hung like an anchor round his neck, but his face wore a relaxed, generous smile.

It was the smile, more than anything else, that Romany homed in on. The smile of a child. An angel. A smile that should have put her entirely at ease, but didn't. And despite everything she should or should not feel, despite everything she should or should not have expected, it was a smile for which Romany Chase was entirely unprepared. For in spite of all its physical beauty, it was a smile of absolute evil.

"How rude you are, Umberto. Are you not going to introduce me to your lovely companion?" His voice cooed softly in the large vacant space of the Chapel.

"*Scusi,* Your Eminence. Signorina Romany Chase, may I present Cardinal Vittorio DeLario."

A low sky like a square blue lid was pressing down on the high walls that surrounded the Cortile di San Damaso, as Cardinal Vittorio DeLario made his steady way toward the courtyard's eastern end. It was a fairly long walk from the Sistine Chapel to this part of the Old Vatican Palace, especially in the heat of late June. But the enforced exercise of walking from place to place within the Vatican enclave was probably what accounted for so many still-active octogenarians among the Roman curia.

The ranks of windows rising on all sides of him stood blank in the glare, like blind eyes sensing by preternatural means his silent passage beneath them. And Vittorio felt an unacknowledged relief when, nodding to the Swiss Guards at the portal, he passed through the large double doors.

The air inside the Apostolic Palace was always cool, air that seemed to have seeped for centuries through the cold filters of stone and marble. An atmosphere of oppressive secrecy was how he'd heard outsiders describe it. For Vittorio it was the very breath of life. He smoothed the hair from his forehead, damp with his perspiration, and pausing for a moment in the dim vestibule, he inhaled long and deeply. As if having labored here for half a century in the vineyards of his own ambition, it was the secrets now as much as the oxygen that sustained him.

A wily young priest from Salerno, he had vowed to seize the chance that his uncle's influence had brought him when he'd come to Rome so many years ago to serve as a secretary to the newly elected Pius XII. And quickly he'd become the keenest spectator of all that passed within the labyrinth of the papal court. A voracious collector of all the social and moral detritus of other men's lives.

A keeper as well as a collector of secrets, he was reminding himself now, as he started down the long vaulted hallway. For a good secret, like a fine wine, improved with age, and the most powerful were often the oldest.

The most powerful and perhaps the most bitter, he thought, for the wine could also sour, as the whole elaborate structure of a man's career might be destroyed by one who possessed the killing secret. Blackmail as an aid to diplomacy was an art he had learned early and well. Cardinal Vittorio DeLario was the power behind the Vatican throne, the man who ruled the rulers.

Still he had not become Pope himself. The acknowledged front runner at the death of Martin VI, he had been outmaneuvered in that summer of 1978 by a coalition of noncurial Italian and foreign cardinals. When on the third ballot it became apparent that he could not assemble the necessary two thirds plus one votes, he had had to accede to the election of the patriarch of Venice, the dark horse, Alessandro Cardinal Rossario.

A disturbingly unknown quantity, this Rossario had been. A man of no secrets. A simple holy man, by all accounts. Discounting the *holy,* Vittorio had allowed himself to be reassured. He was still Papal Secretary of State, after all, and *simple* he interpreted as easy to control.

But he had been wrong. The obedience that Rossario had previously brought to his dealings with ecclesiastic authority no longer contained him. The "smiling Pope," as the press had immediately dubbed the seemingly ingenuous Rossario, had had his own plans. When it became quickly clear that the new Victor Paul I was not such a *simple* holy man, but a dangerous intellectual bent on reform—he had been just as quickly dealt with.

His sudden death in the early-morning hours, a scarce thirty-three days after his election, had aroused suspicion, and public outcries of "murder" echoed in the popular press. But the Pope was dead, and the Vatican was still the Vatican.

As Secretary of State and *camerlengo,* the man officially in charge until the election of a new pope, Vittorio was naturally the first one called by Rossario's aide on his discovery of the Pope's lifeless body. And he was the first beyond the Pope's household staff to be allowed into the bedroom. It had been remarkably easy to remove the bottle containing what was left of Rossario's doctored medicine. Easy to take with him the papers that would have confirmed what had already reached his own ears as rumor, the order for his immediate dismissal as Secretary of State.

If Victor Paul I had been an ordinary citizen of Rome, he could not by Italian law have been embalmed for twenty-four hours. But the Vatican was still the Vatican. And Vittorio DeLario was still the Secretary of State. Death from myocardial infarction was the announcement given out, and most within the curial hierarchy were only too glad to believe it. Within fourteen hours the Pope who had said that the two things in shortest supply in the Vatican were honesty and a good cup of coffee, was already embalmed. There was no death certificate. And no autopsy.

The conclave to elect the new Pope was held a bare ten days after Rossario's burial. This time Vittorio had no false illusions about his own chances, and he was prepared for the challenge that would come from the foreign cardinals, especially from those of the Third World.

The vote had been very close. For a time it had seemed that the smiling Pope would be followed by a Polish one. But that absurdity at least they had been spared. The votes DeLario commanded were the decisive factor in saving the papacy for the Italians and for the Curia. And even after his retirement, they had not been allowed to forget it.

But lately it seemed that Niccolo was forgetting himself. And the truth was it was hard to threaten a pope. Whatever one had on a cardinal, one had better make good use of before his ascension to the Throne of Peter. Despite piranha instincts, to the curial mind the Church was but the hierarchy, and the system that sustained it must forever remain inviolate. Pope for life was the incontrovertible rule. And though Pope Gregory XVII might owe his election to the back-room politics of which Vittorio was the master, it was but a semblance of honor that required a man, once he became the Supreme Pontiff of Holy Mother Church, to stay bought.

Vittorio stopped at the end of the hall and looked behind him. There was no one else in sight. Somewhere he had read that there were thirty secret staircases within the precincts of the Vatican. As if someone from within would ever tell such a thing to a journalist. And only thirty. He allowed himself a smile. He had been here now for more than five decades. Fifty-odd years of ferreting out tunnels and passageways, and even he did not suppose he knew them all. This one he knew well.

He turned back to the painted panel before him, feeling the wooden framing for the catch. With an always surprising silence, the panel swung out, and Vittorio slipped behind it. For centuries a lantern had hung here. Now there was a flashlight. He flicked the switch and played the beam up the stairway, but he wasn't thinking of hidden passageways now. He was remembering the day his troubles had begun with his first doubts about Niccolo.

He ran the scene in his mind as he moved up the narrow staircase, the beam from the flashlight flowing against gravity, step by step. It had been early in December, and the papal apartments were too warm, though never warm enough for Gregory XVII in the winter. He was always thin and cold. The Pope had the look of an ascetic, like John in the desert living on locusts and honey. But it was a false impression, as Vittorio knew well. Niccolo Fratelli loved to eat. Nothing stuck to his bones. He remembered the china teacup that had rattled in the frail hands, as the Pope had announced his personal commitment to what would come to be known as Arte per Pace.

That had been the first shock, that Niccolo Fratelli would undertake such a project without first seeking his prior approval. And that negotiations with the Americans could have gotten so far without coming to his attention.

He stopped now for a moment on the small landing where the stairwell turned into a long, twisting corridor. It was not so cool here in the low tunnel-like space despite the dampness of the rough stone. The Byzantine cross seemed heavier at his neck. He took another breath and continued.

The second shock from Niccolo, he remembered, had been the appointment of Julian Morrow, and this time when he'd met with the Pope, there'd been little tone of apology. Anger was a stepchild of fear, he knew, but Vittorio had been angry. An anger that he had not hidden well. Niccolo's smile had said that.

Still he must keep things in perspective. Except for these isolated outbursts of independence, his relationship to the Pope remained the same. He was sure he had been correct in his assessment to Brisi. Arte per Pace was Niccolo's baby, his one great chance at history. Certainly the Pope's insistence on personally running this show could cause problems. But was it any real threat?

The papal liaison was a nuisance, but probably nothing more than that. A sop to American money, and one more instance of the papal proclivity for kissing Jesuit ass. Still he had his feelers out on Morrow.

And despite what he had said to his Director General, he was hardly thrilled with the inclusion of the Caravaggio in the Vatican exhibition. It would never have happened had he been in total charge. As Prefect he could still stop it. But it would only draw undue attention if he made that kind of objection. And the copy was perfect. There was no cause for anyone to suspect.

Still, it never hurt to be careful. That was one reason for his success, that of all the secrets he guarded, his own were the best kept. It had been ten years since he became the Prefect of the Vatican Museum. Before then, for thirty-five years, there had been the easily replaceable pieces that he had managed to steal, small things for the Baron's own pleasure. Only after he had gained complete control, with Brisi in place of Scotti, had he begun the forgery of major paintings.

And even now Brisi knew little. Nothing at all of the Baron. Only that art went out and money came in, and he got his share. Monsignor Brisi might be ambitious, but he had too little imagination to be dangerous.

He wondered about Romany Chase. The assertive modern woman was another scourge let loose on the world by the Americans. When he'd seen her today, the Acquisitions Director had been standing excessively close to Brisi in some ridiculous feminine version of a business suit. And certainly the monsignor seemed to like her well enough, to judge by his fawning and drooling. Although he doubted the woman would provide the monsignor with an easy conquest. Still, whether fending him off or giving in, Signorina Romany Chase should remain effectively distracted.

And then too there would be Brisi's administrative end run around Father Julian Morrow. Any separate relationship, business or otherwise, that the Director General cultivated with Romany Chase would only usurp Morrow's authority. Dear Niccolo would not like it, but that was too bad. He was still convinced that he could handle the Pope. And if it proved that he could not, there was always a more final solution.

The corridor had dead-ended, and he positioned his hand on the latching device before hanging up the flashlight. He liked to stand for a moment in the utter blackness before he made his entrance. As always when the panel opened, Niccolo was patiently waiting, alone in the little salon that was part of the papal apartments.

"Your Holiness." He swept in with conscious irony, and kneeling down, he kissed the papal ring.

CHAPTER 8

Romany came in from the brightness of the Roman afternoon. The long drapes in the living room stood drawn against the sun, and it took her a minute to make out the dark blur of the figure on her sofa.

"You don't look too pleased to see me," he said.

It was true. Her first reaction wasn't pleasure. She had left the office early with her mind focused, heading straight for her apartment. The last thing she needed was something to distract her from what she was supposed to be planning. And David ben Haar was a major distraction.

"It's not that, David," she said a moment too late. "But I am in kind of a hurry. I have a business appointment. At six."

David was stretched out with the big sofa pillows bunched at his back. A glass of wine from the open bottle in the refrigerator sat next to him on the table. He hadn't moved at all since she'd come in, but he wasn't really relaxing. David never relaxed. His eyes followed her as she walked into the kitchen.

She cracked some ice cubes into a glass and poured herself a Coke. Mineral water was supposed to quench thirst better in this weather, but she didn't really believe it.

She moved in the general direction of the balcony.

"Don't pull the curtains," David said.

"I won't."

She knew it wasn't a good idea they be seen together, and she wondered that he'd taken the chance at all of coming in the daylight. He'd been lying here, for who knew how long, waiting in her closed-up apartment. But David was a desert creature. He liked the heat.

She had been on her way to the thermostat. She turned it down to seventy. The air-conditioning unit drew a long, shuddering breath as she walked over and sat down next to him. He took the Coke out of her hand and put it on the table. She saw him make a face at the ice in her glass. An American indulgence like the air-conditioning. He drew her toward him and kissed her.

"I've got to get a bath, David." She half pulled away.

His hand was under the tight hem of her skirt where it had risen against her thigh.

"David . . ." He was kissing her again, his hand working its way higher.

"Can't bathe with this on." Now his hand had moved away, and he was kissing her again while he worked to unfasten the hook that held her waistband. He stopped, pulling back, his eyes familiar in their intensity. "Let's both have a bath," he said, tugging at the buttons of his shirt, ". . . after."

She stood up, undressing in silence while he watched her. Trying to understand what she was doing. There wasn't time for this now, and it wasn't what she wanted. Not the smart part of her. Rome wasn't going to last forever. At the end would be another airport. And David alone on the plane.

Later they sat facing each other in the marble tub, her bath crystals making a moonscape of bubbles on the water's oily surface. She reached for two large bobby pins on the edge of the basin and twisted her hair into a thick knot on the top of her head. She wouldn't have the time to wash it now.

"Where are you going tonight?" David sank down in the water up to his chin, his knees islands rising in the foam.

"To Tivoli. The Villa d'Este." She ran a soapy cloth against her neck.

"You said business."

"I've never been there." She moved the cloth downward, began to soap her breasts. "The papal liaison is taking me in his car." She explained, "A goodwill gesture."

"Papal liaison to Arte per Pace. A Jesuit. Father Julian Morrow." He ticked it off like a list.

"Right." She looked up at him sharply. "What do you know about him?"

"That's it. Except that his appointment took your guys by surprise."

"And yours?"

He shook his head. "The Vatican scam is Washington's side of things, Romany. The Mossad's got bigger fish."

"Like the neo-Nazis."

"Sully fill you in on that?"

She nodded. "I saw him Monday night. He said he was worried Mossad would . . . 'jump the gun and screw it.' "

David made a disbelieving noise. "Sully's got it a little twisted. We're the ones who've been on this. . . ." He stopped. "Things have changed since Sunday," he said now. "Word's come down our agencies are supposed to 'coordinate our operations.' " He had managed to pack a lot into the last three words. And acceptance was a very grudging part of it.

"It makes sense, David," she said to him. "And *we* manage to work pretty well together." Beneath the bubbles she was poking a toe inside the curve of his thigh.

"Yeah, well . . . you're a lot better looking than Sully." The green eyes had narrowed. Calculating.

"Uhn-uhn, David." She had guessed his intention. "No, don't. . . ." Too late. He had grabbed on to her ankle. "No!" She was screaming and laughing as he tugged her forward. "David . . . my hair."

Her back was sliding inexorably down the slick curve of the tub, and she'd barely time to close her eyes against the soapy water. When he let go, she was gasping, trying to reach a towel on the floor with one hand, wiping at her eyes with the other.

Then David had her by the shoulders, ignoring her protests, pulling her to lie back against him. She felt him hard again in the water between her legs. His hands cupped her breasts, and he lifted her.

Pleasure shot upward, a lightning stroke along her spine as he entered her, guiding her down to rest against his chest. There was a wonderful weakness in her limbs as she lay against him, buoyed in the body-warm water, as up and down he rocked her, his hands still cupping her breasts. And then so unlike David, he began whispering in her ear. In Hebrew. Not one of her better languages.

Strangely, like a sharp assault, she thought of Julian Morrow. Imagined him standing here in her bathroom bound in his Roman collar. Watching her now with David, wanting what was forbidden.

It was a kind of betrayal, one that should not have heightened her pleasure in this moment with David. But perversely enough it did. David was clutching her now, thrusting hard against her. Her own climax came as a burst of light and a sudden exultant conviction, like laughter filling her head. That tonight could work. That, after all, she might find in herself something sufficiently wanton.

With one small edge of the curtain rolled back, David ben Haar could just see through the balcony railing where the red Alfa Romeo Spider was waiting to park in the street. Romany had been flying about the apartment when the car had first driven up, still cursing him for her half-damp hair, amusingly anxious to keep the priest from getting as far as her door.

"I could hide in the bedroom." He had said it from his comfortable position, lying still naked on her sofa. Laughing at her as she went past buttoning her dress, hobbling on one shoe back to the bedroom.

"I don't trust you, David ben Haar." She'd come back with her other shoe and was throwing a hairbrush into that satchel she called a purse.

"Romany?" He had concentrated on the intent face, the wild curls threatening to break loose from the scarf that bound them. "Morrow one of the bad guys?"

Picking up a sweater, she had looked over at him then, with something remarkably like guilt. "I don't know." She was going for the door. "That's what I'm supposed to find out."

Then she was gone, her heels rat-tatting down the stairs. High heels at Villa d'Este. Just like an American. They never took anything seriously, then covered it up with a cynicism they hadn't earned. Romany was the flip side of that, of course, all earnestness and innocence. She was smart and she had guts. But it wouldn't be enough to protect her. He got up.

As he watched now, the Spider was swinging into the parking space that had finally become available at the curb. The door opened and a man got out, turning to where Romany had just emerged from under the balcony overhang. The man didn't exactly match the car, he looked far too American. What he didn't look like was a priest.

He watched them greet each other. Very friendly. The compressor on the air conditioner picked that minute to kick in again, so he couldn't hope to hear what was said. The man opened the passenger door for her, then walked around to get in. They didn't pull out right away, and he was wondering why when he saw the canvas top go down. The engine roared up as they shot away from the curb. He could tell by the tilt of her head that Romany was laughing.

Rushing, gushing, tinkling waters. Babbling waters rippling and cascading over age-worn stone, misting magically among the shadowed greens of lichen, moss, and fern. Frantic and romantic waters roaring in the mouths of dragons, spouting decadently from the multi-teated breasts of sphinxes, warbling in the rich bronze throats of owl-startled birds. The fountains were every-thing that Romany could have wished. And more, the history of Villa d'Este seemed fraught with teasing iro-nies.

Built for Cardinal Ippolito d'Este in the sixteenth century, the palace and water gardens were the work of Pirro Ligorio. Brilliant and complex, an archaeologist as well as an architect, Ligorio, like his contemporary, Mi-chelangelo, included among his many talents the faking of classical antiquities. Indeed, his name had once been called "the blackest in the calendar of Renaissance forg-ers."

And then there was the composer Liszt. Hiding be-hind an abbé's robes, he had fled to the Villa d'Este hoping to find a refuge from the women who pursued him. One, a Russian countess and his former music pu-pil, had not been in the least deterred. Dressed as a gardener's boy, Olga Janina had sneaked onto the villa grounds and succeeded quite easily in his seduction.

Maybe I should have carried snippers, Romany thought, watching Julian Morrow.

They had not spoken for some time now, standing among the tall cypress, looking out below to the valley. The dying sun had painted everything in a kind of satu-rated light, and he seemed almost surreal standing next to her, his fair aureole of hair and tall body in light-colored shirt and slacks glowing against the blackness of the trees.

They had played today, she and Julian Morrow. Like happy strangers who had met in Rome, with no history and no future. She had felt it immediately, the playful-ness, implicit in the red car, in the way he wore the light, casual clothes. Like an emblem, like a costume at a party.

She had sat in the red car, letting the wind blow everything away from her mind, letting it rip David from her body. Forgetting the job. Forgetting that the man beside her was a priest and a suspect, and she a paid agent of the United States government.

It had all been wonderful. The rapid change in the landscape as the city fell away into ancient olive groves and farmsteads. The blast-furnace air growing cooler with the miles, as they climbed toward the Sabine Mountains.

They had reached Tivoli and the Villa d'Este well before dusk, but by the time they had left the palace frescoes, the lights in the gardens were on. From the terrace she had caught her first glimpse of spraying fountains, like the plumed heads of leaping stallions white among the trees.

They had played today. And she had liked this uncomplicated persona better than any he had so far let her see. Liked his ease and his sense of humor, and the pleasure he had seemed to find in their joyful sharing of this place. She had to stop playing now, but this was the Julian Morrow she must hold in her mind. Not the priest. Not the suspect in criminal forgery. But a Julian Morrow to whom she could want to make love.

He turned to her and smiled. For a moment the truth of her treachery rose to stick in her throat. But she forced it down. This was her job. She was committed.

She smiled back, moving closer, as if she might want a better view, or perhaps some little shelter from the wind. He must have thought the latter, because she felt his hands draping her sweater more firmly around her shoulders.

Time to take the advantage. And shifting backward, she pressed herself lightly against his chest, her eyes closed. She was barely breathing, feeling for any answering strain. But she could find no sense of any rejection in his posture.

She turned. He was looking down at her. His eyes, so close, were unreadable. She would never remember exactly what had happened next, but she knew when her arms went around him. And the small moment of her triumph when she felt him hard against her. Then she was pulling him down toward her, her fingers tangling in his hair, her mouth moving on his.

At the moment when she ceased thinking at all, he let her go, suddenly, with a gesture almost brutal that set her tumbling back. His hand reached for her wrist, didn't let her fall. But the grip was not kind or gentle.

His face was closed. Completely. Anger would have been better. She was glad when he turned away from her, walking back in the direction of the car. There would be no dinner tonight at the wonderful terraced restaurant he had talked about today. Of that she was perfectly sure. It was going to be a long drive back to Rome.

The waves were, as always, dark and hungry. Like great sucking mouths devouring him. Their terrible coldness eating at his flesh. Seeping inside to the marrow of his bones. And there was no end to it. Boundless, without definition, the water was eternal. As in the beginning before the hand of God had set the seas to rest.

He could feel water filling his mouth like fresh blood, and the pitiful thing, a heavy weight at the end of his arm. Again he was grasping, trying to pull, force the body above the wall of black wave. Only once had he been able to wrap his arm about the neck, see for one instant the face, that face which was an exact mirror of his own. Then his arm failed him, and he'd lost his hold. *Jeremy* . . .

Julian shot up in bed, his body wet as though he'd just come up from a great dive into a pool. He had had the dream again.

He stripped the sheet away and got out of bed, pulling at the tight band of his jockey shorts, sliding the underwear down his legs. There was the fresh taste of blood in his mouth. At some point he had bitten his lip in his sleep. Slowly he ran his hand over his stomach, trying to ease the thudding pain in his gut. He never had any trouble imagining what a boxer felt like when a good one had been landed to the midsection. Yet he knew from experience, the pain had a will of its own, and he could do nothing but simply wait it out.

He moved into the bathroom and turned on the water inside the shower stall. For a moment he waited for the hot water to make it through the pipes, then stepped inside.

How many months had it been since he'd last had the dream? He couldn't remember. He thought it had been almost a year. But why now? He let the warm water beat against his face, taking in a mouthful and spitting it out. Like most things from his past, Julian Morrow knew better than to try to put his memory to the test.

He stood listening to the sharp zinging sound of the shower, and just beneath the topnote, a soft gurgling escaped the force of the nozzle. He stared at the small, slow stream running like a tongue from a fountain.

He looked down at his erection.

It was his old enemy. The old battle. The one he'd lost more than he'd won. And like the pain in his gut, there was nothing to do for it but give in. Be done with it. He reached for the bar of soap and lathered his palms. Then he lowered his arm and took hold of himself. He stroked slowly at first. Precisely. Watching the controlled movement of his hand as though it were not his hand at all, but someone else's. On cue the muscles of his stomach began to constrict, pull up and away from his groin. He focused his concentration and began to work faster. Reproducing the old rhythms, the old pattern that his body had long ago come to expect.

He felt himself slump against the wall of the shower. The water beat a hard path down the sharp angles of his shoulders. He sucked in a deep breath. There was always, with the release, a price to pay. And over the years he had almost come to terms with the burden of his sin. But this time there was that which had never been before. Something inside of him for which he was infinitely unprepared. Something new to be added to the old store of guilt. A thing he understood as fear.

Perhaps it had been the dream. Or the soft dripping stream of the water from the nozzle. Like the water from the fountains at Villa d'Este. He had no reason for it. But this time his passion had a new face. The face of Romany Chase. But how could he have been so stupid as not to have seen it coming? Had he not been working up to it, sending her signals all night? He could still feel her mouth on him. The exact pressure of her breasts against his chest. But he had been good this time. Had he not in the end pushed her away? He could hear his dry laugh reverberate inside the stall. Pushed her away, Julian? If she only knew how much he'd wanted her.

And how he'd hated himself after. Seeing her face. Her confusion. And was it not pain too he'd seen there in her eyes as the shadows closed in on them? He shut off the water and got out of the stall. Always he marveled at his great capacity to hurt.

Now in the darkness of his room he stood with a towel wrapped about his waist. He hadn't bothered to dry off, and beads of water slid down from his hair into his face. He ran a hand over his eyes, pushing away at the wetness.

In this place of assumed and actual holiness, the ghosts of his past lay in wait for him, in the company of all the angels and saints of this his Holy Mother Church. But there would be no passing of judgment this night. Judgment would come later. After all had been done. After all the sins of Julian Morrow had been tallied.

But he had to see things as they were. Here and now. And that brought him inevitably back to Romany Chase. He had to try to understand what was happening. Apart from the old demons from the past. Apart from his own sins, his own guilt. More than anything, he had to come to terms with the events of the last days without the burdens of Switzerland, without the pain of that sailing trip almost twenty years ago. He had to put

Romany Chase where she belonged, evaluate her in terms of where he was now, and what he must do.

It was important that he stay close to her. And that was the rub. Stay close to her. He laughed again, that same dry, mocking laugh. Come on, Julian, old boy, you can do it. She's not the first woman to get under your skin. Stop thinking with your dick.

He moved to the window and pushed aside the heavy drape. Somewhere in the distance, some part of Rome was still awake. He listened to the muffled sounds, then let the curtain slide from his hand. It was never an easy thing for him, pinning the blame on someone else. Sinners had a way of getting comfortable with their own guilt.

Yet if he was going to deal with it, he had to face the undeniable—it was Romany who had made the move on him at the Villa. But why? His good looks and charm? He had to laugh again. He supposed that was an outside possibility. He was not so stupid as to underestimate his effect on women. It had certainly happened before. But he didn't figure Romany Chase for that kind of woman. She was too smart, too focused. So why the come-on?

It didn't make sense. Not in light of their responsibilities to Arte per Pace. My God, the woman was a professional. The two of them would be working together for months. How in the hell could she expect . . . Unless Romany Chase *was* doing her job?

He didn't like the way that sounded. Things were complicated enough as they were. He was just being paranoid, he told himself. There was no reason to think that anybody suspected anything. He rubbed his forehead; he was feeling the beginnings of a headache. In the old days he would have been able to meditate, and the pain would have gradually faded away. But those days of prayer and fasting were a lifetime ago. That small monk's cell a universe away.

Yet he wanted to pray. Surrender himself to faith. Let God take care of it all. But it was a man's world, and a man's game he had decided to play. For a moment he thought of the last time he'd put on vestments to say Mass. Even then it had given him some small comfort. Yes, he made himself believe, that was what he most needed. To say the Mass. But that, unfortunately, was not possible.

CHAPTER 9

Romany was late. And like Cinderella in reverse, she found herself hurrying upward along a weather-worn marble stairway to the rooftop garden of Count Klaus Sebastiano. His apartment, it had turned out, was the entire top floor of a sixteenth-century Roman palazzo, and the long ascent through the terraced landscape provided her with a perfect twilight view of the Tiber.

She could hear the party as a murmur from above, the sound rolling down to her, distant and muffled in the warm night. Bursting into sudden volume as she reached the top, a buzzing like the noise of insects rose from the multilingual crowd. Caught in that first flash of perception, the guests on the cobbled pathways seemed as carefully arranged as the topiaries, like a scene from *Last Year at Marienbad*.

An attendant in livery was waiting to exchange her invitation for a shawl of patterned silk, one of many which lay piled on the table beside him. It seemed a very eccentric if expensive party favor, until she remembered the rumor that Linda had passed on to her that morning on the phone. The Pope himself was supposed to make an appearance at this party. She draped the shawl to cover her bare shoulders as the women around her had done, and edged into the thick of the action. Heads turned as she moved along the crowded walkways, but she saw no one whom she knew.

Elliot would be getting anxious. She hadn't gone into the office, hadn't spoken to him at all today, letting

Linda believe she'd work to do at the Vatican. She had wanted to avoid her boss until she'd had some time to consider how she was going to repair the damage with Julian Morrow. But time so far hadn't provided her with any easy answers, and she was hoping against hope that the subject of the papal liaison would not come up tonight. She'd have the rest of the weekend to plan. Maybe she'd have a better grip by Monday.

She stopped where she was for a moment, still searching through the faces. A waiter came by, offering her a drink from his trayful of glasses. It was asti spumante. A good one, rich and fruity. Things were looking up.

". . . So, the Count Sebastiano. He is not Italian?"

The woman, one of four people standing in a little knot near to her, had spoken in heavily accented English. Her floral dress, two decades out of fashion, clashed horribly with the complimentary shawl. A diplomat's wife—Eastern European, Romany guessed. She lingered shamelessly, sipping at her champagne. She decided she wanted to hear this.

"The Count is Austrian, actually." The man who answered had the air of an elder statesman. Certainly he was the oldest in the group. His own evening clothes seemed of an even earlier vintage than the woman's, but Saville Row rather than Budapest.

"The title comes from his mother's side . . . and she was from Liechtenstein." It was the other woman who spoke now. "And his father was most certainly Italian." She had stressed that final word, as if delighted to be contradicting what the older man had said. A good bit younger and not so painfully British, but probably his wife, Romany concluded.

"What I really wonder is how old he is," said the woman in the floral dress. "Milos Cherezenski's wife told me tonight that the Count is in his sixties. But Gregor said more like seventy-five."

Romany had given up pretending to stare into the distance. None of them had even noticed she was there, except the younger man among them, and his smile of amused tolerance said he didn't care. American, she thought, until he opened his mouth.

"The Count's age, like everything else, is meant to be a mystery." His accent was French. "You'll hear everything from fifty-five to ninety."

"Ninety! Don't be absurd." The English woman made it sound as if he were personally accountable for the exaggeration.

The Frenchman ignored her. "What bothers me is the eye patch," he said laconically.

"Oh, no mystery there, Leclerque." The elder statesman blustered his way back to center stage. "Sebastiano lost that eye in the war."

"Oui?" Monsieur Leclerque was giving a good imitation of surprised innocence, but his smile seemed more amused than ever. "Then tell me," he said, "were you not all here for the party in December? The patch that night was velvet, I believe. And the Count wore it on the left." His smile for a moment seemed about to break into open laughter, but he turned and walked away. Romany thought she saw him wink at her as he passed.

So he had not been serious. But if what he had said about the Count was simply as outrageous as it sounded, why then were the others so startled? The elder statesman in particular seemed disturbed, as if he actually were remembering the patch on the wrong eye. *Wait and see for yourself* had been Elliot's advice about Klaus Sebastiano. Well, she was more than ready now for an introduction. So where was her boss?

Not anywhere near the tables of food, she discovered, stopping to have her champagne glass refilled. It really was a good vintage, but she hadn't had an awful lot of food since lunchtime yesterday. Better take it easy, Romany.

She found the Pope before she found Elliot. At the southern end of the garden, where the marble balustrade overlooked the Tiber, he stood as the focal point of a sort of clerical island. DeLario was there, right next to the pontiff, his cherub smile working overtime. And Monsignor Brisi out on the fringes, working everybody. And there too, talking to another priest, was Father Julian Morrow, looking clerical at long last, cassocked and collared to the nines. Straight as an arrow, his eyes went to hers. She held her ground. Stared back.

"Romany."

She spun around. Elliot's secretary was at her shoulder.

"Have you seen the boss?" Linda said. "He's looking all over for you."

"No, but I've been trying to find him since I got here. There are so many people . . ."

Her eyes, with a will of their own, had drifted back to Julian, but the priest he had been talking to stood alone. She could still see DeLario near the Pope. He was with someone new now. A man with silver hair and an elegant posture, though she could see him only from the back.

"That's our host. The Count Sebastiano." Linda's gaze had followed hers. "The boss will introduce you. To the Pope too, I imagine. . . . Oh, listen to this"— Linda was giggling—"about the shawls."

"What about the shawls?" She felt herself already beginning to smile. Linda's stories always made her laugh.

"Giuseppe Aldano . . . you remember, he's the Director of the Italian pavilion. Well, he was standing near the doors when the Pope came in, and he overheard him ask why all these women were so covered up." Linda's brown curls bounced as she laughed. "Funny, huh? And he seems such a dry old stick, not as if he'd like to see a little cleavage. . . . Come on, girl," she said, "I better get you to Elliot."

The last time Romany looked back, Julian had not reappeared. She caught a glimpse of Cardinal DeLario laughing. And the Count Sebastiano bowing low over a woman's hand.

"Romany . . ." Linda was calling her.

They found Elliot in a large group that included Giuseppe Aldano and several other members of Arte per Pace's international staff. She had to meet them all, and it was some time before she and Elliot spoke alone.

"Sorry to be late," she began, "but I had trouble getting a taxi. And then when I finally got here, there were so many people."

"I know," said Elliot, "and a lot that you need to meet. . . . Did you see the Pope?"

She nodded. "Just before Linda found me."

"We'll go back over there in a minute. Sebastiano made a major contribution last week toward the construction of the Vatican Pavilion. That's what got Gregory here. You've got to meet him, Romany. Sebastiano, I mean. You can meet the Pope too, of course."

She'd never seen Elliot this effusive, but of course he was excited, justifiably happy with the attendance at this party, and what it meant in terms of Arte per Pace's success.

"Do you want to grab something to eat before we start making the rounds?" He was speaking again. "Oh, did you know that Antoine Nassif is here? Says he met you a couple years ago."

"No . . . I don't remember. . . ."

"Good evening once again, Elliot."

The voice behind her could only be described as cultured. The five words, in perfect English, held the barest hint of an accent, but one she could not define. She turned to see the man who had spoken them.

"I was just talking about you a moment ago." Elliot was smiling broadly. "Count Klaus Sebastiano," he said, "may I present the Acquisitions Director of Arte per Pace. Ms. Romany Chase."

The Count stood before her. Taller even than he had seemed when she'd glimpsed him earlier in the intimate little circle around the Pope. *Correct* was the word that applied to his bearing, as *cultured* had applied to his voice. The patch was on the right eye, she noticed. The other, of a clear and startling blue, was regarding her somewhat strangely.

"Miss Chase," he said, allowing his voice to linger over each of the syllables. And still watching her with that single eye, he took her hand and brought it to his lips.

The Count Sebastiano was hungry tonight. Or what passed in him for physical hunger. Even in his youth he had never required much food. But of course, then as now, there were other appetites to satisfy.

Hans knew he never touched food at the parties he hosted at the Palazzo Rozze, and the steward entered quietly now with a silver tray, placing two covered dishes and a decanter on the table in front of him. A glass of wine was carefully poured, and Hans stood at attention, waiting near the floor-length drapes that concealed the nearby wall. There was never a need to speak. He simply nodded and Hans pulled the cords. The drapes sprung apart, the two halves darting away like startled beasts toward the corners.

With eyes averted, the steward left the room. And now alone, the Count drank a bit of the wine. There was no detectable aftertaste, and the temperature was perfect, which pleased him. He set the glass down and began with his soup, while Wagner stirred in the speakers.

From inside the room beyond, the intervening wall appeared as a mirror. On his side, the parted drapes revealed clear glass. And it seemed that had he wanted, he might only reach out and touch the woman on the bed.

The bed itself was huge, stagelike, with a pedimented headboard and Doric columns for posts. The woman was slim and athletic, with a blond waved bob so popular during the war. Nude but for a filmy toga, she stood upon the mattress, reaching to test the noose that hung above the very center of the bed.

He could see with perfect clarity the spidery webbing

of blue veins in her upthrust breasts, the tiny imperfection of the mole that lay in the depression of her spine. Like all who worked for him, even those here in the Palazzo Rozze, her people had been in service to his family for centuries, for over fifty years now solely to himself. He had personally engineered the coupling that had produced this nearly flawless conjunction of skin and bone, and it came to him in an afterthought that it was his steward Hans who had sired her.

She got down from the bed and lit the tall braziers that stood at each of the bedposts. As she finished, a brunette entered the room, wearing nothing but jewelry that gleamed on her oiled skin. She was leading a man who wore only a black hood, the kind that executioners placed on the heads of condemned men. And she laughed as she pulled him along toward the bed.

Her laughter did not penetrate through the thickness of the glass. And this was as he wished it. Except for the Wagner, these dramas progressed in silence. He returned to his supper and poured for himself a second glass of wine.

When he looked again, the blond woman stood alone at the headboard. The other two lay together on the bed—the hooded man face down upon the mattress, the brunette astride. She was moving like a serpent on his body, her hands gliding from his back to his buttocks, slipping like errant birds between his thighs.

The Wagner welled in the speakers, and he watched, recalling his mild surprise the first time that he'd seen the priest naked. *The priest.* It was not often that he broke his own rules. But allowing this outsider a part within his menagerie had added a certain spice, and was, after all, merely secondary to the man's primary role of spy.

The minutes slipped past. The priest's face still hidden by the hood, his arousal was yet plain in the tension of his cording muscles. And even as the brunette slipped from his hips and guided him to turn upon his back, his sex sprung engorged from the thatch of coarse hair between his legs. And still he made no single move that was his own. The priest had one condition in these little dramas. He blankly refused to penetrate his partners. At his own request his role remained an essentially passive one.

It had seemed strange until he had puzzled out what vow the priest's crude rationalization was meant to preserve. How twisted were the corridors of men's minds, including, of course, his own. That he understood the nature of the mind's internal game, that he used it, manipulated it even in himself, was the very measure of his superiority over such as the creatures on the bed.

Beyond the glass the brunette had helped the priest onto his knees and was busy now binding his hands behind him. The blonde had moved to loosen the rope from its ring in the nearby wall. She lowered the noose over the priest's head.

Without haste, the Count downed the last of the wine and felt the drug begin to take effect. Familiar and quick, the shock of double perception, his consciousness and the priest's melding into one. He could see through the cold glass the brunette now crouched upon her haunches before the kneeling figure. Could now hear the man's accelerated breathing straining against the music overhead. Could smell the cloying incense from the braziers, blending with the odors of his dinner. He closed his eyes to heighten his union with the priest.

Sensation overwhelmed in the now suffocating blackness. An unbearable tension building in his muscles. In his spine. In his penis like a hot iron in the tight space of his crotch. Somewhere, in some small place, some part of his mind at least was free, free enough to rate this performance as possibly one of the best.

And then the tightening rope, greedy as her red mouth. And the cortoids in the neck compressed, the oxygen disappearing from the brain. The fear and the pleasure nearly unendurable, the slide into ecstasy in pace with the slide into death. For one split second there was nothing. Then the rebound of terrifying fear.

And the orgasm, physical this time. His own body convulsing in rhythm with the man on the bed and the Wagner exploding from above.

When his eyes reopened, he saw that the priest lay still. And the women, together now on the bed beside him, had begun to minister to him as though he were a patient. As silently as before, Hans appeared with the final course of his meal. It was the only dish from his native land that he treasured, and expectantly he watched as the steward removed the silver dome. *Blutwurst.* The blood sausage. He plunged his knife deep into the casing, for the quick rush of hot metallic stink.

CHAPTER 10

She'd had to get out of the apartment. Couldn't sit, couldn't think. Couldn't shop either, it had turned out, when she'd found herself staring blankly into the store-front windows on the Piazza di Spagna. Though it was hardly the time to be making snap decisions, she had walked on impulse into some place called Prossimo. Evidently the very last word in Italian hair design.

She'd been sitting here now for more than thirty minutes, waiting near the marble slab of the reception desk for a stylist who could see her. A large style book was open in her lap, the faces staring back at her safe and bodyless under perfect helmets of hair. Did she really want to do this? Or had coming in here been merely symbolic? Did she just need to prove, at least in some small way, that she still controlled her own life?

Her own life. Her *own.* That was the problem, that it didn't feel like her own anymore. Somehow, some*when* there had been a subtle shift. Like a secret thief, pulling away inch by inch the magic carpet she had always taken for granted beneath her feet.

Well, she was stranded now. The limitless world she'd always imagined was gone. When had it begun to disappear? Was it after that stupid college affair with Alan, when she'd decided she hadn't enough talent to make it as an artist? She'd had some talent. Maybe it was guts she'd lacked.

Come on, Romany, you're being too hard. It was a carefully made decision. Nobody can do it all. That damn little voice in her head that was always second-guessing was now trying to console her. Shut up, she told it.

That cocktail party last night had been a perfect illustration of how wrong things really were. It had been a great party with a cast of characters who, even by her own jaded standards, were interesting. She'd met the Pope *and* the mysterious Count Sebastiano. So why hadn't she really enjoyed it?

It was too easy an answer to say that the pressures of her work were responsible. She had chosen both her present assignments precisely because they were the kinds of high-level, high-action jobs she had thought she would enjoy. But then that's what she always thought, wasn't it? She had taken the teaching job at Georgetown because she wasn't getting enough out of her position at the National, taken the Arte per Pace post because teaching had begun to be just a bit of a bore. And agreed to spy because . . . Why had she agreed, really? She'd never answered that question even in her own head. How many other questions hadn't she answered?

What do you want? Yes, that was one of the questions. The big one. And "too much" was her probable answer. She knew how glamorous her life must look to someone on the outside, knew she had no right to complain. But she *was* complaining, had been complaining for a long time. She just hadn't been listening to herself.

Well, she had to listen now. Had to get this thing straight before she went completely off the track. Her monumental failure with Julian Morrow had really shaken her. Besides the fact that she had blown it with him so badly, it really bothered her, trying to seduce a priest. And that it did bother her so much called into question the whole of her involvement with the CIA. What was her moral position in all of this? That she'd left it unquestioned for so long was appalling.

And there was something more. Something else that cut deeply. She was attracted to Julian Morrow for real. Thursday had been wonderful until he'd pulled away. It was incredible when she thought about it now, that in spite of what she'd known she had to do, she had relaxed with him that afternoon. Had been . . . herself. Whatever that meant.

Maybe it had been the setting. The Villa d'Este was a special place. Though she couldn't imagine that sort of day with any other man. There could never have been that kind of playfulness. Not even, she had had to admit, with David.

The truth was that she had seen things in Julian Morrow. Things she liked too much. She didn't want him to be a crook. More than that, she didn't want him to be a priest. Well, he was most definitely the second, and very probably the first. But he had still made her laugh, still made her feel . . . what? As if he could want to know her. The real her. The one even she hadn't figured out yet.

Oh, Romany, listen to yourself. What you're saying is that you need some man to make you complete.

Not need. *Want.* There was a difference. And it wasn't a crime, was it? To want some man to love her? Like her father loved her mother.

It came back to her like a blow, that she'd thought that man was Alan. A professor of sophomore English. And married. It was painful still to imagine that she had ever been that foolish or naive. She had never really dealt with her feelings about Alan's betrayal. Probably because any sort of analysis would have threatened her tidy image of a strong, smart, and sophisticated Romany Chase. If there had been something as simple as a wrong turn, then that was when she had taken it.

Poor little Romany, she laughed at herself now, only you could be having a midlife crisis at twenty-seven in a beauty salon in Rome. Heidi would laugh too. But her best friend was back in the states, and this was all too complicated for a transatlantic heart-to-heart. And, of course, she couldn't talk to Heidi about what she was doing in Rome for the CIA. She couldn't tell anybody about that. Not even her father.

Her father. She'd almost forgotten. Her parents would be here in a few weeks. One more reason why she had to get her act together, and quick. It was fine to admit that her decisions in the past might not have been the best ones. But no one had forced her to do what she was doing. She had led both Elliot and Andrew to expect that she could be counted on to get the job done. And she could. She still believed that. Any personal crises, whether emotional or moral, would just have to wait.

Except for one emotional crisis, she reminded herself. Her hair. And the moment of reckoning was now. One of the receptionists was coming for her from behind the marble desk.

"Signorina . . ." The girl's extremely short hair was worn like a badge. "Follow me, Signorina Chase. Raphaelo can see you now."

The huge partitioned work space had the same Euro-modern glossiness as the black-and-white reception area, a machine-edged sterility that reduced the human hum here into something faintly robotic. The brunette led her through the maze of busy cubicles to one empty mirrored box with a contour chair like a dentist's.

She sat down. Confronted her reflection. Strange that the hair she had hated only this morning in her bathroom mirror now looked suddenly fine. Had, in fact, never looked better. The length perfect. The style just right for her face.

"Signorina Chase . . ." Raphaelo, thinly smug in

something stretch-knit and black, appeared behind her. His eyes questioned hers in the mirror.

"I want it cut. Cut short." It came out very quickly. Then, ". . . No," she said, "wait."

Behind her, Raphaelo was losing his grip on cool. He hadn't even directed her to where she was supposed to have her hair washed, and already she was starting to panic. She saw his eyes roll upward in a perfect display of Roman exasperation.

"Oh hell," she said. "I don't care. Do whatever you want."

Vittorio sat back in the warm cocoon of water, examining his reflection, tiny replicas of himself, duplicated thousands of times in the mountain of bubbles that floated like vanilla gelato over his belly. The installation of the generously oversized tub had been the first of many alterations he'd made to his apartment in the Apostolic Palace. The first of many indulgences. He stroked the fine marble at one end of the tub with a fat wrinkled toe and heaved a long sigh. Old age had its compensations. Of course, the mere accumulation of years had not given to him all his rewards. Hard work had done most of that.

He poked one hand out of the soapy froth and reached behind him to turn on the jets. Immediately the water hissed and churned, the solid mound of suds whipped into choppy little islands of foam. Vittorio closed his eyes, surrendering to the force of the streams that prickled and prodded the soft pads of flesh along the flanks of his body.

Yes, the other day he had overreacted. He was wont to do that lately. With Niccolo showing off half a mind and more balls than he'd ever assumed the man had. But Niccolo was still Niccolo. And if he imagined that the pontiff had somehow acquired a genius for independent action, he was mistaken. He could still twist the little man like a lump of clay. Why, Niccolo had almost asked his permission to piss the other day when he'd visited him. And his mind instantly fixed on an image of Gregory XVII jamming his hand between his legs, squirming on his feet.

He allowed himself to laugh out loud, snuggling deeper into the warm swirling water like a bambino in a womb. He was a happy man.

And then there was Sebastiano's cocktail party last evening. Oh, how splendid it'd been. With everyone kissing his ass, deferring to him. Even in the presence of the Pope of the Holy Roman Catholic Church. It still felt good after all these years. That surge of power, that feeling of absolute control. He moved his thick thighs beneath the water, feeling just the delicious beginnings of an erection. But at his age, his penis was something he could well ignore.

He had to congratulate himself. Brisi was not such a miserable choice after all. The priest was a complete and utter whore, who would have Signorina Romany Chase between his legs before the *puttana* could even think about making trouble. And he had Signor Elliot Peters eating out of his hand. Just like a pigeon. Coo, coo, he heard himself gurgle. Just like a pigeon.

Then he sat up and frowned. The water was getting cold, and the Jacuzzi had suddenly become more irritating than soothing. He reached back and turned off the jets. He couldn't fool himself. He understood what was really eating away at him. What was boring an exact and even hole through his skull to the inside of his brain like a worm.

Julian Morrow. Julian Morrow was the worm inside his head. Why he had finally concluded that Morrow was someone to contend with, he wasn't sure. But of one thing he was certain, the man was not what he appeared. The priest was a fake and a liar. And he, Vittorio DeLario, should know.

He could smell it on the man. Deceit had its own peculiar odor. An attar Vittorio could sniff all the way down his throat. And too, he had looked into the man's eyes last evening. After the smell, it was the eyes that gave away secrets. Morrow had seemed so priestly, standing quietly at Niccolo's side. Fawning, like a paid lover. Now that was a thought. No, no, that wasn't it. But there was something there. There in the priest's eyes. There in the very air that he, Vittorio, breathed. Something that said, "I'm not what I seem. Catch me if you can."

He doubled over and grabbed a towel from the top of the toilet seat. He wiped his hands and reached for the telephone on the wall next to the tub. Another of his little indulgences. He was fucking tired of waiting for the call. He wanted to know. Needed to know Morrow's secrets.

He dialed the number from memory and left a message on the answering machine. Always the same message. It was their prior arrangement. He hoped he wouldn't have long to wait.

Less than five minutes passed before the telephone rang.

"Yes." He spoke into the mouthpiece.

"I was going to call." The voice at the other end of the line.

"I am not a patient man." He didn't try to disguise his anger.

A long pause. Then, "This isn't easy."

"But not impossible."

Another pause. Shorter this time. "He seems to have been able to cover his trail. Or someone has done it for him."

"Explain . . . 'cover his trail.' "

"You know, hide things along the way. And it appears he's come a long way."

"A long way?"

"He's been involved in many things."

"Tell me."

"Well, he's certainly the perfect Jesuit. Intelligent, personable, from a wealthy American family. You understand." A dry laugh.

"Yes."

"Seems to have been, as we say, 'on the fast track'—being groomed for high places in the order. But something happened. Something serious. Something nobody wants to talk about."

"Nobody?" He sounded like a parrot repeating the words. Having to drag everything out.

"Nobody. Whatever happened, happened a while back. He seems to have disappeared after that. There's something about a monastery somewhere."

"A monastery?"

"You understand, sent by the head doctors, the psychiatrists." The voice at the other end waited.

"Why is he here?"

"No one knows. Except he seems to have worked really hard to get here. To get the Pope's favor."

"How?"

"Obviously he is good at what he does. Public relations, you know."

"Scarcely qualification enough for what he is supposed to do here."

"Oh, but he is qualified."

"This, I do not understand."

"It seems to be his little secret."

"His secret?" Finally.

"Yes, that he's something of an art expert."

Romany readjusted her Holly Golightly–sized sunglasses from the bridge of her nose to the top of her head as she cleared security and the ticket takers at the entrance to the Pinacoteca. She turned slightly and glanced over her shoulder. She'd recognized the guard on the left. *Frankie.* She liked him. Luckily he hadn't noticed her as she'd merged in with the last wave of tourists entering the museum. Her first break. She'd need a couple more before the night was over.

She fiddled with the back of her hair as she stopped for a moment to examine a painting. As Romany Chase,

Acquisitions Director, APP, she could come and go at will within the Vatican Museum complex. But as Romany Chase, her comings and goings would be duly noted. Right now she required anonymity. The new haircut would help.

Summer hours meant the museum stayed open until five o'clock. Though it would still be a long wait till dark. But she could do it. She moved into one of the smaller exhibition rooms with some Japanese tourists. She gazed around. Damn, she was at least a head taller than everyone in the group. She stood out like a sore thumb. Frankie wasn't the only guard who'd be able to spot her. She'd better find some Americans or Swedes to circulate with for a while.

Ten of five. Time to make her move. The inner offices were just around this corner, down a short hall. She looked over her shoulder. The Japanese she'd tried to tag along with earlier were having an animated discussion just behind her. Her Japanese was rusty, but she got the general idea. They wanted to be sure to purchase slides since photographs were off limits.

She stopped before a large door marked Personnel Only. A solitary light lit the hall; her fuzzy shadow trailed out after her. She reached out and turned the knob. It twisted slowly in her hand. She let out the breath she'd been holding. Break number two. The doors had not been locked for the weekend.

Once she was inside, it was darker than she imagined. But most of the offices were blocked off by windowless doors and faced a solid corridor. She reached inside her purse. She knew Julian's office was just down the hall to the left, and she aimed the beam of the flashlight ahead of her.

She stood for a moment before the door to his office. Her hand limp at her side, yellow light pooling at her feet. For a moment she imagined that he was just on the other side, sitting at his desk. His blond head tilted slightly downward, his hand marking small X's on the blotter before him. When he looked up, his face wore that same cold expression he'd shown her last night at the cocktail party, the one she'd first seen at the Villa d'Este when he'd pushed her away from him.

She shook away the image and prayed for break number three. The knob turned easily. Julian Morrow was a trusting man. She closed the door softly behind her.

He'd made no changes since the time she'd been there. Spare and tidy, the office could have belonged to anyone. She moved around the desk, sat down, switched on the fluorescent lamp.

She opened the drawers one by one. Rifled through the contents. Nothing of interest. Just the usual. She flipped through his appointment calendar. Most of the dates were blank. Julian hadn't had many engagements since he'd arrived in Rome. At least not many he cared to note. Then today's date. Saturday. The word *Switzerland* scrawled across the page. So that's where he'd gone. Switzerland.

She frowned. Angry that her search had turned up nothing. Aggravated that she had a long time to sit around Julian Morrow's office with nothing to do but wait.

It wasn't footsteps that alerted the monk. There were no footsteps. He simply sensed a presence. Another intruder like himself flitting from shadow to shadow in the dark precincts of the museum.

Not a ghost. The Pinacoteca was too young for that. For all its pretending to a Lombard elegance, the building was scarcely sixty years old. And Vatican ghosts preferred the ancient more than most.

A guard, perhaps. But not on the regular schedule.

Forewarned, he had slipped through the far doorway before the slight figure entered the dimly lit room. He stood now, unmoving, just beyond the open blackness of the threshold. In full sight, had there been any source of light behind him. But there was not. And he watched, satisfied that he was invisible in his dark robe and hood.

There had been no footsteps because the woman wore crepe-soled shoes. In a few short instants she had crossed the space of the room. He waited for a moment, then followed. Watched as she passed out of the Employees Only door. She was staff. Pia Venza from the Vatican Cataloging Department had a reputation for working late. She would be lining up replacements for pieces on their way to Arte per Pace.

He sank back into the shadows, savoring a moment's relief. He had thought for an instant that he recognized the body beneath the dark sweater and pants, but Pia's bare white neck above the black turtleneck had convinced him he was wrong.

CHAPTER 11

"Good, you're still here, Romany." Elliot threw himself down in a parody of exhaustion in the chair that fronted her desk. "What did you do to your hair?" He sat staring up at her.

"Why, don't you like it?" She had answered with a question of her own, the same she'd been using all day. Her voice, she noticed, was beginning to have a bit of an edge.

"Looks nice." Elliot didn't sound too sure. "I miss the long hair, though."

That was predictable. Every man in the office, even the most sophisticated ones, had said the same thing. The women had all said they liked the new style. *She* liked the halo of soft curls framing her face. Raphaelo had done well. She forced a smile. "You said you were glad to catch me . . . ?"

"Oh, yes." Elliot seemed relieved to be off the hook.

"I wanted you to know what a hit you were at the party Friday night. Nice job, Ms. Chase."

"Thanks."

"Good job on the letter, too. I'd like to get it mailed out as soon as possible. How are we doing with the translations?"

Mentally she crossed her fingers. "I'm getting that lined up now," she said. Then she sucked in a breath. "The party Friday was wonderful."

"A total success." Elliot had taken the bait. "The Pope stayed almost two hours. What did he say to you that time you laughed?"

"He said to take off the shawl so he could see my dress."

"Oh." Elliot laughed now, too. "Pope Gregory's not at all like I thought he'd be. But then I've never met a pope. . . . What did you think about Klaus Sebastiano?"

It took a moment before she answered. "I've never met a count before," she parroted his own line. "I don't know what to think." It was true. She didn't.

"Well, the Count certainly seemed to like you. He couldn't take his eyes off you, Romany."

"Eye, Elliot."

"What? Oh, yeah"—he smiled—". . . eye."

"Elliot?" She was hesitating again. She knew this was going to sound silly. "Elliot, how many times have you seen the Count?"

Elliot shifted slightly in the chair, his mouth twisting in the equivalent of a shrug. "Not too many I guess. Why?"

"It's just something I overheard at the party, something . . . Hi, Linda." She had glanced up to see Elliot's secretary hovering at the door.

"Sorry to interrupt." Linda came into the room. "But Signor Barelli's here to see you, boss. He's in your office." She turned, tossed an envelope on top of the desk. "Looks like somebody made a conquest."

"What is it?" Romany asked her.

"Invitation for you. Hand delivered by the same creepy guy who brought the ones last week."

Elliot had gotten up to leave. Now he stopped. "Really, Linda . . ."

"Well, he is creepy." Linda wasn't giving in. "Looks like his name should be Igor."

Romany had begun tearing open the envelope. "Nobody else here got one of these?"

"Nope." Linda shook her head.

"It's for dinner Wednesday night at the Palazzo." Romany looked up at her boss. "You think I ought to go?"

"Of course." Elliot sounded surprised. "There's no telling who else he's invited, and having you there has got to be a plus for Arte per Pace. And it's a chance for you to see his art collection."

Elliot stopped again in the doorway. "I told you he couldn't keep his *eye* off you."

"That's what bothers me." Romany had made the comment to his back, as little more than a murmur, but the sharp-eared Linda had heard.

"Why, Romany Chase," she said too sweetly, "such deliciously naughty thoughts. The Count's probably old enough to be your grandfather." She started to leave, then turned, still grinning. "By the way," she said, "I've been meaning to tell you all day that I like your hair."

The Mezanotte was a long low cave, dark and cool, with at least the illusion of a dripping dampness. Its brick vaulted ceiling seemed just high enough to clear the bar, just wide enough to accommodate a shadowy row of rough wooden tables. Guttering candles made the features of the few scattered customers more uncertain than the dark. At the last table in the back, Romany sat waiting for Sully.

This morning when she'd arrived for work there'd been a flower seller with a red scarf in front of the Arte per Pace building, the signal that instructions had been left for her at the dead drop nearest to her office. At lunchtime she'd bought a sandwich and gone to eat in a small piazza a couple blocks away, where she'd sat on the bench, a shopping bag set close at her side. She'd eaten slowly, taking time to tear pieces of bread for the pigeons, and to make certain as she could that no one had followed her.

The precautions seemed unnecessary, but she had observed them to the letter, sitting idly, watching the birds strut and flutter around the remaining crumbs of her sandwich, while under cover of the shopping bag, her fingers had been busy prying loose the slip of paper stuck to the underside of the slat. Quickly she'd palmed the folded note, slipping it into her purse as she pretended to fumble for a tissue. The whole by-the-book performance had made her feel ridiculous. Who would be watching her? She was relatively clean in the jargon of the trade. It was a major reason why Andrew had decided to use her.

Back at the office the note had had to be decrypted, and she'd holed up in a stall in the ladies' room with the little tablet that Sully called a one-time pad. Identical to the one he kept, the tablet held over fifty numbered pages with a different code on every sheet. Each message used one sheet, and then the page was discarded. It made for unbreakable code.

Sully's note had been short—the time, the name of the bar and directions. It had taken her only a few minutes to get it written out, memorize it, tear it up with the code sheet, and flush both down the toilet. The rest of the afternoon had been spent deciding how much to tell Sully about what had happened between her and Julian Morrow.

She'd intended to see Julian today and make her apology in person. After worrying about it all weekend, she'd convinced herself that he would have to meet her halfway. True, he had avoided her like the plague Friday night, but the party hadn't been the best place to talk. Problem was, when her secretary had called for an ap-

pointment this morning, the man who answered said
that Father Morrow would not be in his office all day.
She would have to try again tomorrow.

So her plan for tonight was to tell Sully nothing.
Why borrow trouble? And besides, she was still having
second thoughts about this grand seduction scheme anyway, qualms that had nothing to do with ethics or mo-
rality. She was simply not convinced that seducing
Julian Morrow was the way to get an angle on the Pope.

One thought nagged at her. If seduction was the way
to go, then the obvious candidate was undoubtedly
Umberto Brisi. For unless her Italian did not extend to
Roman body language, the Director General was clearly
interested. She had a duty, she supposed, to tell this to
Sully, but the thought of jumping into bed with Brisi was
something quite different from the thought of making
love to Julian Morrow. And it was Sully himself who
had insisted that Julian and not Brisi should be her focus. She would salve her conscience with that.

She was on her second glass of Chianti when Sully
finally showed up, stopping at the bar for a drink. He
really was the perfect agent. Totally forgettable. Average
height, average looks. Definitely American, but even in
this place he simply blended in.

"You're late," she said, as he slid into the chair beside her.

"You should be facing the door," was his answer.

"There's a door in the rear, too. Which I'm sure you
know. And with my chair like this, I can cover both.
And, Sully"—she gave him her sweetest smile—"no one
could have followed my taxi driver."

"So what have you got for me?"

"This." She took the small tubular package out of
her purse. "Be careful with it. It's the layer sample from
the Caravaggio."

"Good." He slipped it quickly into the inside pocket
of his sport coat. The cigarettes and lighter came out.
"How's it going with Morrow?"

"Fine," she lied. Then, "A little slow maybe. It's not

easy, you know, seducing a priest on a timetable."
Damn. Why had she felt the need to add that?

"Look," she began again before he could make a
comment, "let me ask you this. Why aren't we going
directly to the Pope? Hell, if he's guilty, he's guilty,
Sully. Once he knows that we know what's going down,
guilty or innocent, won't he have to play ball?"

Sully had been busy lighting up. He took another
long drag before he answered. "Sure," he said finally,
"but we still want this thing nailed down solid as possible before we go in. That's why I'm glad to have this."
He patted the front of his jacket. "It's not completely
necessary that we know if the Pope is innocent, Romany. But it would be nice. Sort of smooths out the approach."

She looked down into her wine. She was beginning
to see things more clearly. They were hoping she'd
come through for them, Andrew and the rest. Even
Sully. But her end of this was comparatively small pota-
toes. She wondered suddenly what David was doing, but
knew she couldn't ask. "I might have something else for
you," she said instead.

Sully raised an eyebrow.

"I think I know where they're doing at least some of
the forgery."

"Where?"

"The Vatican Restoration Department. It's perfect.
You send a canvas or some other piece of art in for
repairs . . ."

"And when it comes back, it's a copy." Sully had
finished it for her. "But then how do they get the real
one out of the building?"

"Easy. I figured when I took the paint sample that
I'd have to stay overnight in the Pinacoteca. Then walk
out the next morning with the first group of tourists."

"But . . . ?"

"There's a door in the first-floor office section that's
locked only from the outside."

"And there's no guard?"

"No." She shook her head. "Not there. Which I'm certain is no accident. Same deal, I'm sure, with Restoration. There'd be no major problem getting out at night with one of the smaller pieces or a rolled-up canvas. Even one as large as the Caravaggio."

Sully set his cigarette in the chipped saucer that held the candle and picked up his glass. She remembered it was Scotch that he drank. The one that used to do the magazine ads with the insufferably upscale people lecturing on the proper pronunciation of the brand name. She imagined Sully wearing a trench coat, his brown hair slicked straight back. *Hello. I'm a case officer in the Company. That's the CIA to you. After a hard day of covert operations and black-bag jobs, I like to relax with* Paris Match *and the perfect Scotch. . . .*

"I understand you went to a little party Friday night." It was the real Sully interrupting her thoughts.

"That's right," she said. "A P.R. thing for Arte per Pace. Ambassador Gilchrist was there. I thought you might show up too."

"Couldn't get an invite. Too low-level for the jet set. And besides"—he made a crooked smile—"everybody these days automatically assumes that most foreign-office types are spies. Which is why this may be our last personal contact, Romany." He was suddenly totally serious. "You haven't seen ben Haar again, have you?"

"Why? He's not missing?"

"No. That's not what I meant. We're working together on this thing now. It's my business what ben Haar does. I just want to make sure he's not stupid enough to be jeopardizing his cover. Or yours."

Sully had hovered over the "stupid" as if he'd really wanted to say something else. He leaned back in the wooden chair, waiting for her answer.

"I haven't seen David since that time I told you about," she said. It was her second lie, and easier than the first.

Sully seemed genuinely relieved. "Ben Haar's good," he said, "even if I'd never tell him to his face.

But he's an arrogant son of a bitch. And frankly, when he gets around you, Romany, he starts to think with his dick."

"Fuck you, Sully."

The eruption of words shocked her, maybe more because she'd had to keep them to a hiss. But Sully laughed out loud. "Tell me about the party," he said. "The Pope was there. DeLario. Morrow. All of them, huh?"

"Yes." She kept her voice even.

"What did you see?"

She should have been the one to bring this up, but she'd been working too hard at what she *wasn't* telling Sully. She made herself drop the anger. "The Pope and DeLario seemed pretty chummy," she said. "But we knew about that going in."

"What about Morrow and DeLario?"

She shook her head. "They were both there Friday night. Both close to the Pope. But they didn't interact at all. At least not while I was watching."

"And Brisi?"

"He was there. Made an obvious point of ignoring Morrow. But like I told you before, all that could be an act."

"Maybe. But it's looking less likely now."

"Oh? And what does that mean, Sully?"

"That we've had time to do a more thorough check on Morrow, and his appointment as papal liaison is beginning to look like a fluke." He stopped. Chain lit a second cigarette. "Did you know that Morrow had a twin brother?"

"The brother who died."

Behind the cloud of smoke, Sully's eyes were running some kind of total. His mouth curled in the corner that held the cigarette. Apparently she'd come up on the plus side.

"Morrow tell you about him?" he asked her.

"Not very much."

Sully leaned forward. "The Morrows are wealthy

people," he said. "Mother's family's been prominent in Philly since before the Liberty Bell. Father's money's not that old, but old enough, and he inherited one of the biggest corporate law firms in the city. The twins were the only children."

"Identical twins?" It was a question she hadn't asked Julian.

"Yeah," Sully said. "A matched set. Rich. Smart. Impossible to tell apart unless you really knew them. Had a great time, apparently, keeping the debutantes guessing. Then it all blew up."

"How?"

"Boating accident. Two of 'em were out sailing when a freak storm came up. Boat capsized and Jeremy Morrow drowned. Body didn't wash ashore for over a week. It was Julian who ID'd it."

"Not the father?"

"No."

"The family must have taken it pretty hard."

"Real hard according to the report. Mom and Pop drop out of the social scene almost completely, for years as it turns out. Julian starts acting weird."

"Weird? How?"

Sully shrugged. "People our guys talked to weren't real specific. Just said Morrow changed, began acting more and more like his dead brother. Company shrink claims it's not that strange, though, with the death of an identical twin, the survivor trying to keep the dead 'half' alive."

"I guess not," she said.

"But there's still the zinger." Sully drew on the cigarette. "Out of the blue Morrow informs his parents he's not going back to Harvard in the fall. Instead he's transferring to Catholic University. Chucking Daddy's law firm. Little Julian's decided he's going to be a priest."

"And what has that—"

"The Jesuits." Sully said it like an answer. "Mummy, and especially Daddy, were plenty upset, but the Jesuits were glad enough to get their hands on Julian Morrow. At least at first."

She ignored the last remark. "I don't understand what this all has to do . . ." She stopped again at Sully's look. He was going to tell it his way.

"Once Morrow becomes a priest, the sources start to dry up." He began again. "Like I told you before, our access to Church records isn't all that good, though everything looks like roses at the beginning. Morrow throws himself into his studies, graduates in record time with honors and several degrees, including the canonical. But then he starts dropping out of the record. A lot of sudden transfers where he disappears from one place, then suddenly pops up months later in another with no official explanation. The kind of thing that is usually a smoke screen for disciplinary action. Then six years ago there's a period where he simply vanishes."

"What do you mean 'vanishes'?"

"No record on him at all until he turns up at that monastery I told you about. Nobody's talking exactly, but the rumor seems to be that Morrow was sent there by his superiors after some really major fuckup."

"So how did he end up with the Arte per Pace post?" Maybe at last they were getting to it.

"It wasn't the Pope's idea. At least originally," Sully said. "The Jesuit Superior General made a special request. Asked the Pope to appoint Morrow as a favor. That's what I meant when I said it was more of a fluke. It's a rehabilitation project apparently. The order's way of giving their whiz kid one last chance to make good."

"So Morrow's not the key, then." She said it softly as the full meaning sank in. "My orders have changed." She looked up.

"Not at all. We can't be sure about any of this. This entire Morrow deal might still be some kind of setup. For all we know, the whole damn Jesuit order might be involved." Sully was jamming the burned-down butt of his cigarette into the saucer that held the candle. The light flickered like fingers over his face.

"And besides, Morrow's smart," he said, "and from what we can piece together, odds are he isn't a saint. Even if he's clean now, he's a good bet to smell out what's rotten. You've got to be there when he does, Romany, and watch which way he jumps. Jump with him if you can."

Sully's eyes were watching her closely now. For the first time she noticed the defect, like a little black ink mark at the edge of one iris. She wondered if it was real, or just some trick of reflection.

"We need you at a ringside seat for this thing," Sully was saying, "and Morrow's still your ticket in. You do understand that, Romany?"

"Yes, Sully," she said, "I understand that." It was easier just to repeat his words. She would have another sleepless night in which to think about them.

In the oldest portions of the Apostolic Palace, in what had become a wing in the Palace of Sixtus V, a lone figure in the brown robe and cowl of a monk carried a candle along a darkened hallway. The rows of colonnaded windows, blind eyes in the black moonless hours before dawn, looked down unseeing upon the silent plaza four stories below. More immediately real were the faded frescoes on the corridor's arched ceiling, flowing in and out of life with the light from the passing candle.

From a place deep inside himself the monk watched everything. Observed the gloom, the candleglow, the crumbling beauty. Watched himself, a ghost flickering like the scenes on the ceiling above his head. Insubstantial one moment, too crowded with life and feeling in the next.

He stopped. He had been counting unconsciously the doors along the passageway. Now he drew a key from the pocket of his robe and unlocked the door before him. The chapel inside was as old as the building itself. In the light of the votives that burned before the

rail, it was just possible to see the altar fresco, the Cruci-
fixion as conceived by some forgotten thirteenth-century
master. He lifted the candle and stared into the eyes of
the Christ. Dispassionate. Byzantine. So different from
the later more sentimental depictions.

He walked across the room to the tiny wooden confessional, a fragile structure to have borne some seven
centuries of guilt. A bit cynically he reminded himself
that the sacrament was no longer called Penance but
Reconciliation. He liked the older concept better, the
baring and stripping of the soul. But that was all out-
moded now, like the Byzantine Christ. He blew out the
candle and slipped behind the heavy velvet curtain.

"Bless me, Father," he spoke in the discarded phra-
seology of the old ritual. "I have sinned."

The dark roared about his ears in the pause. Then
from the blackness of the cell beyond the grate came
the expected answer. "We have all sinned, my son."

Father. Son. No other names or titles would be spoken.

"You are getting along in the work, my son?" The
voice came again, whispering at him in its soft-spoken
Italian.

"Yes, Father, as slowly as our haste permits." He
heard the answering sigh, could imagine the small self-
ironic smile, which even in the glow of day would barely
light the long Umbrian face.

"It is our way to move slowly," the voice said, "but
we must know, and soon, my son, if what we have been
led to believe is true. Have you found nothing at all to
confirm our suspicions?"

His eyes had had time to adjust to the deeper darkness inside the box, but there was simply not enough
light here to see. He sensed rather than saw the impatient shift in the older man's frail shoulders.

"It has been impossible as yet, Father, to take anything major from the museums," he said. "But I did
borrow some minor things. A Roman terra cotta, icons
. . . some other small pieces."

"And?"

"The majority were unquestionably genuine."

"And the others . . . ?"

"Fakes? Yes, but it doesn't prove anything. It's not surprising, my Father, that some of these pieces should turn out to be copies. There's nothing new about forgery. Even Michelangelo is known to have tried his hand at it."

"You are keeping your eye on the priest?"

"As well as I can."

"And what do you plan next?"

"I must get to the Caravaggio. If *The Deposition* is a fake, we'll know the rumors are true, that the real canvas has been auctioned."

"The Caravaggio. Yes. It was a mistake perhaps to have it on the exhibition list. If anyone from Arte per Pace should begin to suspect what's happening, we may lose control entirely. This woman, this Romany Chase, she's a danger to us, my son."

The monk had come to expect it in their conversations, the point when the soft almost unctuous voice took on an implacable authority. There was an unpleasantness about that sudden shift that had given him the audacity to admit to himself that he did not always like this man.

"I don't think we have to worry, Father," he said after a moment's hesitation. "Miss Chase's credentials are excellent, but if *The Deposition* is a copy, it's a nearly perfect one. She won't see what she's not looking for. I've looked, and I can't tell a thing without the tests."

"When will you be able to do them?"

"I'll have to get samplings of the paint layers first."

"Are you still so certain, my son, that the Cardinal suspects nothing?"

"Almost certain. He didn't balk at the Caravaggio remaining on the list."

"Perhaps that's an indication of innocence. Perhaps the Brotherhood is wrong. . . ." The voice, which again had softened, stopped midsentence. The mention of that which was not to be so lightly spoken had been an uncharacteristic slip.

"Perhaps we are all wrong." The voice, recovering itself, spoke again. "Perhaps it is all nothing . . . a bad dream."

"You don't believe that, Father."

"No, my son, you are right. I do not believe it. And that is why at all cost we must succeed. We cannot afford exposure now. There is the world at stake."

The words, invisible wraiths that shivered in the blackness between them, seemed absurdly grandiose. The monk closed his eyes, though it made little difference in the dark. Absurd was the way the words had sounded. The absurdity was, they were likely to be true.

CHAPTER 12

Even the hate could not keep him from enjoying the game. David ben Haar loved playing with men like Anton Arendt. Pawing away, like a cat with a mouse, waiting for the right moment to go in for the kill. And Arendt was better prey than most. Such a self-consumed little prick.

But he had to practice patience if this particular game was to go down as planned. And he'd learned patience. Learned it years ago. Learned to hold back, keep the adrenaline in check, suck up the anger and hurt. Sublimate the pain to careful strategy.

Yet the old thoughts that cut into his gut were never far away. Thoughts of Rebecca and Seth. Thoughts of what men like Arendt were capable of doing. He could still see in his mind the exact angle of Seth's broken neck. Becca's beautiful breasts chewed away as though by rats. Yes, the hate was useful. Fuel for the game. Keeping him razor sharp. Ready. And today he was playing for high stakes. Both professional and personal.

He was tracking a Jew-killer. Not too different, he imagined, from Becca and Seth's Jew-killers. From a different place, wearing a different face, posturing a different cause. But the same. Always the same.

He watched now as Arendt bit into his sandwich. The man's sharp teeth cut a wide circle into the bread. Strange how stickmen like Arendt devoured their food. Ate as though no matter how much they consumed, their hunger would never be sated. Arendt's Adam's apple quivered as he swallowed. Then, setting the remnants of his meal on the plate, he seemed hopeful that his belly might possibly be satisfied this time.

David fiddled with the olive before popping it into his mouth, worrying about the fake black mustache that Chaim had insisted he wear. A Greek like Stephanos Severnos would have such a mustache. So went the logic of Chaim. David never argued with him; he wasn't hungry anyway.

Chaim hadn't wanted David for the assignment. Said he wasn't right for it. Too aggressive, was Chaim's estimation. No matter how much David tried, Chaim Lieber always compared David ben Haar to a rabid dog. But Chaim was two generations removed from death by Jew-killers. Of course, Austerlitz and Dachau were not forgotten, but not so fresh as the Palestinian and Iraqi attacks. And Chaim had a wife and daughter who still breathed.

But in the end, Chaim had given up his opposition. After all, David had kept the low profile needed for the job.

David watched Arendt wipe his hands on a napkin, rubbing the tips of his long, narrow fingers as though polishing the skin. The German was saying something about how integral was this phase of the master plan. The "master plan" of course being an eventual neo-Nazi takeover of Europe. He had to wonder how long before this fucker would be devising some kind of scheme to "contain" undesirables.

Right now, however, this Nazi had other ideas on his

mind. Specifically the acquisition of a spy satellite to monitor the superpowers when his little group finally came into power. Stephanos Severnos was the broker he hoped would be able to get him what he needed.

As David listened to Arendt, he had trouble keeping his mind off how he would like to castrate this skinny bastard. He could feel the mustache tickle the line of his upper lip as his mouth twisted into a smile. He could almost get a hard-on just thinking about it. A real trophy it would be too. For the longer he sat in this shit-hole of a restaurant, sat across from the skinny Herr Anton Arendt, he became more certain that here at last was the link between the neo-Nazis and whoever it was that was black-marketing Vatican art.

Down the rabbit hole again, this time without a guide. Romany had entered the Vatican at St. Anne's Gate, assuring herself that she could remember the way to Julian Morrow's apartment. And so far so good, she thought, certain that the door she had just passed was one that she knew, the door that Sister Clemensia had once swung so firmly closed on the promising patch of garden.

Her secretary had finally gotten through this morning to Julian's office at the Pinacoteca and had set up an appointment for Ms. Chase to meet at two o'clock this afternoon with Father Morrow. But just before she'd left her own office, a call had come with the message that she was to meet with him instead at his apartment. All the way to the Vatican, Romany had wondered about the switch. His apartment seemed the last place that Julian Morrow would want to see her.

She had spent two weeks now, she realized, trying to figure him out. Only this morning, sitting at her desk, she'd rerun all their meetings in her head. Rehashing every word and gesture. Wondering suddenly if he was equally puzzled by her. She'd supposed he had a right to be. From his point of view, her own attitudes and actions could seem pretty inconsistent, too. Realizing that had been a major revelation.

One thing she had figured out in the sleepless hours last night as she'd replayed her meeting with Sully. Forget she was working as a spy, forget whatever it was she felt for David ben Haar. If it weren't for the fact that he was a priest, Julian Morrow would already be in her bed. It was what they both wanted. She could admit it. And in that first moment, when he'd given in to her kiss at the Villa, he'd admitted it too. No matter what kind of picture Sully had painted last night, no matter what kind of trouble Julian Morrow might have with his priesthood, he'd wanted her—yet he had pushed her away.. His vows must still mean something.

It was a thought that made her uncomfortable. Going over it all again, she realized she had not been paying attention. She stopped walking, aware suddenly that she'd taken a wrong turn. Two German seminarians in their distinctive red cassocks came out of a shadowed doorway and crossed on the path ahead of her. *Gamberi cotti.* Boiled lobsters. From someplace the Roman slang had popped into her head. Fitting enough in this heat. Other than herself, the seminarians were the only ones moving out of doors, and they at least seemed to know where they were going. She turned around and began retracing her steps.

Fifteen minutes and a little luck later, she was standing in front of the big double doors she remembered. She'd allowed herself plenty of time leaving her office, and was still a few minutes early according to her watch. She took a deep breath, and knocked.

Julian Morrow opened the door. He looked surprised to see her. Shocked almost. Then she realized he was staring at her hair.

"I cut it," she said quickly, unnecessarily.

"I like it. It looks cool."

Spoken like a P.R. man, she thought uncharitably. But then he just kept on staring. Was he going to make this awkward after all?

"Come in and sit down." He seemed to have read her mind, and welcomed her into the apartment. "I asked you to meet me here because my office is a mess."

"Oh?"

"They're trying to find space for another desk. His Holiness decided I needed some help," he said. "So he's given me a secretary. Father Vance."

So that was who her secretary had talked to the last couple days. Romany followed Julian over to the sofa and sat down.

He was still standing. In khakis and a blue chambray shirt, he looked excessively American beneath the gilded ceiling.

"Sister Clemensia isn't around today," he said. "No Orangina in the fridge. Wine okay?"

"Yes, fine."

He left her for the kitchen, but was back almost immediately with the glasses already poured.

"Here." He handed her one, sat down in the chair across from her.

"Thank you." She took a sip, not really tasting it.

"Italian Riesling." He lifted his own glass.

"It's very good." She had answered automatically. Despite his apparent goodwill, she was feeling a little shell-shocked. She set her wineglass down on the table and concentrated on opening her briefcase.

"This is the letter I've prepared for the exhibitor countries." She handed him the copy. "The one I had spoken to you about."

He took the letter from her hand. Aware, she was sure, of her trouble in meeting his eyes.

"And this is the list of translations I still need." She took another typed sheet out of the briefcase, forcing herself to look up at him.

He was watching her, the copy of her letter held lightly in his fingers, one leg crossed over the other at the knee. A pose of relaxation. She held out the list to him. He uncrossed his leg before he took it.

"If you could let me know as soon as possible

whether the Vatican Translation Department can help us with these . . ."

"It's no problem, Romany." He smiled now. "How soon do you need them?"

"Yesterday?" She hoped her own smile looked more natural than it felt.

"How 'bout two days?"

"That's fine," she agreed, still holding on to the smile. "It will be nice," she said, "when we start getting a response to those letters. We'll have an idea then of what this exhibition is actually going to look like." It was her first venture into real conversation, and now he had no comment. He seemed to be waiting.

"Julian," she said it quickly, "there's something I need to set straight." She had to struggle again to keep her eyes level with his. "I owe you an apology—"

"No." He said it so forcefully, she fell silent. "I owe *you* an apology." He sounded almost angry. But clearly not at her. And now he was the one who looked away.

"I've always preferred the company of women," he said. "All my life. But it's not a harmless preoccupation for a priest. It leads to trouble."

He had turned to her again, and she noticed that his lashes seemed golden as a young boy's in the strong afternoon light. "What I'm trying to say, Romany, is that what happened the other day was more than half my fault. I'm sorry for that. And I'm sorry for the way I acted Friday night. I had thought things were in better control," he said. "That I was in better control. I'm sorry . . . for everything. I really like you, Romany."

"I like you too, Julian."

What else was there to say? It was the last thing she'd expected. That he would apologize to her. That Julian Morrow would be confessing to a weakness, a weakness that by implication he was asking her help to control. It wasn't how it was supposed to go, the fly begging the spider for some friendly assistance. Just what in the hell was she supposed to do now?

. . .

"Here." David handed Romany her glass of unfinished wine. "I'll do these. You cooked. I'll wash." He walked over to the sink and turned on the tap. "Take long to get hot?" He looked back over his shoulder and smiled.

"Hot? The water? No, not usually." She smiled back, propping her feet up on a chair.

"Good. Sometimes you don't get so lucky." His hand went under the faucet.

Suddenly she burst out laughing.

"What's wrong?" He'd turned to look at her.

"You."

"Me?"

"Yeah, you washing dishes."

"I could say the same. You cooking dinner." He flashed her another smile.

"Hey, I'm a good cook."

"Hold on, Romany." His arms were now elbow-deep in suds. "Dinner was great. I just didn't have any idea you could cook."

She almost said he hadn't given her much of a chance, but she didn't. Maybe it was the wine, but she didn't want to get into anything with David tonight.

"You know, I'm really pretty good at this. Washing dishes. I used to do it all the time." The tail end of his last sentence seemed to drag a bit.

"I'd have never figured you for the domestic type, David ben Haar." She could hear herself laughing again.

"When I was married, I used to wash dishes all the time."

He hadn't turned this time to look back over his shoulder at her. And she couldn't quite tell if he expected her to say something, something about not knowing that he was ever married. But there was a sliver of something in his voice, something that finally made her keep quiet.

"It was when Rebecca and I would talk." He was speaking again. "She'd sit just like you're doing now and we'd talk. I guess we never said anything too important. Just little things. About how things were going for us. Mostly about Seth." He turned then. "Seth, our son."

She nodded and watched him run a soapy sponge across a plate.

"I was away a lot. You know, the job. So it was nice just to be home and do little things for Becca. Things I never got a chance to do. I became real expert at washing dishes." She heard him laugh. A soft sound.

"After she died, I would go home at night and cook myself something. Then I would wash the dishes. Sometimes I would imagine she was in the kitchen with me. And I would start talking. Tell her things that happened. Just like before." He stopped, reached for another plate. "I guess I wasn't doing so well. I mean talking to myself in the kitchen. Anyway I quit after a while. Sold the house. Moved into an apartment. Ate out."

She listened as he sloshed the dishes in the water. Then, "Do you want to talk about it, David?"

She thought he made a kind of shrugging motion with his shoulders. But she couldn't really tell. It seemed a long time before he spoke again.

"I was away. But I'd heard the rumor. That there was going to be a raid on the school. The school where Becca taught." He paused for a second. "Actually it had worked out well." He seemed to have changed gears. "Seth in the first grade. Becca teaching just in the next building. I'd liked the thought of the two of them together when I was away." Another dish went onto the drying rack.

"I told myself I wasn't worried. That there was plenty of time to get everybody out. Even if the raid was really going to happen. But I was wrong." He turned now, and she saw that his face looked drawn, pulled tight by everything she knew he must be feeling.

"The bastards surprised us. Nobody had a chance." He was looking down into the water again. His shoulders seemed overburdened, and he made a kind of leaning motion into the sink. "The PLO were good at that.

Playing dirty. Treating people like garbage." The last sentence was mean. Then he made a sound that might have been a laugh. "It's strange, but I could have accepted it if they'd planted a bomb. It's not so personal that way. I mean that's the way things are. . . ." He was staring at her, his green eyes asking her to understand this kind of twisted thinking.

"But they had to make us really feel it. Rub our faces in dogshit." He turned back to the sink. When he spoke again, his voice was less sure. "They raped Becca, did things to her . . . before they killed her. Made her suffer. Humiliated her. But Becca was proud. She would never let them feel they'd taken anything from her." He stopped, and she could hear the clink of one dish against another. Then she heard him inhale, exhale slowly.

"I guess it all happened so fast," he was talking again, "but Becca had somehow made her way to Seth before they got to her. She'd run all the way to the next building. Their bodies were found together."

He'd finally come to the end of it, and for a while she merely watched him standing very still before the sink. At last she made her way to him. Pressed herself against his back, ran her hands down his arms. Then, reaching into the warm sudsy water, she found his hands, threaded her fingers through his, and held him.

Romany sat naked in her bed watching David sleep. Their lovemaking had been different tonight. She had led the way. Taken charge. David had been the follower, the supplicant.

In all the time she'd known David, she'd never guessed. Guessed that he'd been married. Had been a father. He'd had her fooled. But that was David.

She shook her head and ran her fingers through the short hair at the sides of her head. She loved a man she hardly knew. But of course, that had always been part of it. The mystery.

She closed her eyes and listened to him breathe. Deep, relaxed breaths. She was glad. He needed to sleep. Tonight had been hard on him. But then, every night was probably hard on David ben Haar.

Tonight for the first time she saw David's obsession with Israeli vindication as more than political fanaticism. It was a personal war. The pain ran hard and deep. The casualties of war were more than comrades-in-arms. Yet despite everything she now knew, it didn't make her any less afraid of David's recklessness. If anything, she was more frightened.

She reached down and traced a light finger along the line of his jaw. He sighed, seemed to smile. She smiled back. David ben Haar, I do love you. The words welled up inside of her. It was a difficult admission, perhaps the most difficult choice she'd ever made. And loving someone was a choice, a conscious choice. Before, she had refused to allow herself to feel anything more than sexual intensity for David. Her instincts had told her that anything deeper would be dangerous. Obviously she was willing to take the risk now. For she'd come to love David, love him more than she thought possible.

She eased herself back down under the covers, let out the breath she'd been holding. She didn't want to wake him.

The pillow felt cool against her cheek, and she gave herself over to its softness. After they'd made love tonight, she'd stayed in his arms for a long time. David never talked much after sex. So she'd been surprised when she heard his voice. He spoke quietly, in a kind of throw-away fashion. But what he told her was anything but casual. "I was dead before I met you, Romany." Just those few words. Nothing more.

She suspected that was the closest he'd ever get to telling her he loved her. But she'd settle for that. It was the best David could do. Yet there was one thing she knew she could never accept. David's dying. Getting himself killed.

She shut her eyes. It was a thought that wasn't going

to make falling asleep easy, but she'd just have to force herself to do it. After all, she'd have to force herself to go on if David did die. And that was a distinct possibility.

At two A.M. the Vatican natatorium was a black indeterminate space haunted by the strange acoustics of enclosed water. The only lights on were in the pool, a glowing rectangle of aquamarine that quivered, suspended in the dark. Julian Morrow sat completely still at the deep end. But the water moved to its own interior rhythms, its wavery shadows crawling on the tile walls.

Abruptly Julian stood up, dove in. The water crashing for one split second past his ears, he sank to near the bottom—eyes closed, arms encircling the knees he held pressed against his chest, a tight ball tugged from side to side in the water. Finally, his oxygen depleted, he exploded upward through the surface. Gasping in deep breaths, one, two. Then down again. Kicking. Arms cutting forward. Head moving in precise arcs, bisecting space. Up, down. Dark, light. Air, water.

He swam laps until he was exhausted. Then floated on the light that billowed below his outstretched limbs, face and body naked to the dark. Body-warm, the water seemed to disappear, as invisible to his skin now as the darkened ceiling above was to his sight. It had taken a long time to love the water again. And he was grateful that he could come here to swim alone at night. But even so, the water brought it back. Made him remember Jeremy.

His brother hadn't wanted to take the sailboat out. But it was their last summer weekend before Jeremy went back to his school in London, and he went back to Harvard. And so he had insisted, laughing at his twin's "bad feeling" about the weather. But as always, Jeremy had been right. A front had blown in from nowhere, black and cold, with gusting winds that tore and flapped like something wounded in the sail.

He hadn't the sense to be frightened. And Jeremy's only "I-told-you-so" had been the familiar twist of his smile as he'd tossed him his own spare jacket. He remembered himself laughing again as he'd struggled with the wind to get it on over his bare chest. He'd been happy, not afraid. Not even when the wave came that threw them over like a toy boat in a tub. Not until the next cold swell had separated them, and he'd heard the sickening crack of the boom connecting with Jeremy's head.

What he felt then was something worse than fear. Something unnamed that had taken hold and never left as he'd fought his way back to Jeremy, lifting him that one brief moment from the sucking water, holding on as long as he could to what he knew already was dead-weight.

A feeling . . . like death. His own as well as his brother's. That was as much as he knew. Jeremy could have said what it was exactly. But Jeremy, the analytical one, was gone.

There was one thing he remembered clearly. The moment when his parents had found him sitting numbly in the hospital corridor, the exact relief that he'd seen within their eyes. His mother's voice saying, "Jeremy, thank God," and his not understanding till he had looked down to see himself still wearing his brother's jacket.

He remembered the explanations. Not theirs to him. Once they had understood their mistake, it was never spoken of later. The explanations had been the ones that he'd made to himself. Explaining that it was natural, that his parents hadn't known when they'd found him that either one of their sons was dead. It was true. Factually true. And yet it didn't matter. He knew, and they knew too, that the wrong brother was dead.

CHAPTER 13

"Here," the Count held out the brandy to Romany. "Let us walk a bit. It is good for the digestion." His one eye smiled at her.

"I certainly could use a walk. Everything was delicious, Count Sebastiano. I feel stuffed like . . ."

"A Christmas goose?" He'd finished for her.

"Yes." She laughed as she felt him lightly touch the exact small of her back.

"This expression . . . Christmas goose. It is English, is it not? And the name *Chase,* is it not also English?"

"Yes, Count. My paternal grandfather was English. And a bit of Black Irish." She was moving at his side, walking out of the large dining hall, into an adjacent room, a kind of salon. All of this tonight was alien territory, rooms she hadn't seen the evening of the cocktail party. Now he stopped.

"And your father's mother?" His face was suddenly very close to hers; she could smell the rich brandy on his breath.

"My grandmother was Russian. One hundred percent Russian."

"So . . . ?" He seemed to be asking for some kind of qualification for her last remark.

"My father has nothing of the English in him. No, that's not exactly true. He has the English sense of humor."

"I approve. The Russians are a somber lot." The one good eye smiled again.

"But in most other ways," she heard herself going on, "my father is very much Russian."

"And your mother?" He had shifted on his feet away from her, and she watched the light from the wall sconces leave shadows on his face.

"My mother's people were mostly French."

"Ahh, so that accounts for your beauty, Romany Chase."

She didn't quite understand why, but the compliment suddenly made her feel uncomfortable. She looked down at her shoes.

"I can't believe I've embarrassed you, Signorina Chase. I would not have thought you could be embarrassed. I see I am wrong."

He was playing with her. She knew that. Like a cat with a mouse. Not quite going in for the kill. But dragging the game out. Enjoying how the smaller animal squirmed.

"And you, Count?" She looked up sharply and her voice came out sure of itself.

"I?"

"Yes, are you as much of a mystery man as everyone seems to think you are?"

Now his smile turned into a laugh. A much heartier laugh than she would have expected. "I wish I had experienced half the stories that are told of me, Romany Chase. What a life I would have led. But as it is, I'm afraid I have endured quite an ordinary existence."

At the last of his words, Romany arched her brows and gazed about the room, taking in the king's ransom in art that lined the walls.

"Please, Signorina Chase, exteriors can be deceiving," he spoke sweetly, continuing the charade. "I have been but a fortunate man to have acquired some small wealth." He waved the arm holding the brandy to include the whole of the room. He wore a fixed smile.

In her quick survey, Romany had seen what she most certainly believed to be a da Vinci, a Titian, a Raphael, several sketches by Michelangelo, and though it seemed completely impossible that he should have acquired it, Vermeer's *The Music Lesson*.

"Well, Count Sebastiano," she said coyly, deciding to go along with whatever game he was playing, "despite your rather monkish existence, I must nevertheless compliment you on your excellent taste in art. You have a most extraordinary collection."

With that he bowed. "I am humbled, Signorina Chase. Praise from one such as you is most gratifying." Then without another word, he escorted her about the room. Stopping before each work, making a few unassuming comments. Her mind reeled at the thought of any one person possessing such a collection. For an instant she suspected that all of them were nothing more than very good copies. But immediately she dismissed the thought. There wasn't a fake in the bunch.

"Count Sebastiano . . ." She'd turned to say something. But he was gone. Vanished, like a puff of smoke. One moment he was there, then he wasn't.

"Signorina Chase . . ." she heard him call her name, his voice muffled, slightly distant. Then he was there again, restraining a sliding panel, a kind of hidden door. He smiled, offering her his hand. For an instant Romany stared at the white unlined palm; then she put her hand into his.

She stepped into a small chamber, a kind of anteroom, where there was less light. And for all its architectural detail, the room was entirely empty except for a single canvas dominating one wall.

It was a huge painting. More than likely an altarpiece. Italian Renaissance. Midfifteenth century. Madonna and child were seated against an almost mythical landscape, a labyrinthine villa dominating the background. For a moment she determined it was the work of Filippo Lippi, the lady's countenance wearing the same distracted gaze of another of the artist's more familiar madonnas.

But in the next minute it was the work of Bellini. As in another of that master's works, the landscape was luminous, chilly, under a pale winter sky. Yet curiously unlike the Bellini madonna, there was no tenderness or solicitude on the woman's part for the child seated in her lap. This madonna was remote, detached, as though caring little for the son she held. Rather she clutched a crude earthen jar in her right hand.

Then suddenly Romany's focus was pulled into a tight composition of line and form. Lying across the Madonna's lap was a mantle of complex design, its disturbing pattern in complete contrast to the eerie serenity of the rest of the painting. But as she stared at it, the pattern receded, and the queer curves and angles again were merely brushstrokes.

"Well, Signorina Chase?" He was waiting for her reaction.

"I eliminated almost immediately Signorelli and Botticelli," she said after a moment. "And for a few minutes I thought it a Filippo Lippi. Then I changed my mind. 'No,' I said to myself, it is a Bellini. But that isn't right either." Romany frowned.

The Count smiled. "My dear Signorina Chase, it is not an old painting at all. But something I had done for me quite recently. It is remarkable, though, is it not?"

It was very late when the Black Baron returned to the Villa Bassano. In most ways it was a needless trip. He could have slept in Rome in the Palazzo Rozze. But he had had to come here tonight. Besides, now that he'd gotten older, he actually required very little sleep.

He made his way up the long flight of stairs, moving on the balls of his feet. He hoped that none in the household should discover him till morning. The bane of the very rich—ubiquitous servants.

The room was blacker than the night he'd just left, but he preferred the darkness. Maybe the light of one candle . . . He moved to the sideboard and struck a match. Instantly her face came to life behind the glass in the frame. Beautiful, his perfect Lise.

He lifted the photograph from its exact resting place behind the vase of roses. Wolfgang had done well all these years. Never was the vase without fresh roses. He angled his head, enjoying how the watery light swam across her image.

Yet why was it he never trusted the gods? Too capricious, he'd decided. He trusted only himself. But of late the gods had smiled upon him. Had seen fit to favor him at this the last turn of the wheel.

"What game do you play that this Romany Chase should look so like my Lise? What game do you play?" he whispered to the unseen gods.

He examined the fading photograph once more. Silly old man, he cursed himself. No gift of the gods, but a willful trick of his own mind. Romany Chase did not in the least resemble his Lise. But he knew even as he thought it that his words were lies.

He shifted the picture under the candlelight. What is truth? And what is not? he wondered. No matter, he concluded at the last. The important thing was what he believed. And tonight had been wonderful. He liked having a woman of real flesh and blood across from him at the table. The Chase woman was delightful. Not as close to physical perfection as Lise, but surely more intelligent, more charming. He could feel the slow constricting of his anus. In another moment there would be an erection.

He closed his eyes and regained control. He would not be stupid. Romany Chase was Arte per Pace. Romany Chase could be dangerous, could betray him. Betray him as Lise had done. He would not be made the fool twice. He would not be deceived again.

He touched the photograph, Lise's mouth. "My precious one," he muttered, the German rattling in his throat, "you should not have kept your secret from me."

CHAPTER 14

The dream fled even as she woke, and Romany, blinking in the morning light, lay grasping at half-remembered images. But the substance of the dream was gone, like tasteless wisps of cotton candy dissolving in her mind. A kind of hollowness was all that remained, and the certainty that the dream had been of David.

In the days since he'd told her about the murder of his family, David ben Haar had haunted her thoughts. And now, it seemed, her dreams. Not the erotic dreams of the months she had been without him, but strange disjointed dreams of anticipation and loss that she could never quite remember. What was David doing to her, letting her in so far? What was she doing to herself?

She sat up in bed and shook her head, as if to free her mind of thought. Then, brushing her hair away from her eyes, she turned to look at the clock. It had been a good decision last night not to go in to the office this morning. She'd gotten some rest, and there was plenty of time yet to try to get her focus before this afternoon's meeting with Julian Morrow.

Thank goodness she hadn't panicked at the first sign of trouble and gone running either to Elliot or Sully. The first bad patch with Julian had been nicely muddled through. The question was, what came next? For one brief moment, when Sully had said that Julian's appointment was probably a fluke, she had thought she was off the hook. But no such luck. Her assignment remained the same. *Get as close as possible to Father Julian Morrow.*

But who was Julian Morrow? That was the question she'd played tag with again in the long hours before she'd finally fallen asleep, the same question she'd been toying with now for weeks. Because the clues just didn't add up. As a mystery story, the priest was either an exceptionally clever piece of work, or very poorly plotted. The problem was, it was taking too long to get to the end of the book.

She thought about the portrait that Sully had sketched for her on Monday night. A young Julian Morrow who'd acted "weird" after the death of his brother. A son who'd defied his father's wishes to become a priest, who was anything but a saint. Julian Morrow as a picture was an equally puzzling study. Rendered not so much in black and white as varying shades of gray.

Jump with him, Sully had told her, with the implication that if the priest stumbled into the Cardinal's plot, he would most likely turn the discovery to his personal advantage. Maybe. But Sully was a professional cynic. Something in her still resisted, something that kept wanting to give Julian Morrow the benefit of every doubt. Perhaps part of the problem was that she still had no real feel for where the priest actually stood in relation to the Cardinal and to Brisi.

And the bad news was that Sully still expected a seduction. Well, her new plan was not to hurry that. What she needed was to know Julian better. Learn how to put him more at ease. No more sudden moves like at the villa, but a logical progression, step by step. It made more sense to become his friend, before she tried again to get Julian Morrow into bed.

For a moment before she got up, she thought again of what Julian had said to her at his apartment. Hadn't there been as much calculation as sincerity in the way he'd implied that it was partly her responsibility to make sure things didn't get out of hand?

Well, tough luck either way, Father Morrow, she thought as she bounced up and headed toward the bathroom. The straight and narrow would have to be his choice. She planned on looking gorgeous today.

He was late. Not a new experience, but today, waiting in the chair in front of Julian Morrow's desk, Romany could make no practical use of the time. Not with Father Vance clacking away at the keyboard on his own crammed-in desk. It was a bit unnerving to have him there working so close behind her back, even though she wasn't doing any spying.

They had introduced themselves when she'd come in, and the new secretary was pleasant enough, explaining that he was expecting Father Morrow any minute. Father Richard Vance, it turned out, was also a Jesuit. Younger than Julian, she'd guessed, and kind of Midwestern collegiate with his wholesome smile and neatly combed hair. Only his eyes didn't fit. An ordinary light-brown color, they were not ordinary at all. *Old soul* was the phrase that had popped into her mind when he'd looked up to shake her hand.

She could imagine those ancient eyes watching her now as she reached down to smooth her skirt and steal a look at her watch. But the clacking at the keyboard went merrily on, and it was probably just her guilty conscience. The last time she'd been in this office, after all, she'd been waiting to steal the paint. And then came a stray thought, much more to the point. If Julian Morrow were in fact the reclamation project that Sully supposed, was Father Vance the Jesuits' watchdog?

"Sorry I'm late."

She turned to see Julian at the door. Father Vance had risen. So the watchdog, if that was what he really was, was leaving them alone. It was surprising just how glad she was of that.

Across from her, Julian sat down, pulling papers out of the file drawer in his desk. "Here they are." He laid them in front of her. "The translations that you asked for."

"Thanks, Julian." She reached down for her briefcase and opened it in her lap. "I have to admit I was surprised when you called yesterday," she told him. "I know we said a couple days, but I really didn't expect to get them all so quickly."

"Well, there are still one or two to go. But I should

have them for you sometime next week." He was leaning back in his chair and he was smiling. This open, boyish Julian Morrow seemed to feel none of the tension that had underscored their last meeting. It was as good a time as any for this.

"Julian," she said, shutting away the translations in her briefcase, "what do you think of the Director General?"

"Brisi?"

His smile got wider when she looked up, but something shadowed his eyes.

"Yes. What do you think of him?"

Julian shrugged. "The monsignor's not a subject I've given a whole lot of thought to."

"He wasn't happy about your getting this job. You told me that, remember?"

"Yes." The shadow in his eyes got deeper. "But I don't understand what you're getting at."

"Can *you* get me into the Restoration Department?"

"The Restoration Department?" He parroted the words back.

"Yes. Naturally, like everybody else in the field, I had wanted to come to Rome while the work on the Sistine was in progress. Now that I am here, I'd at least like to have a look at the facilities."

"I see."

"I asked Monsignor Brisi about it, but he just put me off. Perhaps I should take the direct approach, go straight to Cardinal DeLario."

"No."

She wondered which one of them had been more startled by the force in that single syllable.

"The direct approach in Rome?" His voice was softer, and he'd forced the smile back. "I'm sure I can set something up for you, Romany. Just give me a little time. All right?"

"Of course, Julian," she said easily, but her mind was decided. She was going to get in there tonight.

·   ·   ·

An immense marble-enclosed silence pressed hard against her ears as Romany moved quickly down the dim branching corridor. With her crepe-soled shoes, and her oversized purse tucked tight against her body, she moved as noiselessly as her haste would allow, aware that any sound made here would echo like in a mausoleum.

She really didn't like this. Not one damn bit. It was scarier than the last time in the Pinacoteca, the chances greater here that she'd run into a guard in what was largely unfamiliar territory. Her staff ID just might get her through if it was necessary, but her best defense was not to get caught.

After long minutes, when the beat of her blood became louder than the silence in her ears, she stood before the door to Restoration. It was no surprise to find that it was locked. She hadn't supposed that anything about this second reconnaissance mission was going to be as easy as the first. She listened, but there was no sound except for the battering darkness. No time like the present to find out if all her little toys really worked.

She took from her purse the small black box that measured electric current and ran it around the door. No current, no alarm. The black box went back, and the flashlight came out along with what looked like an ordinary manicure kit, but was actually a set of picks. She stopped again. One more minute to look and listen. No movement. No sound. She turned on the flashlight and played it over the lock.

The light went back into her purse. Feel, not sight, was important. The right touch. But it was never smart to leave prints. She struggled as quickly as she could into the latex gloves. If doctors could do brain surgery with these things on, then surely she could pick a simple lock. She took a calming breath and knelt down. In a matter of moments there was a satisfying click. She tried not to be too surprised that she'd actually done it.

She relocked the door behind her, resisting the

temptation to turn on the overhead lights. She would have to rely on the flashlight.

What she saw in the first moments surprised her, although there was certainly no logical reason why. The medical laboratory look of chemicals and computers was typical of modern restoration. What had she been expecting? Monks with tiny brushes? The question that really bothered her was how Cardinal DeLario could control all the men and women, many with international reputations, who worked in the museum's Restoration Department. And yet she could remember certain rumors that the major shake-up in personnel after the Sistine Chapel restoration had been anything but amicable. She wondered now if it might not explain how the Restoration Department, or at least a part of it, could have become involved in the commission of the forgeries.

She stopped at a table where cleaning was being done on a small Etruscan statue. There was nothing about it that appeared at all incriminating. She went on to the other rooms, work spaces, and offices stocked with cabinets and files. It made her head ache even to think about plowing drawer by drawer through a mountain of Italian paperwork. Better to use her time in searching for physical evidence.

After a complete circuit of the department, she sat down to think in the dark. Slowly, methodically, she retraced the last half hour in her mind. Her gut was telling her that something was here. Something her brain had seen and missed. She was up and moving before the decision was conscious.

She had seen the room only in the patches picked out by her flashlight. But she had suddenly remembered it as the only office with no cabinets or files, no name or title stenciled on the door. She walked over and sat down in the chair. The desk appeared unused. No marks on the blotter. No papers in the trays. The drawers were all locked, but she could take care of that. Though right now she just wanted to sit there and look. Something was still nagging. But what?

A grab bag of coats and umbrellas hung from brass hooks screwed into the ugly dark paneling. Just a pile of clothes, Romany, she cautioned, but intuition was already prodding her toward the only haphazard element in the room. The jumbled mess was a disguise for a set-in door. She swept aside a raincoat and tried the knob. It turned in her hand.

She reached inside her purse. At the bottom was the .22 that Sully had insisted on her taking at their last meeting. She had never really faced the reality that the gun represented. Certainly not then. Perhaps not even now. For a moment her fingers closed tightly around the hardness of the grip. But her hand, when it came out, held only the flashlight.

The door in the paneling swung noiselessly open into black space. A low corridor led to a narrow flight of stairs. She followed them down. At the bottom, tucked into the basement, was another large work space, the perfect setup for the production of forgeries. And yet it couldn't be easy to keep a secret this size. So the old question came back. Could the Pope really not know what was happening beneath his nose? And what of Julian Morrow? If Julian was truly an innocent set down by Pope Gregory inside this den of thieves, then De-Lario had to be really sweating over the Jesuit sitting in his little office at the Pinacoteca every day. It came to her with sudden force that an *innocent* Julian Morrow was in danger.

With the flashlight sweeping ahead of her, she moved from table to empty table. It was just what she'd been afraid of. The Cardinal had quit while he was ahead. Maybe in the cabinets . . .

The first held chemicals. The second, other supplies —brushes, pigments, the usual kind of stuff. The third was nearly empty. It had the look of being stripped. There was only a pile of rags now, and a few jars of paint that looked like ochers and umbers. And leaning against the bottom shelf nearly hidden behind three huge jugs of solvent was a very old and dirty piece of paneling.

Of course. For the forgery of an old painting, you needed authentic wood. She pushed aside the heavy jugs. Turned the board around. And almost laughed out loud.

An envelope was attached with tape to what looked like the underpainting for one of Giovanni di Paolo's *biccherne,* a small panel once used as a cover for an account book in the public treasury of Siena. She peeled off the envelope and opened it. Inside were a disk and a pack of complex schematics—computer mappings of the paint layers of di Paolo's original. She recognized the program. It was part of the software that had been devised for the restoration of the Sistine ceiling. No wonder the forgeries were so close to perfection.

Her first impulse was to stuff the envelope and its contents into her purse. But that was a bad idea. Whoever had done her the favor of leaving the panel behind might very well have second thoughts and be back. It was important that the Cardinal go on believing he was safe. Everything must look the same as it was.

She propped the artwork on the nearest table and set up her light. The camera could focus on only a small area at a time, and she had been rushing through the painting and several pages of schematics when she thought she heard something. No, not something heard, she told herself. More like an impression. Eyes. Watching her. With a sudden move, she gripped the flashlight, swung it around in an arc.

Nothing.

She'd been holding her breath. She let it out. God, it was true. The hairs on the back of your neck really could stand up. And her hands were sweating away like crazy in the tight-fitting gloves. It was the tension. She'd been down here way too long.

What was that? A real sound this time? She waited, stock-still, with the flashlight off. But the sound, if it was anything more than nervous imagination, did not come again. She switched the flashlight on. Hit the stairs with the beam. Bottom to top. Down again. Played it around in a circle. Nothing.

She gathered the papers and the disk into the envelope and taped it carefully into place. The panel went back to the cabinet. Another sweep with her flashlight, and she headed up the stairs.

At the top she stopped abruptly, swinging her light one last time into the well of blackness below. And saw, or thought she saw, for one lingering instant, a flickering at the edge of her light's penumbra. Like the ghost of a deeper darkness. Like the fleeting shadow of some monstrous bat.

CHAPTER 15

Romany was tired, dog tired, and glad she'd been able to make it to the dead drop and leave Sully what she'd gotten last night, before collapsing into bed. Just a little shut-eye, one of those catnaps she'd become famous for during her days in college. She had to smile even now remembering her old roomie complaining she didn't know "how in the hell Romany did it."

"Just close my eyes, Jenny," she said half-aloud to a roommate, too many miles and too many years away. She slipped off her shoes and stripped down to her underwear.

It was strange, but the older she got, the more vivid the dream became. She imagined a psychoanalyst could make something of that. She, however, had no theories. And always, the line between dreaming and waking was never crossed. She simply acknowledged to herself that this was a dream, and she should just relax and go along for the ride. Observe the pictures playing in her head. Watch the movie.

She dreamed the dream now.

The day was hot, and fat white gulls sailed over where she squatted, filling her little tin bucket with sand. She was seven years old, and it was only the second time she could remember going to the seashore with her parents. She looked over now to where her father sat sprawled upon a canvas lounger, under the shade of a large yellow umbrella. He'd fallen asleep with one of his big books propped against his broad belly. She watched the pages flutter in the small wind that was trying to find its way through the dense balloon of heat that surrounded everything.

Daddy was certainly her favorite friend. He told the best stories, even better than the ones she read in books. She giggled under her hand. He did look funny in his swim trunks. The wide red and white stripes made him look something like a giant peppermint stick.

A bird screamed overhead.

She shielded her face, making a kind of salute with her fingers, her eyes following the path of the gull. White wings beat against a cloudless blue sky. Its destination was not far, and she watched the bird swoop and land like a small plane precisely upon the single exposed tooth of rock. A sudsy wave crashed against the gull's breast.

"Romany . . ."

She heard her name, and from a distance she could see her mother bobbing out of a rich green wave. Her thick hair had come loosened from its braid and spread like feathers across her shoulders. She wore a plain black suit, not unlike those worn at the turn of the century. Romany had seen pictures of young women strolling along the boardwalk at Atlantic City long before the great war had broken out.

But Mother looked pretty anyway, in her old-fashioned suit, her golden-brown hair sparkling under the hot sun. She ran her fingers across her eyes to remove the last bit of water from her face and waved.

Romany dropped the small shovel she'd been holding and waved back.

"Come into the water, Romany . . . ," her mother's voice called.

And in an instant she was in the ocean, forcing her seven-year-old young girl's legs against the pressure of the tide. Then she let the waves buoy her up and out, and she began moving her thin arms in long strokes, swimming to the wave where her mother waited.

The end of the dream was always the same. Romany locked in her mother's arms, her mother's cool wet lips kissing her neck, the soft spot on her shoulder. The two of them laughing, laughing and fighting to stay afloat.

She never knew what happened after that, because the dream always ended there. With the two of them laughing in the water. Never once had she ever dreamed her mother out of the water, out of the ocean and walking with her along the shore. And because of this, a very young and imaginative Romany Chase had christened this her "mermaid dream."

Romany opened her eyes. In her waking hours she had never spent a single summer's day with her mother on a beach. Marthe hated the sun. So whenever she had gone swimming as a child, it had been with her father in the faculty-club pool.

But it was her mother's arms about her and the soft kisses that were the most alien to Romany. In all her years Romany could never once remember her mother cuddling her, kissing her like in the dream. In reality Marthe rarely touched Romany.

It wasn't that Marthe was cold or unloving. She adored her daughter. It was that she was never comfortable with any kind of intimacy. To Romany she seemed almost frightened. As though you might erase her if you touched her.

It had at first been hard for Romany to understand this. Her mother's routine, protracted life. So different from her father's spontaneity. And whatever magic she'd been able to work on her father, she longed to work on her mother.

But she never did.

As she grew older, she saw the wealth of kindness and gentleness in Marthe, and she found some comfort in the simple explanation: "It was just Mother's way."

Later when she became a woman and suspected her mother's behavior might involve something far more complicated, she would quickly discount the idea, and find new relief in a much safer conclusion: "Mother has never been well."

Marthe was particular about her things too. As a result Romany rarely went into her parents' bedroom. She could remember once spying on Marthe through a partially opened door. Watching for what seemed like hours, watching her mother brush her long, impossibly thick hair. It was strange to see her mother's hair spread as it was down her back, across her shoulders. She'd never seen it in anything but the tight knot at the back of her head. Except of course, in the dream. But she didn't think that counted.

She remembered being enchanted that afternoon, following her mother's hand as it moved the brush. Mesmerized by twin images—her mother's straight back supporting the fall of thick hair, her mother's solemn, pretty face reflected in the mirror.

She sat up, thinking now about her father, thinking that he hadn't called lately. If she was anxious to see him, she also felt some misgivings about his coming. He was so good at reading her. And with all that was going on . . .

Oh well, she'd just have to cross that bridge when she came to it. Right now she needed a hot bath.

Gina di Lorenzo had been watching him stroke the erect phallus of the small bronze since she'd arrived at the palazzo from her office in the Arte per Pace building. He had not asked her to sit down, had not in any way acknowledged her presence, and she shifted once more on the balls of her feet. Some women were prone to buy shoes that were too narrow or too short and suffered the misery of corns and bunions as they hit thirty. Gina was such a woman.

"Such a prodigious penis for one so small, do you not think, Gina?" Count Sebastiano had finally looked up, his middle finger resting on the bulb of the statue's exaggerated sex.

"I . . ." She had no idea what he expected her to say. But Gina di Lorenzo was anything but timid. In fact, Signorina di Lorenzo, in somewhat dated but nevertheless accurate idiom, "knew the ropes." However, this man, this pretty old man, made her sick in the stomach.

But she saw he'd ignored her. "The men of the Italian Renaissance had a special fascination for dwarfs," he continued. "Why, some of the princes kept them as pets." He fondled the underside of the disproportionately large member. "I can imagine what tricks these poor unfortunates were forced to perform." His good eye trapped her in his line of vision.

"It is not so easy being chattel. I hope that you never think of our relationship in that light, Gina." The lower portion of his face took on the expression of a man who'd unexpectedly tasted something bitter.

"No, of course not, Count Sebastiano. I have never thought of our relationship as anything but satisfactory."

"I would never want you to think of yourself as being used"—his fingers gave a final lingering caress to the bronze genitals—"like a pet."

"We have a very efficient business arrangement, Count Sebastiano. You want something that I am able to provide. And for that I am highly paid."

"Good, good," he said, his mouth finally smiling. "I am glad we understand each other. But please sit, Gina, I have been most rude. Sit and tell me everything you know about your boss, Signorina Romany Chase."

.   .   .

"Bless me, Father. I have sinned."

"We have all sinned, my son."

The ritual complete, the voice in the dark cell of the confessional fell silent, waiting for the monk to begin.

"We have a problem, Father." He said it quickly.

"A problem?"

"It's the woman, Romany Chase. I'm afraid she is more than she seems."

"A danger, my son. Did I not say it? Tell me what my fear already knows."

"The first night I tried to get a paint sample from the Caravaggio, I was interrupted," the monk said. "At the time I thought it was someone from the regular staff, but now I'm sure it was Miss Chase. It appears that she and I are on the same track. Last night she turned up again. This time in the Restoration Department."

"In Restoration?"

"Yes. I'd begun to suspect that that was where at least some of the duplicates were being created. Miss Chase had obviously thought of it too."

"What did she find?"

"A small panel, the beginnings of another forgery."

"And you could do nothing to prevent this, my son?" The worried words were a whisper.

"Nothing that would not have meant revealing myself, Father."

"Are you sure she understood what the panel meant?"

"Completely sure, Father. She had a small camera. She took pictures." He waited for some new reaction. The prolonged silence was worse. "Perhaps, Father," he suggested, taking the initiative, "this is not the worst thing that could have happened."

"How not, my son?" The voice was again a whisper, but velvet over steel.

"It seems obvious that Miss Chase had a running start, that she arrived in Rome already knowing about these forgeries. The most logical conclusion is that she was planted in Arte per Pace. Perhaps now, Father, it is time that we could . . ."

"No more, Zuriel." The monk heard the swish of the heavy robes, saw the hand come up, cutting off any possibility of discussion. "Indeed, it *is* time." The voice was pure steel now.

The monk leaned forward in submission, his brow resting against the cruciform pattern of the grate.

"It is time." The words were repeated again. "No doubt can remain now that we stand in the gravest peril. Pass the word quickly to your brothers, my son. Tomorrow night we meet."

CHAPTER 16

The Brotherhood met as they did with no actual belief in any of it. That is, no precise faith in the exterior. The exterior was a mask, a means to an end. A device, a mechanism. Mere ritual to advance them to where they must be.

The true reality lay in their will.

From the beginning there had always been twelve in the highest order of the Brotherhood. The Thirteenth, not of them, but above them.

Always and always the Twelve had served the Thirteenth. And over the years they had come to be what they were now. But there were times in the long-ago past when the Twelve had no place. And the Twelve, and the followers of the Twelve, hid from those who misunderstood and would seek to destroy them. They even hid from the Thirteenth.

But those times had passed. And today the Twelve and the followers of the Twelve served the Thirteenth and the descendants of the Thirteenth well.

The guttering candles mixed light with flames from braziers. The scent of tallow mixed with frankincense.

The carpet with the great circle lay upon the floor, its once dark colors fading. But the stations could not be mistaken, and each of the Twelve took up his place. Twelve signs. Twelve houses. Twelve men.

The Brotherhood dressed as monks now, having forsaken long ago the vestments of knighthood. But knights were they still. Pledged to protect the Thirteenth and his kingdom on earth. Aries to Pisces; the Angel Machidiel to the Angel Barakiel.

Then the Thirteenth, who was called Metatron, spoke.

"He has more than one Swiss bank account."

It had been a simple statement of fact. Not a question. But Verchiel elaborated. "Yes, three to be exact. The third opened only recently."

"He is wealthier than we first thought," said Zuriel.

"And greedier," said Machidiel.

"That point was never contested." Asmodel's words brought forth a round of laughter.

"Ambriel," Metatron addressed the monk standing in the house of Gemini, "is it worse than we thought?"

"No, Metatron, we have always understood that the situation with His Eminence would be difficult. We have never had any illusions." Ambriel frowned behind his cowl. He hoped the Thirteenth had not taken notice.

"But this evil is surely greater than one man. We are almost certain of this now." There was just a trace of impatience in Muriel's voice.

"Yes, Muriel, we are sure there are others who must profit from His Eminence's activities," Ambriel spoke to the monk standing in the house of Cancer.

"And the woman?" Muriel's question was directed at Ambriel.

But it was Zuriel who answered. "There can no longer be much conjecture. She is CIA."

"Forgive me, Metatron, but I feel we can no longer stand by and wait. Our hands in our pockets. We must do something . . . before it is too late." Muriel's last words fell to a whisper.

"I have no quarrel with your position, Muriel."
Metatron's voice seemed to rise with the smoke from
the candles. "But we cannot be premature. We must act
only from a position of strength."

"So it is most likely that she is CIA?" Hamaliel
asked.

"Yes," answered Ambriel. "But there are certain
contradictions . . ."

"Contradictions?" Barbiel asked.

"Nothing specific. Nothing I can yet elaborate
upon."

"She must be watched closely, this American
woman," Metatron said, looking again at Ambriel. "We
must do whatever is necessary."

"We surely cannot think the interests of Rome are
not the interests of Washington, Ambriel?" said Ad-
nachiel.

"I think we can assume their interests are one
if . . ."

"If the Americans believe His Holiness is not himself contaminated." Metatron himself finished Ambriel's sentence.

"Obviously," said Haniel, "they are uncertain of the
Pope since they have not tried to communicate with
Rome."

"So the Americans do not know everything,"
Cambiel said.

"But exactly what do they know?" asked Barakiel.
"Our options are quickly collapsing. Perhaps we should
approach the Americans."

"No." Metatron bellowed the word. "Rome must
clean its house before guests may be invited in."

"But surely, Metatron, the success of Arte per Pace
is something the Americans want very badly," Barakiel
was speaking again. "We cannot be so naive as to think
it is but an art exhibit that brings the world to Rome."

"We are all very much aware of the significance of
Arte per Pace, that it is a seal upon the new world order." Metatron's words sounded kinder than any of

them might have expected. "But again I must advise patience lest Rome bring down its own house upon itself.

"Ambriel?"

"Yes, Metatron." The monk bowed in obedience. "I shall do what is necessary."

There was no electricity in the long passageways of the hidden library. Electricity had been unknown in the century when the library had been founded to hold the precious volumes salvaged from the destruction of the Templar priories. And within the century of electricity's invention, only recently had there been one among the Twelve with the menial skills to himself install the wiring—to none else but the Twelve could the existence of the library be trusted. And still there was no electricity. The Thirteenth did not wish it.

Through the narrow corridors formed by the towering shelves, Metatron moved in his white robes like a night-treading spirit, like a rat in its maze, his attention focused not upon the dusty manuscripts that rose in ponderous rows above him, but forward upon whatever small patch of wooden floor where fell the light from his lantern.

There was no map, no pattern to the path that the Thirteenth walked. His conscious intention was to randomize his steps. To give free reign to his daemon. Compelled, he stopped. Reached down blindly among the nether shelves. Let his finger touch . . . there.

He lowered the lantern to see what volume had thus been chosen. A slim one, coarsely bound, very dusty. Unread, like most of what was here, for centuries.

He carried the book back to a table, set down his lantern, and settled himself in the chair. He did not believe in this, he told himself, this divination by book. And still he did it. Again and again. Drawn here as if by some perverse magnetism. Or more likely by the rankling impossibility of the position into which God or his blind ambition had thrust him, of the tasks that plagued him, of the tests to which he was not equal.

He fought it down, the anger that gnawed like a pestilence from within, an insistent and impotent rage whose only real object was himself. And with a sudden force of will that swept clear his mind, Metatron lifted the book within his hands and let the pages fall open as they would.

He read:

October 1307

This terrible night has not been without its beauty—horses and riders moon-pale in the soughing darkness as we fled like specters along the forested roads leading out of Paris. Fled southward to the ancient mountain strongholds. South to where the stars low-twinkled above the horizon, yellow and warm as the light of distant torches.

And I, Jacques de Beauvacque, Knight of the Temple of Solomon, one among three, crouched low against the neck of my straining steed, remembering other stars. Stars like dagger points in the indigo vault above the seawalls of Acre. Last great citadel of the Templars in Outremer. The land beyond the sea. The Holy Land, fallen once again to the Saracens.

I was sixteen years younger on that long-ago night, and what I wanted most was to remain with my brethren, fighting to the last man against this final victory of the infidels. But the first rule of the Brotherhood was always obedience, and mine was not to be a martyr's death. Not then and not now. The fires of the Inquisition will no doubt pass me by as did the Moslem blade. For tonight as in Acre, my superiors did once again see fit to entrust into my care that treasure most singular of the many that the Templars possess, more sacred than the cloth of Veronica, more precious than Solomon's gold.

And yet 'twas but a simple touch upon my shoulder that awakened me tonight, summoning me from the barracks, where even a message of some urgency must not be allowed to disturb the rule of silence. I dressed quietly, but in haste, donning my white mantle to follow the brown-robed sergent past the rows of sleeping knights. The night was already cold, the sky above the courtyard starless. The moon, not yet in zenith, cast but a pallid light, and shadows, like evil rumors, ran slithering ahead of us into the deeper dark as we moved in silence toward the Great Hall.

Inside, the scene was hellish—the lurking gloom, the smoking brands in the sconces, the black figures moving like great ants before the fireplace—the knights of the treasury feeding into the orange flames the records and documents of the Brotherhood.

It was the Preceptor himself who beckoned me from his ceremonial chair, reflections from the fire casting his features into a mask of weariness and strain. And I, moving to stand before him, felt the clutch of forgotten fear. That strange falling away of the center that had grabbed at me in childhood whenever some deep-set worry had ravaged my father's face.

The Preceptor's voice echoed strangely in the hollow spaces of the hall as he told of the warning that had come. In his jealousy and greed King Philippe of France would turn his hand against the Knights of the Temple. The secret inner mysteries had been betrayed, and the sacred rituals twisted into something evil. All were to be arrested, branded as heretics who worshiped the demon and denied the salvation of the cross.

Stunned, I no less protested that the King had not the right to call us to account on such a charge. The Templars were not Philippe's vassals, but answered only to the Pope.

Bitterness deepened the furrows of the Preceptor's already haggard face. Pope Clement was weak, he said, and doubtless had been reminded that it was to Philippe's influence that he owed his election. The ax would fall upon us all, and yet the commander of Templar forces at Bezu was the Pope's own cousin. Bezu of all our preceptories in France would the King's seneschals spare. To Bezu was I ordered with that relic I had once already saved, that secret never to be trusted to the popes and kings which in these dark days our God has seen fit to send us.

And so, as once before, I left my brothers to their fate, and set out in company with but two knights who like myself would fight to the death to preserve those sacred things that we carried. And wagons too went out on other roads from Paris, wagons of gold and worldly treasure that make their way even now to the waiting Templar fleet. The King will find but empty coffers as payment for his treachery.

All this I pondered, as tight against the wind I drew the hood of my unfamiliar jerkin. No white mantle proud with its red cross now. Gone too the distinctive beard of the Templars, shaven in haste to leave my cheeks but raw and stinging in the cold. Though disguise was prudent, it was hateful nonetheless. And more hateful that a Christian king should come to destroy what centuries of infidels could not.

And yet was my sword still left to me. Yet was I a Knight of the Temple of Solomon. And within my keeping, the long leather satchel with its holy treasure. I saw that in the east the moon had risen, its light steady now and pure in the late silver hours of its descent. To me it seemed a promise, a sign in the heavens that my journey would indeed be blessed, that in the secret depository near Bezu where tonight I rest, the sacred relics will again find peace. Till that far-off day when kings and popes might prove worthy of mysteries that in this age of barbarity and ignorance they would destroy.

The entry was the last in Jacques de Beauvacque's carefully scripted journal. And the Thirteenth wondered momentarily whether this was because de Beauvacque had in the end been seized by the Inquisition, or simply because he'd had nothing more of significance to write.

He closed the manuscript and stared into the dark.

He had come here for some kind of affirmation, some sense that the course that he now but stumbled upon was right. What answer was there in anything that he had read tonight?

No answer, but a further puzzle. What, he wondered, had been the treasure de Beauvacque carried? That he would never know. So much had been lost or forgotten in the time since the attempted destruction of the Brotherhood.

More sacred than the cloth of Veronica, more precious than Solomon's gold. But what could it have been? He shook his head. He was concentrating on the wrong thing. Perhaps there was indeed a message, that what had seemed of such importance in one age might be but safely forgotten in another. Perhaps. He doubted it.

Other of de Beauvacque's words came back to him. *Till that far-off day when kings and popes might prove worthy of mysteries that in this age of barbarity and ignorance they would destroy.* That far-off day. Was that not what he was working for? The day when there would be an end to barbarity and ignorance? Was that not what Arte per Pace was all about? Perhaps there was an answer here after all, a permit to do what was necessary.

But surely barbarity could not be a blade that exorcised itself. There must be limits. Yet here at the pinnacle where the lines were drawn, the temptations were only more great. Could he ever trust himself?

And suddenly the Thirteenth knew what drew him here. Understood the attraction and the revulsion. Like every form of divination, bibliomancy was a mirror. It was your soul that was revealed when you looked in.

CHAPTER 17

Morrow was damn efficient. Romany had to give him that. He'd promised her the rest of the translations by the first of the week, and here they were bright and early Monday morning. She picked up his handwritten note and reread it: "Hope these meet with your approval. I'll be out of town for a few days. Father Vance will be in the office. Please call him if you run into any problems. *Ciao,* Julian."

More than anything she hated not knowing how she felt. And right at this moment she couldn't decide if she was disappointed or relieved that Julian Morrow was going to be away for a few days. Of course she should be relieved. More time to plan her strategy.

Or more time to stall? She bit her lower lip.

Damn, she was anxious just to get things under way. Get the whole thing over and done with. But she knew that was a lie. She didn't much care for what she was supposed to do. Besides, she wasn't exactly batting a thousand. Why in the hell didn't she just level with Sully? Tell him the whole thing was impossible, that trying to seduce a priest in order to learn his secrets was going too far. But she knew she would never be able to tell him that. She had something to prove to Sully. The old bastard should at least be pleased with what she'd lifted from the Restoration Department, although she knew that the photos would only substantiate what they already knew.

What Sully didn't need to tell her was that the real prize would be the middleman. Finding the broker was critical. And that was where David came in. She knew that David was up to his ass in all this. And very likely to get it blown off.

Get some perspective, Romany. This is business, remember. Julian Morrow is business. David ben Haar is business. All in a day's work, she reminded herself. God, she hated cliches.

Anton Arendt had led him on a wild-goose chase through narrow Roman streets. The first stop had been for a hair trim and manicure. The second, an exclusive tailoring salon. The third stop, a pharmacy. The little Nazi was damn prissy. Hair, fingernails, wardrobe.

David now waited in his car somewhere in the Alban Hills. Fifteen minutes ago a cab had dropped Arendt off at an out-of-the-way pensione. And for what? All that grooming to fuck someone. But why the drive? Even a skinny monkey like Arendt could find all the women he wanted in Rome. No, his gut told him that little Anton was not on the prowl for pussy. He had something else in mind.

He sank lower in the seat of the rented car and tried to maneuver his legs across to the passenger side. He cursed the cheap compact, but everything had gone cold. Nothing had turned up on the identity of the mystery middleman. And Chaim had told him to stay cool. "Don't force anything, ben Haar."

He lit a cigarette. He hardly ever smoked. In fact, he hated the taste of nicotine on his breath. But it settled him on stakeouts. Smoothed out the rough spots when he got fidgety. Or when he was likely to think too much. Like now.

He didn't want to think of Romany. Not how she felt. Not how she tasted. Or the smell of her. Like warm sunshine on clean clothes. Fresh. Yes, thoughts like these were decidedly bad for him, made him soft. He didn't like to admit weakness. But damn it all, Romany Chase was his weakness.

The other night when they'd made love, when he'd told her about Becca and Seth, he'd gone too far. Things with Romany were never supposed to get out of hand. He'd promised himself that a long time ago. But things had gone too far. And despite all his resolve, he had no will to stop any of it.

He loved her.

He closed his eyes a moment and saw Rebecca the last time in life. Her mouth inches from his, her white teeth bright in a wide smile. Her dark eyes, slanted, teasing. She'd bitten his chin before she'd sent him off. He crushed out the cigarette, twisting the butt between his fingers.

Shit, he could use a good night's sleep. He never slept well away from home. Home? Where in the hell was home anyway? Surely not Tel Aviv anymore. He shoved his sunglasses back on and tried to get comfortable again. It was likely to be a long wait.

He hadn't exactly counted the minutes, but he knew he'd been sitting too long. His legs were getting stiff. He glanced down at his watch. Fuck, it was almost two o'clock. Arendt had been in the pensione for almost two hours. What the hell? Was it possible that he could have missed him coming out? He didn't think so.

He opened the car door, got out, stretched. He'd just have to go in himself and see what was keeping little Anton so busy. It would have to be a real piece of work, though. If Arendt was up in one of the rooms, it'd be hell finding out. Maybe the little monkey was just having one of those typically Italian marathon lunches.

The place was like most pensione. Simple, but with a kind of insinuating personality. Like its concierge, Signora Agostina, who showed him into the dining room. The place was almost empty, except for a couple at one of the back tables. The best cacciatore in all of Italia, the *signora* boasted. He was hungry. He didn't need much convincing.

He sat down, pocketed his sunglasses, looked around again. Definitely no Anton Arendt. But that meant nothing. He could be upstairs in one of the rooms.

A waiter, no doubt a relative of the *signora* with the same apple cheeks, set a basket of bread in front of him.

Yes, of course, he would try the house specialty. But first, the water closet, *per favore*. To wash up a bit.

He moved back out into the entrance hall. Empty. Off in the distance he could hear kitchen sounds. The voice of Signora Agostina. He took the stairs by twos. He wouldn't have much time.

The pensione was small. He counted eight rooms on the floor. He pressed his ear against the first door. Nothing. Slowly he twisted the knob. Vacant. He moved to the next door. Listening first, then twisting the knob. Vacant.

Rooms three and four were empty but occupied. By some young Americans no doubt. Both of the rooms were littered with dirty clothes, Coke cans. He picked up a pair of discarded jeans. He knew these would have brought a bundle on the black market a few years back. He tossed the jeans onto the floor and closed the door.

He checked his watch, moved to the other side of the hall. He put his ear to the first door. He could hear voices coming from the other side. English. But not American. A woman was talking softly. Trying, it seemed, to get a small child to go to sleep. He moved to the next door. Vacant.

The last two rooms were also vacant. Signora Agostina was definitely not doing the best of business. He worried the bridge of his nose. So where in the fuck are you, little Anton? Was it possible he'd given him the slip?

He knocked on the WC. No response. He opened the door. As he expected. Primitive, but clean. He washed his hands and went downstairs to try the best cacciatore in all of Italy. Wherever Anton Arendt was, he was not inside one of the eight rooms of the pensione. And that was very strange indeed.

Basco had been working the same flesh for almost twenty years. Well, not quite the same flesh. There was more of it these last years. In the old days his sure fingers penetrated layers of thick muscle. Now he had to work hard to find firm tissue. Often he wondered if there was any of it left. If now there was nothing but soft flesh.

He reached for the oil, warm and heavy like syrup. Tilting the jar, he drizzled a small quantity into the palm he'd shaped like a cup. He spread the liquid evenly across his hands and reached for the hump of flesh that now grew in the approximate center of the Cardinal's back, just below the neck.

He'd straddled the naked prelate as though he were a horse.

"It is insufferable that I should endure such things in my last years, Basco." Cardinal DeLario stuttered into the sheets as the masseur kneaded the fat at the top of the spine, the fat that always seemed so tense these days.

"Niccolo is off to Castel Gandolfo, and where this Julian Morrow is . . ." He coughed up a curse. "Not so hard, Basco, are you trying to kill me?" Basco eased up a bit and smiled to himself. Always the same, *Are you trying to kill me, Basco.* Such a thought.

". . . and no one seems to be able to find out where the American has gone. What fools surround me, Basco." A deep sigh. ". . . and an art expert! He is an art expert, Basco. And what does that mean, tell me, my friend, tell me . . . ?" The old masseur smiled again. He was never expected to answer.

"Why does Morrow keep such a thing a secret? For what purpose? It is not a rational act." But of course Basco knew the Cardinal understood the mystery. He only needed to hear himself say the words, fit the pieces together in the air like a puzzle.

"He wants us to think he is stupid, Basco. Julian Morrow wants us to think he knows nothing about art." There, the answer to the riddle.

"But why must we think he is stupid, Basco?" This time Basco did not smile, and he could feel the lump of flesh beneath his fingers harden as the Cardinal reared his head. Another curse. Another sigh. Then the prelate eased back down, flattening himself once more against the padded table. This time he would not work out the puzzle for Basco.

"And Brisi's an idiot," he suddenly started again. "All he seems to think of is his own position. Such vanity in a man I have never before seen, Basco."

Basco nodded and poured more of the oil into his palm. He began to work the spinal column, playing the vertebrae like keys on a piano. Running scales up and down the broad back. For a moment he thought the prelate had fallen off to sleep.

"Ahh, Basco, you are the only one I have, the only one I can trust. If only you could speak, tell me your thoughts. But alas, the gods are cruel, Basco, very cruel."

This time Basco had to agree.

"Who are you really, *señor?*"

The words had seemed to force themselves through a guard of frozen civility. The effort left Don Alonso Valdez de Renoza's petulant lower lip quivering beneath the upturned points of his mustache.

"Surely you understand why I cannot answer that, Don Alonso." The American's smile had widened. "Let's just say I'm a connoisseur, like yourself."

Americans, the Spaniard was thinking. They were like puppies or kittens, expecting you to like them, no matter what preposterous or disgusting thing they'd done. Well, he didn't like any of them, small animals or Americans. And especially not this one.

He looked up, at a more than half-foot disadvantage, and studied the man in front of him. Blond. Almost disdainfully handsome. Clothes too casual, if expensive. The voice was casual, if expensive, too. Well-bred by American standards. But no real clue as to who this man might be, or how he could have learned of one highly secret purchase made more than six months ago.

But the fact was that he knew all about it, as this morning's telephone call had made clear. And now he was here, confronting a Valdez de Renoza in the library of his own country house. The man was insufferable.

Don Alonso turned away without speaking, marching off to perch himself on the taut skin of the library's long leather sofa. For all the hauteur he had managed to put into the gesture, he knew that to the American's eyes he must appear like little more than an angry bird. And that was insufferable, too.

"So many years it took to find it." His words were bitter if filtered through barriers of reserve, his glance pulled reluctantly to the black-figured amphora that sat by itself on the table. "There are only eleven known pieces with Exekias's signature as master potter." He leaned forward, not lifting the vase, but matching his palms to its gleaming curves, as if to absorb some lingering comfort.

"Is there nothing else I can offer you?" He had let his fingers slip away as he turned abruptly to the American. The question was as close to a plea as any words he had spoken in his life.

"I regret your loss, señor." The American's smile had gone. But pity made the words more hateful.

"I can still refuse."

"Yes, Don Alonso. But I think you know better than I how much you stand to lose by a word leaked here or there within the international community. And besides your reputation, there is the remainder of your collection to consider. Unless I am very mistaken, the drinking bowl that stands in your hallway has been missing for three years from the *Kunstmuseum* in . . ."

"Enough."

The American inclined his head. Perhaps, after all, he was not so obviously gauche as most of them. He at least knew when to quit. Without another glance toward the table, Don Alonso rose to his full height and walked to the window that looked out onto the family vineyards. When he turned again, the American had already placed the amphora in a sack. He was glad. For a few short months the *Homecoming of Castor and Pollux from the Hunt* had been his. He could not have borne seeing it in the hands of another.

The American had a deep leather case, which he placed upon the now empty table. He snapped open the lid and emptied out a pile of bundled bills. "Swiss francs," he said. "Paid in full."

Hardly true. No amount of money could ever compensate for the loss of his collection's crowning jewel. But it seemed, indeed, the amount he had paid. And he had to admit, if only grudgingly, that it was a very strange kind of blackmail that reimbursed where it might have simply stolen.

The American waited for a moment, as if he might have actually expected the satisfaction of seeing a Valdez de Renoza counting out the bills. But at last he placed the sack with the amphora into his case.

"Before I go, Don Alonso," he said, "I must remind you how unsafe it would be to mention this, and how very unwise for you to buy again on the black market." The insulting American smile, at once both friendly and dangerous, had been switched on again to full effect.

Driving south through the rugged passes from Andorra, Julian Morrow was wishing for his much lighter Alfa. The Mercedes that he'd rented at the airport in Barcelona did not seem to have near the maneuverability of the Spider. He geared down as if to test this theory on the bend of a hairpin turn, laughing as the car threatened to fishtail out of control.

He fought to straighten the wheel and shook back the hair that had fallen into his face. He had always loved fast cars. The physicality of real driving was his kind of Zen—a total absorption that could keep his thoughts on the surface. Too bad he couldn't spare the time to drive all the way back to Rome.

Yet his plan was proceeding, and whatever might

come later, today with Valdez de Renoza had turned out
easy enough. The amphora was his, and he might as well
admit there'd been a few moments of honest cruelty
he'd actually enjoyed. Still, handling the Spaniard was
only a dress rehearsal for the main event.

CHAPTER 18

"I hated to drag you out this late at night, but . . ."

"No problem, Romany, I had a few things I needed
to check up on anyway." Julian gave her what passed for
a smile.

"You certainly were missed earlier this week." Her
words hung in a kind of no-man's-land, half waiting for
some kind of response.

"Oh, that. I had some loose ends to tie up." It wasn't
much of an explanation, and to make matters worse, he
wore that little-boy-lost expression that could make her
forgive him anything.

"Well, as the Brits say, we muddled through. Actually, Father Vance was more help than he'd admit. Very
careful about not overstepping his authority. He was
really kind of funny the way he kept deferring to you."

"Richard is a good man. I'm sorry if I messed things
up." Instantly he seemed to know how inadequate his
apology sounded. "I had to make a quick trip."

"Oh? You left Rome then?" She could hear the
transparency in her voice.

"Yes. Some personal business, nothing really important."

Important enough to make you drop everything else,
Julian Morrow. But she let it go. "Oh, by the way,
thanks for the rest of those translations. The letters
went out today. I sent copies over here this afternoon.
Father Vance probably has them."

"Good. I'll take a look at them tomorrow. Not that it

makes any difference." She saw that he'd seated himself behind his desk and was worrying the eraser end of a pencil.

"Doesn't make any difference?" Her look had turned into a stare.

His reaction was immediate. "That didn't come out exactly right. Of course, it makes a difference, Romany." The pencil slipped from his fingers as though it had somehow lost its density. "Everything about Arte per Pace is important. I just meant that I'm sure the letters are perfect, that my input couldn't make any difference." He finally did smile.

"Grazie mille, Father Morrow . . . I think." And she returned his smile. "Now about this mess with the architect. Did Father Vance have a chance to tell you anything?"

"Enough to know it's business as usual."

"I guess we should have expected a hitch sooner or later. Elliot said just last week he was worried because everything was going too smoothly."

"The general contractor is really giving the architect a rough time."

"And the architect is giving the general contractor a rough time. Technically I don't think there's a problem that can't be resolved. What we have here is more a confrontation of principles, or at the very least, 'style.' Elliot is trying to set up something early next week with Fallco and Pritisi. He's a pretty good arbitrator."

"Settling right-brain, left-brain differences."

"Exactly. At any rate, he wanted me to run some things by you before the meeting next week."

Romany reached inside her briefcase and dumped a heavy file on Julian's desk. He moved from his chair and began to help spread out a set of blueprints.

"This is of course only a partial rendering, but right here is the sticking point." She targeted one of the areas with her finger. Julian bent over to get a closer look.

In the soft light coming across from one of the lamps, she studied his profile. Sometimes it was hard to get a handle on Julian's age. She had the number all right. She'd gotten that from Sully's report. It was the physical encounter that constantly threw her. Right now, at this very moment, Julian Morrow looked all of eighteen. Blond hair, shiny clean, brushing against his forehead. Plaid-printed shirt opened at the neck just barely revealing smooth tanned skin underneath. The blue, blue eyes, clear and wide with a child's curiosity. And he smelled of something good. Like Ivory soap.

"You smell good." Her thought had slipped into words.

"Thank you, but I'm surprised." He gave her one of his smiles that crinkled the corners of his eyes. "I feel like we've lost the air conditioning in here. Are you warm?" He was really facing her now, the slant of lamplight shaping his features into a wholly different cast.

"Well, now that you've mentioned it, it doesn't feel as cool as it should be."

He stood and walked over to check the thermostat. "No wonder. It's eighty-two degrees in here. Something is definitely wrong. I'll have to get someone over tomorrow to see what's going on."

"So what did people do before air-conditioning?"

"Sweat a lot."

"Right, and took lots of baths. Well, that's not exactly true." She paused a moment thinking. "Invented perfume."

Julian was laughing.

"Speaking of baths . . ." She'd begun folding the blueprint. "We can finish this up later."

"How about a swim?" he said suddenly.

"A swim?" He'd taken her by surprise. "Where?"

"The Vatican pool."

"The Pope's pool? Isn't it part of the exclusive men's club around here? You know, restricted, no women allowed."

"Come on, I'll sneak you in." And just as before, his expression was that of a little boy, a little boy hell-bent on getting into trouble.

· · ·

The thing to do, Romany had decided, was to shut off the *why* part of her brain and concentrate on the *how*. Don't worry about why Julian Morrow should suddenly propose skinny-dipping together in the Vatican pool of all places, just focus on using it to her advantage.

Except that focusing on anything was proving pretty difficult with a constant barrage of water in her face and a chlorine-and-mascara cocktail stinging her eyes. The stuff was supposed to be waterproof, and she hoped to hell it was. Black gunk dripping down your face in streaks was not exactly sexy.

If only Julian would stop splashing her like some silly kid. He'd started out okay, leaving her on some excuse to get undressed alone by the lighted pool. She'd felt truly naked in the vast darkness, wishing for her favorite suit, a black maillot sexier than skin. Still, she'd reasoned, if things went well, there'd be literally nothing in the way to give Julian Morrow time for second thoughts—she couldn't have planned it any better.

She had smiled then, remembering very deliberately her first image of him coming in from tennis, stripping off his sweat-soaked shirt. Remembering the way it had felt in the garden at the Villa at the moment when he'd begun to return her kiss. *Oh, yes* had been the words in her mind as she'd uncrossed the arms she'd been holding protectively about her chest and waded down the tiled steps into the green-lit pool. Just far enough to let the water perfectly define her cleavage.

And then, the next thing, Julian Morrow came cannonballing out of the dark to land like a beaching whale behind her. The impact had engulfed her in a tidal wave that pushed her forward into shallower water. Eyes stinging, hair plastered across her face, she had been choking, trying to get her balance when he'd exploded upward beside her.

"Wait a minute," she had shouted. Or something like it. But already he'd been laughing, shooting hard sprays of water that hit her square in the face. Finally she'd ducked down, come up waist high in the water, smoothing her hair back, shaking the water from her eyes.

"Wait . . ." She put her hand up now, protecting her face.

"Romany."

She turned to see him looking unselfconsciously at her breasts.

"You're beautiful."

His tone was serious. Almost . . . reverent. The thought must have made her smile, because he glanced up at her suddenly. Smiled back.

"You're so beautiful," he said again.

She didn't answer, only looked at him, wondering what was really going on, wishing there were nothing more to this than the single dimension of this pool. She closed her eyes, wiping out Julian's questioning face. *Don't ask. Don't let me be the one to start this.* Her words. In her mind. She didn't want to know what they meant.

She felt him come closer, the water lapping between them.

"Romany, look at me." His voice, still so serious.

She obeyed, and it was there for her to see. He wanted her. His eyes were as naked as his body.

"Julian . . ."

She had not intended it to sound like that. Like a wail, like an apology. But whatever he heard, he moved. It was nothing like at the Villa, where at least she'd had the illusion of control. His intensity was almost frightening as his hands gripped her shoulders and his mouth came down over hers. She felt him hard in the water against her, his arm around her, pulling her close. Then his hand was between her legs, and she was rising, weightless, the pleasure spreading outward, as consciously she let go her will.

"Julian . . . ?"

The shock of the voice calling out from the darkness was immediate. He pulled back. She floated away.

"Julian, are you there?" It was Father Vance, his footsteps echoing hollowly as he emerged from the lobby.

"I'm coming." Julian had turned, was moving off toward the steps.

She sank noiselessly, swam to deeper water where dark bands of shadow rippled beneath the diving board. When she came up, the two men were standing together, yards away from the lighted pool. In the reflected glow, Father Vance's face shone eerily above his black cassock. Julian, in a white towel, seemed to be talking to a disembodied head.

She could hear nothing of what was said, which was odd because it was the effect of amplification in the hollow space that had made Father Vance's calling out seem so doubly threatening. They must be whispering, and after only a few moments they walked together back toward the lobby.

She didn't think that Father Vance had seen her. It hardly mattered. A different Julian Morrow would return. Sharply in the distance, she heard a door. She was already dressed when Julian walked back to her.

Cocooned in white linen, Colleen Shaunessy lay dreaming. . . .

No moon. The country road lay dark beneath a black shroud of sky. But at least there was no fog tonight, and the Fiat's headlights shone a clear beam to light her wild flight through the bogs. For the space of time it took to cross herself, she allowed the fingers of one hand to pry themselves from the wheel. These days, when she was more than half-agnostic, the gesture was as much superstition as prayer, and her hurried plea that she might *please, please make it to Frawley in time to save Michael,* was as much addressed to the Celtic Bridget as it was to the Virgin Mary.

Would any of this be happening tonight, she wondered, if she had only said yes to Brian McLaurie like her Da had wanted? Dear God, how she hated it, the talk as much as the actual violence. That was the fog you could never escape, not even out here in the country, the ancient hatred like an evil mist permeating everything in Northern Ireland, turning the very beauty of the land itself to a poison that killed men's souls.

And if she had ever doubted it, then her mother's meaningless death had been the final proof. Both her parents had died that day. Her mother, a physical death; her father, a living one. It was not the IRA that her father blamed, not the senseless violence. His curses were solely for the British. Da vowed vengeance. But she'd made a vow to life.

She would try to make a difference. That had been the essence of her vow. It was get out, or change things. And though she didn't have it in her heart to blame anyone who left, she knew it would feel like cowardice if she was just to give up on her country. At least in this she was Niall Shaunessy's daughter.

It had been a relief when, after her mother's funeral, she'd been allowed to go and live in Belfast with her Aunt Fiona. What she had never planned on was Da becoming ill. Nothing life threatening it had turned out, but serious enough for him to require her return after all these years to help him in the pub. "Just till you find yourself a husband to take over the place" was what he'd said. She had never seen Da so angry as the day when she'd turned Brian McLaurie down.

She'd been stalling for time in the months since then, trying to get up the courage to tell her Da that she was going back to Belfast. A new term would be starting soon at the university. Before then, she'd have to find a way to explain it to her father.

That was how it had started, watching Da, observing his moods, waiting for the perfect moment. She'd noticed the new faces in the pub before, the city faces, but she'd been too caught up in her own problems to pay that much attention. Still, it was obvious from the beginning that Da didn't want her in the stockroom. And once she'd become suspicious, it didn't take her long to figure out the rest. It had all become real when she'd found the cache of guns and ammunition hidden under the loose boards in the stockroom.

The next Sunday, she'd gone alone to Belfast to meet with her friend Duncan Bryant, leader of one of the Catholic peace groups. If there was some way out of this mess that would not destroy her father, then Duncan was the one to find it.

Duncan had been sweet. He'd told her to go back to Ballybarrit and stay put. He'd see what he could do. And then one night, there was Michael Casey.

She would never forget her first glimpse of him. He'd seemed somehow illuminated despite the dim tavern light, with his perfect white smile and that gleaming thatch of blond hair spilling from under his cap. Like an angel of God, had been her first impression, when he'd turned the smile on her. Then her second, that her thoughts about this man had nothing of the angelic about them.

"I'll fetch the order, Da," she'd said, going to the tap, smiling her own smile as she'd wiped the counter before setting down his beer. He'd lifted the glass and winked at her over the rim. And easy as that, she knew. This was the man that Duncan had sent to help her.

Oh, Michael, what went wrong? The fear surged up like a black wall, and she pushed the little Fiat till it whined. She couldn't be too late. Not when fate had intervened so perfectly to warn her of betrayal. She had not had time to think. She had simply run as quickly as she could down the back stairs to the car as soon as she'd heard enough. It had seemed as if she'd never get there, and then suddenly the sign for Frawley was looming up at her.

No time to slow down now. No time for caution. "Michael. Michael," she screamed as she stopped the car and ran toward the old abandoned barn.

"Michael?" She took a few steps through the open door. No answer but the desperateness of her own voice wavering in emptiness, and the old grain sourness growing stronger in her nostrils and her throat.

It was the grain smell that made her remember.

This was past. She had been here before. A hundred times. A million. An immense and terrible sorrow gripped her even as the explosion of light came again. And the noise. Ripping her back into blackness. But this time, even as the dark tide caught her, Colleen Shaunessy fought to make it through.

"Mich . . . ael."

Sister Lucienne's head jerked in surprise. It had been one of the more fitful nights. She looked over at the pale oval face, hazy and indistinct in the furzy glow of the night lamp. *Michael.* Only a name, but the first word that her patient had spoken since she'd come here. A small thing. But something.

For a long time Sister Lucienne sat in the straight wooden chair next to the narrow bed, while the roosters stirred in the convent yard and the predawn light swept the last of the shadows from Colleen Shaunessy's face. He had been unable to be here last weekend as he'd planned, and it was hard to be sure at all when he would visit again. Besides, it would be wrong to stir his hopes so prematurely. The decision was a hard one, but her better judgment prevailed. She would not after all be phoning Father Morrow this morning.

CHAPTER 19

David pushed the release button and let the clip slide out the bottom of the grip, pulled back the bolt, and ejected the round from the chamber. Taking out the bolt, he unscrewed the silencer and put it down on the table.

The Ruger didn't really need cleaning. With no desert handy for weekly target practice, the semiautomatic hadn't been fired since he'd arrived in Rome. Still, preventive maintenance never hurt, and he'd wanted the familiar ritual of cleaning the gun while he waited to ring Rachael back.

He had phoned her this morning at the resettlement office in Tel Aviv almost immediately after Mika's little bombshell call. Rachael had been his mother's friend since the two had been girls together in Haifa. Tante Rachael to him ever since he could remember. Even after his mother's death, Rachael still kept in touch. And if anybody could confirm what the tail on the Klimpt woman had turned up, that person was Rachael Levy.

He'd made a quick pact with himself. Until Rachael had his answer, he would not try to analyze or evaluate what Mika's information meant. It might not be true. But if it was true . . .

He picked up the cleaning rod and fitted the end with the small brass brush dipped in solvent; he loved the smell like some kids loved the smell of gasoline. He pushed the brush back and forth down the barrel of the gun, cleaning out filings that weren't there.

When the gun was finally oiled and reassembled, he let himself look at the clock. Rachael was always a fast worker. He could power up the phone now.

"Yes." Her voice when she answered was "round the block" clear, the uplink working perfectly.

"It's me," was all he said. Even with the impossibility of a bug, it was best to avoid names. "You got what I need?" he asked her.

"Your contact was right, David. The records are there. The trick's just in knowing where to look. Everything was so chaotic at the end of the war."

"And you're sure? The name . . . ?"

"It checks out. The Klimpt woman's a bigger fanatic than any of us, and she never gives up. It's that list of hers, what she calls her *Atonement.* Whoever's on that list, she finds . . . eventually."

He didn't answer. Absorbing it.

"You still there?" Rachael's voice sounded suddenly tinny in the earpiece.

"Yeah, Tante Rachael. And thanks."

"I know I'm not supposed to ask, David, but I do get curious. . . ."

"It's personal." He cut her off. "This one's personal, Tante." He smiled, hoping she could hear it in his voice. "I'll see you when I get back."

He hung up. Heard Mika again in his head, telling him this morning, "This is unofficial, David. Just a random bit of data. I thought you'd want to know."

The Ruger lay where he'd left it on the table. He picked it up. He had killed three strangers with this gun. In the American Old West there would be three notches, three scratches in metal to mark the passage of men who lay otherwise unremarked.

Random. Mika's word. But what if it was more? Even to him, this morning's revelation suggested some kind of pattern. Even to him, with no belief left in God, or will, or destiny.

"I can't thank you enough for your help with this, Julian," Elliot was saying. "It's important that the Vatican and the Arte per Pace staff present a united front when these kinds of problems come up."

"You're welcome, Elliot. But it's my job."

The two men sat relaxed, drinking coffee in the black leather chairs that fronted Romany's desk. She sat in her own chair, trying not to stare too conspicuously at Julian Morrow. She had spent the full thirty minutes of this morning's meeting watching him as closely as she could, trying to see something behind that entirely complacent face. The same face he had worn by the end of last night. Friendly, composed, and shut tight.

He was laughing now at something Elliot had just

said, some remark about the contractors. He seemed at ease, the laugh totally natural, his eyes crinkling at the corners as he turned toward her, including her in the joke. She smiled back, but let her own gaze follow Elliot as he got up and walked toward the window.

"These flowers are beautiful, Romany." Elliot had set down his empty coffee cup and was pouring a glass of ice water from the pitcher on the console. "I saw the delivery boy coming in the building with these yesterday. I wondered who they were for."

"They're from Count Sebastiano," she answered the unspoken question.

"I should have known." Elliot turned back from her to Julian. "Romany made quite an impression at the party," he said, sitting down again. "Dinner last week at the palazzo. And now . . . flowers."

Julian didn't comment, but his smile was amused and, if possible, more annoying even than Elliot's. The best course was to keep her own mouth shut. For some reason she couldn't.

"The Count is very . . . Old World." She heard herself being defensive. "He enjoys making gestures."

The phone rang, and for once she was glad for the interruption. "That was Linda, Elliot," she said, "reminding you about your eleven o'clock."

"I'm on my way." Elliot, already out of the chair, reached down to shake Julian's hand. "Thanks again," he said. "Talk to you later." He threw her a grin and left.

"I have to go too." Julian stood up.

"Oh?"

"Yes. Sorry. But I have another appointment. Something I can't get out of."

"But . . ."

"I know. I told Elliot we'd get it worked out before Monday. Don't worry. I'll come back tomorrow morning. We'll get this problem with the contractor and architect worked out."

"All right."

"And we'll do something fun after."

"Okay."

"Nine o'clock?"

"Nine o'clock is fine, Julian."

"Great." He gave her his biggest smile.

She smiled back but her eyes weren't in it. Watching him leave, she wondered if he'd noticed. Wondered what, if anything, he was feeling. Dammit, he had done it to her again.

Everything had happened so fast last night after Father Vance showed up. She'd gotten dressed and Julian had come back. It was hard to see anything of his face in the darkness, and she'd stood at the edge of the pool's green glow, waiting like a blind person for him to speak, ready for every nuance and tone that might tell her what her sight could not.

"Give me a second to get dressed," he'd said, "and meet me in the lobby. I'll walk you back to your car." That was it. Direct and simple. The words and nothing else.

It had made her wild driving home, thinking how passive she'd been, letting him get away with the simple acknowledgment that they'd go ahead and meet with Elliot in the morning to finish things up. By the time she'd gotten back to her apartment, the questions were lining up for answers in her head. She'd forced herself to go to sleep instead, to wait to see which Julian Morrow showed up the next day at her office. Well, Julian Morrow had come and gone. The time for questions was now.

Was she any closer to her goal?

The answer seemed obvious. If not for Father Vance's untimely interruption, she and Julian would now be lovers. She was positive of that. Strategywise she appeared to have taken a giant step forward. But had she? Even at this late date, Julian was sending mixed signals. Coming on to her, then pulling back. He had cooled it last night and certainly just now, running off before they'd had even a few minutes alone. And yet it had been his suggestion that they spend their Saturday working alone, with something "fun" to follow.

So how should she play it? Passive or active? Let Julian take the lead, or try to push things along herself? And what if Sully's basic assumption was wrong? Julian's behavior was so damn erratic. What guarantee was there that he'd suddenly open up to her simply because she got him into bed?

The questions kept coming. How much of her involvement with Julian was personal? She had to find out what it meant to her. It was her job to be involved with Julian Morrow. He was an assignment, not a boyfriend. But to ignore the emotions he aroused was dangerous, and to pretend they didn't exist was to forget how badly they could cloud her professional judgment, even place her in danger.

And what about what Julian felt for her? What was driving this thing for him? Simple, unadulterated lust? Or something deeper, darker?

She walked over to the window. There were a couple of Cokes on the tray. She opened one, ignoring the ice, preferring it straight from the bottle. Then she sat down at her desk, determined to work out some answers.

One. She could get Julian Morrow into bed, she knew it now. It was true he was leading her in a dance, two steps forward, one step back. Still, her progress was unmistakable.

Two. Sully might be wrong that sleeping with Julian would improve her chances of finding out anything important, but there was no way to know that before the fact. As to how she should play it—she had to stop anticipating. It was impossible to predict, from anything he said, what Julian would do. She must concentrate on his actions, not his words. Let him lead if possible, and improvise from there.

Three. Her feelings. Julian Morrow turned her on, she'd long ago admitted to that. He simply looked so damn good that you didn't stop to think about what you were doing, what you didn't know. Add to that the fact that he was a priest and forbidden . . .

Except maybe that wasn't all there was to it, and maybe it was a big mistake to think of her response to him in such simplistic terms. Because the real Julian Morrow, the complex man she sensed behind the facade, was the real attraction. And that man might well be more than merely sexually dangerous.

"Don't fall for him, Romany." She'd said it out loud to make sure that she had heard. She was certain it was very good advice.

"He seems not so worried. But I know him. I know Cardinal Vittorio DeLario better than he understands. And he *is* worried." Monsignor Umberto Brisi looked particularly handsome in the dark blue silk robe, his hair fresh from a shower.

"Vittorio is an interesting man. I have enjoyed our relationship over the many years." Count Sebastiano did not wear the eye patch this evening. He had no need for the disguise with his guest, the monsignor.

Brisi stared at the older man. He was always amazed at his vigor, the precise exactitude in the almost colorless eyes. "You like him, you actually like Vittorio."

"But of course, Umberto, I like him. Don't you?" The Count lifted his brandy glass and took a small sip.

"Sometimes I hate him. How could he have let all of this happen? Let things get so out of control?" The fold of Brisi's robe had slipped open so the Count could see the priest wore nothing underneath.

"You mean Arte per Pace?" The Count lifted his eyes.

"Yes, Arte per Pace, and the Jesuit." Umberto's lips twisted against themselves.

"Ah, Julian Morrow." It seemed the Count tasted the name with the brandy in his mouth.

"What is this man, Klaus? Even Vittorio does not know. And no matter what face he shows me, your friend the Cardinal is not so happy to have Morrow up His Holiness's ass."

"No, no." The Count considered his words carefully, "Vittorio would not be so happy. He has had the Vatican all to himself for quite some time now."

"And no more money going into his Swiss bank accounts. No more money for anybody."

"My poor beautiful boy, is that what is wrong? You are no longer getting your share of the profits. You know there is nothing I would not give you. Have I ever denied you anything, Umberto?" The last sentence came out much like a cat's purr.

"You know well this is not why I am as I am." Brisi's words came up short.

"No, no, it would never be the money. Like Vittorio, it is the power that gives you the most pleasure."

"Don't be a hypocrite, Klaus, you enjoy the power better than both of us."

The Count measured Brisi's handsome features for a moment. Then he smiled. A truly genuine smile. "Yes, yes, there is some satisfaction in the power."

Brisi let out a grunt of exasperation and stood. The custom-made robe almost pooled around his bare feet. "And the Jesuit disappeared earlier this week. Evaporated. Vanished. Into thin air." Umberto snapped his fingers.

"Now, Umberto, you will have to do better in the future. Is that not why I have brought you into my house, to watch Vittorio and to be my eyes and ears in the Vatican?"

"Fuck you, Klaus, how can I know what even Vittorio cannot discover?" Then suddenly softer, "And you know well there are other reasons why I have been brought into your house."

A second genuine smile from Sebastiano. "Did you enjoy yourself this evening, Umberto?"

At first Brisi did not answer but watched the Count from under the lids of his eyes. Then he walked across the room to where his host sat. Slowly he bent and kissed him hard on the mouth. "Yes, Klaus, I enjoyed myself," he whispered against the older man's lips. "Did you enjoy?"

"Yes, Umberto," the Count whispered back, "I always enjoy watching your little performances."

Marthe Chase gazed out the upstairs window of her townhouse, thinking first of her trip to Italy, then remembering the woman who had just mere weeks ago given her a new destiny. Rome would be the beginning. And the end.

Deliberately she let the drape fall, shutting off the view of the quiet Georgetown street. Her hand moved automatically to attack the now almost constant pain in her thigh, then reached out to feel for the cane propped against the wall.

During the day she made use of the cane, taking the pressure off her leg. Resting when she could. All of this so that when her husband came home, she could make a bit of pretense and move about freely without it. Dear, dear Theodor, how sweet of him never to let on that she was fooling no one.

She lowered herself upon the sofa, lifting her bad leg up onto the cushion. She leaned her head back, closing her eyes for a moment, slowly massaging the space over her heart as if she could somehow ease the pain there too.

It was impossible to think that one minute you were one person, and the next, quite another. But Helena Klimpt had done that to her, had written for her a new history. Had recreated her. Had reassembled all the parts and parcels of her life.

Was it just weeks ago that she'd sat across from that remarkable woman, listening to her strange, unbelievable tale? She'd watched as Helena had brought the cup of tea to her mouth, taking a deliberate sip, pausing a long moment before attempting to say what had to be said. It seemed she'd waited as long as possible to put off what surely must come. And when she finally spoke, the words were terrible ones.

For so many years Marthe had had the dream. Dark things skittering about in her mind, half things hiding in shadows. Dry bone-thin arms going about her. Pressing her to a cold, almost breathless, chest. Squeezing tightly, locking her own breath inside her throat. And lips, crusting and peeling, kissing her cheeks. But the worst of it, in the distance, the tramping of feet marching off to some unknown destination.

But Helena Klimpt had found her. And those desperate arms that had held her now had a name. And those feet had at last a destination. And in mystery's place, there was now a clear and compelling certainty.

Marthe had dreamed of her death so often, that lately it seemed only a vague memory in someone else's mind. But like her other dream, this one too finally had the ring of truth in it. And if before she had been sad because her dying meant leaving Theodor and Romany behind, now she was only frightened. Frightened she should die before she was able to do what must be done. Frightened she should leave this world before seeing the face of the man who had betrayed her.

CHAPTER 20

To Romany, Rome in summer had always been a lion. Imperial, self-indulgent, lazy with a surfeit of food and sun. A big tawny, roaring, stretching beast, the dust of ages suspended in its honey-lighted mane, the color of travertine. And a Saturday in Rome in mid-July could never be a day for business. Even with the central air pouring from the office ducts and the vertical slatted blinds blocking out the lemon sun, something of the carnival leaked through.

Blessedly the work went quickly, perhaps because the day before, when Julian had abandoned her, she'd thrown herself into getting a good head start. For whatever reason, they were finished before one, and Julian, reminded of his promise, had laughed and said he had not forgotten her reward.

Their first stop after leaving the office had been to buy her some flats. Heels would not do, said Julian, on a walking tour of Rome. Had she forgotten that Rome was a city of steps?

They walked everywhere. To churches, and fountains, and flea markets, and she'd been mock-grudgingly grateful for the sandals. Not the pretty strappy ones that she'd cooed over, but the homely comfortable pair that Julian had picked out. She'd made a face and called them ugly, but he'd insisted they were the ones. Insisted on buying them too. It was only fair, he'd said, because they were his choice.

And so the shoes had been the real beginning of the day. The seal on some unspoken pact. They had talked and laughed everywhere they went. It had been as wonderful as the day at Villa d'Este. Better, because she had not spoiled it. Would not spoil it. Anything that happened now was like the sandals. His choice.

After dinner at the Café Greco, they strolled in their first real silence up the Piazza di Spagna to the Spanish Steps where the sun sank in a huge red ball above the old church. The air had cleared, the busy motion slowed, and the clashing colors on the milling tourists seemed to glow with a mellow light. As if, Romany thought, she'd been smoking pot, or were suddenly looking through sunglasses. Maybe it was only the coming twilight that made everything at once so solid and unreal. Or too much wine. Or talk. Maybe it was just Rome getting to her. Or maybe it was Julian Morrow.

He was right there at her side, the rolled sleeves of his light cotton shirt brushing her skin as they walked, the pale hairs on his bare arm molten in the pink light.

She slowed to look up into his face, and as if sensing something in her glance, he took her hand and smiled.

Julian's smile on the Spanish Steps had finally flung wide the door. The door to a destiny that had been waiting from the first. So that the rest of the day passed like a dream, but a dream far more acute than any reality. A dream that would forever cling to Romany like gauze.

She looked up now into the shadowed face suspended over her. In the half dark of her bedroom, the whirring blades of the ceiling fan seemed somehow attached to his shoulders, like metallic wings on the perfectly constructed body rising and falling over hers.

Romany ran her hands over the straining muscles of his back, severing the illusion of wings. Her breath caught in the back of her throat so she could taste him, his own scent and something vaguely citrusy. She could feel him sucking her, the small space of skin between her armpit and breast. His mouth moving, sliding back and forth, but never quite reaching the nipple. Over and over he worked that small, well-defined territory until she heard herself beg him to take her into his mouth.

She pressed hard against his head, her hands knotting in the soft dense hair at the base of his neck. "Yes, Julian," and his fingers made a frame around her breast.

"Kiss me," and she pulled up on his face. For an instant she saw the darkening color of his eyes, the fine serious line of his mouth before his lips came down on hers.

The tips of his fingers centered at the small of her back, and he drew her up a few inches from the bed so that she seemed precisely balanced. She could feel her thighs opening, his body fitting exactly against hers.

· · ·

The oval mirrored doors of the antique wardrobe were eyes reflecting the bed. One swung blankly open, and David ben Haar stepped out.

In the sky outside the moon had risen, and the silver light seeping in from the window made the room seem cool and blue in contrast to the hot and heavy darkness where he'd crouched for hours breathing in the scent of Romany's clothes. He walked to the foot of the bed. The rumpled sheets were stark and glacial, the sleeping bodies swallowed up in ice.

He should get out. Now. He'd been lucky so far, and he knew it. But he still didn't move. Letting some very stupid instinct take control. The one that wanted the man in the bed to wake up.

Is Morrow one of the bad guys? he had asked her that day while she'd rushed around getting ready for the priest to pick her up. *That's what I'm supposed to find out* had been her answer. He'd been in this game for a whole lot of years now. He knew how it worked. What he'd seen tonight was business. So why did it feel so much like a kick in the gut?

Because she'd liked it. Yes. Romany had liked fucking the priest. He put it in the coarsest terms, rubbed his own nose in it. But why shouldn't she like it? Hadn't he always liked screwing in the line of duty well enough? If you had to do it, you might as well enjoy it had been his own rationale against thoughts of betraying Becca.

And Romany was not Becca. That was another thing to get straight. Right here. Right now in this room. The things he loved in Romany were nothing like what he had loved in Becca. But love was love, and the hot white anger threatening to blank out his thoughts was not rational. So why wouldn't the Jesuit bastard wake up so he could find some good excuse to kill him?

He smiled, a grim rictus that stretched his lips across his teeth. Chaim was right, he was a rabid dog. He had come over here with the vague idea of maybe telling Romany what he'd found out yesterday. So in some sense he'd deserved just what he'd got. He had no business even thinking of telling her, at least not without a whole lot more thought.

He looked at her sleeping face, smooth and innocent beneath the halo of tumbled curls. He loved her. What did that mean? He hadn't even begun to figure it out.

CHAPTER 21

The heat of a Roman Sunday in July was expected. Julian Morrow's visit was not.

Cardinal Vittorio DeLario smoothed the hair at the sides of his head and fumbled with the tie of his robe. He was more surprised than annoyed by the Jesuit's intrusion.

"You are, I see, accustomed to sleeping late on Sunday, Your Eminence." It was a statement of fact that in no way could be construed as an apology.

"For so many years I had to rise early to say Mass, that it is a small sin I now commit in allowing this old body to remain in bed past ten o'clock. You understand, of course." There was a smile that seemed to be asking for something more than Julian's understanding of his indulgent routine.

Julian's returning smile said he understood nothing. "It is warm out today."

"Excuse me, Father Morrow, I am most rude. Please let me get you something cool to drink."

"Call me Julian, Your Eminence. And I really don't care for anything. *Grazie.*"

"Please." DeLario motioned to a chair and fixed his robe again before he sat. "You are finding everything you need here in our Vatican, Julian." Another smile that made his round face seem all the rounder.

"*Your* Vatican is not so easy."

"Not so easy? *Scusi,* but I do not understand." There

was just a trace of a genuine frown forming on the cherubic face.

"There are so many mysteries here, Your Eminence."

The frown completed itself. "Mysteries?"

"Yes. Why, just the other day I had the pleasure of visiting someone who was in the possession of something that I found quite interesting. Extraordinary actually."

"Yes." The word was flat, expectant.

"At first, I was sure the thing had to be a fake. After all, the Vatican owned the original. But . . ."

"But, Father Morrow?" It was back to "Father Morrow."

"Well, Your Eminence, see for yourself." And with these words Julian almost threw the package he'd been holding into DeLario's lap.

For a moment the Cardinal stared at the soft padding that surrounded the object. Then slowly he loosened the string and let the paper fall to the floor. It was the Exekias that he'd marketed last year. His stubby fingers traced the thin black figures silhouetted against the vermilion background. Then he looked up.

"What do you want, Julian Morrow?"

"I want in, Vittorio."

CHAPTER 22

Romany reached for the dictaphone switch and turned the machine off. She couldn't concentrate, even on the routine letters that Gina was waiting to type. She glanced at the clock. Well past one on Monday afternoon, and she still couldn't think about anything else but the weekend.

Why hadn't Julian called? Disappearing from her bed had been bad enough, but not even to call her?

In the very first seconds when she'd awakened alone, she'd doubted her lingering memories. It could happen sometimes with the things she obsessed on, that she'd dream about them in a detail so convincing, that even after waking she'd go on believing they were real.

So she'd sat up, and immediately she was absolutely certain. Julian Morrow *had* been in her bed. What had passed between them the night before went beyond imagination.

So where was he now, and what was he thinking? In terms of her job for Sully this was either a triumph or a disaster. But more than that, she needed some answers for herself. She'd never been made love to by a man like Julian Morrow.

She looked at the telephone. You're a grown-up, Romany. You have every right to call. And besides, anything's better than waiting.

The phone buzzing made her jump. He'd read her mind, like before. "Hello." Had that sounded just a bit too breathy?

"Romany?" It was Elliot, sounding quizzical. So her voice had indeed been funny.

"Hi, Elliot." Rebecca of Sunnybrook Farm, now. She had to find some kind of medium.

"What are you up to?"

"Dictation," she lied. "Just some minor stuff that needs to go out."

"Good, nothing that can't wait. Grab that suitcase you call a purse and let's go. We're having lunch with Fallco and Pritisi."

"Both of them? Together?"

"I talked to them on the phone this morning, going over the compromise that you and Julian worked out. They agree to it. In principle."

She breathed a sigh. She'd almost forgotten that they had *worked* on Saturday, she and Julian. She had put their proposal on Elliot's desk herself before they'd left the office.

"This little lunch date is to seal the deal," Elliot had

gone on speaking. "You've got to charm them for me, Romany. Keep them distracted, or they'll be at each other's throats again before we even get to cappuccino.

"I tried to reach Father Morrow, get him in on this, too," Elliot added. "But he's not in his office."

"Well, I'm on my way now. Meet you by the elevators." She hung up, then stopped to put on a fresh coat of lipstick. *Not in his office.* What did that mean? Nothing, probably. Julian had been away from his office most of last week.

She flung her lipstick back loose into her purse and stood up, smoothing her jacket. Any other time this luncheon would have been one gigantic pain. Today she was glad for it. Fallco and Pritisi were not the only ones in need of distraction.

The first thing little Vito ever stole was the rosary from his mother's hands as she lay in her coffin. It was a sin he hadn't really wanted to commit. Nothing he'd actually planned for any length of time like one plans a real crime. Little Vito wasn't a criminal, or a sinner. But in his seven-year-old mind, Mama's rosary was something he had to have. And since Lucia would not give it to him, had insisted Mama be buried with the crystal beads blessed by the Pope, Vito had had no choice.

For four days he had begged Lucia for Mama's rosary. Begged for it from the moment Dr. Fontana pronounced Mama had gone to the angels, till she had been taken away to be powdered and rouged and dressed for her funeral. Of course, he understood he had no real claim on the rosary. Mama barely knew Vito. It was his sister Lucia who had raised him. Poor Mama, already tired from too many babies, and Vito an unwanted surprise coming after her fortieth birthday. But he'd loved Mama anyway, and more than anything he had ever coveted in his young life, he coveted her rosary.

In his small boy's heart, he wanted to hate Lucia for her treachery against him. But it was hard to hate her.

She who had coddled him, protected him from all the petty jealousies of his older sisters and brothers. *"Basta,"* Lucia would say, "there is enough love to go around."

Surely there was enough money. His father Angelo had done well with his little manufacturing business. The world had changed beneath his very fingers, and he'd made his own magic of the metamorphosis. No one wanted to work with his hands any longer, Angelo would preach, machines are the "new hands." And he had been absolutely right.

Yet young Vito had always felt deprived—deprived of Mama's love, of Papa's respect. So it was with great regret that he finally forced himself to hate the only person who had been loyal to him. And hate Lucia he did as he'd slipped his chubby brown hand into Mama's thin white one and tugged on the rosary till it had come free.

Lucia shared in his sin, he'd decided in the end. She, who could have made it very simple for him, given him the rosary. Mama's legacy to her bambino, she could have told them all. But his sister was always one for justice. It was not right that he should have the rosary. It was only fitting Mama be buried with the beads that never left her fingers during the last days of her life.

He could still see Mama lying inside the pink satin-lined casket, her white skin made whiter by mortician's powder. He had sucked hard on the thick knot of saliva that had formed in his throat as he'd looked down into her face. He had willed himself not to cry. If only she had worn a smile, he had wished to himself, one last smile for him. But her milky face was a mask that said nothing.

The rosary had sparkled like a circlet of small stars on her breast, and the beads had clinked together like wineglasses as he pulled them into his hand. It was a thing of beauty, this rosary of Mama's. And beauty was the thing he held sacred above all else. Beauty was to be treasured and nurtured, he'd told himself many times in his child's way. That Mama's beautiful rosary should be buried was a sin greater than any theft.

Sì, sì, it *was* Lucia's fault. His sister, twice guilty in his eyes. First, for denying him this small remembrance of Mama, then for a stupidity that would insist upon the sacrifice of something so beautiful.

So Mama's death had had the added tragedy of unsolved mystery. And though he'd feared discovery, Vito secretly enjoyed the audacity of his act. He was excited and anxious all at once. Had he been older, he might have appreciated the feelings as something very close to sexual arousal. He recalled that someone eventually had been punished for the theft. He could not now remember who it was or what had followed, but he thought many times over of the delicious moments that had finally delivered Mama's rosary into his hands.

Into his hands Cardinal Vittorio DeLario slipped Mama's rosary from the small leather pouch. Calculating, not praying, he began worrying the beads like a Moslem, not a Christian. Julian Morrow was his anguish. And though Vittorio's mind railed against the priest's challenge, his implied threat, a small island inside of him shivered in a kind of perverse delight at this new danger.

Yesterday he'd talked very little. What indeed was he to say? He pinched one of Mama's beads and frowned. It was impossible to know how much of what the Jesuit had said was bluff, how much was earnestness. But the simple reality was that the American knew enough. Enough to hang him, Cardinal Vittorio DeLario, from the cupola of St. Peter's by the balls.

Yet Morrow had seemed to hold nothing back. He'd told him how he'd found out about the forgeries, how he'd wormed his way into Gregory's favor, had won the Arte per Pace position. All of it for this very moment. For this opportunity.

Sì, he'd smelled secrets on the man from the first. Still, Vittorio DeLario had not gotten where he'd gotten because he was a fool. Despite everything the Jesuit had told him, despite the unspoken threat that lay in half sleep between each of his words, Vittorio would not allow the priest to come into his house so easily.

Morrow must wait for his answer. He could not, he'd told the priest yesterday, make such a decision so quickly. There were other people to consider. Situations even he, Julian, could not know. Surely the priest could appreciate his position. Morrow had smiled then, looking nothing but priestly in his simple black clericals, and said he would not have expected anything less of His Eminence. The whole of it very civil, almost congenial. But it was nothing more than a cat-and-mouse game. And too many years since Vittorio had not played the cat.

Yes, Julian Morrow must wait. Wait for Cardinal De-Lario to make sure of his thief's heart. He placed Mama's rosary on the small table and dialed the number. As usual he left a message and waited for a return call.

Five minutes later the telephone rang.

"I was planning to call this week." His informant's voice on the other end.

"Our situation has changed."

"Changed? I don't—"

"The priest seems to have discovered certain matters."

"How?" Genuine surprise.

"That is of little importance now."

Silence.

"What is important is how we are to proceed."

"Sì." Resignation.

"He wants to come into my house."

"You will allow this?" Again surprise.

"He has placed me in a very delicate position. I'm afraid I have little choice."

"What is it that you want me to do?"

"Certain accommodations will of course have to be made. But I can do nothing until I understand about this priest. You understand, I must know all of this man's secrets."

"Sì, sì, I understand. I will try . . ."

"You will not try. You will do. And soon, very soon."

Lunch had gone on forever, and now back at her desk, Romany loosened the waistband of her skirt, swearing that this was absolutely the last time she would eat so much food in the middle of the day. She reached for the phone and dialed the number for Julian's office. It would be perfectly normal, of course, to have Gina set up the appointment, but she had something to prove to herself. Still she was glad enough for the reprieve when it was Father Vance who answered.

"Father Morrow's office."

"Romany Chase, Father Vance. I'd like to speak with Father Morrow."

"I'm sorry, Miss Chase, but he's out for the rest of the day. May I help you?"

"Yes, I'd like to make an appointment. For tomorrow afternoon, if I could. I need to fill Father Morrow in on what's been happening with the contractor and architect."

Now why had she had to add that? So Father Vance would pass it along, and Julian would know that she was calling him on business?

"Two o'clock, all right?" Father Vance was speaking.

"Yes. That's fine, Father. Thank you."

"You're welcome, Miss Chase." The priest hung up.

Lord, this whole mess was really getting to her. She was hearing things that her better judgment told her weren't there. Like the wink and the leer in Richard Vance's voice.

CHAPTER 23

"Come on over here, Richard," was the first thing Julian said. "You need to hear this too."

Julian had greeted her with a smile and a nod as Romany came into his office and took her seat in front of his desk. Now Father Vance tagged obediently after her with his ancient swivel chair. It squeaked and groaned as he pushed it more than rolled it.

"Good," was Julian's pronouncement as Vance wheeled the thing finally into place beside her and sat down. Julian sat down too.

"So what have you got?" he said.

"Nothing," she heard herself give a short, nervous laugh. He had made it sound as if he expected something on paper. "I don't have a report or anything," she said. "Elliot just asked me to tell you what was happening with Fallco and Pritisi."

"The head contractor and the architect." The flat explanation directed from Julian to Father Vance.

"Yes," she seconded him unnecessarily.

Julian was doodling on the blotter now. A new green field for the fresh production of X's. Father Vance was watching the pen move, in total repose, his own hands in his lap, folded.

"We had lunch with them yesterday, Elliot and I," she said. "Elliot tried to call you, Julian. To join us."

"Oh," Julian looked up. Gave her a completely normal smile. "Sorry I missed it."

"Yes. Well, it went well. They liked what we'd worked out. Although they had to gripe and complain through five courses to make it official."

"Has a date been set for breaking ground?" Father Vance spoke.

"No, but we should have one by next week," she answered.

"That's good." Julian again. The X's had turned into loops that repeated endlessly.

"Yes, it is good." She picked up her purse from the floor. She was ready to end this.

"Are you leaving?" This from Julian.

"Is there anything else?" she said.

"I was wondering about the translations."

"What about them?" she asked flatly. Hell, she was as capable of making things tedious as the next guy.

"When are you planning to send the letters out?"

"They went out last Thursday, Julian. Remember? I told you that here in this office."

"That's right. I guess I forgot." The easy smile again. "How long do you think before we start getting some responses?"

Why was Julian prolonging this? Unless he was hoping she would stay long enough for Vance to leave? But he was the one who'd asked the priest to join them.

"It's hard to say how long," she answered. "Some of the smaller countries will probably get back to us first. I'm sure it will be quite a job trying to get a finalized version of this whole thing together before the official deadline. But that's what you and I are getting paid for. And now you too, Father Vance." She smiled, including him.

He smiled back, but not with his eyes. His eyes still gave her the creeps. It was not a wink and a leer she had heard in his voice yesterday, she decided, but a certain too-knowing tone.

She looked at her watch. Stood up. "I really do have to run," she said. "I'm behind on my dictation."

Julian stood. And a fraction later Vance stood too. He had to move so she could get out, but he made no attempt to go back to his desk. It felt to Romany like a full-out retreat, so she slowed her steps consciously before she reached the door. When she glanced back, Julian was staring down, as if trying to guess how the marks had appeared on his blotter. But Father Vance had turned to watch her go.

. . .

Wash her hair, that was the thing to do. Wash her hair and clear her head. Damn, she didn't understand why she was so . . . What was she feeling anyway? Anger seemed to fit the bill. But that wasn't the sum total, and she refused to lie to herself. Anger and hurt. Now that was a more complete picture. Anger and hurt over what had happened in Julian Morrow's office.

All right, Romany, what's the real problem? Why was she angry and hurt over what happened? What had she expected, that Julian would take her in his arms right in front of Richard Vance? What if the two of them had been alone? Now that was a question with exceptional possibilities.

She reached for the bottle of shampoo she'd let Raphaelo talk her into buying. It cost a fortune and didn't seem to work any better than the cheap stuff. She plunged her head under the tap and wet her hair. Then she fumbled for the shampoo, squeezing a dollop into her palm. She rubbed her fingers over her scalp. The warm water brought the shampoo to a frothy lather. One good scrubbing was enough now that her hair was short. A cool rinse. She'd condition next time.

She checked herself out in the mirror over the sink. She looked like an oversized rabbit in the white terry-cloth robe, the towel turbaned into pointy ears above her head. Her face had gotten wet, and her eyes were ringed with remnants of mascara. The giant rabbit suddenly resembled a giant raccoon. She reached for the cleansing cream.

What in the hell was it with Julian Morrow? Sure, he was her assignment, but *he* didn't know that. So what was it with him anyway? Obviously he could turn it off and on like a switch. And why should she have expected anything different? He was a man, wasn't he?

But he was a priest. The papal liaison to Arte per Pace. That should have really told her something. But it didn't.

She ran her fingers through her hair. It settled into a halo of loose curls all over her head. This idea to get her hair cut short had definitely been inspired.

The knock on the door sounded too soft at first. Then, again, insistent. She gave her hair one more tousle and tightened the belt on her robe. She checked the digital clock as she walked through the bedroom to the living room. After nine o'clock. Late, but not that late. Sully would never show up at her apartment. Knocking wasn't David's style. And she didn't think Elliot would just drop by.

"Yes?" she asked through the door.

"Romany, it's Julian."

Julian Morrow at her doorstep. Well, speak of the devil . . .

"Hi, Julian," she said as soon as she pulled open the door. "Come in." She sounded cheery enough.

But he had ignored her invitation. "I'm sorry . . . ," he said, standing outside the door, staring at her still damp hair, the terry bathrobe. "I should have called first."

"But you were just in the neighborhood? Come on in, Julian. You're not disturbing me." She watched him step inside her apartment, then stand like a teenager called into the principal's office.

"Make yourself comfortable. Gimme a sec, I'll throw something on." She'd already begun fumbling with the tie on her robe.

"Take your time," he said.

She gave him one of her best smiles and walked into the bedroom, closing the door behind her.

Well, wasn't he just full of surprises? She threw the terry robe over a chair and rummaged in a drawer for panties and a bra. She'd noticed he was in jeans and a polo. She opened the armoire and reached for a white cotton sundress.

"Be out in a minute," she called. He didn't answer.

She walked back into the bath and checked herself out in the mirror. Maybe a little lipstick would help. She found something orangey and pressed her lips together, spreading the color. It'd have to do. Besides, this was an unscheduled stop. Sully would just have to forgive her if she didn't quite look the part. This seduction business was a hell of a lot more than she'd bargained for. Hell, Julian Morrow was a lot more than she bargained for.

"Hi, again," she said as she opened the door, giving him another of her best smiles.

He smiled back this time. "Hello, yourself."

She walked to the sofa and sat down next to him. After a moment she nervously touched the back of her neck.

"I like it," he said.

"Like it?" she asked, watching the smile expand on his face.

"Your hair."

"Oh." She pulled her hand away, suddenly self-conscious.

"You still have gypsy hair, Romany Chase."

"Julian . . ."

He'd heard it in her voice too. "That's why I'm here, Romany. We need to talk. Work some things out."

"Work things out?" Repeating his words suddenly seemed easier.

"I've never been very good at this, Romany. I mean, facing things. It's usually kind of hit and run with me." His smile had lost something.

"Julian—"

"You're beautiful, Romany. And intelligent. Which of course makes everything more complicated. You see, I can't seem to be around a woman like you without wanting to . . ." He didn't finish, but this time his smile moved up to the corners of his eyes. "I'm sorry, I told you I wasn't very good at this." He turned away in a kind of frustration, and she had the chance to study his profile. He was perfect, she decided. Classically handsome. A Greek god. And tortured, and mysterious, and a thousand other romantic attributes that made him lethal.

But this wasn't romance she reminded herself. Julian was an assignment, and right now she needed to deal with his ambivalence. Her own feelings weren't important.

"Julian, I can appreciate that what's happening between us affects you differently." She stopped. Suddenly there was nothing to read in his expression. "I mean, I understand you're a priest." The words hung like deadweight in the air.

He didn't say anything.

"Julian, I know this may sound awful, but I can't allow myself to get caught up in guilt about this. I have a job to do in Rome. And the simple truth is that what happened, happened. And there's nothing we can do about it now."

"Romany, please." His voice was soft, but his eyes were huge, intense. "You don't understand. I don't regret what happened between us. That would be a lie. I wanted it, Romany."

"Wanted, Julian?"

He took her hand and pulled her to her feet. *"Want,"* he said, and drew her toward the bedroom.

They undressed together standing by her bed. He stopped her once, as she was reaching to unhook her bra. "I love these," he said, kissing the tops of her breasts. And then he helped her, sliding the straps down her arms, pulling her down beside him on the bed.

He looked so tan and blond against the crisp white of her sheets. He waited, watching as she removed her panties. "Come here," he said, and drew her close, full-length against his body.

She was not small, Romany thought, but lying with him made her feel . . . not frail. Oh no . . . but sheltered. She held her breath and felt his erection hard against her thighs.

He was making her crazy, his mouth moving from her eyelids to her neck, but teasing, not kissing. She was wild, so glad when his mouth had at last found her breast, and his fingers slipped inside her, finding her ready. She arched against him, her eyes opening to see him smile at her response to him.

"Romany," he laughed, and pulled her beneath him.

God, it was good, even better than Saturday. More natural now, the two of them together. She wrapped her legs around him as he rocked against her. Pleasure washed over her in colors.

But later, when he was gone, she confronted herself in the mirror. "Well, so you've done it," she said to the naked stranger. "Father Julian Morrow has become your lover. Now what?"

Cardinal DeLario's thick fingers grabbed the phone before it had a second chance to ring.

"Sì."

"It is a great mystery how your Jesuit is still a member of the Church, much less a priest," his informant said bluntly.

"Do not speak to me in riddles."

"If half of what I have been able to uncover is true—"

"What . . . what have you found?"

"It was not easy. As I have said before, anything that concerns this priest is most difficult. Things are kept very secret, hidden in trunks, buried in holes."

"I am not interested in your difficulties." The son of a bitch was turning into a poet. "You are paid well for your difficulties. I am not interested in puzzles. I am interested only in answers. You have answers for me?"

"Sì, sì, I have answers."

He mustn't let this little bastard tease him like a cheap whore. "Well . . . ?"

"Your man is very very smart, or has someone who guards his back like an angel." A self-satisfied laugh. "He has done well, your American Jesuit."

American Jesuit. The little shit was getting careless. He might as well have said Morrow's name. He was fast losing his patience. Yet what choice did he have? "Sì," he said, "go on."

"The priest put to good use his talents as an art expert." Another short dry laugh. "It seems he ran a very profitable black-market operation ten, twelve years back. Import-export of stolen antiquities. Mostly jewelry, gold coins."

"Black market? How is this possible? How would I not know this?"

"As I said, your Jesuit is very smart. Dangerous too, perhaps. The word is he became very upset with one of his brokers a few years back before he got out of the business."

"And . . ."

"The man turned up dead."

CHAPTER 24

Large, but quietly tasteful with its spillover pieces of art—mere tag ends from the Museum's extensive collections—Cardinal Vittorio DeLario's office stood in modest contrast to the opulence of his Vatican apartments. Its message was clear. Here was the office of a man selflessly devoting his final years to his Church. A man who, quite forgivably, could not resist surrounding himself with a few borrowed tokens of the beauty that was his province.

What was more obscure was the inside joke that the artwork represented. The office treasures were nearly all fakes, reproductions of some of the very earliest works that the Cardinal had stolen.

He was sitting now, smiling benignly from behind the solid wood of his desk. With his deep leather chair canted backward, his toes but barely brushed the floor. Still, from the vantage point of his visitor, there was only the impression of his scarlet-clad torso riding high. A king secure on his throne.

Monsignor Brisi was pacing in front of the desk, moving from border to border on one of the priceless rugs. He was mad as hell.

"So what are you saying, Vittorio? That Morrow is to be let in on our operation? Just like that?" The pacing stopped for the single beat it took to snap his fingers.

"Why do you upset yourself so, my dear Umberto," the Cardinal said mildly, "when it seems clear that we have no choice?"

"How big a piece does he want?"

"That has not yet been discussed."

"But there is no money coming in now. Did you not tell Morrow that? Even a hundred percent of zero is nothing."

"Oh but, Monsignor Brisi, surely you are not thinking. With the Jesuit on our side, why should we not go on with the forgeries?"

Brisi stopped dead. Greed seeped into his eyes like groundwater swelling in a ditch.

"Ahh. So now you begin to see, dear Umberto, even a smaller percentage is something *more* than nothing."

"But how did Morrow discover us?" Brisi had changed tack. "I thought you said that this arrangement was foolproof." He was moving again in front of the desk.

Vittorio sighed. "Proof against fools? . . . Perhaps. But whatever this Morrow is, he is smart. And there was always the risk that one of our patrons would find irresistible the temptation to show off an acquisition."

"You are saying that this Jesuit was shown one of our pieces?"

"No." Vittorio shook his head. "It seems that a friend of Morrow's father told the priest about something he'd seen in Spain. A piece he had always thought to be in the possession of the Vatican. This piece."

Oh. Brisi's mouth formed the word, but didn't say it.

He had finally stopped pacing long enough to take in the presence of the vase on the desk.

"Sì," the Cardinal answered the unspoken question, "the original. Castor and Pollux have indeed come home. So kindly returned to us by Father Morrow." He gestured with a stubby finger toward the amphora. "Switch it back and destroy the fake."

"Destroy it?"

"Of course, Umberto. The black market for works like this is small. We cannot afford embarrassing questions as to why the same work by Exekias is offered for yet a second time."

"What about the buyer? How did the Jesuit get it away from him?"

"That I do not know. But Father Morrow has assured me that the Spaniard will not talk."

"And you trust him? Morrow, I mean?"

"Of course I do not trust him, Umberto."

"But you do plan to agree to his terms?"

The Cardinal gave an expressive shrug. "I have said there is no choice. At least for now. Father Morrow has the goods on us, as the Americans say. While we, Umberto, know so very little of him. *Che pecatto!* It is a sorry thing, no?" He smiled again in total contradiction of the words.

"So, what are you going to do?"

"Ah, you know me so well, Monsignor." The Cardinal fingered the Byzantine cross below the level of the desk. "I have devised a certain plan. A test."

It was just the sort of thing to catch the Curator's florid imagination. "A test?" he demanded. "What kind of test, Vittorio?"

"One that kills two birds with one stone." He smiled again.

The monsignor opened his mouth with yet another question, but the Cardinal held up a hand.

"Truly, I am sorry, dear Umberto. But just for now this must remain my little secret. But I promise that in due time, you shall know everything."

• • •

Marthe's hair had not aged with the rest of her. It spread itself like a bright fan on her pillow, but her face was somber even in her sleep. Somber, but as yet unlined. It wasn't wrinkles that betrayed Marthe's fifty-odd years, but something else—a weight, a gravity, that had pulled on her delicate features far more relentlessly than the single G-force of this earth.

Theodor set down his journal and smiled at the thought. Trust the English rationalist to try to put into scientific terms something that was essentially mystical in nature. He had always known that any satisfactory theory regarding his Marthe would have to emerge from that half of his brain that was Russian.

This new idea cartwheeled across his mind connecting another circuit. *A mystery wrapped in an enigma.* Yes, that was right. Churchill's familiar quote was an apt enough description of his wife, swaddled in her blankets beside him, despite the summer heat.

Mona Lisa he had named her that long-ago day on the Washington Metro when from some three rows back, he'd felt the pressure of her eyes. And looking up from his book, had caught the merest trace of some expression on her face. So that what lingered was the distinctive impression of a smile, though he knew that he hadn't actually seen it.

It wasn't exactly shyness, he'd decided, that had made her look away. Rather, in the weeks that followed, he always thought she seemed somehow amused at finding him there in the car with her each time, though her smiles were like ghosts that only he could glimpse, and then only from the corner of his eye.

He was surprised the first time he caught himself daydreaming about the girl on the Metro. And then he had to wonder if the strange unspoken connection that seemed to leap between them was not simply the product of his own imagination. Manufactured from that loneliness, which he seldom allowed himself to even acknowledge was real.

For despite his many friends, despite his popularity with his students, Theodor had always seemed to himself to be waiting. Waiting back then at thirty-four, for whom, he didn't know. *The last of the romantics*, he'd been accused of that. And there he was in love with a face in the underground. He was Orpheus. That was it, of course.

But Theodor Chase, if not habitually a man of action, was neither an idle romantic. And so finally he had simply sat beside her. And talked to her. And been surprised again. Marthe Rignaud was as delightfully unfathomable a creature as ever his imagination could provide. And though in six short months they were married, had been married now for almost thirty years, never had he solved her central mystery.

"Theodor?"

He looked down to see her emerging from her fuzzy cocoon of blankets, sitting up to arrange the pillows against her back.

"I thought you were asleep," he said.

"I was. But I'm awake now." She smiled.

"Pleasant dreams?"

"Interesting dreams. . . . Theodor?"

"Yes, my love."

"Have you called Romany? To tell her when we're coming."

"No. Not yet. Is something wrong? Have you changed your mind?"

"About going? Oh, no. I'm looking forward to it." She hesitated. "It's just that I was wondering, if you had talked to her again, how she'd sounded."

"You're worried about her."

"Well, it's only . . ."

"Marthe, you're always worrying about her."

"I know." She gave a small sigh. "She's grown-up now. We don't have to wrap her in cotton." She was repeating his oft-spoken litany. "It's just that I have . . ."

"I know. A feeling." He laughed, reached over, and

pulled her into his arms. His dear Marthe was such a purely instinctive being. Only after their friendship had begun, had he understood what a singular thing their unorthodox meeting had been. Despite an extraordinary wariness, Marthe had more or less *chosen* him on sight. *But I knew you* was the way she had put it, explaining.

He took her hand. "You know, my love, I learned a long time ago to trust those feelings of yours. It's just that with Romany . . ." He smiled to take out the sting.

"I know, you think I'm overprotective."

His words again. He let go her hand, planted a kiss on her brow to smooth her frown. "We should let Romany know exactly when we're coming. Why don't you phone her tonight? Ask her yourself how she's doing."

"No." Marthe smiled now, but he noted that the habitual sadness remained in the set of her mouth. "No, Theodor, you talk to her. It'll be late here when it's a good time to call Rome. I'm sure I'll probably be asleep again."

"You're very tired?"

"No more than usual. Less tired, really. Haven't you noticed?"

"I've noticed this whole week." He grinned. "I like that we're getting a head start for the trip. Our second honeymoon?"

She blushed. Surely Marthe Chase must be the very last woman to do it so prettily. He was overcome by a rush of emotion so strong, it stung his eyes.

"I love you, Marthe."

"I love you, Theodor."

He knew that she did. Her love for him was like a set of keys that she gave to him one by one. Through the wonderful years of their marriage he had moved through door after door of her, and every room had been a fresh surprise.

Today he'd uncovered another secret, another mystery solved. He had spoken to Dr. Weissman about this sudden burst of energy in his wife, this seeming reprieve in her decline. And though the physician would not directly betray his patient's wish for silence, there was no doubt left in Theodor's mind that for him and his beloved Marthe there was only this last room now.

Vittorio floated on his back. When he opened his eyes, he saw a splay of summer constellations shimmering across the vaulted ceiling. An intricate mix of azure and gold. He thought the design must mimic the artistry of some Islamic mosque. But no mosque this, but the Villa Bassano. He sighed silently. The Baron had spared nothing. The enclosed pool was inspired.

He shifted his bulk slightly. Yes, there was much to be said for being fat, Vittorio decided. A skinny man could never stay afloat so well. He paddled his feet a bit and felt the water lap warmly over his belly. A perfect day. The Baron had accepted the news about Morrow with little more than the arch of a single brow. Herr Friedrich was a reptile. But of course this little matter could very well have gone differently. One never knew with the German.

"You are comfortable, Vittorio?"

The Baron's voice. Invading the tight seal that the water had made against his ears. He forced his feet down and found the bottom of the pool. His hands worked against the moisture at his hairline, his eyes.

"You said something, Friedrich?" he sputtered.

"I asked if you were comfortable." The Baron stood by the edge of the pool. Dressed in a pale-blue suit, with matching shirt and tie, he had not joined his guest in the water. Vittorio tried to remember if he had ever seen the Baron in anything but a suit or a uniform. He thought not.

"Ah, it is like paradise." He smiled his cherub's smile.

"Here, I've brought you a robe. Put it on. Fritz has brought us champagne."

"French champagne?" He could risk the tease. The Baron had never been in a better mood.

"But of course, Vittorio. Every nation must excel at something. The French are good wine makers." He extended his arm and held out a striped caftan.

Vittorio stepped out onto the cool marble lip of the pool and worked his way into the robe.

"You look like an Arab, Vittorio."

"An Arab with no harem." He laughed, feeling the spongy limpness of his testicles and penis bobbing inside his wet trunks.

"That could be arranged if you wish." The Baron was pouring the champagne that Fritz had brought. "Very easily."

"Oh, Friedrich, but I do wish. Unfortunately at my age, wishing is all I am able to do." He lifted a glass from the tray and raised it. *"Prosit,* Friedrich."

"Salute, Vittorio." The crystal of the glass shimmering at his thin lips. He sipped sparingly and set the champagne down. "So you are satisfied that Morrow is telling the truth."

The Baron had decided to return to their earlier conversation.

"We have little choice but to trust the priest, Friedrich. But we must not let him swell up, the only rooster in the henhouse. My little test should determine his loyalty."

"Ah, this test of yours, Vittorio. You will tell me nothing?"

"As I told Monsignor Brisi, you must wait and see, Friedrich."

The blue eyes measured him for a moment. Then the narrow smile came to his lips. "What if we play the game? What if I choose to ask about the test?"

Vittorio felt a tight knot bloom instantly in his bowel, and then as quickly disappear. "Oh, no, Herr Baron, you will not ask this question." He was laughing now. "You relish surprises as much as I do. And I promise you, this surprise will be worth the wait." He raised his glass to the Black Baron once again and drained the last of his champagne.

. . .

The monk felt the robe fit like a membrane this night. The confessional made a larger womb around him. Perhaps it was only the summer's heat that caused this unaccustomed claustrophobia. Maybe the insanity clicking inside his brain. He looked down and saw even in the dimness dark blotches of perspiration spreading like blood from the tight cord binding the wool habit at his waist. His tongue licked the thin line of moisture above his lip; his hair was sticky beneath the cowl. He lifted the hood from his face and inhaled stale, humid air.

"Ambriel." It was Metatron's quiet voice. "Is it truth that you tell me?"

"Yes, Father, it is true. Julian Morrow has joined with the enemy."

CHAPTER 25

With the sun but a haze of pinkish light beyond the Vatican walls, it was actually cool in the gardens. Julian Morrow stood in shorts and tank top leaning with his palms against an oak, relaxing and stretching the muscles of his calves. Despite his eagerness to get on with his run, he forced himself to continue through the warm-up. The next exercise was thankfully the last, and he lay down on his back in the damp morning grass, slowly lifting his legs above his head in parallel with the ground. Knees straight and together. Holding it, holding it, till he felt the expected tug along his hamstrings. Then at last he was up and running, flat out along the trails, the cypress trees nodding past his shoulders in the semidark like sleepy chenille-robed strangers.

During his two years with the Cistercians, he had not run. And he had missed it, taking it up again as soon as he'd come to Rome. There was nothing to match it, the sensation of being sprung from a trap. Especially if you'd constructed the trap yourself.

The light was widening now, pouring in a spread of wine across the eastern sky. He opened his mouth wide, gulping the air that rose like breath from the earth. The world was simple; it was humans who were complicated.

And not only men. The Cardinal was hardly his only concern now. He glanced at his watch with its automatic readout of his pulse rate, and increased his speed. But not even the physical effort could blot out the image of Romany Chase pinioned, like a trembling white moth, beneath him. Or erase from his mind the feel or the taste of her. Or the perfume scent of her arousal—a vixen's musk cut with the fresh remembered greenness of his mother's lilies.

Breathless, he pushed through the pain, waiting for his second wind. He would sleep with her again. And not only for his pleasure. After all, he could trust himself not to let whatever he felt get in the way of what he had to do. There was Colleen Shaunessy to stand as proof of that.

For a skinny man, Anton Arendt looked almost massive riding in the open train Gustav was driving. Perhaps it was the strange interplay of light and shadow within the tunnels that gave the false impression. Perhaps it was the manner in which he sat—spine ramrod straight, chest ballooned out, shoulders splayed back like stiff little wings. Anton was a happy man.

A trip to the Villa Bassano was not usually something Anton enjoyed. Herr Baron was not the easiest of men. And on more than one occasion he'd wished for another to go in his place. But then he would remember the cause and force his feelings down into his bowels. Many a time, a journey back from the Alban Hills was followed by a severe case of diarrhea.

But he wouldn't be shitting today. Today he would be eating, and drinking, and perhaps even. . . . The thought of putting his long, skinny penis inside Margarite's pretty ass made him squirm on the hard seat and wish that Gustav would make the car move faster.

Ja, wonderful surprises had greeted him today at the Villa. First, Herr Baron telling him that the black-marketing operation would not in all likelihood have to be curtailed. That new monies would be filling their special accounts before too long. He'd given him no details as to what circumstances had brought about this sudden change, but Anton never expected to be privy to all the confidences in this particular arrangement. Besides, he didn't care to know anything beyond the probability that more money would be forthcoming to support the party's efforts.

However, the most astonishing aspect of his meeting this afternoon had been the Baron himself. Never had he seen Herr Friedrich in such good humor, never had the man displayed such enthusiasm for the cause. He had spoken boldly of the necessity of a new world order, a renaissance of the lost German *Gemeinschaft.* And though he knew the old Prussian aristocrat didn't accept the neo-Nazis as equals any more than he had accepted the old, it did Anton's heart good to hear the Black Baron call for the glorious restoration of *Blut und Boden,* "blood and soil."

Anton took in a deep breath of the rich underground air. Tonight was definitely a night for celebration. A night for a good German wine and Margarite's beautiful ass.

He wasn't going to be cramped this time. No more sardine tins for stakeouts. David stretched out his long legs in the luxury-sized rental. He figured on a long wait.

He hadn't seen Romany since that night he'd hidden in her bedroom and watched her and Morrow make love. Had it been any other woman in the world, he would have enjoyed what he'd seen. Voyeurism wasn't exactly his thing; he was too much of a player for that.

Yet on the three or four occasions he'd done it, he surprised himself at how quickly he'd come. But he hadn't even gotten an erection watching Romany and her priest the other evening.

What he'd gotten was angry. Angry at himself for caring, for being there in the first place. Angry at Romany for doing her job. And that was the worst. What was happening between her and Morrow looked too personal, too damn real. Romany hadn't faked anything the night they'd made love. He knew her too well not to wonder what was going on.

He figured Sully had been pressing Romany pretty hard. So she was better at her job than he'd thought.

He wanted to see Romany for a thousand reasons other than he "just wanted to see her." Ever since that call from Rachael, he hadn't been able to think of much else.

He had to wonder if what Helena Klimpt told Marthe Chase had been something she'd already known. He knew Romany's parents were planning a trip over soon. Would Marthe tell Romany when she got here, or keep what she knew a secret?

He thought again of Romany, the way he'd seen her the other night. Her long, honey-brown legs wrapped around Morrow's waist. Her hands working the muscles of his back. Her opened mouth, the soft purring sound coming from deep inside her throat. He'd been flaccid when he'd seen it then, but now remembering, remembering Romany, he could feel himself grow hard. God, he wanted her. Loved her. And though he knew what Rachael had told him shouldn't make any difference, it was now the single thing in his entire universe that did matter.

A sudden movement caught his eye. He pushed his sunglasses down the bridge of his nose. The skinny Jew-killer was coming out of Signora Agostina's. Pay dirt. Obviously Arendt went somewhere inside the pensione. There was no way to know where today. He'd just have to follow the Nazi in next time and find out in exactly which hole the little rat-fucker was hiding.

It had come full circle again. Like the phasing of the moon. Like the menses of a woman. But not in units of twenty-eight days. Thirteen. Thirteen days.

He would call Lise back from that aethyr where she now dwelled, to this temporal plane where he would confess to no living soul that he had at last grown weary. He had in truth experienced it all; there was nothing left for him.

He looked across the shimmer of crystal and silver spread down the length of the table. The flowers seemed sweeter this night, the wine more intoxicating. He repeated the ritual words, evoking his beloved. And like each time before, he experienced the flimsy reality of the room slip away. His body arc and twist into a self that was Friedrich but not Friedrich. Then he felt the familiar tightening in his anus. He sniffed the air. Lise sat smiling before him.

"Lise . . ." Her name a benediction.

No answer. Never did she speak to him. But his soul understood her special language. She stood and stretched out her arm. A delicate flower balanced in the space before her.

He followed.

It was their *Verlobung,* the passage of their engagement, and the Berlin August of 1939 was hotter than he could ever remember.

Friedrich glanced across the room to where his future father-in-law Herr Schulen stood, a dutiful Nazi, his party badge pinned to the lapel of his evening coat. His beautiful wife Hilde, dressed in the latest Parisian fashion, had chosen, however, to ignore the Führer's suggestion that only German couturiers be patronized. Unfortunately, in the Third Reich it was the male gender, strutting for the most part in the plumage of well-cut uniforms and polished boots, who appeared fashionable. Only English women, Friedrich believed, could look dowdier than German *Frauen*.

He watched as trays of lobster and venison, champagne and caviar, were ferried among the guests. Herr Schulen had spared no expense, and understandably so. Schulen was one of the wealthiest men in the capital, a man who could well afford to spoil his only daughter on the occasion of her betrothal to a baron. Friedrich tested the edge of the fine linen napkin he was holding. Linen, according to his now dead Nanna, was what elevated a party to an event.

The Führer's "uniformed peacocks" circulated from room to room among the crowd. To be sure, there existed now in Germany a new kind of elitism that had nothing to do with titles or wealth. Friedrich smiled his spare smile, thinking that it was a perfectly agreeable accommodation, this Third Reich of Adolf Hitler's. The opportunistic upper classes neatly goose-stepped behind the Nazis, who in turn were granted a kind of legitimacy by association.

And though this new elite seemed wholly manufactured, lacking measurably in the proper bloodlines, it embodied a style that well-suited Friedrich's own patrician tastes. Indeed the *Schutzstaffel* with its black uniforms, death's-head insignia, and jackboots, projected the precise mix of power and mystery that had drawn Friedrich like a magnet. And Reichsführer Himmler had been most eager to recruit aristocrats to the ranks of the SS.

But he had forsaken his officer's uniform this evening, and chosen instead black tails and the royal insignia of his mother's house. He moved toward the outer doors. He had tired of the conversation inside. How incredibly naive the German people were. How stupid this talk of Poland. The Nazis didn't give a damn about Danzig.

The gardens outside were strewn with colorful Chinese lanterns; roses and lilacs amassed in pots and jars. He took a deep breath and wondered where Lise was.

The strains of a particularly sentimental tune made him want to take her into his arms and dance.

"So here you are."

He turned at the sound of her soft voice.

"I have been looking for you everywhere." She wore a false little pout on her lips.

"I came outside for some air. It has grown cooler." He smiled. "Listen."

She closed her eyes to better hear the music, and in an instant his arms were around her and they were waltzing. Her bare shoulders seemed waxen under the yellow glow of the lanterns. The same light turned her auburn hair to gold. She smelled of vanilla.

Her hand pressed against his chest, and she pulled away slightly, looking up into his face. "This engagement gift, Friedrich . . ."

"You do not like the slippers? But it is an old Merovingian custom, Lise." He tried hard to keep his voice serious.

"I am quite aware, Herr Baron, of the Merovingian custom. A custom that makes a bride the chattel of her husband. Binds her to his house. His will." The pout had returned to her beautiful mouth.

He bent and kissed her. "You are bound, my Lise, bound only to my heart. . . ."

A sudden constriction in his chest, and he sensed the present slowly propelling him forward. He bit the thin line of his lip and tasted the metallic flavor of his own blood. This was the part he hated most. Remembering, remembering that it wasn't long after that he had learned of her betrayal.

The pounding at the door got Vittorio naked out of bed. Not that he'd been sleeping. Bright cards had scattered like a flurry of frightened chickens as he'd flung back the coverlet, destroying totally the solitaire he'd been winning. For a moment he'd fumbled with his hastily gathered robe, wrapping and tying the dressing gown around him. Like a sausage in red silk, he thought, catching sight of himself in a gold-framed mirror as he hurried down the hallway from his bedroom. Anything to stop the goddamned pounding.

Was the whole place on fire? Had Niccolo died? Despite his recent doubts about the Pope's reliability, the thought of his sudden demise was not altogether pleasant. His control on papal politics, Vittorio was beginning to admit, was not what it had once been.

The noise, when he reached the foyer, was nearly intolerable, the heavy paneling seeming almost to bow with the onslaught of sound. Though he knew this was only illusion.

"What is it?" He flung the door open.

"Buona sera, Eminenza. I hope I am not disturbing you." Julian Morrow stood on his threshold looking like a lost tourist in blue jeans and a short-sleeved knit shirt. A dripping umbrella was furled in his hand. For a moment in the dim light of the hallway, it had almost looked like a sword.

It was the iron ferrule, Vittorio realized, that had been beating against his door.

"It's raining outside," Morrow said, pushing past. The explanation was hardly necessary. Water glittered on the polished floor like jewels marking his trail.

Vittorio was forced to follow. "Why do you come here at such an hour?" he said. If the priest's behavior was calculated to anger him, certainly it was succeeding.

"You said you'd get back to me," Morrow turned, answering his question. "I just got tired of waiting." He sat on one of the living room's richly brocaded sofas. Leaned back with his arms along its spine.

Insufferable Jesuit cowboy. Vittorio eased himself onto an adjoining chair, settling his robe as though it were edged in ermine. He reached for the cross that was absent from his neck, ended by patting his hair. "It is perhaps good that you came tonight," he said finally.

"Sì," Morrow agreed. "So let's get down to business.

I tell you what I estimate your operation is making in a year, Vittorio. Then we talk about my percentage."

"You go too fast, Julian." The cherub smile was a laser cutting him off.

"And you are stalling, Vittorio. Which is not smart. You don't cut me in, I go straight to Pope Gregory."

"And what will that get you, do you think?"

The tanned arms lifted in a shrug. "The gratitude of His Holiness."

Vittorio's smile turned almost genuine. "Are you so sure that His Holiness will thank you, Father Morrow? You have a saying, I believe, that ignorance is bliss. Even if he were grateful, Niccolo's gratitude is but a poor coin. And one that must be very quickly spent."

"Are you saying you refuse—"

"I am saying, Father Morrow, that I have doubts. I cannot help but wonder if this is not some kind of trap."

"Trap?" Morrow shook his head. "You Italians. You think everything's a conspiracy. It's simple. I just want to make some money."

"Why? Your family has plenty."

"You said it. My family's got money. Besides, you never have enough. You ought to know that." The priest's own smile was back. "You've been checking up on me, Vittorio. What did you find out?"

"Nothing to make me trust you."

Now Morrow laughed. "What can I tell you, Vittorio? I never claimed to be a saint."

"I don't need a saint."

"Right." The priest was immediately serious. "What you do need is somebody who can cover your ass with Arte per Pace. You need me."

"I have Monsignor Brisi."

"What? Brisi's no help. . . . What are you saying?"

Oh, the Jesuit was quick. He would have to give him that. Maybe it would not be so bad in the end. If only he were not so American.

"Monsignor Brisi has been my right hand." Vittorio spoke carefully. "A man cannot have two right hands."

The Jesuit was frowning. "Say it then."

"I want you to rid me of him, Father Morrow." The Cardinal smiled. "I want you to kill Umberto Brisi."

CHAPTER 26

It was late in the afternoon, but still breathlessly hot, and even in the short distance between his apartment and the waiting limousine, Cardinal Vittorio DeLario had begun to sweat. In the car's full blast of air-conditioning his skin had turned almost instantly clammy, as if the solid black door slamming home had been sealing him into a vault. A tiny pain ran out to join a shiver of cold at his spine. And for the briefest moment it crossed his mind that this uncustomary twinge might be a warning of the prostate trouble his doctors had long predicted, or even a presentiment of something worse. But he had outlived three physicians in the last twenty years, all of them younger than he. And rearranging his damp soutane where it clung against his shoulders, he leaned back more comfortably into the deep leather seat, settling in for the twenty-minute ride that would bring him to the Pope's summer residence.

The black Mercedes had sped its way through several manned checkpoints and was already climbing into the green hills when the Cardinal looked back. In the darkened rear window Rome shimmered through a veil of sunlight and dust, the domes of her churches like the blunted spires of some half-imaginary kingdom. But the image, for all its shadowed potency, was lost upon Vittorio. He was thinking only of Umberto Brisi, and wondering just where it was his Curator had disappeared to this morning.

Not in his office, Your Eminence, the monsignor's secretary had said with a cringing apology that offered no further explanation. A scheduled absence, blocked out on the Curator's calendar, the priest had added when pressed. But what the appointment had been, Father Grimaldi had no idea, the inference being that one should not presume to ask such things of Monsignor Brisi.

Well, Monsignor Brisi would soon be disappearing for good, Vittorio reminded himself. Not that Julian Morrow had committed himself verbally to the little assignment he'd been offered last night. The Jesuit was too cool for that. No, what Father Morrow had actually done was laugh. But a laugh with enough self-mockery at its core, so that his listener could not take offense. Indeed, Vittorio had been smiling rather smugly as the Jesuit had risen to go.

"Later," was all that Morrow had really said before he left. But the implication was clear. Umberto Brisi was now as good as dead. In the cool isolation of the limousine, Vittorio pushed aside any lingering regrets for the loss of his court jester, and concentrated instead on the question that had kept him up till morning. If Umberto Brisi was a self-important ass, he was at least a predictable one, and therefore easy to control. Could the same ever be said of Julian Morrow?

If he were truly the outsider he appeared to be, then the American could be disposed of when his usefulness was served. But what if he were more? What if he had allies in this thing? Morrow had called him paranoid, but Vittorio had not gotten where he was by trusting too easily.

But surely a conspiracy against him was impossible. In the arena of curial politics Vittorio DeLario was undisputed master. Who among his fellow prelates would so recklessly oppose him, when an exposure of his crimes could endanger them all? Endanger the very Church?

Julian Morrow had to be a renegade. What had he called him last night? A Jesuit cowboy, out only for himself. Everything he had so far uncovered about the priest confirmed it, though it was still not precisely clear to him why Niccolo had picked Morrow for the Arte per Pace job. It was the purpose of today's visit to find that out.

The limousine was slowing, making the turn onto the private road that led up to the villa. At the gateway a uniformed guard nodded in recognition, and the Cardinal sat forward, impatient now, as the Mercedes drove to the terraced end of the long tree-lined roadway. Here the driver parked and, getting out, opened the door for Vittorio.

The air outside the car was pure and much cooler than in the city, as it always was here in Castel Gandolfo. The Cardinal ignored the view and went instead to the short stone steps that led to the formal gardens. He walked on quickly down the familiar branching pathways, passing at last through a thick screen of hedge.

A statue of the Virgin stood near a fish pond in the tiny hidden garden, and quite unconsciously Vittorio glanced, as indeed he always did, to see if there were flowers in the stone Madonna's hand. There were not. For it was only Eugenio Pacelli who had once picked them for her.

The Pope had not seemed to hear him enter, but remained gazing down into the pond, his back toward Vittorio. And despite the lack of flowers, it was easy for a moment to believe that the white-clad figure in the gloom was indeed the sad and emaciated Pius XII that Vittorio remembered from the years that had followed the war.

The Pope turned.

"Vittorio."

"Your Holiness." The Cardinal walked forward, knelt to kiss the ring.

As always the hand was half pulled away as if Niccolo were embarrassed. The fingers, nervously moving, motioned him up from his knees. "Sister Maria has put out food and wine for us," the Pope said. "Come."

In the shade was a little round table where they sat

on wooden chairs. Dishes with cheese and green olives rested on a spotless cloth of carefully pressed linen. There was freshly baked bread and butter. And a bottle of Frascati, Vittorio's favorite Alban wine. One always dined well with Niccolo.

Vittorio took charge of uncorking the bottle; the Pope broke a heel from the loaf. Fragrant doughy steam like the smoke from an offering rose up in a cloud between them.

"You must remember, Vittorio," said Niccolo, "to take milk and eggs from the farm. Guido is so proud of our dairy and chickens. He will pout, if you forget." He reached for the butter. "You seem well."

"I am fine, Niccolo." The Cardinal passed the Pope a glass of the wine. "But you are looking tired, I think."

"Am I? Perhaps it's old age."

Was the barb intentional? Niccolo Fratelli was twenty years his junior. Vittorio pushed the thought aside, eating and drinking and talking to pass the time till he could finally broach the question he had come to ask.

"Your Holiness," he began after Niccolo's rambling monologue on the disintegration of Catholic education. "Your Holiness, there's something I wanted to ask you, about Julian Morrow . . ."

Niccolo was instantly alert, his face set in that look it always assumed whenever anything to do with Arte per Pace was mentioned—the expression of a child who may be asked to share his favorite toy.

"The Americans like him." A matter-of-fact statement.

"Of course, Niccolo." His own tone was conciliatory. "It's just that certain rumors have come lately to my ears."

"Ahh. Rumors among the Curia. That is a surprise."

Sarcasm, and now irony. The Cardinal reached for a piece of the bread, took a moment to spread it with butter.

"Well, what is it you have heard, Vittorio?"

He did not answer the Pope at once, cutting a slice

of the cheese. "Smoke and shadows, Your Holiness," he said, looking artlessly upward. "But I fear some hidden scandal that could cause embarrassment to Arte per Pace."

A smile he did not at all care for hovered ghostlike on the Pope's thin lips, leaving him to wonder if he'd seen it at all.

"I think I can guess what you've heard about Father Morrow, Vittorio," the Pope said. "And it's no real secret. There was a problem. Years ago. With a woman." Niccolo lifted his wineglass, took a healthy sip. "It's nothing for you to be concerned about now," he added a little testily. "As I thought I'd explained before, I appointed Father Morrow at Felipe Constanza's request. Surely you'll agree that the Jesuit Superior General appreciates as well as anyone the importance of Arte per Pace."

Vittorio was still chewing his bread and cheese, which avoided the need for an answer. Niccolo's version fit well enough with Morrow's side of the story, and the woman explained what the Jesuit had been doing in the monastery. That had been penance, and the Arte per Pace job was obviously his chance to redeem himself. How deliciously devious of Morrow, and it made perfect sense.

He looked across at Niccolo. Gregory XVII had put down his wine and was chewing on an olive. He seemed entirely undecided as to what to do with the pit, and he smiled uncertainly when he saw that Vittorio was watching.

The Cardinal smiled back. If Julian Morrow was a trap, then who could have sent him? Certainly not Niccolo Fratelli. Some things were just too hard to believe.

"I do not give a fuck for Vittorio's little test. And I do not give a damn about the money. What I wish for is Julian Morrow's head."

Umberto Brisi strutted as he spoke, moving before

the sofa where the Count Sebastiano sat comfortably reading a book. The monsignor's robe was crimson, an embroidered Chinese silk, whose open throat revealed a fresh striping of welts. Today the rope had bitten deeply, but he was little concerned, since the damage was so easily concealed beneath his Roman collar.

There was the rustle of a turning page. Then a ripple in the perfect posture that might have been Sebastiano's equivalent of a shrug. "I don't kill people, Umberto, if that is what you are asking."

The monsignor did not believe him. At best the denial was a half truth. Umberto had not the Count's intellect, had only a fine animal instinct as his guide. For a moment he was still, checking and weighing internal currents while he watched Sebastiano's face. "The Jesuit is a danger," he insisted.

"I respect your intuitions, Umberto." The Count looked up from his reading. "And surely you did not believe that I would simply take Vittorio's word that this Jesuit priest was harmless?"

"No . . . but sometimes I get impatient." The admission brought a smile. "You have found something out?" He sat down now on one of the formal chairs.

The Count laid down his book. "The world so quickly forgets," he said, "but the Führer came to power on the votes of the Catholic Zentrum. There were Jesuits in those days who supported the Reich, as long as its aims remained in accord with their own plans to consolidate a Catholic central Europe. Most of those priests whom I knew are long since dead. But I am not entirely without resources. Father Morrow, it seems, is indeed a very bad boy."

"You cannot think that you will leave it there, Klaus. What does this mean, 'a very bad boy'?"

"Involvement in a ring that imported illegal antiquities. The murder of an inconvenient partner. Father Morrow has been busy. And very, very clever."

"He cannot be trusted. Get rid of him."

The Count's hands were long and tapered, with little

sign of age. Brisi watched the fingers fan in a gesture of regret. "Beautiful Umberto, I cannot."

"What you mean is that you will not."

Instantly he was sorry for the stupid show of temper, but Sebastiano had not seemed to take offense. On the contrary, he smiled. "I want the money to continue."

"Why? You don't need it."

"Personally? No. There is plenty to sustain all this, all this and more. For my lifetime and indeed forever. The money from the forgeries is for my heirs."

"You have children?"

"Spiritual children, Umberto. Stunted offspring, to be sure. But they are the last hope of a world that is mired in chaos."

"The Germans!" He could not hide his disgust.

"You don't approve, Umberto. You are such a pure little hedonist. It is, of course, why I love you."

"Then help *me.*"

The Count simply looked at him while his eyes grew unmistakably harder.

"Remember the money, Umberto." The voice was immediately soothing. "And forget your pride. It is the only thing that has so far been hurt."

The Count had risen from his chair and now walked toward him. "What shall I perform for you tonight?" One hand stroked Umberto's face, the fingers cool against the cheek, which still burned with his anger.

"You decide for me, Klaus," he answered. "I enjoy whatever you play." The statement was true despite the fact that his mind was racing with resentment. He would never accept Morrow as a part of the operation. Never.

The Count sat down at a harpsichord that he'd once claimed had belonged to Beethoven himself. Very softly he began to play the first haunting notes of the *Pathetique.* But Umberto refused to be comforted. He fidgeted for a moment on the rigid chair, then reached for the book that the Count had been reading, examining the printing on its spine. Children's tales! The Grimm brothers. An ancient and rare edition no doubt, to have absorbed the Count's interest.

He turned the volume over in his hands. The printing inside was small and difficult to read even had his German been better, but the copperplate illustrations were disturbingly graphic despite the parchment's age. In morbid fascination he brought the yellowed pages closer to his eyes, surprised at how grossly detailed such black-and-white drawings could be. Wolves glutting themselves on the carcasses of goats and old women. Kings chopping off the hands of weeping maidens, throwing cronelike creatures into barrels spiked with nails.

And the worse perhaps, because she seemed so innocent with fat blond curls and chubby knees, was Hansel's little sister Gretel, her cherub's face distorted with malicious glee as she pushed the unsuspecting witch into the oven's maw.

A bloated moon lay behind a ruff of bruised clouds that somehow made the Italian sky seem dirty. And the air was too hot, too thick for nine o'clock in the evening. Even for Rome. Romany checked her watch for a third time. Damn, Sully was late.

But Sully was never late.

Something was wrong. Or if not wrong, changed. She could feel it. A slight shift in her universe. She had always been able to tell when something was going to happen. Could read the atmosphere like a pack of tarot cards. The short hair at the nape of her neck prickled.

He came from behind her. From a direction she had not anticipated. But she was ready for his voice when he spoke.

"Sorry."

She'd turned to face him. He looked like a poor man's version of Columbo if that was possible. Rumpled, but wily. Always that hard intelligence behind those brown eyes, which in another face might have been called "sexy."

"No problem, Sully. Anything up?" Of course there was something, but he was going to make her go fishing.

"In this business, Romany, something's always up." He cracked a smile. She could almost hear the wrinkles as they formed around the edges of his mouth.

"I'm listening, Sully." She waited for what was coming next.

"You wanna take a little ride? Too hot outside."

"Sure. My car or yours?"

"We'll take mine. Just up the street."

She could see the instant they arrived that someone else was in the car. She flashed a look over her shoulder to Sully. He shrugged and opened the back door of the sedan for her.

"Hello, Romany. Sorry about the cloak and dagger." His face smiled that same smile she'd first seen over twenty years ago in her father's library.

"Andrew." She settled herself on the seat next to him, returning his smile.

He bent over and gave her a peck on her cheek. "You look wonderful, Rom. New haircut."

"An impulse," she said, touching the back of her neck as if to confirm at least half of what he'd said. "Good to see you, Andrew. It's been a while. Here to check up on me?" She could hear Sully at last grinding the engine to life, switching on the radio. He was going to give them some privacy.

"I was in Rome." His response was a throwaway, his gray eyes trapping twin points of passing headlights.

"I'd assumed that Sully had—"

"I wanted to see for myself, Romany." His words suddenly conveyed an earnestness that hadn't been there before.

Then she understood, understood that this little impromptu meeting had more to do with her personally than professionally. Now that he knew she was sleeping with Julian Morrow, he wanted to see how she was handling it.

"I'm okay."

"You can call a halt any time you want, Romany. Just do your job with APP and walk away from the rest."

"I'm your best shot at the Vatican, Andrew. I can't walk."

He didn't say anything for a moment but seemed to be listening to the music that came from the radio. Then, "We understood from the beginning that you were a bonus, Romany. Knew your work for us could never be any kind of binding arrangement. There were certain boundaries that we just could not expect . . ."

She looked over to Sully as he brought the hot orange rosette of the car's lighter to the cigarette held between his lips. "There can't be any boundaries, Andrew. You know that as well as I do." Her voice sounded more serious than she wanted.

"Romany . . ."

"Listen, Andrew. I could have backed out of this long ago. Backed out when Sully proposed that the best way to get an inside track on the Pope was to sleep with Julian Morrow." She'd come right out with it. "I promise—I'm not doing anything I don't want to do."

He reached and pressed her hand inside his. She knew in this exact moment he was thinking of Theodor. Thinking what his best friend would feel if he knew what he'd gotten his daughter into.

"Sorry, Romany. I just wanted to make sure everything was all right with you."

"Thank you, Drew." It was the first time she'd called him that in a long time.

He smiled. Then he seemed to alter in a subtle way. Transform as she'd seen him do many times before. Deliberately he straightened his back against the car seat, neutralized the set of his face. She felt his hand loosen its grip on hers. "If we only knew how far up this forgery business goes," he said.

"I guess we'd all better pray that 'His Holiness' is just that."

She heard his dry laugh, but he didn't comment. Everyone understood that if Pope Gregory was involved, all the pieces on the board would change. That they would be playing a new and more dangerous game.

"Theodor and your mother should be here soon." He'd switched subjects. "Are you surprised that Marthe's coming?"

"You know I am, Andrew, but Daddy says she's never felt better."

"She's beautiful." His words were too soft and didn't seem to have any relationship to what they'd been talking about. She stared at his face, searching in the half darkness inside the car for some kind of clue. Then suddenly she understood. Understood something that had been so obvious all these years that it had entirely escaped her notice. She wondered if her father knew. Her mother, of course, would never have guessed. And she had to wonder if Andrew himself knew, knew that he was a little in love with Marthe Chase.

She shouldn't be analyzing her feelings about Julian Morrow's making love to her. Not when David ben Haar had just pulled out of her, was lying naked next to her in the bed. But she couldn't help herself. Her relationship with the Jesuit had been occupying center stage in her thoughts lately.

Of course her meeting with Andrew hadn't helped. But she'd certainly talked a good game. Yet the truth was she'd never been very good at casual sex. Not that going to bed with Julian could be theoretically classified as casual sex. It was part of her job. An integral part. Technically, it should at least feel like "screwing." Yet it didn't. And that was the real problem.

She felt David's warm palm rest against her stomach. In a moment she put her hand over his. She should say something, but she knew that whatever she said wouldn't come out right.

"What's wrong, Romany?"

"Nothing, David." It even sounded like a lie.

He threw his legs over the side of the bed and stood, his back to her. Even in the diffused light coming from the bath, she could see the perfect outline of his body and understood just how much of her attraction to David ben Haar had always been physical. He turned.

She smiled and sat up. "Don't move. I like looking at you."

"Romany . . ."

"But you knew that already. Please . . . don't move." Now she could hear something in her voice that signaled they were coming dangerously close to the edge. She glanced away.

"It's no good, Romany."

She turned away.

"You have to say it, Romany."

"David . . ."

He shook his head and walked over to where he'd left his jeans. He reached and pulled them on. In a moment his eyes sought her out in the semidarkness. "Not even with Becca was it as good as it is with you, Romany."

She could feel her stomach tightening in on itself.

He moved closer. "It's the priest."

"What?" The word got tangled in her throat. "No. No, David, it's not Julian. It's everything. You of all people should understand how it is."

She heard him make a grudging noise. "Yeah, I know how it is. Know how this business can eat out your insides." His green eyes flashed hard in the near blackness of the room. "But this is something different, Romany."

"Hell yes, this is different, David. Before it was just small stuff. Helping Sully out every now and then. But this—"

"This is the big time. Right, Romany. Playing with the big boys. Fucking Julian Morrow."

"How did you know that?" She hadn't meant it to, but her question sounded more like a confession.

His laugh was ugly. "I have my sources."

"What sources, David?" The tightness in her belly was turning nasty.

"You know that's privileged, Romany."

She watched his face for a moment. And then her universe shifted again. Hairs prickled on her skin. "You . . . you were in this room. You were right here in this apartment. Watching us."

"You surprised me. At the time the armoire seemed like a good place to hide."

"You son of a bitch." It was all she could manage.

"Yeah." And he smiled again, but this time there was no trace of meanness. Instead, a kind of resignation played out in his features. "You were quite convincing, Romany."

"Get out, David."

"Okay." Then he bent down and twisted her face up to his. She thought he was going to kiss her, but he just stared at her for a long moment. When he finally released her, she fell solidly against the headboard. She could hear him mumble something harsh in Hebrew as he walked out of the bedroom.

CHAPTER 27

Finding somewhere to pray in the Apostolic Palace was simple enough. But Julian Morrow preferred it here. The Church of San Francesco a Ripa was one of his favorite places in all of Rome. Perhaps his affection had much to do with the Bernini statue.

Of late the tourists had discovered the Blessed Lodovica Albertoni in droves. But Julian didn't mind.

He could easily remove himself from the distraction of feet shuffling on marble and not-so-quiet whispers, and concentrate wholly on the absolute beauty of the master's work.

His eyes lifted, seeking out the hidden window. But as always he was defeated in his search, and satisfied himself gazing at the secret play of light and shadow on the turbulent sea of robes engulfing the reclining widow.

Lodovica Albertoni, the Roman mistress who had given all her worldly goods to the poor, had been captured by Bernini in the last moments of life, when death kissed the flesh like a lover and hovered about like a lady-in-waiting. The woman's mouth was parted in some final and silent utterance of agony, her fingers tearing at her breast as if to quiet some relentless sorrow. Yet about the half-lidded eyes there was a small promise of distant peace, as though Lodovica glimpsed at the end of her terrible travail the Beatific Vision.

As always Julian was disturbed by the inherent contradictions he saw in the Bernini work. The passionate contest of flesh and spirit, the concrete and the mystical. Death was surely not the easy surrender the Christian fathers had extolled.

Thus the work gave Julian no peace, at least not in the conventional sense. Yet it reaffirmed his own spiritual struggle, holding out for him, if not solace, a firm hope. Hope that there must be victory, if indeed there was strife.

He would pray now.

He lifted his head to the Blessed Lodovica and felt eyes upon him. He gazed over his shoulder and saw the familiar tall dark figure kneeling midway down the aisle, black eyes cursing him even in the dim and sacred sanctuary.

After a moment Julian rose and went out into the bright Roman sunlight, into Piazza San Francesco d'Assisi. He took a deep breath and waited for the inevitable footfalls.

His visitor did not disappoint him.

He turned abruptly and smiled. "Monsignor Brisi, what a coincidence."

The dark eyes in the sunlight lost none of their malignancy.

"It is no coincidence, Julian Morrow."

"Oh, then I have no choice but to conclude that you have followed me to San Francesco a Ripa, Monsignor."

"I am not a stupid man, Julian Morrow. I am not amused by your sarcasm."

"A thousand apologies, Monsignor Brisi. I did not mean to be disrespectful."

"*Basta,* I will not chase you like some lap dog. I have come here to say something. I will speak it and you will listen. Then I will leave."

Julian watched red color suffuse Brisi's olive skin. Ropy veins pulsed beneath his restricting Roman collar. In the distance a siren sang, and he saw that the pigeons scurried like beggars around the monsignor's long cassock.

"I do not know what game you are playing, Julian Morrow. But it is not a game you can win."

"I don't know—"

"Do not speak it. Do not lie into my face. You know well what I speak. You may put the dagger to His Eminence's throat, or you may decide to kiss his ass. But neither will work. I say again, Julian Morrow, you will not win."

Then suddenly he smiled, perfect white teeth shining in the hot sun, and pressed closer. "You think you are so clever, Jesuit priest. Yet there are things I know of which you cannot dream." Then he bent and placed a kiss on each of Julian's cheeks.

His mouth was very warm, and Julian felt a sting of heat even as he watched Umberto Brisi move off into the distance. In his mind he saw Judas kissing Jesus, giving his rabbi the kiss of death.

.   .   .

Julian, with a string sack of groceries on his arm, was waiting for Romany at her door. He wore white shorts and a polo shirt, and his white smile shone down on her. "Hi," he said. "I hope you haven't had lunch."

"No." She came the rest of the way up the steps, fumbling in her purse for the key. "I've been out running errands all morning," she said. "I just brought home stuff for a sandwich."

"No sandwich today." He followed her into the apartment. "I'm going to fix you something Sicilian."

She heard herself laughing. "I didn't even know you could cook." She walked ahead of him into the kitchen and put her groceries down.

"There's a lot you don't know." Julian was still smiling when she turned around to face him. "Spaghettoni with olives is just one of my secrets."

"Olives, huh? Sounds good. I like anything with olives." She smiled at him. "Julian, will you excuse me for a minute?"

"Sure. I'll just get started." He had already put his bag down next to the stove. Now he got busy lining up ingredients on the counter. "Go ahead," he said to her. "I'll find whatever I need."

Still she hesitated, stopping to put her perishables away in the refrigerator. When she did leave, Julian was tying the big kitchen towel like an apron around his waist. "There's wine in the pantry," she said to him. "And wineglasses over the sink."

"I got us this." He took a bottle out of the bag.

In the bedroom she went to the mirror, but her face couldn't tell her what she felt. That was good. There was nothing there for Julian to read either. She tossed her head and ran her fingers through her hair, tousling the curls that had tightened in the outdoor heat. Her cosmetics bag was in her purse. She got out a lipstick and some blush.

In the last few days, she had talked to Julian a lot on the phone, but mostly about Arte per Pace business.

There'd been a surprising amount of early response to her letter, which kept her busy. And Julian had been commandeered by Elliot to take up the slack with Fallco and Pritisi at the site.

If Julian had seemed to pull back again the last few days, then she should have moved forward. Finding him on her doorstep just now had unaccountably thrown her. She couldn't let it. This was not a surprise visit from a lover, but an opportunity to get on with her assignment.

She finished with the makeup. And, gathering her scattered clothes from the last few days, she tossed them into the bottom of the armoire before heading back to the kitchen.

"This mine?" She picked up the glass of wine that was sitting by itself on the counter.

"Yes." Julian in his makeshift apron was cutting up tomatoes. He turned to watch her.

"It's good." She smiled. Found that she meant it, and made herself relax. "Sometimes I forget how nice the Italian whites can be. At home I seem to always buy German."

Julian was fishing in her silverware drawer, his back to her again.

"What are you doing?" She walked over.

"The olives." He'd gotten out a small paring knife and had begun removing the pits. "I'm going to throw these in the oil with the tomatoes and some seasoning." He motioned with the knife toward a skillet he had warming on the stove. "It'll cook for about ten minutes, then I'll add a little milk. You have some?"

"Right here." She went over and got him the carton from the refrigerator. "Anything else I can do?"

"Yes." He pulled her toward him, kissed her. "The parsley," he said after a moment. "Could you wash it? Chop it fine."

The parsley was sitting in a colander in the sink. "Sure," she said, and reached to turn on the tap. Not thinking about the kiss. "All of it?" she asked over her shoulder.

Julian's fingers were playing on her spine. "No, just about half will do." He let his hand drop, turned up the fire, threw garlic and some chili pepper into the oil. She dried and chopped the parsley, watched him stir in the tomatoes and the olives.

"I'm impressed," she said. "You look like you know what you're doing."

He laughed. "You haven't tasted it yet."

But when they did sit down at the table in her living room, she was still impressed. Julian was a good cook, and when they'd almost finished, she said so.

"It's only one dish," he pointed out.

"Maybe so, Julian Morrow," she teased him. "But you're just so damned good at everything."

He didn't stop smiling, but something changed in his eyes.

"Julian," she said, placing her hand over his on the table, "what you said before was right. I don't know very much about you."

Now his eyes laughed too. "What do you want to know?"

Do you know about the forgeries? Is the Pope involved? Are you? "Did you always want to be a priest?"

"No." His hand was sliding from beneath hers. She felt it grip her wrist. He was rising from his chair, pulling her up with him.

She glanced at the ruin of dishes. "Julian . . ."

She was in his arms, his hands turning her face. "Later," he said.

"I was late going into the seminary."

In the drowsy hush of evening, Romany had only just awakened. Lying on her side, half dreaming in the air-conditioned coolness of the room, she had been conscious of Julian on the bed beside her, the rhythmic comfort of his deep, even breathing. She had thought him still asleep until he spoke. Her first impulse now was to turn to him, but some instinct held her back.

"I told you I had a brother," he spoke again. "Jeremy. My twin. I went into the seminary after he died."

He stopped. She waited.

"The Jesuits had taught us in high school," he began again. "There was one Brother . . . he came to dinner with us at my parents' house sometimes in the summers. After Jeremy died, he was a friend.

"Do you know the definition of a Jesuit? He's a servant, a man who has put his complete life at the disposal of Jesus Christ. He has no needs, no desires, no responsibilities of his own. That was a life I wanted."

She fought the need to touch him. Whatever had been his reason for telling her this, she knew it was not sympathy he wanted. In the new silence that had begun to stretch, she struggled to find something safe to say.

He spoke before she did. "I'm going out of town for a couple days, Romany, leaving early in the morning."

"Where?" She turned toward him.

He lay on his side, his head propped up, supported by one elbow. Blond hair spilled into his eyes.

"Richard will be in the office to help you with anything that comes up." He hadn't answered her question.

"Julian, how did you get the APP job?"

The noise he made was a laugh, with no clue to its meaning.

"You came out of nowhere. Everybody thought Umberto Brisi was going to be Pope Gregory's appointment."

"Who's everybody?"

The blunt question took her by surprise. No wonder, she was totally winging this. *"Everybody,"* she said, as if repeating the word explained it.

He was watching her. He looked amused.

"Well, like Elliot. . . . It's not a trick question, Julian. I'm just curious."

"It was political," he said.

"Oh?"

Her inflection made it a question. Julian ignored it.

"Let me see these," he said. He was pulling the sheet from her body. Bending his head to her breasts. His blond hair was a curtain cutting off the sight but not the sensation of what he was doing.

"No, Julian. Stop." He had found out from the first how easy it was to torment her. She was trying not to laugh, trying to wriggle free, her hands pushing on his shoulders. "Julian!"

His head came up for a moment. But he was already grabbing for her wrists. He pinned them with one hand above her, flattening her knees with his body.

She was really laughing now, gasping for air. "No," she pleaded.

"Yes." The blue eyes were full of devilment. They watched her as his head moved back to her breast.

She struggled harder beneath him. "Julian!"

His mouth turned up in a smile. The free hand made a little stroking run, and her nipple stood at attention. She was lost and he knew it.

He let go of her hands.

The Roman night was warm and brown, a fuzzy kind of heat that wrapped Romany's bare shoulders like a blanket. Standing in her nightgown, she leaned upon the balcony railing, looking out to the street where Julian's blond head was already disappearing into the Alfa. In a moment the engine coughed to life, and the car swung from the curb, headed back toward Vatican City.

The air stirred, humid as breath, ruffling the loose curls at her neck. She shivered as if she were cold.

She felt a little strange. Exhausted and exhilarated. Like coming home from a party. All those hours spent with Julian in her bed. And that last time, making love to him. Sliding on top of him, she had seen the catch of pleasure in his face, had felt some larger connection. An energy that moved with him inside of her.

Great sex. So it was great sex, Romany. So what?

Julian Morrow turned her on. Or maybe it was playing spy that turned her on. The bad news was that she had learned exactly nothing.

She turned, went back through the French doors into the artificial coolness of her apartment. The dishes were still on the table. The kitchen was a mess. Julian had offered to help clean up before he left, but she had told him it was all right.

She walked back into the kitchen and poured herself a glass of wine. Rinsed the pots and dishes, and put them all in the sink to soak. She'd do the rest tomorrow.

After her bath she went to the bureau in her bedroom. In the top drawer was her good hairbrush. Her hand was on the brass pull when it froze in reaction. The strand of hair she'd left stretched between the drawer and its cabinet was gone.

Dammit! Dammit! Dammit! She pulled her hand back. Tried to think. Was it really possible? Had someone been in here?

Shit! There'd been a tell-tale on the door too. But Julian had surprised her, and she'd totally forgotten to check it. She opened the drawer now. Everything was the same as she'd left it. But what did that prove?

She walked over to the big trunk she used as a night table next to her bed. It had traveled with her from the states, complete with a false bottom where she could store all the little toys and tricks provided by Sully. It was the only place in the apartment there was anything to find. On top of it was a scarf and a glass and a lamp, and a lot of little knickknacks, all of which at least seemed perfectly undisturbed. She turned on the lamp and got down on her knees for a look.

Thank God. The hair in the corner by the brass fitting was still in its place, and so was the other strand nearer to the lock. She flopped to a seat on the carpeted floor and took a deep breath. Maybe she had overreacted. Maybe the tell-tale on the bureau drawer had just fallen off. But that was doubtful. One of the things they taught you was how to make the damn hair stick.

David? Maybe. But she didn't think so. The most likely scenario was the obvious. Julian Morrow had used his little lunch ploy to search her apartment first.

Marthe Chase sat in the big comfortable chair on the second floor of the town house. She often sat here near the window in the small parlor, especially at night when pain would not let her sleep. The chair, in which she rested as best she could, had not been reupholstered in nearly a dozen years, and yet the needlepoint cushions retained a strange newness, as if the embroidered fabric and the padding beneath could manage to absorb but little impression from her body.

She had been here for hours tonight, listening to the drifting choirs of weekend traffic, watching in unlit corners where memories like ghosts struggled for form in the whorls of moonlight and dust. Now it was nearly morning, and the room hung poised in that slow urgent moment before sunrise. The long cool heartbeat of the world, which was neither darkness nor light.

From somewhere an image came to her. A perfect picture of Romany at four glanced through the kitchen window of the house in Chevy Chase. Her daughter was laughing, her penny-bright head thrown back against the wind that streamed an iridescent trail of bubbles from the green plastic wand in her hand. Romany had thrived in the beautiful white colonial that Theodor had bought for them. But Marthe herself had never been able to love the house. The rooms, too big, had made her feel exposed.

She had cherished instead that first apartment rented after their marriage, the tiny kitchen where on Sundays Theodor prepared for her the Russian favorites taught to him by his mother. It was on a Sunday that she'd told him about the baby. She could smell the cabbage steaming even now, could still feel the happiness blazing out of him like the heat from the old gas oven.

He'd been bending, carefully sliding a braided loaf

into the stove, when she'd mumbled the words softly to his back. She'd known in the way that his shoulders moved that he'd heard her. He'd nearly slammed the oven door in his haste to see her face. *Marthe, a child.* And he'd grabbed her laughing, his big hands leaving huge floury prints. And still laughing, he had dragged her to a mirror to see for herself the mess he had made of her dress.

She'd laughed with him then, wanting his baby, wanting to share his happiness. Yet her pregnancy had filled her with a fear she could not explain. Not to Theodor, nor to the doctor who smiled and said that everything was fine. Only as her belly swelled with the undeniable reality of her child, did she finally have the words. Something would be wrong. Something terrible was going to be wrong with her baby.

But Romany had been born whole and healthy and perfect. And holding her daughter for the first time, she had felt such a surge of love and fierce protectiveness. No one was ever going to hurt her child. And that had become her new terror. That a moment's guard let down, and something bad could happen yet to Romany.

Now Romany was grown, and she was still afraid. Afraid that love too openly expressed could tempt some unknown power. Marthe did not ponder or brood so much as hold herself open to the vague and piercing revelations of her heart. Now, at this moment, she was seeing Helena Klimpt's face again, hearing her story. And suddenly she understood that the baffling incompleteness and the formless terror she had really always felt had not so much at all to do with Romany. The child for whom she'd most feared was herself.

With a sigh of resignation, she shifted in the chair, trying to ease the throbbing in her thigh. On the table beside her were a glass of water and the small amber army of plastic containers that ruled her nights and days. The pain pills were not scheduled for nearly another hour, but she took them now. She needed to get some sleep. She wanted to begin her packing this afternoon, and Theodor must find her beside him when he woke.

Slowly she stood, beginning the slow journey back to her bed. Some things at least were clearer. The German woman had given her fear a form. And now, at its end, she must make somekkind of justice for her life. She had only a name and a city. But the city was Rome, the one place to which Theodor would bring her without question. God or something darker must mean for her not to fail. There would be records somewhere, and she would search until she found them. And when she found the man, she would know then what to do.

CHAPTER 28

The bed he slept in was fit for a Borgia, but not at all out of place in the rooms he'd been given by the Pope. Romany, all in black, felt like a crow on the golden brocade of the coverlet. She was imagining Julian, coming here from her bed to this bed last night.

Who was Julian Morrow? That was still the question.

He was her lover. He was a priest. Propositions that should be exclusive, but weren't. Very probably he was the person who had made an unsuccessful search of her apartment yesterday morning.

What was now also clear to her from the photos spread before her on the quilt was that Julian knew about the forgeries. The evidence was a group of pictures she had found among his papers—detailed copies of portions of *The Deposition*. There was nothing written on them to indicate that he knew they were pictures of a fake. But despite that, she was certain. Julian Morrow was perfectly aware that the Caravaggio was a copy.

The question remained whether he had just innocently stumbled onto this fact. But how, if he were not an expert in art? The copy was far too good for an expert, let alone an amateur, to easily detect. No, his knowing about the forgery could not be innocent.

On the table next to the bed was another photograph, framed. She picked it up, careful not to disturb any layer of dust on the glass. Julian smiled up at her, a younger Julian, college age, standing on the banks of the Seine with Notre Dame as a backdrop.

Julian in Paris. What exactly had he been doing there? And wasn't it a little odd? Men didn't normally display photographs of themselves. And then she understood. Of course. The young man in the picture was Jeremy.

Jeremy Morrow. The dead twin. She remembered Julian's voice from yesterday, *I went into the seminary after he died.* The words had sounded like a confession. But a confession of what?

She set the picture back into its place. Opened the drawer in the table. Pens and pencils. Odds and ends. The tag end of a notepad. With the flat of a pencil, she grayed the topmost page. And just like in the movies, writing came up. Stark white against the graphite. Airline reservations made for this morning—a flight number and time. The name of a hotel in Fribourg.

She looked at her watch. Sully had once explained the problems in putting a man on Morrow inside the Vatican grounds, not to mention the impossibility of getting a tap on his phone. If there had been time to alert him yesterday that Julian was leaving town, he surely would have had him followed.

As if it hadn't registered, she looked again at her watch. A decision had to be made. She was not completely finished here. An outside chance existed there could be more to find.

She got up from the bed. Gathered the photos quickly and placed them back carefully in the cabinet in which she had found them. Her mind was made up. With a little luck it was going to be as easy getting out of here unseen as it had been breaking in. Still, she hoped it was the last time she'd have to dress as a nun.

Romany unfastened her seat belt and settled back. Through the window the late-evening sun skittered and bounded off clouds. She pulled the shade down to half-mast.

If she had any luck, she wouldn't be too late to pick up Julian's trail in Fribourg. Though he did have a twelve-hour jump on her, she knew where he was staying. If she had to, she would just camp out across from his hotel and wait for him.

What in the hell was he doing in Switzerland anyway? She had to laugh, thinking that this latest disappearance was just another piece of the puzzle that was Father Julian Morrow. And to her growing store, she now had to add the photographs of the Caravaggio she'd found in his apartment. Curiouser and curiouser.

What did it mean that Julian knew about the forgeries? And why had he been searching her apartment? And why was he screwing her, compromising his priesthood? And apparently without guilt.

He had told her about his problem with women as if that meant he intended that nothing should happen between them. Yet what had been going on for the last week hardly looked like he was trying to keep any kind of rein on himself. Her fatal charm? Love? Hardly. The whole thing circled back to one point and one point only —Julian Morrow was guilty. Guilty of something. She was sure of it.

CHAPTER 29

The weather had turned queer. The temperature had dropped overnight, and there was still a crisp chill in the air. Romany had packed only a light sweater and was forced to buy an overpriced parka in the hotel gift shop. It was the only place open when she left that morning before dawn.

She wasn't going to take any chances on Julian giving her the slip. She'd done some sleuthing after she'd arrived, and knew he'd checked in yesterday afternoon, had had room service for dinner, and was now in his room asleep. Something she very much wished she were doing.

Although she detested "jock" type sportswear, she had to credit the windbreaker with pulling double duty. It kept her warm enough as she sat in the rented compact across from Julian's hotel, and it certainly helped to augment her not so clever disguise. The wig was a mess, and she was glad to pull the parka's hood over her head.

She finished the last of the airline peanuts. Next time she had to plan a little better. It was eight-fifteen and she was starving. God knew when she'd be able to eat again.

Even though her primary focus the past several hours had been Julian Morrow, David ben Haar lurked just beneath the surface of her thoughts. Always before there had been so much distance between her and David, both physical and emotional, that there were never any real disagreements. But now that they were together again, had gotten closer, things were so much more complicated.

She shook her head. Dammit, she'd been wrong to get so angry with him. After all, what should he have done when she and Julian showed up at her apartment?

"Hi, Father Morrow, I'm David ben Haar. The Mossad. You've heard of us." She knew he'd done the only sane thing he could do.

Yet thinking about David hiding in the armoire, watching her and Julian . . . She groaned.

And just what had it been that David said before he'd left her apartment? Her Hebrew was terrible, and he had been halfway out the door when he'd mumbled the words. Something about how she couldn't possibly know how different everything was between them now. Different? How?

Things were beginning to come to life around the hotel. A middle-aged couple was checking out, and she could see the doorman helping a bellman load luggage into a taxi. Even from a distance she could tell the husband was aggravated. Something about the mountain of luggage. No doubt the same scene was replayed at every departure.

The fussing over the baggage almost caused her to miss him coming out of the hotel. He was wearing a pair of slacks with a shirt and a pullover sweater. Obviously Julian knew something about the vagaries of Swiss weather she didn't. The taxi with the couple had finally pulled away, and she saw him speak to the doorman. The man nodded and disappeared into a small alleyway flanking the hotel.

Julian whistled as he waited. She'd never seen him do that, and she thought it oddly out of character. But what did she know, really, when it came to Julian Morrow?

In a few minutes the doorman drove up the hotel's circular drive in a bright-red Alfa Romeo. The car was almost a dead ringer for the one he drove in Rome. She watched as he walked around to the driver's side, tipped the doorman, and got into the car.

Luckily her car was pointed in the right direction, and the bright red car would be easy enough to follow. She glanced down at the fuel gauge. Full tank. With luck she wouldn't need to fill up. Of course she had no way of knowing that, since she had no idea just where Julian Morrow was taking her.

Outside the city the roads were little more than small byways with practically no traffic. She'd have to maintain a reasonable distance, or he might just pick up her tail.

She settled back, pulling off the hood. The wig and dark glasses should do it. She rolled down her window. She hadn't slept much, and the cool air felt good.

They hadn't gone very far when she lost sight of him as he rounded a curve. She checked her speedometer. She never had gotten a handle on the metric system. But even by her less than perfect calculations, Julian was doing well over eighty miles per hour. She'd have to step on it to keep up.

She rounded the curve. The Alfa was dead ahead. Then suddenly the car made a sharp left, disappearing into what seemed a stand of thick trees. She accelerated, then slowed.

Down a sliver of a dirt road, she caught sight of the red rear end of the sportscar. One thing was certain: unless you knew where you were going, there was no way to spot this turn-off. She followed, grateful for the cloud of dust as his car churned up the road ahead.

She guessed they'd gone about five miles when the dense growth broke. Beyond, the land had been cleared, manicured. And far to the right stood a chateau on a rise. She'd visited Chenonceau, most of the other chateaux in the Loire, and this one was as beautiful as any she'd ever seen. The perfect embodiment of every fairy-tale castle she'd ever imagined.

She had stopped the car just as the dirt road met a paved drive leading up to the chateau. Julian had already parked his car near the front and was walking toward the entrance. She watched for a moment longer, as the sun, gathering steam, ignited the smooth surfaces of the structure. In the distance she saw topiaries. Heard pigeons coo.

She crossed over onto the pavement and followed

the drive to the entrance. A small discreet sign stood to the right. A bed of bright flowers bobbed around it. *Le Centre de Postcure de Sainte Cecile.* A sanitarium.

She looked across to where Julian had parked the Alfa. Turning her car into the parking lot, she pulled into a space several yards away, alongside a large Volvo sedan. She'd have to give him some time to get wherever he was going.

Julian Morrow visiting a sanitarium. This was certainly an interesting development. An act of charity on the part of the good Jesuit? She thought not. Why fly all the way to Switzerland? There were plenty of hospitals in Rome where he could practice the corporeal works of mercy. No, Julian Morrow had come to Fribourg on a specific mission, to see a particular person. But whom? A doctor? A patient?

She glanced at her watch. He'd been in the chateau at least fifteen minutes. That should be enough time. She got out of the car and removed the parka. She gazed around. The place certainly seemed peaceful enough. Almost deserted.

She ran her fingers through the wig. Smoothed her lipstick. Realigned the strap of her shoulder bag, and walked toward the chateau.

Coming in from the bright sunshine, she took a moment to readjust to the gloom inside. Her ears pricked at the silence. She caught herself tiptoeing as she moved toward the small reception area. A pretty young woman, reminiscent of the put-together girls one saw in the Paris shops, sat behind a desk working on a file.

"Pardon." Romany heard herself whisper.

The girl smiled, stood, walked to the counter. *"Oui, mademoiselle.* May I help you?"

"I certainly hope so. I am trying to locate the mother of a good friend. I'm almost positive she said her mother was a patient here at St. Cecile's."

"I know most of the patients here, mademoiselle. What is the name of your friend's mother?"

"Moncel. Andrea Moncel."

"Moncel, *mademoiselle?* We have no patient with the name of Moncel at St. Cecile. Perhaps she is in the public hospital."

"No, I am sure she is in a private sanitarium. Would you please check your records? Maybe she was once here and . . ."

"I will be happy to check for you, *mademoiselle.* If you will please excuse me, I will have to look at the files in the main office."

"Merci, merci beaucoup."

The young woman smiled again, and Romany watched as she moved back toward her desk and exited through a small door at the rear of the reception area.

For the first time Romany looked down at the registry she had been fingering all the while she'd been talking to the receptionist. She glanced over her shoulder. There was still no traffic into or out of St. Cecile's. She turned back to the book. Julian's name was last on today's log. She moved her finger across the page. Colleen Shaunessy. Room 230.

Julian had visited Colleen Shaunessy for a little over forty-five minutes. And now Romany followed him down another country road that twisted and turned through forest.

Switzerland had always impressed Romany as a country that was almost too perfect. Almost artificial in its pretty postcard beauty. She had hoped for more. Had always yearned for some unexpected and hidden mystery beneath the happy facade. Julian Morrow was certainly granting her wish.

She watched the landscape move across her windshield and remembered one of her favorite books. *The Animals' Ball* was the story of a little girl who had been put to bed, and because she could not sleep, crept down the stairs to discover a shocking sight. Her home, taken over by animals. Wild animals who walked on their hind legs like humans, sported beautiful costumes, fanciful masks.

The little girl had moved slowly down the stairs to get a closer look. In the living room a masquerade had begun, and as the first haunting strains of music swirled about her, the child became frightened. What would her parents do with wild forest animals dancing about in their home? It was at that moment that the child spied her mother, in the very center of the room, dancing with a tall handsome wolf. She heard their giddy laughter, saw kisses. Could this be? The little girl rubbed her eyes. What was real? What was not?

Romany smiled. The ultimate questions. And who had the answers? She thought no one had. And until these last few weeks, answers to questions had not been important to her. Now they were everything. What was real? What was not?

Julian had turned down a side road. She followed, slowing as she saw him drive ahead to a large chalet. There was nothing else she could do but pull off to the side and walk the distance to the house if she was to get a closer look.

She backed up a few yards, found a level shoulder, and parked. She hoped no one else would be coming down the road on the way to the house and spot her car.

She decided to forgo the wig, but kept on the sunglasses. She left her purse behind under the seat, pocketed the car keys, and got out. She walked about a hundred yards before she found a good hiding place—a clump of shrubbery.

Julian was getting something out of the trunk of the Alfa. From the brightly colored paper and ribbons, she could see that he'd unloaded a stack of presents. Suddenly a young voice cried, *"Mon oncle Julian. Il est arrivé."*

Then as quickly the voice had form, as a small boy came bounding down the steps of the house. Bright red curls bounced around his head, and chubby hands balled into fists as he ran toward Julian. *"Mon oncle Julian,"* the child squealed, *"mon oncle Julian."*

Gina was tired and her feet hurt, yet she could not bring herself to sit. That she preferred to be standing was possibly a reaction to the salon's museumlike formality, which contrasted so sharply with her simple linen sheath—crisp and sexy when she'd put it on this morning, damp and decidedly wrinkled now with the sultry heat and a day spent before her keyboard at the offices of Arte per Pace. Yet the desire to remain upon her feet was more likely atavistic. In the lair of the Palazzo Rozze, Gina di Lorenzo seemed always poised for flight.

This was not, however, a picture of herself that Gina would ever consider. In her own eyes she was clever and tough—the only one of her family to escape the poverty in which di Lorenzos had lived and bred and died for generations. Deciding to be bored with the paintings that encrusted the walls, Gina walked to a gilt-frame mirror to inspect herself instead.

Despite what the long day had done to her dress, she was pleased to find that her makeup at least was intact. She was admiring the natural wave of blond hair that curved over one eyebrow, when Count Sebastiano appeared within the mirrored room.

Gina always took careful note of his clothing, having calculated that just one of his suits cost more than what she made in several months. Today the suit was navy with the dull luster of silk. It looked perfect and unwrinkled, as if still on a mannequin in the shop. She doubted that Sebastiano would ever perspire even outside the coolness of the villa. She could not imagine he ever took a shit. It was a wonder he had a reflection.

He did not greet her. He never acknowledged her presence at once, as if she were of such insignificance that many minutes were required before he could register her existence. She watched in the glass as he took his seat on one of the brocaded sofas.

A servant followed with a bottle of wine, poured two glasses, and left. This was new. She had never been offered anything to drink. The Count, however, continued to ignore her, lifted a glass, and sipped.

She wanted to sit down now, and she wanted the wine. God knew that she could use it. Why should she continue to stand here tired and thirsty, when common sense screamed that she had only to turn and walk across the carpet?

But Gina di Lorenzo had not gotten to where she was without instinct, and instinct warned that this absurd pantomime was really a kind of test. She had been in Rome for years now, and was sure she had heard every ridiculous and contradictory rumor about who or what Klaus Sebastiano really was. She had believed little of this gossip, but suddenly she knew absolutely that the Count was far more than an infamous old eccentric. This game was real, and dangerous. In the moment when his one eye met hers inside the glass, she could feel the chill in her heart.

"*Buon giorno,* Gina."

She found she couldn't speak.

"Come and sit." His lips smiled.

She turned at last, walked to him, sat down on the facing sofa. The blue eye followed hers to the glass of untouched wine. The cold gaze offered nothing.

"You have something to report, Gina?"

"Signorina Chase was not in her office today." Amazingly the words came out, her voice the same as always. "She called this morning to say she would not be coming in. Maybe not even tomorrow. She asked me to tell Signor Elliot Peters that she would explain it to him later."

"She was calling from her apartment?"

"No, from out of the country. The operator who connected us was Swiss."

"Switzerland." She watched his mouth stretching out the word as if he could taste the syllables.

"You knew nothing about this trip?" he asked her.

"I listen in to all her calls. She made no reservations from the office."

He was nodding. "An unexpected trip, perhaps. Did Signorina Chase seem upset or anxious?"

Gina paused, considering her answer. "No, not that. She just seemed in a hurry."

"And the last two weeks, Gina?"

"Nothing," she shrugged. "There've been a lot of letters to get out, a lot for me to type. She's been working a lot with Father Morrow."

"You have not yet met this priest?"

"I saw him once," she said. "She goes mostly to his office. But a couple of . . . Fridays ago, I think it was, he came to meet with her and Signor Peters. He's not much like a priest."

"What does that mean, 'not much like a priest,' Gina?"

The crack had come out of her mouth offhandedly, without her thinking. *Stupido!* she berated herself. One thing was sure. It was safer to stick to the facts than to try to justify her opinions.

"Gina . . . ?"

"He didn't wear a cassock." *That was a fact.* "And he's American," she said. "Good-looking. He's . . ." She allowed herself another shrug. "Like a movie star."

At least he smiled. A real smile. And suddenly she had a picture of what Klaus Sebastiano had once been years ago. Pretty old man, she had always called him in her mind. It had been almost a term of derision, as if the fact that he was still so handsome made him somehow less. But now she imagined him young. The white hair— of course it had been blond. And the eyes, two of them then, so blue. *Bello uomo* . . . Unaccountably, her fear of him increased.

"And this meeting? You were there?" The question brought her back. His smile was gone.

"No, not in her office," she answered him. "But I left the intercom open. I heard almost everything." Heard, sì, but not always understood. Her English was good, but Americans just talked too fast sometimes. But that she didn't tell him.

"Excellent, Gina."

"They talked a lot about some problem with the contractors," she continued. "Then they mentioned your name."

She watched him as closely as she dared. But there was no reaction, no extra note of interest. He simply continued to stare at her, waiting. His gaze was like his voice, which seldom changed pitch whether asking her about Signorina Chase or talking about the weather. Strangely the mildness of his tone seemed to magnify the implication of a threat. You never could guess where you stood.

"You had sent flowers to Signorina Chase." She hastened to close in the silence. "Signor Peters commented to Father Morrow that she had obviously made a good impression on you. Signorina Chase was . . . I think she felt they were teasing her. She said: 'He enjoys making gestures.' That was when Signor Peters's secretary called for him, and I had to close the line. I was afraid Signorina Chase might notice then if my light stayed on. But the meeting broke up after that."

"How do they react to Father Morrow? Signor Peters and Signorina Chase?"

"React . . . ?" The word seemed to die.

"I'm *asking* for your impressions, Gina."

So much for sticking to the facts. What good was caution, anyway, if he could read what was in her mind? Could feed on her fear like a snake?

"Signor Peters seems impressed," she answered him.

"And Signorina Chase?"

"She likes him too. I think she's glad the Pope picked an American."

She had not lied. She had simply not said all of what

she thought. That Romany Chase liked Father Julian Morrow more than just a little.

The Count Sebastiano was staring through her now. She couldn't guess what he was thinking.

"I'm so sorry that you didn't care for your wine, Gina," the voice said when he spoke. "Maybe next time we could try another vintage. Something red."

When she stood to leave, the high heels hurt more than ever. Still, it was hard for Gina not to run.

Romany scarcely breathed as she flattened herself against the wall of the small linen closet. So far so good, but she wasn't about to press her luck. There was still too much activity on the second floor to try for a go at room 230. Through a small seam around the molding of the door, she'd been watching white-robed nuns move like wraiths on silent, unseen feet up and down the long darkened corridor.

Within the blackness of the closet, she was unable to see her watch, but she knew it was well past the witching hour, and that Julian was already back home in the Vatican.

Silence. She pressed her eye closer to the opening near the door. Empty. At least what she could see of the hallway. She squeezed the knob and cracked the door wider in order to get a clearer view of the corridor. Her limited vision had proved accurate. The floor was deserted. She opened the door and slipped outside into the hall.

Room 224. 226. 228. Room 230. She glanced once more down the long dark passage, as if by doing so she was somehow protecting herself against detection. What she would actually do if she was caught, she had no idea. Still empty. She pressed against the door leading into room 230 and watched it give against her weight.

There was a nightlight burning, and almost instantly she detected the scent of flowers. A large vase of white roses, already showing signs of decay, stood by the bed.

Petals littered the tabletop, were scattered about the floor.

Then a stirring in the bed. A soft moan. And Romany watched her own feet as she took her first steps inside the room. Slowly her eyes shifted to the figure lying beneath the starchy crispness of hospital linen.

Colleen Shaunessy was beautiful. A child. And not a child. Young, but not young. Her tongue worked the flesh at her lips; a small blue vein throbbed in her temple. She moved a pale hand to her hair—long, curling, darkly red, flung like wings across the ghostly pallor of the pillow.

Then a word. A single word, unintelligible at first. But repeated, again and again, until Romany at last was able to make sense of it.

"Michael, Michael," Colleen Shaunessy called. Called a thousand times in her sleep, cried out a thousand times to a man who wasn't there.

CHAPTER 30

Had she been dreaming she'd gone to the dead drop to leave Sully a message? No. No, she'd done that. Right after she'd gotten off the plane. And when was that? Romany squinted at the digital readout on the clock. Almost ten. She threw a pillow over her face and moaned. Just five hours ago.

Apparently Gina had gotten the message she'd left on her machine, because no one had phoned from the office. She uncovered her face and did a cat's stretch under the sheets. God, she was tired. But what she couldn't decide was whether it was mental or physical. Probably a combination. A lot had happened in the last forty-eight hours.

Julian Morrow. The name played like an old forty-five record in her brain, a forty-five with a very long scratch. The background music for images of Caravaggio photographs, a redheaded boy, and the woman she'd found at St. Cecile's. Any connections? The forgery operation and the trip to Switzerland? Apples and oranges. At least on the surface. The boy and the woman? Possibly. The red hair was certainly an obvious link.

A loud knock on the door shut down the projector, yanked the needle off the record. Elliot? She didn't think that too likely. Elliot had enough on his schedule to keep three people busy, and he wasn't inclined to play nursemaid lately.

"Coming . . . ," she mumbled, as she climbed out of bed and threw on a robe. She hadn't even bothered to put on a gown this morning.

When she finally managed the door, she saw Julian Morrow, dressed in the black suit of Roman Catholic priesthood, standing on her steps.

She spoke first. "Julian . . ."

"Are you all right, Romany?" He was staring at her, with not quite a frown on his face. Some part of her brain noted he hadn't even said "hi."

"Yes, of course. I just slept in this morning." What *was* he doing here?

"I'm sorry I woke you. This is a bad time. I'll check with you later." He was already back-pedaling down the steps.

"I was up, Julian."

"No, you go on back to sleep."

"I'm not going back to sleep. Please . . . come in." She opened the door wider.

"I feel kind of foolish." He stumbled over the words as he made his way back up the steps and into her apartment. She thought he looked entirely too young for the severe black clericals.

"I phoned you several times . . ." He was talking again, not any more effectively than before. She watched his face. God, was he blushing? That's ridiculous, Romany. Anyway, who could tell with the tan?

"I haven't talked to Gina this morning . . . ," she

said. It sounded like an apology, and he seemed to be waiting for some further explanation. "I . . . I was out all day yesterday. Up too late . . ." Now she stumbled. *God.* "Hey, I could use some coffee. Want some?" She moved toward the kitchen.

"Okay. That'll be fine." She watched him debate between the sofa and a chair. He finally decided on the sofa.

What was he doing here? She started the Mr. Coffee, trying to distract herself by recalling how difficult it had been to track down this particular model in Rome. How she'd been delirious with joy when she'd finally found it in a little out-of-the-way shop. *What was he doing here?*

"Be ready in a sec," she called out.

"No rush."

Now what? Walk back into the living room . . .

"As I was saying, I was out all day yesterday." She made her voice chatty. She sat down in a chair. "I think I told you my parents are coming over for a visit."

"Theodor and Marthe." He'd remembered their names.

"Yes. Well, I think they're going to stay for a while. Dad's doing some kind of research. Etruscans." She was reaching, trying with little success to fill the silence between them. "At any rate, Mom couldn't bear it in a hotel all that time. So . . ."

"You're looking for a house?"

"Or a large apartment."

"Maybe I can help." His voice sounded impossibly sweet, sincere.

She shook her head. "Thanks, but I think I located something yesterday. It's just about perfect too. There's even a small garden."

"Sounds wonderful." He hadn't stopped staring at her. And there was still that expectant look in his face, and something else, something she didn't want to acknowledge. Julian Morrow knew she was lying.

She looked away, began to fiddle with the nap of the

towel she'd brought in from the kitchen. Damn, this was harder than she thought.

"Is there something wrong, Romany?" Sweet words again.

"Wrong? No, no, nothing's wrong." She'd glanced up, thinking how totally unconvincing she sounded.

Suddenly he was kneeling, kneeling on the floor at her feet. For an absurd instant she thought he looked very much like a man ready to propose. Then she felt one of his hands pressing hers together, a light touch on her cheek. She looked into his smile.

"Julian . . ."

"It's okay, Romany. It's okay. . . ."

She found it impossible to separate his words from his breath as his mouth closed over hers. She knew she should have questioned how easy it was to just let him kiss her, touch her breasts, carry her into the bedroom. And she should have asked why she wanted it so much, wanted him so much. Of course, she could have simply told herself that she was doing what was expected of her. Doing her job. But like so many other things she'd said and done lately, it would have been a lie.

The Mezanotte to Romany seemed even more cave-like than before, the wavering candles like tiny Neolithic fires. Sully's cigarette decaying in the ashtray sent signals in stuttering smoke.

"Okay, Romany," he was saying, "let's go over again what you've told me. Take everything step by step. You say that Morrow knows about the forgeries. What do you think that means?"

"It means he came into APP already aware of the Cardinal's operation." She shifted backward in the chair, reaching for her wineglass.

"Maybe." Sully shrugged. "But Morrow's sharp. And he's there at the museum every day. Are you *that* sure he couldn't have just sniffed out what was going on?"

"It's too quick," she said without hesitation. She was through being defensive with Sully.

"Okay," Sully answered. "I'll buy that. The question then is how did he find out."

"I have no idea."

"Is he free-lance?" Sully was pushing. "Or working for someone else?"

She felt herself frown. "More questions."

"There are always more questions, Romany." Sully took up his cigarette, dragging on it hard. "That's just the way this business is," he said. "The more you find out, the more you find out you don't know." He blew out a thick stream of smoke.

"What do *you* think, Sully?"

"About Morrow?" Now he smiled. "You know, it's weird," he said, "but I can't get a fix on him either. My gut usually tells me things, but on this one . . ." He was watching her closely. "I blamed that on you, Romany."

"On me?"

"Yeah, on your being an amateur. I figured that was what was making things confused."

"But you don't think that now?"

"Naahh, Morrow's just a strange one. And his being a Jesuit . . . it just fucks things up worse." Sully had exchanged the cigarette for the glass of liquor in front of him. "You did a good job, getting into his place. Following him."

"Thanks," she said, "but I didn't find out much. Things just got more mixed up. And I don't know what to think about the woman and the boy."

"Yeah. Well, I'll get somebody right to work on that. In the meantime, you need to be careful."

"Why, because he searched my apartment?"

"Yes."

"You think it means . . ."

"I think it means you've got to be careful." He drained the rest of the Scotch.

"I am careful, Sully."

"I know that. And it's good that Morrow didn't find

anything in your apartment. Most probably he was just doing the basics."

"Checking me out?"

"Yeah. He just wants to be sure you're nothing more than you seem. Reassure him, Romany."

"I will."

The cigarette was down to the filter now. Sully went for one last puff before stubbing it out in the ashtray. "I'm going to give you a number." He got out a pen. "Memorize this now." He wrote on the inside of a matchbook. "This is your cut-out," he said. "You call her, she gets in touch with me. It's faster than the drop, but use her only in an emergency. Like if Morrow decides again that he's going out of town. I can have someone put on him immediately."

When she was sure that she had it she tore up the matchbook. Put the pieces in the ashtray and burned them. When she looked up, Sully was looking back, grinning.

"Sunday," he said, "you got into his place dressed as a nun?"

"That's what I said, Sully. It's busy inside the Vatican on a Sunday. I wanted to make sure no one noticed I was there."

"As a nun," he repeated.

"Something wrong with that, Sully?" She worked to keep her voice neutral.

"Not a thing, Sister Romany." The grin got wider. "I just wish I had been there to see it."

CHAPTER 31

"Gina," Romany spoke into the intercom, "could you come in here when you have a minute?"

"*Sì*, Signorina Chase."

Romany sighed. Why did her secretary always sound like that with her? So precise and cold and . . . un-Italian.

Gina di Lorenzo had not been her choice, of course, had already been hired and in place when Romany had arrived in Rome. She knew she had only to ask, and Elliot would authorize a replacement. But she didn't want to do that. Gina was fine, except for that hint of attitude.

Still, Romany was human. She liked to be liked. And she'd found herself more than once lately trying to imagine what she might have done to alienate the woman. She could swear that there was nothing. Gina just didn't like her, and that was that.

There was the expected tap on the door.

"Come in," she said.

Gina walked in, notepad in hand, her mouth working on a strange pout that seemed to be an effort not to smile. "*Grazie,*" she said. ". . . for the flowers."

"Oh." Romany made a throwaway motion with her hand. "I didn't know they'd come."

"They're beautiful." Gina did smile now, her mouth giving up in a bloom of fuchsia lipstick. "I like lilies." Her voice was almost shy.

"Well, great." Romany smiled back. "I thought they'd look good on your desk. And you deserve a little something special, Gina . . . my leaving you in the lurch like that."

Gina's glance skittered away. Already retreating, she gave an indifferent shrug before she took the chair that fronted Romany's desk.

Romany held on to her smile, determined not to let her frustration show. The flowers had been a thank you, not a bribe.

Gina sat waiting, canted sideward in the chair, the notepad poised in her lap. The blond hair hung in a crescent against her downturned cheek. At least it hid the hardness in her eyes.

"No dictation, Gina," Romany said mildly. "I just need you to fill me in on anything that's happened."

". . . Excuse me, Ms. Chase." One of the receptionists stuck her head in at the door.

"What is it, Natalie?"

"This just came for you." The woman walked in with what looked like a present. "The messenger insisted we give it to you immediately."

"Is he waiting for a reply?" Romany took the package from her hand.

"No, I think he just wanted to make sure you got it. I recognized him; he's the same man who delivered the invitations that time from Count Sebastiano."

Igor. Romany remembered Linda's appellation for the man. Her first stupid reaction had been that the gift had come from Julian. "Thank you, Natalie." She put the box down on the desk. She didn't want an audience when she opened it. Except that Gina was still there and watching, with an expectant curiosity on her face.

Oh, why not? Romany reached in a drawer for her scissors.

The box was not very large, but the wrappings were elaborate—rich gold foil with a burgundy satin bow. She opened the card first.

"How odd," she said aloud.

"What is it?"

Romany looked up. Gina's expression was almost apprehensive.

"I don't know," she said with a sort of laugh. "It's part of a famous quote in German. But he's changed it. *Zwei Seelen und ein Gedanke.* That's what it should be. Two souls with but a single thought," she translated.

"But what this says is something more like two souls with but a single form." She tossed the card on the desk. "It's signed, Klaus. Do you know the Count?"

"No," Gina said. She made a moue of distaste that might have been designed to cover some stronger emotion. "Everybody in Rome knows about him," she said now. "He's cuckoo . . . you know, strange." Her eyes went back to the package.

The package. Romany picked up the scissors and snipped through the ribbon. Folded the paper back. The box inside was black velvet. It did not look new.

"My God!" She had opened the catch to a flash of emeralds and diamonds. A necklace, totally lavish. Not quite an antique, but old. "What on earth can he be thinking? I can't accept this." She turned the box to Gina. "Look."

But her secretary's face was a blank now, as if she too were scrambling to understand what such a gift could mean. Romany snapped the box shut. Damn Klaus Sebastiano. She didn't want to have to think of this kind of foolishness now. Not on top of everything else.

"It's getting late, Gina," she said, looking at her watch. "Why don't we wait till after lunch for you to catch me up." And deciding that she had better ask Elliot to help her with this mess, she locked the box away.

Friedrich rubbed the loofah harder against his skin. Milky-white flesh bloomed rosy-pink. He watched in renewed fascination as his hands made large circles over the cage of muscles at his abdomen. His body was still beautiful. His penis, when fully erected, still rose straight till it flattened neatly against his belly. And his testicles had remained firm, nesting like marbles inside his crotch, nothing like the baggage that dangled between the thighs of most old men. Touching himself as he did now, rubbing the loofah harder, he imagined Michelangelo must have felt the same energy as he wrestled perfect form from stone.

He reached forward and brushed the mirror once more with a towel, sweeping clean the second, lighter layer of steam that had concealed his reflection. He moved in closer and set aside the towel, allowing the loofah to slip from his other hand to the floor. Slowly, in another precise exercise, he traced the sharp angles of his face like a man who'd just finished a shave—jawline, cheekbone, the bridge of his nose, testing the taut column of tissue and cord at his throat. Then he stepped back and contemplated. Not his own image, but another that was just as photographically precise inside his brain.

Her throat was slightly tawny from too much sun, but still unlined, gracefully supporting the uninterrupted oval of her head. At first, he'd mourned the loss of the hair, but not any longer. He'd grown accustomed to the rather androgynous quality the new style had given her.

He closed his eyes, imagining the cold hard stones chilling, constraining the carotid pulse at her exposed neck. Yes, he would have given half his worldly treasures to have been there when Romany Chase opened his gift.

His gift. His gift that had lain unopened for so many years. Lise's gift, put away, gathering must and memories. But no more. No longer to be cheated. Finally he'd found someone worthy of the emeralds, and Lise's betrayal would at last lose some of its sting.

Betrayal. That was the correct word for what Lise had done to him. Though she had never been able to see her sin. Never understood her transgression. Perhaps the whole of it was nothing more than the gods teaching him a lesson, reminding him of the imperfection of nature. For despite her completely unearthly beauty, his Lise was stupid.

He moved out from the bath into his bedroom, glanced at the robe that Rupert had laid out upon his bed. Such beautiful things were his, and though he relished the caress of smooth silk on bare flesh, he would forgo the dressing gown tonight. He would enjoy instead the sensation of his exposed ass upon the springy cushion of a chair, the pawing of the soles of his feet across the woolly nap of Persian carpet, the meeting of the tip of his sternum to the acute edge of his writing desk. Tonight he would keep to his nakedness, shed the stricture of layers of clothing that daily encased his body like mummy's wrappings. Tonight he would be free as he remembered his Lise's betrayal.

Like many sons of German aristocrats, young Friedrich had ridden the surging tide of Hitler's Nazism at its crest. He had supposed his reactionary contemporaries found some political rationale in allying themselves with the new right, staffing key military positions, manning critical bureaucratic posts. He, however, had been simply looking to cut the best deal.

Sieg heil-ing and boot-clicking had seemed small tokens measured against the retention of family wealth and social status. And true to his breed, class-conscious Friedrich had regarded Adolf Hitler and his band of goose-stepping boys as nothing more than bourgeois swine to be merely tolerated.

In the beginning Friedrich had reveled in the pomp and circumstance of the Third Reich, the glorious talk of Fatherland, the splendid uniforms, bright flags and banners high-flying. It was a magnificent Wagnerian opera, the wooing wings of Valkyrie sweet music to his ear.

Later, however, when Friedrich had become more serious, cultivating a reality that was an appropriate mix of Prussian patriotism and egoism, he joined the elite *Sicherheitsdienst.* As an officer in the SD corps, the security service of the SS, he was responsible for party intelligence and maintaining secret dossiers on everyone, including the Führer himself.

The *Sicherheitsdienst,* like other specialized divisions in the Third Reich, was expert in *Gründlichkeit,* "German thoroughness," and was determined to make Germany *Judenrein*—"free of Jews"—although, by the 1930's, most Jews had undergone rapid and extensive cultural assimilation, abandoning religious orthodoxy and their identification with anything even slightly "Jewish."

On the day that Friedrich learned of Lise's betrayal, he was working on a file that linked one of Hitler's inner-circle boys with a prostitute. A prostitute whose birth name was one Fritz Wexler. As far as Friedrich could determine, Fritz Wexler had been born with a penis and a set of testicles, and had grown, as the years progressed, a massive amount of dark hair on his chest. The real challenge for young Friedrich was to discover if the officer in question was a homosexual or had been duped by a very clever Fritzy. Either way, Hitler's boy was in trouble.

"Friedrich . . ."

He glanced up from a photograph of a very blond and a very pretty "Fräulein" Wexler. Stuben Kleinert stood in front of his desk, looking paler and more beautiful than usual. Had it not been for Lise, Friedrich imagined he would have taken the younger Stuben to his bed by now. He noticed that the officer's lower lip, the one that begged to be bitten, trembled slightly.

"Yes, Stuben," he answered nastily. It always gave him intense pleasure to have the poor boy think he disliked him.

"This"—the young security officer waved a brown folder—"is . . ." He stopped, looked down. "No one has seen this but me, Friedrich." His voice was a small boy's. "It seems impossible that I should be the one . . ."

"What is it that you have, Stuben?" He should be irritated with this cat-and-mouse game, but something made him hold back, grow cautious.

Stuben walked away, moved to stand before a bare window in the small, cramped office. He looked out at nothing. "No one would have ever known, had it not been for Frau Schulen's kind heart. We never checked so closely, Herr Baron. After all, Lise Schulen was *your* fiancée." He shifted his attention, examined a thumbnail. "But the frau's kind heart betrayed her."

Friedrich said nothing. And though he still held the photograph of Fritz Wexler between his fingers, the only evidence that registered in his brain was that there was something incredibly lyrical about Stuben's little speech.

"Most have left the old ways. Most are not even Jewish any longer. They are like us, Friedrich. German." He turned, one of his thin fingers pointed to his heart. "But some only play at being German, while they are still Jews. They marry other secret Jews. Have Jewish babies."

Stuben's lower lip quivered in earnest this time. "She is Jewish. Your Lise is a Jew, Friedrich."

For a single blinding instant, Friedrich felt completely comfortable with what Kleinert had said. Felt as though the man had related something totally unextraordinary, something that he, Friedrich, had known and accepted for a very long time. Then the layers of his brain peeled back so that the core of his mind blistered and festered with Stuben Kleinert's truth.

"You son of a bitch," he said quietly.

"Friedrich, please, it is all here," Stuben was now pleading. "I followed her mother. She goes to the old quarters. Where the poor Jews live. She takes in food, medicine . . ."

Friedrich jerked his hand up as though he were giving the *sieg heil.* Then slowly he lowered his arm so that it rested on top of the papers he'd been studying. He stared ahead.

"I am the only one who has seen this file, Friedrich." The young officer's voice was a tiny whisper now, but his message roared inside Friedrich's head.

"Nein!" The word, like the blow of a hammer, striking at what had been perceived as a kind of insult. Then softer, like a mew, "I do not wish the file destroyed, Stuben."

.   .   .

It was a singularly perfect circumstance.

Julian Morrow let Umberto Brisi's head slip from his fingers. Even through the gloves, he could detect the glassy texture of the priest's hair. The bedside lamp showed the color to be a true blue-black.

The head had rolled slightly against the pillows to show off a distinctively perfect profile, and it seemed to Julian that the monsignor was merely sleeping. But he knew better. He'd made sure.

He could almost wish for a pulse at the throat that now bore fresh evidence of ugly purple bruising. But when he'd tested a few minutes before, the heart had been quiet, though he suspected the flesh still remained warm, full of blood.

He glanced around the bedroom. The surroundings of a man with decidedly patrician tastes. No, he wouldn't disturb anything. He didn't have to. The setting would speak for itself. And he . . . ? No one would ever be the wiser that he'd been in Monsignor Umberto Brisi's apartment on this, the last night of his life.

He'd been straddling Brisi, and now he lifted himself off the body. He noticed the depressions his knees had made in the satin sheets. He would have to smooth out the telltale creases. Carefully he ran his gloved palms lightly over the surface.

Umberto Brisi still looked as if he slept, though in the last minutes, Julian could tell that the olive complexion was beginning to turn pasty. He stood very still and stared. Then he knelt down by the side of the bed.

Julian Morrow crossed himself. Touched the edge of Brisi's lower lip. Moved a finger near one ear. He had no certainty about what he was about to do. Not even the certainty that he had any right to do it. All he had was instinct. A feeling that it was something he must do.

He bent closer, whispering against Brisi's paling face, the Roman Catholic liturgy of the last rites.

"Peace to this house, and to all who enter it . . ."

· · ·

After a satisfying soak in his jacuzzi, Cardinal Vittorio DeLario had settled early into bed for an equally satisfying rest. He had drifted off effortlessly, had indeed been sleeping for hours, when the phone jangling at his bedside had thrust him instantly awake.

The phone rang again.

He reached out. Switched on the lamp. The ormulu clock on the bedside table read ten after two. He lifted the receiver of the French-style phone. "*Si?*" he grumbled into the mouthpiece.

"The monsignor requires your attention." The voice was Morrow's. "I believe you should visit him . . . alone."

The line went dead.

Vittorio sat motionless, feeling the room stir. His hand shook imperceptibly as he laid the receiver down into its cradle. An energy sweet and electric trembled in his body. He held it, savoring its elusive menace before getting up to dress. Murder, even second-hand, had a frisson all its own.

He dressed as always in the red soutane with the only concessions a simple dark cloak and his felt-soled slippers for silence. Morrow had given him no time for questions, but it was logical to assume that Brisi would be found in his quarters. *Requires your attention.* He hoped the words did not mean the priest had left a mess. He had gambled that Morrow would be clever.

He took no light, but the moon was waiting. Its round white face seemed to follow beside him in the vaulted passage, flashing like a semaphore in the long procession of windows. In spite of its brightness, there was no one about to see him arrive at the monsignor's apartments. No one to hear the knocking that went unanswered. The door was not locked. He went in.

Inside, the apartment was darker than the corridor, and preternaturally quiet with an emptiness that was absolute. Vittorio avoided the windows, resisting the temptation to turn on a light that someone in another part of the palace might see and later remember. He waited instead, letting his eyes adjust to the dimness, then crossed to the short hallway that led to the bedroom. A lamp shone but dimly from under the sill. Slowly he opened the door.

And looked away. Even in death Umberto Brisi was handsome. He closed the door behind him. The Jesuit was indeed a devil ever to conceive of so grim and perverted a trick. And yet it was perversion with a purpose. There would be no investigation into Monsignor Brisi's unfortunate death. No danger of discovery for Morrow, and thus no danger to himself. The Curia would tie itself in knots avoiding any chance of a scandal, would scurry like ants in a broken nest trying to destroy any evidence of what it believed was a vile and disgusting accident. And he would supervise it all.

Alone in the darkness of the hallway, as black and narrow as his soul, Vittorio DeLario laughed.

CHAPTER 32

"Very distasteful, Vittorio, this death of Monsignor Brisi's. Very distasteful." Pope Gregory XVII spoke softly from his favorite giltwood armchair while the Cardinal, sitting across from him at the round table, poured them tea.

"*Sì*, Holiness." Vittorio looked mournful as he passed the china cup. "This death has been most bitter. I, who have prided myself on the worthiness of those whom I placed within my command . . . to be so cruelly deceived."

The Pope smiled thinly above his steaming cup. He did not drink, but set the tea down carefully on the table. "Disappointment in a trusted subordinate, Vittorio, is something we have all suffered . . . at one time or another. Do not chastise yourself unduly."

"You are kind, Niccolo, but the monsignor was my

mistake. And it is I who must assume responsibility."
The Cardinal fell silent, stirring cream and sugar into
his cup. "I have already spoken with Dr. Agnelli," he
said, sipping experimentally. "He understands completely what is to be done. Monsignor Brisi's death will
be listed as myocardial infarction on the certificate."

"A heart attack? Was not Monsignor Brisi a bit
young?"

"Oh, not too young, Holiness. And a first heart attack at Umberto's age is very often fatal."

Niccolo's hand hovered like an uncertain insect
above a plate of *biscotti*. He decided on a chestnut
cookie. "I see that you have thought of everything, Vittorio."

"Everything."

"A new curator?"

The Cardinal smiled. He had been waiting for precisely this question. "For now," he said, "I will assume
the duties myself. I have erred once in my choice. I do
not wish to rush the selection of a replacement."

"That is wise, I am sure, Vittorio," said the Pope.
"But are you certain that you wish to take on this extra
burden?"

"The job of working with our priceless treasures is
the one I love best, Niccolo. And my health has never
been better. However, should I encounter any difficulties with administrative duties, you could give me your
permission to call on Father Morrow. His own office is
so close. He could perhaps be of some help."

"I shall be happy to speak with Father Morrow,"
said the Pope. "But truly you surprise me, Vittorio. You
have more than once expressed your doubts about the
priest."

"I have been humbled, Holiness, in this unfortunate
affair with the monsignor. My own judgment has proved
faulty. Who am I now to question yours?" And bestow-
ing on the pontiff his most beatific smile, he reached for
a crusty cookie, plump with fig paste.

·   ·   ·

"So difficult to admit, but I must. My judgment about the American was in error. He passed the test, as they say, with the colors flying." There was no humility in the words, and Cardinal Vittorio DeLario literally smacked his lips after a long pull on his wineglass.

The Baron watched him with small lizard eyes, willing to grant center stage to his old acquaintance.

"It is impossible to know these things, Friedrich. You believe one thing"—he made a flourish with a hand—"something else is true." The old prelate was obviously enjoying himself.

Friedrich glanced down, flicked imaginary lint from his trousers, ignoring the white film of cheese on Vittorio's tongue. "His Holiness does not disappoint. He has once again refused to lift and peer beneath the carpet."

"The Holy Mother Church comes first, Herr Baron. I do not have to tell you this." Vittorio popped a perfect purple grape between his cupid-bow lips, his face growing rosier with the wine.

"So Morrow made the murder appear as an accident. . . ."

Vittorio frowned, as though the wine had suddenly turned sour. "*Si*, but this 'accident' of Morrow's, it . . . it was most distasteful, Friedrich. So distasteful that the Vatican was forced to announce that its Chief Curator died of natural causes."

"So the papers will report that Umberto Brisi sustained a fatal heart attack. Such an end for so young a man." The lizard eyes slanted into a smile.

"Young men die of heart problems all the time, Friedrich. This is scientific fact." Vittorio's words were defensive. "The press will believe whatever I say. They know me." He'd meant the last to be self-explanatory, a summary statement.

"Know you, Vittorio?"

"They will print what I tell them. There are certain accommodations between the Curia and the press." A peevish grunt went up from the great belly.

The lizard eyes smiled again. He was at last beginning to enjoy this performance. "And just how did your Jesuit dispose of Brisi?"

"What?"

"How did Father Morrow murder Monsignor Umberto Brisi?"

"He strangled him." Vittorio bit hard against the words.

This time the blue lizard eyes widened. "Strangled him?"

"Yes." Now there was something very close to frustration in the Cardinal's manner, as though he were trying with great difficulty to explain something to a child.

"More wine, Vittorio?" The Baron had made his voice into a purr as he balanced the Riesling in midair.

Vittorio shook his head, pushed at his glass. "No, no. I have had enough wine today."

Friedrich set the bottle down. Regrettably Cardinal Vittorio DeLario's little theatrical had come to an end.

The Baron had always marveled at the ironies he'd come upon in life. Time and again the universe had not failed him. Irony abounded everywhere. Indeed it followed him like a great high-spirited dog. Yet it was now the case that he could no longer determine who was true master, who was beast. The dog had won more often than not.

Today the great dog had come to sit upon his lap. And His Eminence Cardinal Vittorio DeLario had let the creature into his house.

Umberto strangled. The phrase scratched at his brain like a thorny paw. That the beautiful monsignor should be murdered by strangulation was to Friedrich von Hohenhofen the most unbelievable and impossible of ironies.

CHAPTER 33

Romany worked another stem of pink freesia into the vase. Stepped back, squinted. Still too sparse. She clipped the stems off a couple more stalks. Therapy. That's what arranging flowers had always been. Besides, her mom loved to have rooms full of flowers. She'd just have to be careful and not go crazy. Wouldn't do having Theodor getting suspicious. She could just see those dark eyes of his fixing on her after he'd taken a mental inventory of the various and sundry vases, pots, and jars, brimming with posies. "Arranging flowers, are you, gypsy girl?" he'd say none too subtly.

Dammit, if only both Julian and Richard Vance had not done a disappearing act, her father wouldn't be able even to raise an eyebrow. But the truth was she hadn't been able to reach either priest since Thursday morning. Brisi died Wednesday; Morrow's office shut down Thursday. Interesting cause and effect, she mused.

"Anybody home?"

She looked up and saw Sully's granite-block shape standing in the doorway. She didn't even bother to ask how he knew where she was. "Come on in, Sully. Just putting on some finishing touches before Mom and Dad get here."

"Why didn't you just get them a place in Florence?"

She gave him a nasty look.

"Mind if I light up?"

"I certainly do. I work all day getting the place ready, and you come in and stink it up."

"You're in a good mood."

She stuck out her tongue. "So you tell me then? Where are they?"

"Morrow?"

"And Vance. Brisi bites the dust, and they get the hell out of town. Not much finesse, I'd say."

Sully shrugged his shoulders. "Sometimes, Romany, a cigar is just a cigar."

"Thank you, Sigmund Freud."

"What's the problem? You don't think our handsome monsignor died of a heart attack?"

"Yes. No. Maybe. Hell, he always looked so healthy to me."

"Not good enough. Lots of healthy-looking guys drop dead. Just like that." He snapped his fingers at her.

She squinted at the arrangement again. "What do you think?"

"About Brisi?"

"No, the flowers, Sully."

"I know nothing from flowers. Looks pretty good to me."

"Thanks for the vote of confidence."

He glanced around. "Nice place."

"I think they'll like it. Look around."

She started cleaning up her mess as Sully made a circuit of the house.

"Sure is a lot of room for just two people," he hollered from one of the bedrooms.

"Mom'll love it. Dad could live in a closet. As long as he had his books." Sully made it back into the dining room. "Want something to drink?"

"Naah, I'm fine. Books, huh?"

"What?"

"Your father likes books."

"Yes, he likes books. Listen Sully, you didn't come all the way out here to find out my father's a bibliophile."

"A biblio . . . what?"

"A bibliophile. Someone who loves books." She had now begun to stare holes into him.

"You know a lot of words, Romany."

"Yeah, in about twenty different languages. What's up, Sully?"

"You asked me to see if I could come up with something on the boy and the woman."

"And?"

"She's Irish. Red hair a dead giveaway." He smiled, as though he'd made the deduction of the century.

"The little boy has red hair too, Sully."

"Irish. Her son."

She nodded. Mother and son. That fit. "What are they doing in Switzerland?"

"The woman was injured in an IRA bombing. Innocent bystander as far as we can figure."

"So who's picking up the tab at the sanitarium?"

"There's a kind of blind trust set up for her and the kid. But here's the interesting part." Sully paused for dramatic effect. Gave her another of his big smiles. "The executor is none other than our Jesuit."

"Julian? What's the connection?"

"Don't know. Looks like she's a kind of ward of the Church and Morrow was assigned to baby-sit."

"You mean the boy?"

"Yeah, the boy too. The kid's name is Patrick. How Irish can you get?"

"What about 'Michael'?"

"Nothing on that."

"The boy called Julian 'uncle.' I heard him."

Sully shook his head. "No relation. Kid's living in Switzerland with a foster family. Julian visits every now and then."

"How long has Colleen Shaunessy been a patient at St. Cecile's?"

A third big grin from Sully. "Seems she was transferred from a hospital in Ireland just about the time Morrow arrived in Rome."

Romany stared at Sully till his smile faded, then at the dining-room table she'd just cleared.

"Hey, Sully, hand me that empty vase over there. I think I'll do just one more arrangement."

Strange, but at that moment he felt a pleasant circulation of air come into the darkened confessional. A humid coolness that made the monk think instantly of mushrooms. The brown, fat variety that had marked his boyhood like the freckles scattered across his nose, the deep scar on his left knee.

His grandfather's prized bounty—that's what the mushrooms really were. He smiled now, remembering the many times he'd run into the forest, run until he thought his sides would split, run in hopes of catching a glimpse of the gnomes who were supposed to tend the mushrooms secretly when Pawpaw was busy elsewhere. But he'd never gotten lucky.

And he remembered too, after a long day's harvesting, how he'd put his dirty hands under his nose to breathe in the odor of earth trapped beneath his fingernails. Not the soil, but its scent—that was the real badge of his labor. And it was a smell he'd never quite forgotten. A smell he'd always imagined as the attar of some elusive wisdom that had to be felt rather than understood.

He heard a sigh from the other side. If he was tired, the other man must surely be exhausted. The last days had been trying enough, and he felt an unaccustomed sympathy for the man, who, more than twice his age, had to shoulder alone the burdens that came with his office.

"If I were a younger man, this traveling would perhaps not affect me as much." The Confessor spoke slowly, seemed to have read his thoughts.

"I am sorry that you were unable to stay, remain with Ambriel . . . at least until the funeral."

"You must be tired also. All of this does not touch me alone, Zuriel." He would not be coddled. Then another sigh. Quieter, more concentrated. "I have been praying for Monsignor Brisi, Zuriel. Have you thought of him as well? We cannot allow this to pass without doing that which is of greatest importance—praying for his immortal soul, praying that he rest in peace."

It was the name Brisi alone that he at first heard. Then all else that Metatron had said dribbled into his brain like cold tree sap. He should be more sorry for Brisi. His death—a sad, ugly thing. But he could find nothing that would move him to anything but contempt. His heart was too worn, older than his years, dry as October's driest leaves. Yet he would do no more to cause the Thirteenth pain.

"I have prayed," he lied.

Then another unexpected stirring of air, again of something moist and cool coming inside. He could not tell if the aethyr reached beyond the grille to Metatron. He could only hope.

"I wonder," the Confessor was speaking again, "what changes will occur now that Monsignor Brisi is dead."

"No changes, except for the one. Brisi was his clown. His entertainment. Nothing more." The words sounded too bitter, and he could sense the Confessor's small brittle body shrinking inside his long heavy robes.

A third sigh. "We must retrieve what is ours, Zuriel. What rightfully belongs to the Holy See. The stolen art must come home. Back to Rome."

"There is still the question of who helps our Cardinal broker the art."

"Yes, the mystery man on the outside. We must know who he is, Zuriel. We must find this man before others can get to him."

He knew the Confessor would never name who the others were, but all in the Brotherhood knew well who it was that ran the race with them. The CIA had been in competition with the old society of monks on more than one occasion.

"They are like cowboys, Zuriel." Metatron faked a laugh, which in the end sounded more like a cough. "They come in and make a great deal of noise. Their zeal could cost us everything."

"Yes, my Father."

He understood well what Metatron wanted. The Thirteenth had no desire to see that heads rolled. He sought the attainment of but one goal—the return of the stolen art to the Vatican museums. Retribution had little or nothing to do with it.

CHAPTER 34

Umberto Brisi's funeral held many surprises.

The first shock was a quiet assault of smells and sounds and images that thrust Romany back to childhood.

Her father was so completely eclectic when it came to organized religions, believing that what was best in one was embodied in them all. An active spirituality, Theodor had taught her, was a necessity for living, not a luxury to be tacked on. But ritual was a matter of style.

Still, he had his own favorite church. And on all the Easters and Christmases of her growing up, the three of them would go—Theodor and Marthe, and Romany in her new holiday clothes—to the Russian Orthodox Church in the District. She had missed her parents in the weeks since she'd left home. In hours they'd be arriving at da Vinci.

The thought made her happy, despite the obvious complications of having her parents in Rome. And here in the chapel with the druglike scent of incense and too many flowers, the hypnotic flickering of candles blending the sensations of sense and time and place, it was easy to filter out whatever was disturbing. Only the first mournful notes from the organ were a voice calling her back, reminding her of this morning's real purpose.

She pulled herself up straighter in the wooden pew, scanning the modest crowd of mourners. Attendance at the funeral had been severely restricted, in order, it was said, to avoid unseemly attention from the press. The sad and sudden death of so important a figure as the Director General of the Vatican Museum was just such a thing to draw the paparazzi like flies. Romany had come herself only as representative of Arte per Pace, and it was another tiny shock to recognize Count Sebastiano seated in a pew so near the front. But then she considered the importance that had attached to the party at the Palazzo Rozze, and began to notice just how many who were here had been people she had met there that night. Damn, she hoped the Count hadn't spotted her, and that she could get out of here without talking to him. She wasn't ready yet to tackle the problem of the necklace.

She looked toward Umberto Brisi's family. Large, wealthy, and Roman, dressed uniformly in black, they had gathered like so many fashionable ravens at the front of the chapel. The men stoic in somber ties, the women veiled and weeping around an iron-haired madonna who could only be his mother.

It must be hard for them to believe that Umberto was gone. It was certainly hard for her, who had known him for only weeks. And even in death the monsignor had hustled on to center stage, in a casket whose blatant theatricality he would have approved. Heavily carved and polished, surmounted with flowers, it loomed like a rosewood galleon in the middle aisle. The rumor circulating at the Arte per Pace offices was that Cardinal DeLario had selected the coffin and paid for it himself. It was certain that he would be the main celebrant today at the Mass, and that he would give the eulogy.

There was a dramatic pause in which Romany considered this, as the organ seemed to hold its breath, then launched into the opening chords of Mozart's *Dies Irae*. As the choir joined in, the congregation stood, and Pope Gregory XVII himself, apparently returned from Castel Gandolfo especially for this service, emerged from the sacristy to take a thronelike seat to one side of the altar. A procession began down the center aisle, a double line of celebrants and servers in black and purple. She turned to watch with the others.

At the head of the procession, in front of the crucifix, walked a priest with a censer. The vessel poured forth a dark cloying smoke as it swung to left and right between the parted crowd. Romany sucked in a breath, a reaction of surprise that almost started her coughing. The priest with the censer was Julian Morrow.

Missing for days, and he showed up here. What in the hell was he doing in Umberto Brisi's funeral? On the surface at least, the papal liaison had been no friend of the Museum's Director General. Nor of Cardinal De-Lario, who appeared to be the ringmaster of this show. It made little sense, unless of course the Pope himself had insisted that Julian be included.

Julian's eyes were straight ahead in the moment that he passed her. It was the first time she had seen him since Tuesday at her apartment, and she thought that beneath the perpetual tan his profile seemed almost pasty in contrast to the black chasuble he wore.

What was Julian doing here? And where in the hell had he been for the last four days? Was a *cigar just a cigar,* as Sully had said? Even when the procession had made its way into the sanctuary, the questions looped endlessly in her mind. It was not until after the Offertory that she thought she caught the thinnest glimmer of an answer—a single look that passed from the Cardinal to Julian some distance away at the farthest side of the altar. A fleeting invisible arc. A connection from A to B that carried an unreadable message, which nevertheless she knew she did not like.

"This house is wonderful, Romany."

"Do you really like it, Mother?"

Romany, who had just come in from a tour of the backyard garden, laid her sunglasses down on a table. She was thinking that her mother looked swallowed up in the arms of the overstuffed chair.

"She likes it." Her father walked in from the little stone porch of the farmhouse with another carton of books. "At least she hasn't made the circuit yet. You know, where she looks through all the windows? That's a good sign." He set the carton down.

Romany saw her mother look up at him and smile. "Don't tease, Papa," she said. "I think the house is great. I just hope it's close enough to the city."

"It's only twenty minutes, Rom. And it's near the excavation." Her father had started unpacking his last carton of books, lining them up on the hardwood floor next to all the others. "Elliot did a good job finding this place," he said. "The bookcase is perfect."

"You should call him a little later." Romany plopped down into the sofa. "He told me he'd be at the office."

"Ask him, Theodor," her mother broke in, "about the car and driver."

"I've got Papa lined up with a car," Romany said. "A Volvo. It'll be ready tomorrow. Did you need a driver too, Papa?"

"Not for me, Romany," Theodor smiled, "for your mother. She wants her own car, to do some exploring on her own."

"Oh," Romany said, surprised. Then she turned to her mother. "I feel bad that I'm so tied up with work."

"That's foolish, Romany," her mother said. "I didn't expect that you'd have a lot of time to be with us. Besides, with the housekeeper and cook, I can do whatever I like. I'll be fine."

The flowers in the vase behind her mother seemed to float like a halo behind her head. The color in her cheeks echoed their blush, but her eyes appeared enormous in a face that had grown thinner in the weeks since Romany had last seen her. There was something hectic in her mother's words, as false in their own way as the healthy flush in her cheeks.

She looked at her father, who was still kneeling before the bookcase. He had stopped what he was doing, had turned toward her with a smile. The intelligence and the goodness that were always there shone in his eyes. But there was something new there too. Her own face must have shown her fear.

Deliberately her father turned toward her mother. "Don't worry, Marthe." He got up and walked over to her chair. "I'm sure that Elliot can find someone to drive you." He sat down on one of the well-stuffed arms and, slipping his hand around her shoulder, looked across to Romany on the sofa beside them. "My two favorite women, and Rome too," he said. "How lucky can an old guy get?"

"You're not old, Papa." The same safe words she always used. A charm against change.

"Marthe"—her father was stroking her mother's hair—"why don't you go lie down? Romany and I can finish with the unpacking by ourselves. Then we'll all go out and eat. Antipasto, fidelini, maccheroni, gnocchi . . ." He rolled his eyes heavenward, intoning the names like a litany.

"Papa, stop, I'm getting fat just listening." More of the ritual.

"I think I will rest," said her mother.

Immediately her father stood, helping Marthe up from the chair, making sure she was steady. "Do you need the cane?" he asked her.

"No, Theodor. It's just hard getting out of these cushions. You promised not to fuss." She smiled up at him.

"But I didn't promise not to keep track of your pills." He looked at his watch. "And it's time too. I'll get you some water." He started toward the kitchen.

"If I should fall asleep, Romany, make sure you get me up in time," her mother said when he had gone. "Your father won't want to wake me, but he really is looking forward to dinner."

Her mother's smile, warm and gentle, was now for her. Marthe's hand moved, reaching out toward where Romany's own rested on the arm of the sofa. The invisible barrier, always between them, trembled, but held.

Her father reappeared with a glass of milk. "Better than water," he said. Then, "Your medicine case is in the bedroom, Marthe."

Romany watched them go, her father matching his own strides with the much slower steps of her mother. She kicked off her shoes and curled on the sofa, trying like hell to ignore all the signals she was hoping she'd imagined.

In a few minutes her father was back. "Let's have some of that wine I saw in the refrigerator."

"Okay."

He went to the kitchen, returned with the bottle and two glasses. "What about this funeral?" he said, sitting next to her.

"What?"

"You said at the airport that you were worried you'd be late because you had a funeral this morning."

She finally registered what he was asking. "Monsignor Brisi," she said, "the curator of the Vatican Museum. He died suddenly."

"That's too bad." He handed her a glass. "Does it affect your work?"

"Not really," she answered him. It was probably a lie.

She sipped at the wine. This was hard, having to censor what she said to her father. Especially hard, when her own thoughts were on something else, something she feared he was avoiding. "I deal primarily with another priest, an American Jesuit. His name is Julian Morrow."

"And it's going well?"

"Papa, what about Mother?" She couldn't stand it any longer.

"She's a little tired from the trip. But I think she'll be able to go with us to dinner."

"Papa, something's wrong. She's different."

"I thought that you would see it."

Unexpectedly, he smiled. Which gave her hope. But his next words showed that he was glad only of her sensitivity.

"It's her heart," he said now. "We're not supposed

to know. So don't act like you do, Romany. That's important to her."

"Her heart. Does she need an operation?"

He shook his head. "She couldn't survive it, Rom. You know what her health is like."

"But . . . what are you saying, Papa?"

"We're going to lose her, Romany."

"No." For a moment she existed in a vacuum, in a space she'd created by that word. Ever since she could remember, she'd been afraid for her mother. Now here it was, concrete and real. Her mother really and truly lost forever, and never, never . . .

"I'm so sorry, Romany."

She was in her father's arms. Not alone, not alone. That little girl again.

"Oh, Papa, what about you?" She leaned back to look into his face.

He shook his head, then wiped away the tears that were leaking onto her cheeks. "We have to think of her, Romany. And I know it's hard, that our first impulse is to protect her even more. But that's not what she wants. All her life she's been conserving her strength. This trip may be the only time left for her to spend it. We have to let her do that. Can you do that, Romany?"

"Yes, Papa. I . . . I love you."

"I love you too, gypsy girl."

David ben Haar squatted by the side of the track. Something very small traversed along it, because the breadth of the ties was nothing of consequence. He thought of a toy train he'd once gotten for Seth.

He checked the time. One of the orange lamps overhead made a hotspot on the face of his watch. He realigned his wrist. Although he hadn't actually witnessed its departure, some kind of railcar transporting Herr Arendt had left from this very spot less than ten minutes ago. He'd heard the muffled sounds of the chugging engine as he'd hidden inside the stairwell, waiting to follow the ugly little mole down his tunnel. He'd had to give the bastard some getaway distance. But at least this time he hadn't been given the slip. Actually Signora Agostina had been more of a problem.

The metallic snake wavered in the dull cinnamon glow. Not this time, Anton, he thought, not this time. He'd have to come back without the Jew-killer and follow the trail to its destination, to whomever or whatever it was that lived at the end of the line.

He stood, forcing the stiffness from his knee joints. Just maybe he was finally getting somewhere.

Marthe Chase scarcely breathed. Not that she feared waking her husband. Theodor was a heavy sleeper. It was her thoughts that made her breathless. She didn't think she had a fever, though her body felt as though it were on fire, and her pulse made loud noisy rhythms in her ear.

She found a breath. Took it. Exhaled quietly. Her family was smart. Her Theodor and her Romany were not easy to fool. And it would not be too long before no one was deceived. But she would just have to do her best, do what she could before her body completely betrayed her.

Her new life, which had begun with Helena Klimpt's visit, had taken a giant leap forward. She was in the Eternal City. And she had the name.

Hohenhofen. Legal records were surely the logical starting point. There must be some kind of evidence of the man coming to Rome. She closed her eyes and thanked God that Elliot had a driver for her. A driver who "knows his way around Rome like the back of his palm, and speaks almost perfect English."

It was certainly a good omen.

CHAPTER 35

Caught, Romany. Paralyzed, she stood halfway into Julian's bedroom, her head frozen in a backward glance toward the foyer's double doors where a key scraped noisily in the lock. *Caught, caught, caught.*

It seemed forever, but in an instant she had turned to scope the bedroom, checking out the heavy bedskirt dragging to the floor, the huge rosewood cabinet that she knew held Julian's clothes. Within seconds she had already disappeared into the armoire. The thing was big, on a grand scale like the bed, and so heavy and so old that it was difficult to close the doors properly. Which was good, because Julian had left them hanging slightly ajar. And now so could she.

The bad news was the heat. It was stifling in the interior darkness with a row of pants and jackets pressing at her back. She concentrated on calm and even breathing, then slowly, silently, she pressed her eye to the thin line of light dividing the cabinet doors. She couldn't see Julian—the cabinet had no view of the living room—but she could hear him moving, walking off, probably toward the kitchen.

Shit. She peeled off the latex gloves and stuffed them into her pocket. Why had she worn a jacket? And the purse dragging on her shoulder felt like a suitcase. At least she'd been able to talk herself into the crepe-soled shoes, and she'd remembered to omit her favorite fragrance. If she did manage to get out of here undetected, Julian wouldn't be wondering later why his clothes smelled like the Piguet counter at Bloomingdale's.

If she did manage to get out.

She brushed the dampening curls back from her forehead, and took in another heated breath. It had seemed the right thing, marching over here with a folder full of APP business that needed his attention—as if she needed an excuse at this stage of whatever game they were playing. Julian still hadn't been answering at his office, or even here when she had called. But he could be home and just not picking up the phone, she had reasoned. And if he wasn't in the apartment, she could finish the search that had been cut short on Sunday.

The bottom line had been a need to move, to do something. And she wanted to see him. For a lot of reasons. Something was definitely going on. His sudden disappearance coinciding with Brisi's death. His turning up in the funeral. And that look between him and the Cardinal. She had to know what that meant.

Going over it all, she hadn't heard him coming. Now, suddenly, Julian was in the room. She almost jerked backward in surprise as he flashed in a shadow past her face.

He had walked over to the bed. The lighting inside the room was dim, the drapes pulled tight against the sun. But she thought in his black cassock he still seemed pale, as he had Monday morning in the church. He stood for a moment, not doing anything at all, then started to unfasten the buttons of his cassock.

Quietly, without panic, she started moving, crablike, sideward and backward, pushing herself into the far dark corner of the cabinet. After a moment, the crack of light widened to a shaft. She could see his hands removing a hanger, and then replacing the cassock. Was he always this neat? He didn't take anything else, so apparently he was going to wear the same pants he had on. The doors closed, but again not completely. To the left of her, through the cabinet, came the sound of a drawer sliding open.

Wedged into the corner, she shifted the weight of the purse still dragging on her shoulder, and heard the drawer shuffle back into its slot. Then, for moments, nothing. Then a knock. Very muffled but distinct. Someone at the foyer door. And Julian's footsteps becoming apparent as he moved from the carpet to the hardwood floor. And abruptly nothing. Again.

Damn. He must have closed the bedroom door behind him as he left. Romany moved quickly to the thin seam of light, stuck her head cautiously out. She could hear the faintest hum of voices from the living room. Julian and someone else. The undertow of rolling vowels sounding like Italian. She had to take the chance of leaving the protection of the cabinet before she could be sure, but, yes, the bedroom door was closed. And better, the keyhole was empty.

The decision was instant. Vulnerable or not, she had to gamble on enough time to hide should Julian for any reason take it in his head to return to the bedroom. At least there was no other way in. He could not surprise her from behind. She crossed to the door, got down on her knees with her eye to the keyhole. And was rewarded with a perfect if somewhat distant view of Julian's head.

The back of his head to be exact. And his shoulders. He was wearing a white knit shirt, which must have been what she'd heard him getting out of the drawer. Julian was sitting on the sofa, talking to someone on the facing couch, someone she could not see because of his head. She could hear their words much better now, especially in the brief moments when she stopped looking through the keyhole long enough to press her ear against the wood.

"*Sì,*" Julian was saying. "His Holiness was very generous in providing me with this apartment. But then there are so many benefits that go with the Arte per Pace job."

She was watching him as he spoke this last. The tilt of his head, the line of his shoulders, gave the impression he sat sprawled against the sofa. She caught a brief profile view, a curve of cynical smile. It was a look, a tone, she had not seen in him before. This was yet another Julian.

"Many benefits." His guest echoed his words. It was not a great surprise to hear Cardinal DeLario's voice.

For a moment nothing else was said, as if each man were waiting for the other. She wished she could have heard this conversation from the beginning.

"Let's get to the purpose of this little house call, Vittorio," Julian said. Perhaps she had not missed so much.

"The purpose? To welcome you into the fold."

Julian got up, walked to lean against a long console. His arms were crossed against his chest.

She shifted her head trying to catch more of him. It wasn't easy. You didn't have much range through a keyhole. But she could, when she wanted, see his face. And now she could see DeLario.

The Cardinal canted his head upward toward where Julian was standing. "Your work the other night . . . was a little heavy with the hand. But these . . . these magazines that were found with him . . ." His cherub lips twisted. *"Buono, buono.* To my brothers in the Curia his death was but an unfortunate accident."

"My percentage?" Julian's voice.

"Ten percent of everything we take."

"Twenty."

"Impossible, Father Morrow. Fifteen."

"Twenty, Vittorio. And that's a bargain. You need me."

"I am not . . ." The Cardinal stopped, as if choosing his words carefully. "There are . . . others who must be considered."

"Who?"

"This you do not have to know."

"You're right," Julian said with a shrug. "I don't. And it's still twenty percent."

The Cardinal did something Italian with his hands that signified surrender. *"Venti* then," he said.

"A deal." Julian's face altered to a smile. Beyond that he offered nothing.

DeLario tugged on the chain around his neck. The

soft clink of links melded with the smack of his lips. "Now perhaps we can get back to work."

"To work?" Julian's tone sounded disinterested.

"*Sì,* now that we have nothing to fear from Arte per Pace." There was an implied wink in the Cardinal's words. "We can certainly proceed with another painting. Another Caravaggio perhaps. Maybe a Raphael . . ." He made a series of circles with his fingers. "But I will leave it all in your good hands, Father Morrow. You have, after all, as much knowledge of art as I. . . . No?"

Julian's back stiffened slightly. The Cardinal seemed to have found a nerve. "I know something of art."

DeLario laughed then. A laugh that made his ample belly quake. "You will do, Father Morrow. You will do just fine."

Julian nodded his head. "*Grazie,* Your Eminence, *grazie mille.*"

"And Niccolo?"

Julian allowed another smile. "I can handle His Holiness. He is not a suspicious man."

The Cardinal rose then, smoothing the sides of his hair. "I have appointments," he said, as if his host had rather begged him to stay. "*Arrivederci,* Julian. We will speak again soon."

Even when the foyer doors closed behind the Cardinal, Julian didn't move. Nor did she. Like a penitent at her peephole, she watched, recorded. She realized that she should hide now, do it while she could. But she didn't stir, didn't even really think. No thinking allowed yet.

Finally Julian did move, in a kind of long shudder like a dog shaking itself free of rain. And still she watched, waiting for the moment when he would point himself irretrievably toward his bedroom. But instead he walked out of her line of vision. In a moment she heard his keys like dissonant bells jangling in his hand and the foyer doors grating locked behind him.

· · ·

"Knock, knock." Elliot stood in the threshold of Romany's office, tapping on the frame of the open door as he spoke the words.

"Hi, boss." She smiled up at him, putting down her pen.

Elliot walked in, took the chair in front of her desk. "You look tired," he said. "Am I working you that hard?"

"No." She slumped back in her own leather chair. "It's just that I've had so much going on lately . . . especially with my parents coming in."

"I talked to Theodor yesterday," Elliot said. "It was after you'd left. He sounded great. Enthusiastic about his Etruscans."

"You know Papa." She paused. "Did he talk to you about a driver for Mother?"

Elliot nodded. "No problem. I've known Bernardo for a long time. He'll take good care of her. I just think it's great that she's feeling well enough to want to get around on her own."

"Yes, it is." She felt her smile fading and leaned forward to pick up a stray paper clip on her desk.

"I'm driving out to see them Saturday," he said. "For lunch. You going to be there?"

"I don't know yet. But I did plan to get out there at least one day this weekend."

"We could go together. If you're not going to spend the night. Just let me know."

"I will."

"Now," Elliot had taken an audible breath, "for the bad news."

"What bad news?"

"The Syrians," he said. "They don't like the space they've been allotted. Too small, according to Mahfoud. And too close to the Israelis."

"You're kidding." She was truly surprised. "I spoke to Assad Mahfoud just last week," she said. "He didn't say anything to me then."

"Well, he's threatening a walkout now. And if the

Syrians go, it could be a chain reaction. We could lose all the Arabs. Not fatal when it comes to art, maybe. But as we all keep reminding ourselves, Arte per Pace is a lot more than an art exhibit."

Damn. She really didn't need this. Not now, on top of everything else. "How did you find out about this, Elliot?"

"New York. Gardner called me a little while ago."

"What are we doing?"

"A lot of high-level scrambling behind the scenes. The boys in New York are calling on their friends in Washington. And I gather that Pope Gregory has already been contacted."

"What's our game plan, Elliot?"

His mouth quirked at the corner. "What you'd expect. The money in New York wants us to keep a low profile while they try to iron things out, and *just be ready to smooth some feathers.*" Elliot did a fair imitation of Gardner's deadpan voice. "By the way, did you ever get hold of Julian?"

She shook her head. "Not yet. His office still isn't answering."

"That's kind of strange. Do you have his number at home?"

"I've already tried it. He doesn't answer there either."

"Well, keep trying. This Syrian mess may get out of hand." He gave a sigh and shifted in his chair, getting ready to go.

"Elliot . . ."

"Yes?"

"I really hate to bother you with this, especially now."

"What is it?"

"This." She took the velvet box from the bottom drawer and opened it on the desk toward him.

"My God, where did that come from?"

"I'm surprised you haven't heard. I'd have thought it

would be all over the office by now. Count Sebastiano sent it by messenger last week."

Elliot put on his glasses. He picked up the necklace, held it closer to the light. "This is something." He looked up over the rims. "You're not going to keep it?"

"Of course not, Elliot." She was surprised he had even asked. "I meant to send it back right away, but we've both been so busy, and I wanted to talk to you about it first. I know you don't want me to offend him."

Elliot set the necklace back into its box. The Count's card was there, and he read it. "Strange old bird, Sebastiano. But you're right. We don't want to alienate him."

"I thought of returning the necklace in person," she said. "But I don't want to have to argue with him about it. Besides, I figure a letter would be more his style. I was working on it when you came in."

Elliot hesitated for a moment. "You could soften the blow with an invitation to dinner," he said finally. "Then it won't come off so much like a rejection."

"Dinner, huh?"

"If you don't feel comfortable with it, I'll understand. It's your call, Romany."

"No. I think you're right. But I'll make it *George's*. Very posh. Very public."

Elliot smiled, relieved obviously that at least this problem was solved. "Put it on your expense account," he told her.

"Don't worry, boss, I intend to." She smiled back, then reached to pick up the necklace. The stones shimmered in the air between her outstretched fingers.

"It's a shame you have to return it."

"What?" She looked up to see Elliot watching.

"I said it's too bad you can't keep the thing. It would look great on you, Romany . . . the emeralds with your hair."

"It *is* beautiful. I wonder if it belonged to someone in his family."

"Maybe the Count will tell you about it over dinner."

She shook her head. "No. I think it would be better not to encourage him on the subject." She laid the necklace back into the faded splendor of the satin-lined box, and with a regretful grin, she snapped the lid shut.

The battered taxi skidded to a halt at the curb, and Romany, maneuvering herself gratefully into the backseat, called out her address to the driver. It was nearly seven, and she was exhausted. Elliot had told her she looked tired today. Well, she was tired. Mentally, physically, and in every other way she could name if she'd just had the energy to count them.

She wondered if Sully would try to make contact tonight. After leaving the Vatican this morning, she'd dialed the number he'd given her from a pay phone and left a message that they needed to talk. It was important that Sully know what she'd overheard in Julian's apartment, especially the part about the Pope, but now she hoped he would wait until tomorrow.

She slumped farther into the curve of the seat. She was going to have a huge glass of wine when she got to her apartment. A glass of wine and a bowl of leftover pasta. Throw in a long hot bath between the two, and she might even start to revive.

And she had to. Because after putting it off all day at the office, she needed to digest the scene she'd witnessed between Julian and Cardinal DeLario. But she didn't have to do it just yet.

She was totally unprepared when the taxi stopped, and she saw Julian's red Alfa sitting at the curb. On autopilot, she overtipped the driver, got out, and started toward the stairs.

"Hi." Julian hung over the banister, watching as she walked up. "Hope it's not a bad time."

"No, of course not." She moved past him with the key. "I'm glad you're here." The words came out. "I've been trying to reach you for days."

"Yes, I figured." He offered no explanation, just followed in behind her, settling immediately into the corner of her sofa. He looked comfortable in his slacks and cotton shirt.

"Can I get you something?" she asked him. "Wine?"

"Scotch would be better. And soda. If you have it?"

"I have Scotch. And Perrier."

"That's fine."

She came back from the kitchen with Scotch for them both. He took the glasses from her and set them on the table.

"Sit down." Grabbing her hand, he pulled her next to him on the couch. "You look tired." He put his arm around her, handed her a drink. It felt so incredibly good just to lean against him. He smelled of aftershave, starch, and sun.

"Terrible, huh? About Brisi. Dead . . . just like that." He said it out of nowhere, as if the words had been there waiting.

She pulled a little away. "You didn't like him."

"No." He took a huge sip of the Scotch. "But something like that still affects you."

"Yes . . . somebody that young." She was listening to herself babble. She still didn't know how to react to him. "But not so unusual," she said now. "I mean, a heart attack . . ."

Julian's smile turned thin. He gave a kind of shrug as an answer. Finished off his drink.

"Want something to eat?" She had let him get away with it.

"You hungry?"

She shook her head. "No. Maybe later. Another Scotch?" She looked at his empty glass.

He nodded, and she got up. They seemed to be talking in sign language. What did he really want? Had he felt what she felt curled next to him on the sofa?

He was standing when she came back into the room. Again he took the drink from her hand and put it down on the table. She thought he was going to kiss her, but he didn't. He just held on to her shoulders.

"I care about you, Romany." He smiled, his look genuine. Solid ground in this whole surreal landscape.

"I like you too, Julian."

"Do you?" Her eyes had drifted from his face, and he shook her shoulders, forcing her to look at him again. "Romany?"

"What do you want me to say?" An honest response. She was too far gone to be deceptive.

"The truth . . . about this, Romany."

She made a sound. A laugh? "Julian, you're . . ."

"What?"

She couldn't speak. Thoughts and images ran through her mind in a jumble. Nothing that could ever come out as words.

Whatever Julian wanted, he wasn't angry at her silence. She watched his eyes scanning hers. Again he smiled. An almost cynical expression now, but still with an odd kind of purity. He kissed her, his breath moving near her ear. "I want you so much."

He led her to the bedroom then, and she let him undress her. Somewhere outside herself she was running, trying to catch up. Her body proceeded without her.

Julian lay naked beside her on the bed, kissing her all over, her hair, her eyelids, her mouth. She thought to lift her arms, began to caress his back.

He must have sensed something false in the motion, because he lifted his head to look at her. One hand held her face. "You really are tired," he said.

She tried to protest, but he smiled and laid a finger against her mouth. "Shh. Just relax."

Years ago, while in college, she had studied Eastern mysticism. A thousand times she had lain in the dark trying to destroy the illusion that her mind existed somewhere behind her eyes. It had never worked. Now without effort, she achieved it. A short-circuit of ego and sensation. Only the physical reality of Julian inside her. Suspended above her, around her, cradling her as he moved. A great dark ocean flowed through her. And light, amber and warm.

"Romany." His hands were tangled in her hair. His voice was calling her back. But now it didn't matter. She knew that she wanted him. At this moment there was nothing else.

He had rocked back upon his knees, watching her. She looked into his eyes, and arching her back, she began moving with him now. Slowly, perfectly, seeing her own pleasure twinned within his face.

Julian. She did not say it aloud. He came down over her, his hands hard on her shoulders. And again she let go. Letting what was greater than them both rip through her in the shudder of his flesh inside her flesh.

Later, with him sleeping beside her, she finally had the time she needed to think. And now she could not fool herself about what the scene this morning with De-Lario had meant. Nothing had been said directly, but the implications were clear. Julian had killed Umberto Brisi.

Julian's face was turned toward her now. She watched him sleep. Could a murderer find such peace? A murderer she had just made love to. A murderer who felt safe in her bed.

And he was not the first. David ben Haar was a killer too. For the Mossad, for the *good guys.* Was it really so different?

She turned away toward the welcome blankness of the wall. How had she gotten here? *David. Julian.* Their names whispered together in the silence of her mind. Perhaps only now was she beginning to understand what kind of hybrid creature she really was. Worldly and sophisticated? Perhaps, intellectually. But emotionally she was sheltered. Her father's love and acceptance had given her certain expectations. She had thought to find straight lines when it came to men. Yet some part of her wanted the danger and ambiguity.

I care about you, Romany. She believed him. Believed also that it was important to Julian that she cared about him too. But love? Did he love her? In some way she felt that he did. Could she love him, and still destroy him? She shivered. That answer too was, undeniably, yes.

Romany leaned against the doorjamb and stared into the early-morning dimness of her bedroom. The watery light from the window made an interesting composition of the rumpled sheets on her bed. She closed her eyes, massaging her temples in an effort to drive away the beginnings of a nasty headache.

"Tired?"

She stiffened at the sound of his voice; her hand scrambled for the light switch.

"Don't . . . please."

She felt her fingers go limp, slide down the surface of the wall. "What are you doing here, David?"

"Not what you think."

She moved a bit, trying to see what she could of David ben Haar's face in the darkness. Only the green eyes seemed alive; the rest was gray, modeled clay.

"I waited until he'd left before I came up."

"Julian murdered Brisi." The syllables drew up tight against themselves, the words some sort of justification for sleeping with the priest.

"I'm sorry, Romany."

"Sorry?" Her voice was shrewish. "Sorry for what, David? There's nothing to be sorry for."

"Okay, there's nothing to be sorry for. It's just that I figured you liked the guy."

"Let's get something straight, David ben Haar." She moved in closer. "Morrow is an assignment. An assignment. Got it?" Now that she was right next to him, his face didn't look like clay at all. Just tired. Like hers.

"What's going to happen now?"

"I don't know. I've got to talk to Sully."

"Sully doesn't know?"

"No, not yet." She looked down, pressed on her forehead. The headache was resisting.

"Romany . . ." His voice was close; she could feel his breath.

"Please, David . . ." She stepped back, shut him out.

"No problem." He gave a nonchalant shrug of his shoulders. It was the old David she'd seen so many times before.

God, she had to get past this. "At least the Pope's not involved in any of this," she said.

"How do you figure that?" He was standing by the window now, looking down into the street.

"From something Morrow and DeLario said."

He turned, gave her one of his "what have you been up to" stares.

"I got into Morrow's apartment. Overheard them talking." Dammit, she didn't want to go into any of this with David.

"Getting a little aggressive?"

"I can take care of myself."

The stare intensified.

"Okay, so you had to save my ass once. Once, David, a thousand years ago."

The stare finally collapsed into one of his lazy grins. "Two thousand years ago."

No, Romany, don't walk over to him. Don't put your arms around him . . . or kiss him. "There's been some trouble between the Israelis and the Syrians," she began. It was the best she could do.

A dry laugh wiped the grin from his face. "So what's new?"

"I mean with Arte per Pace."

"Listen, Romany, if you think any shit between Jews and Arabs has anything to do with a fucking art show—"

"No, I'm serious. The Syrians are upset about their space in the Middle East pavilion."

"Space in the pavilion, huh? A smoke screen."

"What do you mean?" she asked.

"Just that something's brewing, and APP is being used as a scapegoat."

"But APP is supposed to solve problems, not mask them."

"Well, baby, maybe you better just take off the rose-colored glasses."

It was her turn to stare this time, and for an instant she hated him. Hated his certain smugness, his safe, cynical attitude. Hated that he was probably right. "You don't cut anybody much slack, do you?"

He smiled for real now. His white teeth showing like a wolf's in his dark face. The green eyes twinkling. He'd seemed almost cornered in that instant, but she understood it was just an impression he wanted to give.

"David . . . ," she called out to him. But he'd already left her, disappearing over the balcony like some hunted animal.

CHAPTER 36

"It is a crime, Signora Marthe, that we accomplish so little."

Bernardo threw an evil look back toward the building they had just left. "Nephews of dogs!" he grumbled, still in English, allowing her to share his outrage. With one huge paw supporting her elbow, the driver opened the door of the big black car with his other, handing her in as carefully as if she were made of china.

"We will do better in the next place." His disgust had split into a smile. He waited, making sure she was settled comfortably into the backseat, then handed in her cane.

"Thank you, Bernardo. I hope you are right."

"You will see. Tomorrow. There's a clerk in the bureau who is my sister-in-law's cousin." He closed her door, then walked round the front of the car to get to the driver's seat.

Through the windshield Marthe watched him. Realized she was smiling. The driver had that effect.

How old was Bernardo? This morning when she'd met him, she had thought him young, still in his thirties. Now she would judge him much older, and wiser, and able to be discreet. All virtues that he had managed to convey within moments of her own faltering attempt to explain to him what she wanted—a guide and translator who would help her trace a man. A long-lost relative, she had said, a member of her mother's family who had immigrated in the early 1950's to Rome. The hardest part, the part she had feared, had been trying to explain her desire to keep this all a secret. A secret even from her husband.

She need not have worried. Bernardo's kind eyes had watched her in the rearview mirror as he drove. It was those eyes she spoke to, and that spoke to her.

"My grandmother was *strega*. A witch. You understand?" His first words when she had finished.

Astonishingly she did. As he, in whatever strange manner, had grasped at least something of her mission. She had nodded her understanding, still watching the eyes as they faded once more to the quite ordinary eyes of Bernardo her driver. And now her friend. Bless Elliot Peters. Bless whatever power. Bernardo had been sent to take care of her.

But would it be enough?

There had been nothing in the immigration records. Or nothing the two of them could find with the less than enthusiastic cooperation of the clerks. Not that she really believed their lack of help had mattered. Files from the years surrounding the last war were neither complete nor reliable. But she had understood it might be like that. She would simply go on to tomorrow.

"It is time, Signora."

She looked up. The driver looked back at her from

the mirror. "Your medicine, Signora Marthe. I promised the Signor that I would remind you."

"Thank you, Bernardo." She got out the bottled water and the plastic bag of pills that Theodor had measured out for her that morning. Her leg ached badly from the hard wooden chair she had sat on the last few hours. But otherwise she felt even better than she had in the weeks before coming to Rome. The trip, despite its tensions, was doing her good. At least that promise had not been another lie to Theodor.

"Signora Marthe."

"Yes."

"Where have we been this morning, Signora?"

"Where? . . . oh, yes . . . Castel S. Angelo, I think."

"You have a guidebook?"

"Not a very good one."

"That is not a problem"—the eyes had crinkled—"when you have the best guide in Rome."

"You will tell me about it then?"

"Everything, Signora. But first we'll drive past from the Vatican side on the Via dei Corridori. I know that you are tired, but at least you will see much that is beautiful, and the outside of the fortress also. I have a friend who is a guide there. He will let me park, and I will be only a moment. I will buy for you souvenirs . . . postcards?"

"Slides. Slides would be perfect."

"Of course. Slides."

He was beaming. Bernardo had pleased her.

"I miss him, Basco." The Cardinal had managed one lachrymose sigh, squeezed out among the heavy-handed slaps the masseur was raining down on both sides of his broad back. "So often our monsignor acted the ass. But truly, I do miss dear Umberto."

Turning on the pillow, Vittorio could just see Basco's own head nodding in mute agreement as the masseur bent again to his work, kneading now with steel fingers the recalcitrant flesh that larded the Cardinal's shoulders.

Was it already the second time he had called for Basco this week? He had been so tense lately, which was surely understandable given this inconvenience with Umberto. And, of course, there was the continuing strain of this new partnership with Morrow. The priest remained a thorn.

"He is suitably greedy," he said aloud, "and yet I cannot bring myself to trust this Jesuit fox, *mio amico.*" With commendable effort he raised his head another inch from the sheets. "The American insists we Italians are 'paranoid,' Basco. But I ask you, can one trust a man whose own motivations appear to be so simple?"

The masseur's only answer was to pound and prod his flesh the harder. Vittorio's head dropped again into the pillow, his beginning protest cut short by the ringing phone. The torture stopped for the moment it took Basco to retrieve it from the table.

"Sì," the Cardinal panted into the receiver.

"I have something."

"Oh, so the ground has not swallowed you up. . . . *Madre mia.* You are killing me, Basco."

"Someone is there? I will call back."

"No, no. It is only my masseur. He wishes to chop me up today in little pieces with his fingers. But I forgive him all, because his mouth is as the tomb . . . eh, Basco?" He cast a smile upward with his little joke, was rewarded with the masseur's crooked grin.

"Go on. Go on," he said into the phone. "What is it that you have?"

"It is about the Jesuit. You remember the monastery . . . I told you he was sent there because of some trouble?"

"I remember."

"The trouble was in Ireland . . . mixed up where he didn't belong in Republican Army business. Mixed up with some woman too. Couldn't keep his dick in his pants."

"The IRA?" Vittorio ignored the last of what the informant had said. The man could be so crude. "What did the Jesuit do?"

"Ran guns, probably. Don't forget, we know he smuggled art. He had the right kind of contacts."

"*Sì.* It makes sense." The final sibilant came out with a rush of air from his lungs. Basco had straddled him on the padded table, was working hard on his spine.

"This priest," said the informant, "he has been allowed into your house?"

"It became unavoidable."

"I see." A pause. "I heard about the Director General. A great . . . tragedy." The word had carried the inappropriate tone of a question.

"*Sì,*" Vittorio said coldly. "A heart attack. I have just now said to Basco how very much I miss the monsignor. But alas, a death too can be sometimes unavoidable . . . do you not think?"

"Yes. When a man does not take the proper care to protect his health."

What was this? Was this worm of an informant suggesting that he had stockpiled some evidence against *him?* Vittorio pushed the thought aside, in no mood now to push it to a test. "Is there nothing more?" he said.

"No. But I'll keep digging."

"I have said it before. I am not a particularly patient man. Earn what I pay you. Give me this priest to the lines in his palm. I want to know it all."

Across from the Church of San Nicola in Carcere, Romany's taxi came to a stop. After paying the driver, she got out and waited for the cab to pull away. Inside her purse was the gun that Sully had insisted she carry. She checked it in case he tested her, then crossed to where he waited for her near the Ponte Fabricio. The bridge spanning the river to Tiber Island was the city's oldest, and more popularly known as Ponte dei Quattro Capi because of the double representation of the god Janus on its parapet. Janus, the two-faced. Another one of Sully's little jokes.

He was stomping out a cigarette as she walked up. "So tell me, what's so important?" he asked her.

"Morrow's back. He killed Umberto Brisi."

"How do you know that?" He hadn't missed a beat.

"I was hiding in Morrow's apartment . . ."

"Whoa. When was this?"

"Yesterday morning," she said. "I'd gone over to try to find him . . . finish my search if he wasn't there. Morrow came back after I'd gotten in, and then De-Lario came calling. I had a front-row seat."

"And Morrow admitted killing Brisi?"

"No. He didn't talk much. It was more what De-Lario said." She paused, but Sully had stopped with the gunfire questions. "The Cardinal said he was there to welcome Julian 'into the fold,'" she began again. "That's a pretty close translation. He told Morrow that his 'work' the other night had been a bit heavy-handed, but clever enough so that the death had been accepted as an accident.

"I don't get the accident bit," she interrupted herself now. "If the murder looked like an accident, why announce that Brisi had a heart attack? And there was something else, something about magazines that I didn't understand at all."

Sully was already lighting another cigarette. The glow from the lighter made his plain face appear for a moment diabolical. "Magazines, I don't know," he said, "but the heart attack is just neater. Accidents need to be investigated. The real question is why kill the monsignor at all?"

"I've thought about that," she said, "and I got the impression that DeLario might have told Morrow to kill Brisi."

"That still leaves us with why. You think Morrow's getting in might have made Brisi expendable?"

"Could be the other way around," she said. "Brisi's death might have been a condition of his getting in. And now with Morrow in, they're planning to continue with the forgeries."

"That's interesting."

"It seems with Julian riding shotgun, DeLario figures they don't have to worry about anybody from APP getting too nosy. DeLario even said Morrow could pick their next project, since according to the Cardinal, Julian knows as much about art as he does. . . . And, oh, Sully, the Pope's innocent."

"You sure, Romany?"

"Let me give it back to you the way I heard it." She thought for a moment. "DeLario had been pumping Morrow up, saying how well he was going to work out. Then he said, 'And Niccolo?' Just like that, a question."

"And Morrow's answer?"

"He said, 'I can handle His Holiness. He's not a suspicious man.' Sounds like the Pope's in the dark to me."

Sully smiled. "Good girl."

She had to fight to keep her own smile down to a reasonable wattage. Somewhere along the line she'd begun to like Sully, but that was nothing he needed to know. "What happens now?" she asked him.

"I'd say that the decision will probably be made to go to Gregory immediately."

"And that's good, isn't it?"

"I don't know." Sully sounded his doubt. "Exposing the art scam doesn't guarantee us proof of what these Germans are up to. And the elections are getting close."

"What about Mossad? I thought they were handling that end."

Sully made a noise. "So they said. But so far nothing."

"David?"

Sully shrugged. "Undercover. He's supposed to have

made contact with one of the Germans. Apparently it hasn't come to much."

"But once we get the Pope's cooperation . . ."

"I wouldn't count on that too much, Romany. Gregory may be a good guy, but the tendency will still be for him to cover up as much as possible."

"Protect DeLario?"

"Protect the Church, which means protecting De-Lario."

"But when Gregory understands what's at stake . . . you do plan to tell him about the neo-Nazis?"

"Not me, babe. I'm just one of the foot soldiers."

"You know what I mean."

Sully shrugged. "Oh, I think our guys'll tell him, but it still may not matter. This might be the new world everybody's talking about, but my hunch is that inside the Vatican things don't change."

She looked away, over the river, to the far end of the island where lights still burned in the dark mass of the Fatebenefratelli hospital. "Maybe I can get you what you need," she said.

"What?"

"It's the middleman you need, isn't it?" She turned back. "Maybe I can find out who he is. Through Morrow."

"What makes you think Morrow even knows?"

"He probably doesn't . . . yet. But they're going to restart the operation. He may find out then."

Sully was shaking his head. "No," he said. "What I want from you is to back off as much as possible. No more heroics."

"You're treating me like an amateur again, Sully. You started me on this. Why stop me now when it's working?"

"Because the truth, Romany, is that you are an amateur. . . . Oh, you're good." He had raised a hand to cut off her protest. "You've got the instincts, all right. What you don't have is experience. I began you on this thing blind, with no real idea how Morrow would develop. He's damn dangerous, Romany. The whole situation is dangerous."

"I'm not afraid, Sully."

"The amateur talking. You should be. But that's not what I meant. The fact is, you're expendable. We all are. The real danger is that if you make a mistake, if you tip our hand, you alert them all. DeLario. The neo-Nazis. We'd never get our proof before the German elections."

"I see."

"Good."

"But you're still wrong."

At least he laughed. "And how's that?"

"Because you're acting like you have options. You've said yourself how hard it is to shadow anyone inside the Vatican. I'm already there, Sully. Already close to Morrow. Like it or not, I'm your best shot."

For a long, uncomfortable time Sully said nothing. Just looked at her, assessing. She stared right back.

"For chrissakes, Romany, be careful. Don't let yourself forget, not for a moment, this priest of yours is a killer."

"I won't . . . okay? Now, what about this woman in the sanitarium? You find out any more about her?"

"Nope. I'm afraid your little jaunt to Switzerland was pretty much of a waste. But that's the business, Romany. Most of what we uncover are just dead ends."

Close beyond the tall field grasses where she lay with Michael was the brook. Colleen could hear it clearly, the quicksilver musings where it bubbled and trilled among the rocks, the softer sound when finally it ran free and narrow to disappear among the moss and bracken. From childhood she had found enchantment in this place. It was fitting that her first time with Michael, her first time with any man, should be within this sanctuary.

Somewhere among the bombs and the bodies and the hate, she had lost her simple faith. But not her virginity. By her early teens she'd given up the notion that God, if he existed, cared at all about the random couplings of human beings. She had sworn then that she'd not be one of those laughable Irish virgins, and yet she'd never seen it through to going all the way. It was not Church strictures that kept her chaste, but a wary self-protectiveness. God might not care with whom she slept, but Colleen Shaunessy did.

There had been none of that with Michael, not from the moment she'd set eyes on him in the pub. She had wanted him. She would have him. In this one thing, at least, she had worn the face of destiny.

The late-afternoon sun was yet warm. Michael lay over her on the quilt that she'd spread for them on the ground. Her blouse was open and his hand was on her breast as he kissed her neck, nuzzling against her shoulder. From a single cloud in the blue sky, rain fell in silver pinpricks on the skin of her arms, on her forehead. On Michael's shirtless back. She heard his laughter, soft and breathless, catch in the web of her hair. And it had never mattered less that she knew next to nothing about him. Nor mattered that reluctance which she sensed in him, a wavering desire to warn her of things she had no wish to know.

With no bridge of time they were naked, her moment of pain melting into shocks of pleasure as she watched Michael's face, seeing his surprise to find her still a virgin. Had he said it aloud? No matter. For he was holding her hard and close, beyond anything now but the goodness he found in her body. She felt blessed, a chalice. And Michael flowing into her. A river, a tree that shook her in its flowering.

Abruptly it changed. She stood alone at the door of the barn. The sour grain smell heavy again in the darkness.

Michael? She stepped through the threshold.

It came as it came, always. The dark emptiness exploding into noise like a thousand trains roaring in her ears, dragging her away from the light.

Michael! This time it seemed she had screamed it, the vibration a shivering live current in her throat and her ears. Her eyes flew open.

"Mich . . . ael?" The actual word was softer, broken, her breathing softly ragged as she willed her vision into focus.

The face that hung over hers was not at all familiar. Nor was the simple room beyond, lamp-lit and cobwebbed with shadows. Her voice croaked from disuse, but the words came out.

"Where's Michael?" she said to the nun.

CHAPTER 37

Romany saw the blinking light on her phone pulse— one, two, three times. She picked up the receiver.

"Yes, Gina."

"Count Sebastiano, Ms. Chase."

"Put him through."

"Signorina Chase, I hope I am not disturbing you." From another man that voice might have been effeminate.

"No, of course not, Count Sebastiano. I was just thinking of you."

"How charming to think of your thinking of me. I shall be entirely content for the rest of the week knowing that I was in your thoughts."

"You are not an easy man to forget, Count Sebastiano." God, everything sounded like bullshit, but the reality was, it was all true.

". . . But you cannot accept my gift." He affixed a slight pouting tone to his words.

"Count Sebastiano, as I explained . . ."

"Please, I quite understand. I would want nothing to jeopardize your position with Arte per Pace. They need you, Romany Chase. Did I ever tell you how very much your name suits you? R-o-m-a-n-y. It rolls down the throat like a fine wine."

This man was impossible. "I'm sorry I was unable to return the necklace sooner. I have been very busy. My parents have just arrived from the states."

"Your parents. Here in Rome. How delightful. Then they shall have to join us for dinner."

"So am I to assume you are accepting my invitation?"

"Of course, how could I refuse Romany Chase?" He'd trilled her name again. "But you and your parents shall be my guests. And I think not *George's*. It has become too public of late. You shall dine at my favorite restaurant. I shall send Jurgen for you . . . say eight o'clock?"

"That won't be necessary, Count Sebastiano, my parents have a driver. If you would give me the address of the restaurant . . ."

"And have you spoil my surprise? I shall not be disappointed twice, Signorina Chase. You have had your way with the necklace. Now it is my turn."

He made it all seem like some kind of game. "All right. But my parents will meet me at my apartment. Your driver will have to make only one stop."

"Good. Then it is all settled. But I must warn you, Jurgen will be punctual."

"Eight o'clock. We'll be ready. But you'll need my home address. . . ."

"Your address? But I already know your address, Romany Chase."

When she hung up the phone, she stared at it a long time after. And of all the things she wondered, she wondered most about how in the hell the old buzzard knew where her apartment was.

It had happened in a brief flash, but the moment Julian descended into the hidden rooms below the Restoration Department, he had a glimpse of his father's wine cellar, of him and Jeremy sprawled out on the floor, too drunk to care. Perhaps it was the coolness, the sense of being underground that had brought back that old memory of his teenage delinquency.

Nino Polidori had said something, and Julian stared at the man Vittorio DeLario had handpicked to coordinate the entire forgery operation. He did not seem a likely choice. Something was out of sync. Julian finally decided on the eyes, small pricks that emanated a kind of intense moral integrity that made a lie of everything he'd been told about the Italian. In another man's face they would have been the eyes of a rat.

Julian nodded his head in reaction to Polidori's comment and glanced around the room. Here and there were artists working on small pieces. He recognized a *biccherne* that could only be a copy of a di Paolo.

"We have resurrected our dead, Father Morrow."

Julian smiled. Integrity and a sense of poetry. "I take it you mean you have resumed work on some of the pieces."

"*Sì,* now that . . ." He made a typically Italian flourish of his hands. He wasn't going to embarrass the priest by saying that now that he was in on the operation, they could continue the process of forging Vatican art.

"*The Deposition* was masterful." Julian knew it had been Polidori who had done most of the forgery.

"We have many talented people in the Restoration Department."

Add modesty to the growing list of the chief forger's attributes.

"I was thinking it was time we begin work on another large canvas."

The pinprick eyes twinkled.

"Perhaps the *St. Jerome.* It would require less time since it is incomplete."

The light faded in Polidori's eyes. "Da Vinci's underpainting is more difficult than the finished work of another."

The man had his own mind. A real challenge for the Cardinal. A pain in the ass for Brisi.

"I also considered Bellini's *Pieta.* . . ."

The light returned. "It is a great painting. It would be an honor . . ."

"And I'm sure you would do the great work justice, Nino. But I think not the Bellini. I think we should attempt something more contemporary. Rouault's *Ecce Homo* is more what I had in mind."

The eyes went dead again. "If you think that best, Father Morrow."

Polidori clearly did not favor the Rouault, but surprisingly he wasn't going to put up a fight. Julian thought his acquiesence might have something to do with the possibility that the forger just might like Umberto Brisi's replacement.

David had been walking alongside the track thinking of Romany. It took him a moment to realize how really mad he was. No one could make him angry like Romany. Damn, she was stubborn. And proud. And . . . and a thousand other things that drove him crazy. This game she was playing with this priest was getting out of hand. The man was a killer. By her own admission. Yet she acted like he was a fucking saint.

He gritted his teeth and looked at his shadow looming against the far wall of the tunnel. A rocky projection at just the right spot made it seem that he'd sprouted a rather large hump on his back. A Jewish Quasimodo. Yeah, and if that pretty Jesuit did anything to hurt Romany . . .

The track was coming to an end. David could see some kind of door in the distance. He had to rather admire whoever it was who thought of this setup. It was a nice little engineering job.

The door was an elevator door. The whole operation was beginning suddenly to turn upscale. He half expected his ascent to be no more than another crude ladder like the one he'd found in Signora Agostina's basement.

Well, nothing to do but press the button and hope that no one on the upper level saw the car take a trip downstairs. He heard the swishing of hydraulics as his fingers left the wall, and he sandwiched himself against the corner, pulling his Ruger from its nest under his arm. Just in case . . .

The elevator opened. From where he stood, the car looked vacant. He kicked out a foot and held the door. Shoulder first, then the arm with the gun . . . Empty. Now he had to get lucky and hope there wasn't a welcoming party upstairs.

The ride upward was surprisingly smooth. A tiny jolt and the car stopped. The elevator had only one route. From the underground tunnel to the first floor, and back again. The door slid open.

In a instant David had the .22 eye-level, finger on the trigger. The face staring into his looked startlingly familiar. It was his own. He eased off the gun and studied his head-to-toe reflection in the large gilt mirror facing the elevator. *Shit.*

His back hit the side of the door, holding it open. He cocked his head one way, then another. The elevator was situated in the exact center of a long darkened hall. A hall that appeared empty.

David stepped out of the elevator car. This place was a piece of work. Small lights that looked like candles flickered in the dimness. There were paintings at intervals and furniture that looked like it came out of a museum.

He had been hearing the music for a long time. In fact, he'd heard its muffled thumping all the way down inside the cave. He'd been hearing, but not listening. Now he listened. The music was classical. Though what he knew about classical music could be put in a pisspot. . . .

The sound was coming from down the hall, to the

right. He listened again, fighting the niggling feeling that this music somehow had some significance for him.

Double doors. He pressed his ear against one surface. The music reverberated through the wood. The hand not gripping his gun twisted the knob. The music bounded out as if it'd been trapped inside a bag. He stepped through the crack he'd made.

A theater. Dark except for the lights coming from the stage. Toward the front, a small audience. Slowly his eyes became accustomed to the dimness, and he saw that there were two staircases, one on each side of the room, spiraling upward to box seats.

He took the stairs two by two. His feet padded on the spongy carpet like a large cat. At the top he walked down a small avenue and went inside the box that hung closest over the stage.

The thick velvet curtain made for a good cover. He wrapped himself like a mummy in its folds and peered around its fringed edge. The music switched tempo suddenly, and when he saw that it was a ballet, he at last understood the music.

Rebecca. Becca had taken him to his first and only ballet. Some Russian company was performing *Swan Lake* in Tel Aviv, and she had begged to go. An early birthday present. He shut his eyes now, seeing her face magically transformed by the movement of the dancers. Of course he'd hated every moment of it. But he had lied afterward. Told her it wasn't so bad. What was good was seeing her face light up like that.

The dancers on stage were performing that same ballet, but not the *Swan Lake* he and Becca had seen. The dancers were completely nude, except for white toe shoes and small circlets of pale down round their heads. Their too-thin bodies had been coated in a fine powder so that with each twist and turn, the dancers shimmered like freshly fallen snow. Small-breasted, with pubic hair shaved clean, the ballerinas seemed more than anything like pretty young boys.

Another shift in the music, and the dancers parted, leaving a wide gap center stage. In a moment she appeared. Pink, where the others had been white. And flesh, where the others had been bone. No tiny cups of white milk were her breasts. But heavy and alive. The nipples ringed in kohl like the edges of an eye.

She moved as though she were a much lighter woman, her arms, rising and falling, fluttering like wings, making love to herself. Then the mist at her feet began to churn, reddened to blood. In an instant he swooped down, a great ugly creature, winged and crowned with dense dark feathers. One twist and his cape fell into the fog. He was all undulating angles, except for muscles that coiled like snakes beneath his flesh. His phallus was large and erect, growing out of a nest of brown woolly hair.

At first the Swan Queen fluttered in a kind of feigned panic. But she was lost from the first. The creature swept her into his arms, his talons raking the soft pads of her armpits. Then he arced himself over her, one dark rainbow over a brighter one.

David gazed down into the audience. There were no more than twenty people. More men than women, though he suspected some had cross-dressed. Each wore a mask. He'd heard about these international sex clubs. Where the membership was exclusive, the dues in the thousands. But he had a difficult time fitting Anton Arendt into the picture. Although the man could certainly afford the membership, had all the other credentials, he seemed just a bit too "bloodless" for this kind of action.

He turned his attention back to the performance. The couple was now into some heavy fucking, porno-movie style. He didn't quite know how he was going to break it to Chaim that the lead he'd insisted on following had dead-ended. No chance of a middleman here. Yet, when he got the time, he probably should check on who owned this prime little piece of real estate.

. . .

"Hope you don't mind." Romany kicked off her shoes.

"Looks like a good idea to me." Julian had turned from the rolls of blueprints strewn across Romany's desk.

"This is impossible," she complained as she bent back over the maze of lines that formed the interior design of the pavilion. "We're playing musical chairs with every damn country in the exhibit."

"The Syrians like being obstinate." Julian's smile was just inches from her face.

"I can't believe they are really serious about this whole thing," she said.

"It's a cover. They've some other agenda going."

"Where'd you get that?" She moved back from the desk and flopped into her chair.

"Spent all of this morning with His Holiness, most of the afternoon. He's putting his feelers out. Nothing really solid yet."

"Any word on what he'd like us to do over here?"

"Just what we're doing. Playing it nice and friendly."

Romany let out a long groan and stood. "Well, let's play it nice and friendly and see if we can accommodate our Arab buddies."

For the next hour Romany and Julian arranged and rearranged space allotment and placement. Nothing seemed to work. A move in one direction only created a problem in another area.

"Okay. That's it for me. Break time." Romany straightened, arched backward, and stretched. "I could use something to drink. How about you?"

"Coke would be fine."

"I was thinking of something a bit stronger, Father Morrow."

He laughed. "Whatever you're having."

"Good. I know Elliot's got some wine stashed away around here somewhere. Be back in a sec."

He watched her move out of the office into another. Then he examined the blueprints again. Romany might just be right. This was impossible. He targeted one of the rooms with the pencil he'd been holding and watched it bound off the edge of the desk.

He slid the prints over and reached for the photograph.

"My parents," she said, coming back into the office.

"I guessed as much. But I can't figure who you look like."

"Neither. You mean I've never told you Dad's story about how I got my name?"

"Romany?"

"Uh-huh. Actually I was stolen from a gypsy camp by a rival band of gypsies and sold to my parents."

Julian arched one eyebrow, but said nothing.

"Of course, after a while, all Mom could think about was the poor gypsy mother who'd lost her child. The problem was, when Mom and Dad tried to return me, my real mother said it had been a blessing having me taken away from her. I was much too precocious for my own good."

"Romany . . ."

"It's true. I swear."

"Seems to me I've heard this story somewhere before. 'The Ransom of Red Chief' I think it was called."

"You're no fun. All you Jesuits like that?"

"Nope. Just me."

She stared at him. Then she threw the corkscrew. "Here, see if you can work this."

He made a grab for it and reached for the bottle of wine.

"So you don't believe my story." She sat on the edge of the desk.

"Not a word . . . and it's a sin to lie."

"I guess you'll just have to hear my confession. God, I haven't done that in years."

"Neither have I." He'd begun working the cork out of the bottle.

"Gone to confession?"

"Nope. Heard confession."

"I thought priests had regular duties."

"It varies. Here." He handed her a glass of wine.

She took a sip. "Hmm, good."

He poured himself a glass and held it up. "Let's toast."

"Sorry, I got greedy." She raised her glass. "You make it."

"To the Syrians."

"To the Syrians." She clinked her glass against his. "I think I just may get drunk."

"You better not. We got work to do." He pointed his glass toward the blueprints curling on the desk.

"Don't remind me." She sat back down in her chair.

He stared at her until she caught him.

"What are you looking at?"

"You. Wondering why you're not married."

She crinkled up her nose.

"Got something against marriage?"

"Not for everybody. Just me. You can surely appreciate that, Father Morrow."

"Ever been in love?"

"Thought I was once. An older man. Handsome in a school book kind of way. He was one of my professors in college, actually."

"What happened?" He took a sip of wine.

"He was married."

"Oh."

"Yeah, I have a habit of falling for the unavailable ones." This time she stared.

He looked down into his glass. "No one since?"

"Maybe. But we're too different. I think we fight so we can make up. That's no way to live." She stretched out her arm, waiting for a refill.

"Romany Chase, you better not get drunk." He poured her another glass.

"I'm not making any promises." She lifted her glass in a mock toast, and drank.

She caught him staring again. "What about you? You ever been in love?"

He smiled, set his empty glass on the desk. "I told you. Women have always been a distraction."

"So that's what I am. A distraction."

"No." The word was harder than he'd planned. "No, you're different, Romany."

She made a kind of giggling noise. "Come on, Julian Morrow, who are we kidding here? You know, and I know, that the only thing going on here is a little fun."

"This isn't any fun."

They were the right words.

He took her into his arms. Felt her giving over her weight to him. And her mouth opening for his tongue.

Blood. Bloodbeat in his ears. A rush. In his head. His chest. Deep in his groin. And she wanted him too. God, she was wet. Warm. But she smelled cool, green. Like mown grass.

Yes, this was what he wanted. Wanted more than Jeremy's life. His parents' love. Colleen. His lost priesthood. What he wanted above all else was Romany Chase. Gypsy girl.

CHAPTER 38

"A fake," Romany pronounced, smiling down at the pottery lid she held in her hand. "It's one of the smallest pieces I've seen produced by the Pinellis, but it has that same weird naturalistic charm. . . . Papa?" She passed the terra cotta to her father.

"I'd say you were right." He handed the lid back to their host.

"Pinelli, certainly," the Count agreed. "These early Etruscan forgeries seem quite obvious now. Though you are right, Signorina Chase, they do possess a certain charm, and now that they are more than a century old, a certain value. But have a look at this." From a soft vel-

vet pouch he removed a golden bowl, which he passed
to Theodor first.

"Seventh century." Theodor was carefully examining
the animal figures on the bowl's handles. "It certainly
looks as fine as anything in the Villa Giulia." He
glanced up at Sebastiano.

"May I see?" Romany took the bowl. "It's beautiful,
authentic or not. Would you like to see it, Mother?"

"Yes." Marthe, sipping her after-dinner wine, was
sitting on the sofa with her daughter. The men sat opposite them both in high-backed brocaded chairs. "It's
very lovely." She held the bowl with its golden surface
pressed coolly between her palms, looked across at the
Count. "Is it real?"

The direct question seemed to amuse him. "No, Signora Chase." He smiled. "The experts here have been
toying with me. The bowl, as your husband says, is as
fine as anything in the Villa Giulia, because the original,
at least, is in that museum. This"—he accepted the bowl
from her hands—"is only a clever, if very expensive,
copy."

"Do you mind it being a copy?"

"Yes, of course, Signora. Though it is strange, is it
not? The distinctions that we make in value between
two things that to our grosser senses appear identical.
For all our modern claims of scientific materialism, we
betray ourselves to be poets yet at heart."

Like his clever forgeries, Count Sebastiano's answer
seemed to have pleased her husband and daughter. The
three of them went on talking about Etruscan art, and
the significance of the new excavations that Theodor
had come to Rome to observe. Marthe let their conversation slip away and thought about the Count.

The most eccentric man in Rome, Romany had said in
coaxing her to accept his invitation. *It'll be fun, Mother.
He's sending a car. And wear something wonderful. With
Count Sebastiano every occasion is formal.*

She was glad she had come, Marthe decided, though
she could not say why. They had not gone to a restau-

rant, as Romany had said, but to the Palazzo Rozze, which overwhelmed her, as had the too-rich food. She was not charmed by the Count. Indeed, she found him threatening in some indefinable way, both repellent and strangely attractive, like a burning house, or a deformity from which you could not turn away.

". . . Third century. That's wonderful, Papa." Romany's words.

Marthe turned to see her daughter's face still glowing with pleasure at something that Theodor had said about his work. The Count was watching her daughter too, Marthe observed. He had been watching her closely all night. That was not unusual in itself. Romany was beautiful, and alive. Men always watched her. But there was something abnormal in the Count's attentiveness. An intensity that bordered on obsession.

Weeks ago now, Marthe remembered, she had had a vague feeling that Romany was in some sort of trouble. She had even told Theodor, though she had known in advance how little he would think of her fears. That feeling of danger was back now, stronger and more frightening than before. But not clear. Tangled. Confusing.

"Mother, what's the matter?" Romany was looking at her. "Aren't you feeling well?"

"I'm fine . . . a little tired, perhaps."

Theodor had risen. "You must excuse us, Count Sebastiano. It is getting late. And Marthe, I know, is tired." He was looking at her fondly. "She's been playing tourist."

"Of course." The Count rose too. "This has been delightful." He was again watching Romany. As if he were seeing her, but also something else. "Perhaps you will all come again, Signor Chase." He had turned again to Theodor. "I want to hear everything about these excavations. . . . Signora." He came to her, helped her to her feet.

It was not until later, lying in her bed, that she let herself relive that moment when he reached to touch her hand. A spark of some kind. Intimate. Inexplicable. She understood only that the darkness around her had spread.

The Black Baron had had to come, drawn here despite the lateness of the hour. And he walked the halls of Villa Bassano thinking, as he so rarely did, of his age. So old, so old now.

The elaborate rituals, the spiritual equivalent of carnival tricks, still worked to preserve his vitality and strength. Energy was all and everywhere. But the instrument grew weaker, the focus harder and harder to bring to bear. Somewhere, long ago, what passed for reality had split away from his dreams. This self-created world, this marble palace, had become a mausoleum.

The Baron Friedrich von Hohenhofen held a candelabra lifted in his hand. Its fantail of yellow light seemed to anchor him in the vastness of the empty ballroom. He moved on, dragging the light through double doors and into a paneled hallway. A narrow passage branched off to the right. At the end was a locked parlor.

From his dressing gown he took the key. The door opened silently inward. And crossing on the thick carpet, he set the candelabra down on the piano, reaching to finger a simple run of notes upon the keys. The sound was thin and ghostly, slightly out of tune.

Have anything that you will from the house, Baron von Hohenhofen. The words of Heydrich himself, clear in his ear as if they had just been spoken.

He had known they would descend like vultures, the high command of the *Schutzstaffel,* grabbing it all—factories, property, assets—all spoils now for the greater glory of the Reich. He would take nothing, he had told himself. Wanted nothing now that had been Herr Schulen's.

The piano, he had answered Heydrich, surprising himself even in the act of naming it. He had not, at least, said Lise's piano—her birthday present at ten, on which, in her mother's favorite parlor, she had played for him so many afternoons—Schubert, Liszt . . . Chopin.

He remembered the day the piano was delivered by three soldiers to his rooms. Its mute presence had not pleased him, and yet that same week he had gone to Lundorf's studio for the painting. It had been meant as a surprise, Lise's gift to him on the day of their wedding. But her little brother had given the secret away, letting it out one day at the house that Lise was sitting for her portrait.

Lundorf had refused his money. It was now the portrait of a Jew, the artist had pointed out with a savage contempt that exposed itself as irony. The Baron could take the thing, if he wished. The painting would never be completed.

As if he had been avoiding it, Friedrich turned deliberately now, lifting the candelabra once more to better see the portrait where it hung upon the wall. Unfinished still, and yet capturing in the daubs and strokes of pigment something of Lise Schulen's spirit.

He had captured that too. In his thirteen-day cycle. Brought back the Lise of the photograph she had given him. The Lise of what had been his innocence.

Why had he come here tonight? Was it Romany Chase in her formal dress looking like the shade of his beloved? Romany Chase of the brilliant father and the mother with the haunted eyes? The woman was dying, did they know it? Did they play their little games, hiding it one from the other? Secrets and falsehoods. Lies in the name of love.

As always in this room, before her portrait, it happened. Time and perspective shifted. He heard her voice outside in the hall. The hall that had for now become the marble-tiled entranceway of the Schulens' Berlin mansion.

"Was ist?" She had come from her shopping to find the staff cars parked along the curb in the front, the

door opened not by Keller—the servants had all fled—but by a Lieutenant in the black uniform of the SS.

"Mutter . . . ?" She swept into the grand parlor, an officer trailing behind her, saw nothing at that moment but Hilde Schulen weeping vacantly on a sofa across the room.

"Mother, what is it?" She had walked to sit beside her. "Has something happened at the factory?"

"It was I, Lise." Her mother had turned to her, a woman drowning, clutching at her arms. "I have destroyed us all."

"What are you saying, Mother? Where is Father? Gunter and Stephan? . . . Oh, Friedrich, thank God, I did not see you."

He had gotten up from his chair by the large formal window. He walked closer now. "Take Frau Schulen to join her family," he said to Brunner, who had remained inside the door. "I will speak with the *Fräulein* alone."

"Don't worry, Mother. It will be all right." Lise held the woman for a moment longer, then helped her to her feet.

Lise's eyes had never left his. They seemed huge in the white face. As the door closed, she came to him. "What is this, Friedrich?"

"I think you know, Lise. An enemy has been discovered in the bosom of the State. An industrialist who turns out to be a Jew."

"My father? You're not talking about my father?" She made a sound of disbelief. "This is stupid. . . . Have you called someone, Friedrich? Told them it's a mistake?"

"There is no mistake, Lise. I turned your father in myself."

The eyes changed. Fear and something else crept in with her confusion. "You . . . ?" Her hand dropped from where she'd placed it on his arm. "But why?"

He had decided he hated her eyes, and he let that emotion further fuel his anger. "Can you dare to ask me that, Lise, after the way you have betrayed me?"

"Betrayed you, Friedrich? I have done nothing but love you. I . . . I still love you."

"Oh, no. You knew, Lise. You had to know what this could mean . . . marriage to a Jew."

"But, Friedrich, I am not a Jew." She sounded so reasonable, even now. "Do I look like one of those creatures that your Herr Hitler describes? I know no one like that. I'm a German, just as you are. You know that."

"Oh, yes, a fine German whose mother brings aid and comfort to the Führer's enemies."

"Oh, that is ridiculous." Despite the fear, there was a sudden spark of anger. "My mother is kind-hearted, that is all. She feels compassion for those who are unfortunate."

"There can be no compassion for the enemies of the Reich. For Jews."

She looked away at last. "I cannot believe this is happening. I know that you love me, Friedrich. How can you destroy me and those that I love, for what? Because I light a few candles at Hanukah to please my mother?"

The eyes had again attached themselves to his face. Whatever she saw there now made her shrink away.

He had told himself he would not touch her, that he did not want to touch her. "You are a fool, Lise." He had grabbed her arm. But only to hold her at arm's length, away from him. "A fool." He forced the cruelty into his voice. It was not so hard. He really did hate her.

She did not struggle, although he knew that his fingers must be hurting the tender skin of her arm.

"What I see," she said to him now, "is that you put on that uniform, and you disappear, no longer the Friedrich who made love to me in the park. You are an officer in the Reich. I am a Jew. But these are only names, Friedrich. You will let names destroy us?"

He smiled. Indeed she was simple. Beautiful and stupid. Unworthy.

"Look at the world, Lise. These names, as you call them, are the children of ideas, and ideas create what is

real. Hitler is real. Our class . . . my class must ride
with Hitler. We will rule. What is anything compared to
that?"

There were tears now on the porcelain cheeks. He
could smell the sweetness of her terror, the full realiza-
tion that all she had known, everything she had
dreamed of, planned for, was lost. Incredibly, she
smiled.

"My poor *lieber* Friedrich, you are the fool. There is
only one thing that is real."

He remembered looking at her throat, the pulse-
point beating in her blue-veined flesh. He had actually
thought about strangling her. He had kissed her instead.
And she had kissed him. Still with those huge eyes, staring at him when he'd let her go. Saying nothing. No
more protest. No begging. Nothing.

He had been the one to turn away. Calling for Brunner. Wanting it to be finished. He would forget her. In
time.

But he had not forgotten. The thirteen-day cycles
when he summoned her were as much her triumph as
his.

It had not been till after the war that first he had
summoned Lise. Not till that god to which he'd sacri-
ficed his dream of her was dead. He had called, and she
had come, the simple and beautiful Lise, the image in
the photograph.

The ritual had always worked, had never yet failed
him. But three nights ago, the thirteenth night after her
last visitation, the shade of his beloved had seemed, very
subtly, to resist him. The inevitable question arose. Was
the ghost of Lise Schulen *real,* separate, or was she simply a projection? It was a question that could never be
answered, as every serious practitioner knew. In the laboratory of the mind, no objective verification was possible.

Practically it made no difference. There were certain
synchronicities, connections through time and space

that one ignored at one's peril. The trick was to know them.

On the same day as the ritual, he had received the necklace with Romany Chase's note. It might be simple symbolism—rejection from a woman whose resemblance to Lise was uncanny, equaling in his mind a rejection from Lise herself. A little joke that his subconscious was playing? Or some much more serious portent?

He looked again at the unfinished portrait of Lise, but beyond the surface nothing breathed. For once he saw only paint.

CHAPTER 39

Robert Cairans, the U.S. Ambassador to the Vatican, was not a man that anyone particularly liked. But he knew his way around Rome's inner circles, and more importantly understood the unique dynamics of Curial politics better than most. He'd visited the Pope at his Castel Gandolfo residence on more than one occasion. Andrew Douglas, however, was a newcomer, to both Castel Gandolfo and Curial politics.

Cairans had done most of the talking so far. Gregory, along with his Cardinal Secretary of State Fabio Antonini, had contributed little more than modest but polite nods of the head. They constituted the precise type of audience the American ambassador liked best.

Drew had nothing more to do this round but settle back into the comfortable chair he'd been offered and sip the excellent wine, a product of the papacy's own vineyards. He'd purposely let Cairans have center stage; time enough later for him to get down to real business.

"Of course, we expected this kind of conduct from the Syrians. Now that the Palestinians and Israelis are finally talking to each other."

"But this was inevitable. Everything else had been attempted but accommodation," Antonini spoke in beautiful unaccented English.

"But that's just the point. The Syrians lose power if peace comes to the Middle East. War keeps them important."

"This is unfortunate. I had hoped that Arte per Pace would offer a refuge of world community where there are no victors, no losers," Gregory spoke with a kind of sad resignation in his voice.

Cairans shook his head. "A most noble effort, Your Holiness, but—"

"I think that we can arrive at a suitable compromise with the Syrians as far as Arte per Pace is concerned." Drew stood, interrupted the ambassador's speech. Like the Syrians, Cairans thrived on conflict.

"I am most grateful for your confidence, Mr. Douglas. And we of course welcome your good counsel." The Pope smiled for the first time, his small hands spread open across his heart.

"Thank you, Your Holiness. I believe that Elliot Peters is a capable man. He works best, as we Americans say, 'when the going gets tough.' "

Gregory's laugh was surprisingly vigorous. "I like your Mr. Peters. I think that he and Father Morrow make a good team. And of course, Miss Chase." There was just a ghost of a twinkle in the pontiff's eyes. "Perhaps we must give the Syrians exactly what they want, if argument is what they desire. Is not the saying, 'Kill them with kindness'?"

"Yes, Your Holiness, kill the Syrians with kindness is an entirely rational strategy at this point."

"Good, then it is done." His Holiness stood. "Cardinal Antonini tells me, Mr. Douglas, that you have another matter of a private nature to discuss with me."

Cairans flashed Drew a surprised look. It did not take long, however, for the shock to turn sour.

"Yes, Your Holiness, I would appreciate just a moment more of your time." He made a sort of a bow, ignoring Cairans's ugly stare.

"Ambassador Cairans, we have some refreshments prepared. . . ." Cardinal Antonini rose, pointed in the direction of the doors. "If you please . . ."

It was no use—the ambassador was finished. He moved forward, knelt, kissed the Ring of Peter, and followed the papal Secretary of State out of the room.

"I think that you have something to tell me that I do not wish to hear, Mr. Douglas." The Pope had reseated himself, was indicating a chair near his for Drew.

"You have good instincts, Your Holiness."

The Pope nodded, a signal for Andrew to begin.

"You have great confidence in Julian Morrow." It came out as a statement.

"The highest confidence. He holds a position of great responsibility with Arte per Pace."

"Why?"

"Why? I do not understand." The Pope's delicate eyebrows floated above his eyes like wings.

"Why Julian Morrow, an outsider?"

"He was the best man for the position."

"An American who understands how American money likes to work."

This time the Pope smiled. "You, too, have very good instincts, Mr. Douglas."

Drew stood, turned his back on the Pope, looked out of the window. When he turned, he saw that the pontiff stared at him.

"Julian Morrow is not worthy of your confidence."

Another arch of the eyebrows, but nothing more.

"Your Holiness, how long has Cardinal DeLario been in charge of the Vatican Museums?"

"Vittorio has always been interested in the art holdings of the Vatican."

"That is not what I asked, Your Holiness."

"Over ten years." The answer came quickly.

"Ten years is a very long time."

"Not so long by Holy Mother Church's standards."
Another beatific smile.

"Very true. But long enough for Cardinal DeLario
to put himself in absolute control of the museum holdings, and to mastermind a forgery operation of international proportions. An operation that has had the
salutary effect of making him a millionaire many times
over."

If Drew had expected a response, he was disappointed. There was not a single change in the expression
on Gregory's face, and the only words he spoke were,
"Continue, Mr. Douglas."

In less than twenty minutes Andrew recounted everything the CIA knew about the forgery ring operating
out of the Vatican's restoration department, including
its ties to neo-Nazis.

"And what has this to do with Julian Morrow?" It
was the first time the Pope had spoken for quite some
time.

"He is, if I may use another American expression,
'the new kid on the block.' "

"The new kid on the block?"

"Yes. A position he inherited after he murdered
Monsignor Brisi."

A long time after Andrew Douglas left, Niccolo sat
and thought. Thought that Andrew Douglas was far too
intelligent to be fooled. But he had done his best at
feigning ignorance, and he could only hope that his act
had been good enough. Time was what he'd asked the
American agent for. Time to consider "these incomprehensible things" he'd been told.

He pressed a small button on his desk. In a moment
Antonini appeared.

"Niccolo?"

"There is no more time, Fabio. We must meet tonight."

"I will make the arrangements." Antonini made a
move to leave the room.

"One more thing, Fabio."

"Anything, Niccolo."

"Pray, dear Fabio, pray."

"You're seldom wrong about things like this, Andrew. If you think Gregory was playing dumb about De-Lario and the forgery operation, you're probably right." Romany handed Drew a cup of coffee.

"You know I shouldn't be drinking this. It's too late. I'll never get to sleep."

"You wouldn't have slept anyway."

"I don't think I like your knowing me so well, Ms. Chase."

"Sorry, but that's the down side of friendship." Romany plopped herself on the sofa.

Drew smiled, took a long drag on his mug.

"What about the neo-Nazi involvement?"

"That I'm sure of. Gregory knew nothing about it."

"What about Julian?"

Drew shook his head. "I got nothing. No impression either way."

"And me?"

"I don't see any reason why your cover shouldn't still be intact, Romany. The Vatican doesn't have any reason to think that you're an operative."

Romany rearranged a pillow behind her back. For an instant that dark-robed figure she'd seen that night she'd broken into the Restoration Department flitted across her mind. "No . . . no, I guess not."

"Even if there's some reason to suspect you, it's not going to make any difference soon anyway."

"How do you feel, Andrew? About this whole thing?"

"There're going to be some sticky moments, but the bottom line is that the Vatican wants the same thing we do. Clean up this whole mess with as few dead bodies as possible."

Romany laughed. She'd never heard Drew really talk that way before. He was always so proper.

"It's critical for all of us that Gregory is protected," Drew was speaking again. "His Holiness made something of a turnaround when he worked out that hostage situation a while back. He's got some real international clout now. Just look at this Syrian crisis."

"It's always been in the game plan to try to keep the papacy clean. It certainly helps that Gregory himself is not involved in the forgeries."

Drew set down his cup. "It's a waiting game now. I suspect the Vatican will come up with some sort of agenda. Just hope it's one we can live with."

Romany stood. "Want another cup?"

"I shouldn't . . ."

She took the cup and moved toward the kitchen.

"What's this that Sully tells me?"

In a moment she'd walked back into the living room and handed him his refill. "I don't know. What has Mr. Charming told you?"

Andrew let a wide grin stretch across his handsome face. "You and Sully act like an old married couple. He said you wanted to try to find our middleman."

"Why not? I'm center stage, and Mossad hasn't produced."

"Let me see 'why not.' How about, it's getting too dangerous?"

"Not you too, Drew. You're as bad as Sully." She sank back into the cushions of the couch. "I've done okay so far. I can handle this."

"You've done better than 'okay,' Romany." He paused. "And it would certainly help to have the middleman loose end tied up. . . ."

"Look, Drew, I know we're walking on eggshells as far as the Pope is concerned, but we're not going to let a bunch of Nazis—"

"No, Romany, we're not."

"Then I can—"

"Yes." He gave her another of his smiles. "Just be careful. This Jesuit priest is a dangerous man."

.   .   .   .

They had made their opening prayers to the Paraclete. And now the Brotherhood stood in the ritual circle, listening to the Thirteenth.

"There is no straying from our initial path. We are bound to serve, to protect the Holy Mother Church. And our commitment to return home those art treasures that the Holy Mother Church has preserved for all of posterity has not been abandoned. Our will is one."

Metatron appeared unearthly as impatient candlelight cast his face into a fuzzy composition of light and dark. The hem of his pale robe ruffled like smoke about his slippers, and when he moved his hands, his fingers made terrible clawlike shadows dance across the wall. He spoke again.

"Yet we cannot draw the line so as to include the papacy's interests alone. Cardinal DeLario must be stopped, our art recovered, but not at the sacrifice of a free and democratic Europe." A single claw skittered higher up the wall, closed into a tight fist. "The neo-Nazis must not succeed."

Haniel spoke. "Metatron, are you saying—"

"I am saying, Brothers, that moral imperatives demand that if revealing the Church's connection to the neo-Nazis is the only path to save the upcoming elections in Germany, then so be it."

"No." Muriel's invective clashed like a noisy cymbal in the hall. Then, repenting, "Forgive me, Metatron, but we cannot forsake our first duty to Holy Mother Church."

"Do you say I am wrong, Muriel?"

"I have made no accusation, but nothing can be done that puts in jeopardy that for which the Brotherhood was made. We must find time, discover the true path. We have not fully penetrated DeLario's operations."

"There is no more time." Zuriel's words were harsh.

"Ambriel?" Metatron spoke the monk's name.

The monk tilted his head upward. Yet his features were still obscured by his deep cowl, and his voice seemed to issue from shadow. "Perhaps speed is what we now need, not delay."

"Proceed, Ambriel."

"We should no longer hold back that of which we have knowledge. Rather we should go to His Eminence, tell him what we know of his activities. Strike a bargain with him. He is a man accustomed to dealing in alternatives."

"A bargain?" Barbiel questioned.

"Yes, inform His Eminence that we will take no punitive action if he will but cooperate. Assure him that no one outside knows of this thing he has done."

"We lie, Ambriel?"

"Yes."

"But this plan of yours will still require time," said Muriel. "And the Americans must be convinced that Gregory be allowed to confront Vittorio without interference."

"Clearly the Americans do not want a scandal any more than Rome does," Verchiel said. "They should be willing to cooperate."

"Then it is settled," Metatron said at last. "Another meeting is to be arranged between His Holiness and the American Andrew Douglas."

CHAPTER 40

"This wine is really excellent, Your Holiness." Andrew lifted his glass to the strong afternoon light. The wine shone clear with a gravid inner glow. Mysterious, like a large and liquid ruby.

"*Grazie.*" The Pope smiled. "The weather remained very good that year. The grapes stayed long on the vine. But you did not return today, Signor Douglas, just to have more of my wine."

"Not entirely." Andrew set down his glass. "I am eager to hear whatever you have to tell me."

Gregory made the protective gesture with his hands, crossing them over his chest. "*Sì*, eager," he said. "So I will, as you say, put my cards onto the table."

Andrew smiled back, but remained silent.

"As I believe you have probably guessed, Signor Douglas," Gregory began, "not everything that you told me yesterday came as a shock. Some of us inside the Vatican had some little time ago learned of Cardinal DeLario's betrayal. Steps were being taken."

"May I ask what steps?"

The Pope's smile turned inward. He gave a little shake of his head. "Let us say simply that a plan had already been put into action—a plan that we hoped would lead to the recovery of our stolen treasures while avoiding any scandal to the Church."

"And you want to proceed with this plan?"

"I ask for time, Signor Douglas."

Andrew leaned backward in the formal chair, high-backed and elaborately upholstered, but smaller than the thronelike affair in which Gregory sat facing him, waiting for his reply.

"The United States has no wish to embarrass either you or the Church, Your Holiness," he said finally. "Nor have we any real jurisdiction in the matter of the art. Our concern now is the German elections. And time is running out. We need names, proof of who these men really are, and what they plan for Europe."

"And you think . . ." The Pope hesitated, not wanting perhaps to plant the words.

"We think," Andrew said for him, "that your Cardinal DeLario is our key. He would almost have to know where such a large portion of his profits were going, would have to have access to the larger network—"

"I see," Gregory interrupted. He sat silent for a moment. Then, rising from the chair in which he had seemed dwarfed, he walked to look out a window. "I like you, Mr. Douglas," he said. "You seem to me an honest and forthright man . . . for a high-ranking officer of American intelligence." He turned with a genuine smile. "I shall therefore return the favor. I shall be as honest with you as I can."

"I appreciate that, Your Holiness."

"I cannot deliver to you a Prince of the Church." Gregory stood still, a figure in white, silhouetted against the afternoon blue of the window.

"What *will* you do?"

"The Cardinal will be confronted. This I promise."

"With all respect, Your Holiness. That is not enough."

The Pope did not speak at once. He came back, settled himself in the chair. "I understand what you are saying, Signor Douglas. But honey, not vinegar, will catch your fly. Your best hope, as well as ours, is for Vittorio to feel that he is still safe in the bosom of Holy Mother Church. Only then may he be persuaded to yield his secrets."

"You will not tell the Cardinal, then, that we are involved?" Andrew had picked up his wine.

"I shall let him believe that only we know about the forgeries and his connection to this neo-Nazi group. Then he will not fear giving up his records, assuming that I will seek nothing beyond the return of the art." Gregory reached for his own glass.

"Will DeLario accept that you would so casually overlook the neo-Nazi involvement?"

"The Cardinal understands that the art is irreplaceable."

Andrew nodded. "I hope," he said, "that it will not be considered in poor taste for me to say this, Your Holiness. But if you ever need a second job . . ."

The pontiff did not answer directly. But the thin lips had widened, and his glass lifted slightly in what might have been meant as a toast.

.   .   .   .

Pope Gregory didn't like the idea of having the Swiss Guard accompany him to Vittorio's apartment. It wasn't the pontiff's style. But his Secretary of State convinced him that it was only politic to do so.

Niccolo watched the toes of his patent shoes slide in and out from under the hem of his long white gown. The swishing of the papal fabric seemed unnaturally loud in the long, quiet corridor, and he marveled at the soundlessness of the two guards who should have clanked as noisily as Don Quixote tilting at windmills as they moved down the hall. They were ghosts at his back.

He paused before the double doors. This was one of the most difficult tasks he had ever set for himself. And his heart was unready for this new sorrow. He did not want Vittorio DeLario to be guilty. He did not want to know this man's sins. He glanced across his shoulders to the guards. They would remain outside the doors and wait. He lifted his fist and struck against the wood.

"*Avanti.*" The Cardinal's voice was cheery.

Niccolo twisted the handle and opened the door.

"*Avanti, avanti.*" The words were repeated, but De-Lario had ignored the opened door. His broad back was to Niccolo as he bent over a long table examining coins.

"Vittorio." The name was spoken softly.

Instantly DeLario recognized the voice and turned. "Niccolo, come in, come in. . . ." He stepped forward. "What a wonderful surprise! It has been too long since you have visited me here. We shall have some wine and talk."

Niccolo shut the door and gave in to Vittorio's embrace. The Cardinal kissed first one cheek, then another. This was to be a meeting of old friends.

The Pope smiled and pushed away from DeLario's arms. He walked to the table where he'd seen Vittorio standing. He picked up one of the coins. He pinched its end and twisted it in the light. "You have always loved beautiful things, Vittorio."

Vittorio smiled his cherub's smile and spread his arms in a kind of feigned bewilderment.

The Pope laid the coin down, picked up another. "Was that the reason, Vittorio, this need for beauty, that caused you to sin, to betray the Holy Mother Church?"

It was only then that his eyes left the ancient coin and found DeLario. What he saw was not what he'd expected. The old prelate seemed to have truly become the child that his features for so many years had only been able to imitate. But the moment passed quickly, and the face rearranged itself into its more familiar parody.

"Niccolo, I do not understand—"

"Don't, Vittorio. Don't accumulate guilt. Don't continue this game of lies."

"Niccolo . . ." The plea again.

"We know, Vittorio. We know about the forgeries. The black-marketing. The money that finds its way into the hands of neo-Nazis." He stopped, wanting all of it to be absorbed at once, wanting never to have to repeat those terrible words again.

Vittorio smoothed back an imaginary wisp of hair from his forehead. "To everything there is a season . . ."

"Do not quote the Bible to me, Vittorio. We want the art returned."

Suddenly DeLario laughed. "Returned? I am many things, Your Holiness, but a magician, I am not."

It was the laugh that finally transformed Niccolo's regret into anger, yet he forced his voice to be very quiet. "The art must return to the Vatican where it belongs, Cardinal DeLario."

"I cannot do the impossible, Niccolo."

"You have records. You are not an inefficient man. We do not care who has purchased the art. Their guilt is of no concern to us. We simply want what belongs to the Holy See. Everything shall be kept secret, but the art must be returned."

"And if I cannot . . ."

Niccolo moved away from the table of coins. Slowly he made a tour of the grand salon. Touching first one beautiful object, then another. His voice from across the room was especially clear. "You have grown accustomed, we see, to certain privileges that come to men who wear the red hat. We think you would find it very difficult to go back to being a simple priest." His thin fingers finally settled on a tiny statue of a nymph.

"A threat, Niccolo? How strange from your lips."

"A proposition, Vittorio."

"Am I under arrest?"

"You may have access to anything that will facilitate the recovery of our art."

"Under guard, of course."

Niccolo nodded his head.

"How long do I have to consider His Holiness's proposition?"

"Twenty-four hours."

Another laugh. "You have grown tough in your late years, Niccolo. Or have I been but a blind man?"

"At first there were many blind men. But no longer." Then, "How far has this disease spread, Vittorio? Is the whole of the Restoration Department infected?"

A practiced smile passed across DeLario's lips, and he tugged once on the heavy cross around his neck before he moved to a small desk in the corner of the room. He slid open a drawer and retrieved a box. He turned abruptly. "Have you ever had your fortune read, Niccolo? No . . . no, of course not"—he waved his free hand—"that would be a sin." A real laugh this time, as his fingers unlatched the lid and lifted a deck of long, slim cards. *"Visconti-Sforza tarocchi.* Very old. Very rare," he said respectfully. Then his full lips brushed against the surface of the first card.

"My fate . . ." Vittorio held the deck above his head like a crown and, with an exaggerated flourish, splayed the cards face down on top of the desk. His hand made an imaginary circle, once, twice, three times. When the ritual was completed, his fingers plucked out one of the cards.

He raised his brows in surprise. Then he turned the

card so that Niccolo could see it. "The Hanged Man," he announced.

The pontiff remained transfixed by DeLario's little show. Watching, waiting for some clue that he knew was certain to come.

"Life in suspension," the Cardinal was speaking again. "Transition. Change. Reversal of the mind. An alteration of life's forces. A period of respite between significant events . . ."

"How far, Vittorio? How far has this thing gone?" He had had enough of the theatrics.

"Do you not accept that there can be honor among thieves?"

The Pope pressed his lips together, determined to say nothing.

"Oh, my old friend Niccolo, what others have done, they have done by my will. They have but followed orders. They are sheep, Niccolo, sheep. Spare them. If a price must be exacted, exact that price of me."

DeLario had transformed himself from carnival wizard to martyr in seconds. Both performances made Niccolo sick.

"Twenty-four hours, Cardinal DeLario," he said abruptly, then turned and left the room.

If he were a different man, Cardinal Vittorio De-Lario might have been praying for his immortal soul. But prayer was the furthest thing from His Eminence's mind. There were important plans to be made, and it was already half past midnight. Time was an enemy now. And the night, with its quiet and shadow, one of few friends.

A noise. Did he hear a noise? No, he was becoming too nervous. And that was dangerous. He had to be himself if he was to accomplish all that had to be done. Now, where did he put . . .

Sì, sì, there was a noise. But where? From whom? The guards? He tiptoed to the doors and placed his ear against the wood. Nothing. Nothing but the sound of breathing. Did they sleep? Niccolo would not like that. But he thought not. The Swiss were proud of their petty little honors.

He slowly turned and leaned his back into the doors. He shut his eyes for a moment. Even pulling on the cross didn't help. One long breath and he opened his lids.

Even though he hid in the dark, away from the half-draped windows, away from the soft-glowing lamps, Cardinal DeLario recognized the tall angular silhouette of the Jesuit. He swallowed the saliva he'd been holding before he spoke.

"How pleasant of you to visit. A corporeal work of mercy?" He laughed softly at his own joke.

Julian Morrow stepped into a circle of light. "A corporeal work of mercy?"

"Visiting the imprisoned." He tilted his head toward the double doors.

"I'd forgotten about the corporeal works." Julian walked in closer. "I'm afraid my priestly instincts are a little rusty."

"I understand this American phrase." And he nodded, self-satisfied. "Please . . ." He indicated a place on the long elegant sofa.

"No, thank you. I'd rather stand."

"So cool, so formal. Not at all what I would expect of our new friendship." DeLario walked closer to the priest, ran his palm over the fine knit of the polo shirt the Jesuit wore. "Not so priestly either." He tested the tips of his fingers, then turned away.

"How?" The first real word.

DeLario twisted back around. "How did they find out?" He shrugged. "Niccolo is a jackal. He is cunning. There are a million paths I could follow to find the answer to your question. But it is of no matter now. We are discovered, and it is at an end."

"Just like that."

"Just like that, Julian Morrow."

This time it was the priest who laughed. "You surprise me, DeLario. I would have expected you to be scurrying around . . ."

"Like a rat?"

Julian arched his eyebrows.

"You can say it. But terrible times also fashion great men." DeLario gave the priest his most cherubic smile. "Now it is my turn to ask a question. What are you doing here?"

"I figure your man Polidori might have something to say to Gregory's people."

"Nino?"

"I was on my way down to see Polidori earlier this evening when I realized the operation was blown . . . found out. Gregory's men were everywhere. I figured it was only a matter of time before they came looking for me."

"I see." The Cardinal's eyes grew smaller. "But you still haven't answered my question, Father Morrow. Why are you here?"

"I'm loyal?"

DeLario's laugh was full tilt this time, came from deep inside his belly. "That's wonderful. I was only just this afternoon reminding His Holiness of the honor there is among thieves."

"I thought there might be someone on the outside . . ."

"Someone on the outside . . ." The Cardinal repeated Julian's words. "Very good, Morrow, very good."

"And I thought that you would like me to deliver some kind of message."

"Oh, but you do not want to do that. Don't you realize the more you know, the more dangerous it becomes for you? I think I shall take care of any messages to the outside, Father Morrow. For your own protection, of course."

"Of course." Julian's mouth shaped itself into a sneer that he passed for a smile.

"But there is something you can do for me."

Julian waited.

"I want you to go to Zurich. Wait there for my call."

"That's it?"

"*Sì.*"

This time it was Julian who moved in closer. He looked down into the fat rosy face. "What's in Zurich, Cardinal DeLario? Bank accounts?"

The Cardinal broke away. "They have discovered the accounts, but I don't think they'll be able to access them."

"But you want some extra insurance just in case something goes wrong."

"*Sì,* some insurance."

"And I am that insurance."

DeLario nodded.

"It's always been for the money, hasn't it?"

This time the Cardinal's face changed, changed into someone the priest had never before seen. "You may not believe this, but it was not always for the money."

He didn't say so, but in that instant it seemed Julian quite believed Cardinal Vittorio DeLario.

"But you, Father Morrow, you are still lean and hungry."

"Fifty percent of what is in the Swiss banks."

"Very hungry." DeLario laughed. "Thirty-three, my Jesuit friend, and not a lira more."

"Where do I go?"

"Here, I will write the address. Remain there until you receive my call." The Cardinal wrote down the address of a hotel.

"You should be able to get a flight out of da Vinci tonight. I don't think Niccolo will have anyone at the airport." He handed him the slip of paper. "*Buono fortuna,* Julian Morrow."

Julian smiled, made a kind of salute. "*Grazie, grazie mille,* Cardinal DeLario," he said softly, disappearing back into the shadows.

CHAPTER 41

Always the same, Sister Annunciata complained to herself as she moved slowly down the long hall, trying to balance the full tray in her hands while keeping the morning papers clamped tightly under her arm. It was enough to make a nun lose her faith. The eggs, not too soft, but not too hard, she repeated the litany under her breath. And the milk boiled, but make sure there was no "skin" floating on the top. Of course, the fruit should always be the plumpest and the freshest from the kitchens. If she was to be condemned to the eternal flames of hell, it would surely be for her impatience with His Eminence. And though she prayed each night for deliverance from the chore of having to serve breakfast to Cardinal Vittorio DeLario, as of yet her prayers had gone unanswered.

Sister Annunciata's ample breasts heaved as she took in a long, exasperated breath upon nearing His Eminence's rooms. She stopped short. But what was this? Papal guards in front of the Cardinal's apartment. This she did not understand. But like so many things in the male-dominated world of the Vatican, Sister Annunciata did not spend much time or energy trying to figure out the puzzle. She had learned many years ago, to be a woman in service to the Holy Mother Church meant to go about your business without asking any questions.

So it was that Sister Annunciata walked up to the Cardinal's double doors and acted as though the Swiss did not exist, and knocked three times. It was the long-ago agreed-upon ritual between her and His Eminence. Knock three times. If the door was locked, she was simply to take the tray away. If unlocked, she was to enter, call His Eminence's name, and begin her preparations.

She would begin by placing a freshly starched linen

cloth on the table nearest the window. Fresh flowers would come next. Set in the exact center of the table. The heavy drapes would be drawn. To let the Roman sunlight in, His Eminence would say. Although she suspected that opening the curtains was just another portion of her penance. In the bright light, Cardinal Vittorio could carefully inspect the breakfast Sister Mary Annunciata had brought in.

"Your Eminence. It is Sister Annunciata. Breakfast, Cardinal DeLario. Fresh strawberries this morning." She was very cheerful in her duties.

One, two, three, Sister Annunciata went about her tasks, getting everything in readiness for His Eminence. Better call him again, she thought to herself. "Cardinal Vittorio. Breakfast."

She didn't like it when he wouldn't awaken right away, and she would have to creep up to his bedroom door and knock. Sometimes she would even have to go in and give him a good shake to rouse him. This she really hated. She had never seen a grown man in bed. Not even her father.

"Your Eminence," she called out a third time, walking toward the bedroom suite. A hearty knock. She put her ear to the door. Quiet. She could curse if she were not a holy woman. She squeezed the knob and turned.

"Your Eminence," she said softly, peeking inside the darkened room. He was still asleep. She could see, even in the dimness, his body in a large tight bundle under the covers.

She moved to the side of the bed. "Cardinal Vittorio?" She reached out a hand to touch his shoulder.

In the instant her hand met his body, she knew something was wrong. This was not flesh she touched. Not living flesh. She jerked her arm away, and for the first time in her life Sister Annunciata really screamed.

"O mio Dio! A'morto. A'morto."

·   ·   ·

Out on the street Romany kept walking, fast. The park was only a couple blocks away, but it had taken her more than an hour to get away from her desk. She wondered what kind of message she would find beneath the park bench—had been wondering ever since this morning when she'd passed the flower seller with the red scarf on her way inside the Arte per Pace building.

The ever-present pigeons greeted her as she entered the small piazza, following her like a small gray army as she made her way to the bench. She flopped down. Took deep breaths. There was no reason to believe the message was especially urgent. Sully could have contacted her through the cut-out if that was the case. Still, things were happening now. Happening fast. And Sully could have some word on Julian.

She opened her purse and took out a package of crackers. Crumbling them up, she began tossing pieces to the birds that fluttered and strutted at her feet, accomplices providing her cover. Casually she glanced around the park, saw no one, and pulled her purse closer, covering the action of her hand as she probed for the note beneath the slat. There was nothing.

She frowned. Wrong slat? She tried again. But still there was nothing.

Steps. On the walkway, approaching from behind. Inside her purse was the gun. She reached inside, her fingers locking on the grip. Slowly, innocently curious, she turned around.

The exclamation came out quietly, beneath her breath, as slowly she withdrew her hand and, turning just as casually back, put on a diffident expression—attractive woman confronted by total stranger in the park. Uninterested. Wary.

Sully sat down at the other end of the bench and opened the *London Times*. His eyes darted for a moment, left, right, then the newspaper covered his face. She began again feeding the pigeons.

"Got any news?" He spoke from the corner of his mouth.

She kept her eyes forward. "Not too much. Talked to my boss this morning. Gave him the stuff I'd worked up with Morrow on the Syrians." She took out another package of the crackers. "Elliot's been trying to call Julian," she went on. "He's talked to Richard Vance and says he gets this funny feeling there might be something wrong. Weird vibes, he called them. That might mean something, but then again, Vance always gives off weird vibes."

"Oh, it means something, I think." Sully's eyes scanned the newspaper as if he really were reading. "Your lover-boy has split," he said. "Flown the coop to Switzerland."

Her eyes cut toward his face. She forced them forward. "How do you know?"

"A tail," Sully answered. "I said it was hard to follow Morrow inside the Vatican, not out. He was spotted leaving through St. Anne's gate late last night. Took a taxi straight to the airport. Got on the first flight for Zurich."

"You said 'flown the coop.' What did you mean by that?"

Sully took his time turning a page before he spoke. "Andrew went back to see the Pope yesterday. A summons."

"And?"

"Gregory wanted time. Said they needed to handle the Cardinal their own way. *They* being the Vatican version of the good ol' boys, I guess."

"What has this to do with—?"

Sully continued, ignoring the interruption. "Gregory's plan seems to be to confront DeLario. Then let him believe it can all be taken care of inside their little club. Catch flies with honey is the way Andrew said he put it. Anyway, maybe Morrow found out which way the wind was blowing and took off. Didn't want to trust himself to the tender mercies of the Curia, I guess."

"Maybe, Sully. But couldn't Julian just be in Switzerland to visit the Shaunessy woman?"

"Could be. But then why is he in Zurich? And just sitting in his hotel room apparently. Last report I had, he hadn't come out yet."

"So what are you going to do?"

"About Morrow? Nothing. Andrew promised the Pope we'd sit tight. The tail is as far as we go."

"And me?"

"You sit tight too. Not much you can do now either, with lover-boy in Switzerland."

"There's something you can do, Sully."

"What's that?"

"You can quit with the lover-boy crap."

"It's just a tag."

"I don't like it."

"You're strung too tight, Romany."

"Why are you hassling me, Sully?"

"Andrew doesn't see it, but I say you're too close."

She wanted to slap him. She crumbled the last of the crackers instead. "Fuck you, Sully." She said it to the pigeons. But when she did turn her head, he was already walking away.

"Why do you stare at me like that, Friedrich?" Cardinal Vittorio DeLario had been laughing. But now he was not entirely sure of the Baron's reaction.

"It is the suit, Vittorio. In all these years I have never seen you in anything but clerical robes. Forgive me, old friend, but the sight of you in a coat and tie is a shock."

"To me also." Vittorio made a kind of grimacing shrug, as if the silk jacket had not quite settled into place upon his shoulders. "I thought it best to make the change, given the circumstances."

"You have thought of everything, Vittorio."

"I have tried. That this day would come, I knew in my heart. And now it is here."

"And you are sad."

It had sounded like real sympathy. The Cardinal

looked closely at the chill blue eyes. No stiletto there. *"Sì,"* he said simply. "I can hide where none will ever find me. I am a rich man. . . ."

"But what is that without your Church?"

"You understand, Friedrich."

"But of course. I have lived in exile all my life. . . . But tell me again, Vittorio, you are certain that only within the Pope's small circle is anything about the forgeries known?"

"Oh, *sì.* Niccolo and the rest of them, they are desperate to keep all of it quiet. They will tell no one."

"And they know nothing of me?"

"They know some money has exchanged hands. But that is not Niccolo's concern. He wants the return of the art."

"Gregory knows about the neo-Nazis? Did he question you about it?"

"Yes, but I know very little. What could I say?"

"Schweinhund."

He had never heard the Baron curse. "Why are you so angry, Friedrich?" he asked the frozen eyes.

"Are you blind, Vittorio? Do you really believe that His Holiness will simply overlook this neo-Nazi connection? He is not, after all, our Pius the Twelfth."

"I did not think—"

"Obviously. But fortunately that does not matter." The Baron unexpectedly smiled.

Vittorio watched as Friedrich got up and walked to the table across the room. He plucked a rose from the vase and, pinching it from its long stem, settled it into the buttonhole of his lapel.

"I have almost looked forward to this day. The opportunity to play . . . a certain trump card."

"Trump card?"

"Yes, Vittorio. Secrets are the most fun when at last they can be shared." He returned now to his chair and sipped at his wine, drawing out the moment.

"It has to do with Himmler," he said at last, "and his search for the Holy Grail."

"You are not making a joke with me, Friedrich?"

"Joke? Oh, no. It was no joke to Himmler. The Reichsführer was obsessed with the legend of the Grail. And the Knights Templar. He modeled the SS on the Knights."

"And what has this—"

"Patience, Vittorio. You will spoil the story. And it is rich in ironies."

Another sip of the wine. "Himmler's grand plan was to carve a Templar-like kingdom for himself and his SS within Hitler's thousand year Reich. He went out and found a castle. Wewelsburg. Had it renovated at a cost of millions. There were ceremonies there, in a secret chamber below the dining hall. You can appreciate that, Vittorio. Secret passages. The use of ritual. Himmler, you may know, had been educated by Jesuits."

"And he sent you to look for the Grail."

Again Friedrich smiled, recognizing the attempt to have him get on with the story.

"Yes," he said. "Himmler wanted the power which he thought that the Grail would bestow, invincible power which would insure the success of his dreams. He had gathered many old manuscripts, one of which revealed the location of a Templar stronghold in France. Himmler convinced himself that the Knights had hidden the Grail there."

"You're not telling me, Friedrich, that you found the cup of Christ?"

The Baron hesitated, seemed to consider the words. "No," he said slowly. "Or rather, yes, if you mean that in the alchemical sense."

"I do not understand this reference, Friedrich. There is a point to this?"

The Baron made a moue of regret. "Forgive me, Vittorio. I have indulged myself at your expense. The Holy Grail was not at Bezu. But something else was. What I found there, what I never gave to Himmler, will do well enough to keep Niccolo Fratelli in line."

CHAPTER 42

It was a shock for Gina, visiting him in this manner. Never would she have thought he would have allowed anyone to see him like this. The impeccably proper Count Klaus Sebastiano. Playing at his game of mystery. Guarding his privacy. Relishing his icon status.

But the Count was a contradiction too. Being unpredictable, his forte. And had she not been so sophisticated, and had not Sebastiano toyed with her before, Gina di Lorenzo would have been utterly embarrassed to find, upon being ushered into the Count's bath, the Count himself submerged in a tub of crystal-clear water.

There was a single chair in the room, pushed into a corner. But the Count did not ask Gina if she wished to sit. Instead she was forced to stand by the side of the gigantic marble tub, forced to look down into the Count's face as they spoke, forced to keep her eyes from drifting down into the water.

She could see he was enjoying her predicament. And to make matters worse, every once in a while he would raise one leg and shift slightly in the tub, so that that fleshy pink island between his thighs rose and fell, bobbed in and out of the water.

"So there is much confusion over at Arte per Pace." The Count was rubbing the side of the tub with his fingers.

"Just when we think we've got the mess with the Syrians under control, this happens." Gina shifted on her high heels. "First, Cardinal DeLario becomes 'indisposed,' then Father Morrow disappears."

"No word on Morrow?"

Gina shook her head. "Nothing. Vance has been filling in."

"Vance?" Another shift in the tub.

"Morrow's assistant. The priest I told you about. The strange one."

The Count smiled, leaned farther back into the water. "Well, Gina, what do you make of all this?"

The woman's pretty face screwed itself into a frown. "Something's going on. But nobody's talking. Nobody."

"Interesting," he said almost to himself, "very interesting." Then, ". . . And how is our Signorina Chase?"

Gina rolled her eyes. "Like always. Nothing ever seems to bother Signorina Chase." There was just a trace of bitchiness in her last words.

He didn't say anything after that, and she watched him for a moment longer. The old man who didn't look like an old man, soaking in the tub, thinking whatever men like Klaus Sebastiano think.

Then suddenly he was out of the water. Dripping, standing stark naked in front of her. Later, when she would remember that precise instant, two things would clearly stand out in Gina's mind. Klaus Sebastiano's smile of absolute self-satisfaction. And the sight of the largest penis she had ever seen.

Julian picked up the phone on the first ring. "Hello."

"You follow instructions very well, Father Morrow."

"Where are you?"

"That is of no importance. But let's say I'm where the papal watchdogs can't find me." Cardinal DeLario made a small laugh. "How's Zurich?"

"I wouldn't know. I've seen only this hotel room for the last twenty-four hours."

"My poor boy, how you have suffered." Another taunting laugh. "But enough, I require you back in Rome."

"Rome? I don't think I want to go back to Rome."

"You need not worry, as long as you are discreet."

"They're looking for me?"

"Precisely. Your sudden disappearance did nothing to aid your cause. I hear Niccolo is not pleased."

"I'm not leaving Switzerland. Not without my thirty-three percent. That was our deal."

This time the laugh was heartier. "I like you, Julian Morrow. You are sufficiently hungry still to make you extremely useful. Come home to Roma. I promise there will be more than enough money to satisfy that young appetite of yours. But you must hurry. I have a message for you to deliver to His Holiness."

"We did not expect you, Father Morrow," Sister Lucienne spoke in her soft French voice, as she led Julian down the sanitarium's long corridor. "We were all very shocked when she came out of her coma, Father. It was surely God's providence."

"How is she, Sister Lucienne?"

"As though nothing has happened, Father. Dr. Armand says she is in almost perfect health. A little weak. The muscles a bit soft. Except of course, our Colleen has not lost a moment of time."

"Hasn't lost any time?"

Sister Lucienne stopped short of Colleen Shaunessy's room. "She is in the past, Father Morrow. Back where she was when the accident happened. Please, do not worry." The nun reached out a hand and patted his arm. Then she smiled. "I told Colleen she had a visitor. She wanted her hair combed. That is a good sign, Father."

Sister Lucienne turned and slowly pushed open the door to room 230. It was brighter than the last time. The overhead light was on, and the blinds were partially raised. Colleen was different too. She seemed somehow younger, a pretty young girl who had been checked into the hospital for some minor ailment. The roses near the bed, like the patient, were fresher too.

"Colleen, here is that visitor I promised." Sister Lucienne moved in closer, stepping cautiously as one would toward a small cornered animal. Her arm stretched backward, beckoning Julian to follow. "This is

Father Julian Morrow, Colleen," she spoke, in heavily accented English. "He has been a good friend while you have been with us."

Then Sister Lucienne's fingers met Julian's, and he stepped from behind her to the edge of the hospital bed.

Even years after, it would be hard to interpret those feelings that crowded inside of him at that moment, but even more difficult to decipher the complex of emotions that crossed Colleen Shaunessy's face when she looked up and saw him standing there. The only aspect of that entire encounter that would ever be clearly articulated in his mind was the single word that finally came from Colleen's lips.

"Michael," she cried. "Michael . . ."

It had been Julian's intention to make a quick trip from Zurich to St. Cecile's before returning to Rome. A quick uneventful trip. But as on so many other occasions, Julian had pulled a con on himself, had failed to face up to reality. A visit to a no-longer-comatose Colleen Shaunessy could never have been quick or simple. Nothing with Colleen ever had. . . .

"Michael . . ."

Sister Lucienne had run up then. Wrapped her arms around her patient. Shushed her like a baby. "No, Colleen, this is Father Morrow, *ma petite.*"

Like the coward he'd always been, he kept silent, allowed the fiction to remain in Sister Lucienne's mind. Then when he could no longer endure the weeping, the calling out of that name that had once been his, he moved toward the bed and took Colleen from the nun's arms.

"I'm here, Colleen. It's Michael." And in the second before he'd tucked her safely into his arms, he looked up to catch the astonishment in Sister Lucienne's eyes fade to understanding.

Colleen gazed up into his face, her blue eyes

clouded by unshed tears. "Michael?" she asked hoarsely, reaching out a small hand to touch his cheek.

"Yes."

"Oh my darling, something terrible is going to happen. . . ." She trembled against him, tears beginning to fall again.

"No, Colleen . . ." He wanted her to know the truth. At least the part that wouldn't hurt.

She pushed out of his arms. Her face was earnest, in pain. She shook her head hard, her long hair tossed like a pink cloud around her shoulders. "You must listen, Michael. They want to kill you. There is . . ." She stopped. Her eyes widened, blazed with horror. And then she screamed.

His arms went around her again. Tightened. "Shhh, Colleen. I'm here. I'm all right." He pressed her head into his chest.

"The explosion?" She wrenched herself away.

"Everything's fine now, Colleen. Please . . ." He felt his throat begin to close in on itself.

"But the baby. *Our* baby . . ." The terror returned as she reached down to touch her abdomen.

"He's fine, Colleen. Just fine."

"He . . . ?" Her face struggled with some kind of understanding.

"Patrick."

"Patrick . . ." She repeated the name. "My baby . . ."

He took her hands into his, stared into her eyes. "You have been asleep, Colleen. Asleep for a long time. Patrick is five years old. . . ."

He had left her with that. Those words and nothing else. He watched as Sister Lucienne took her from him, forced her to lie back, to try to rest. In a moment, she had fallen asleep.

He figured he'd gotten away in time. Gotten away before things had become more complicated. Gotten away before Sister Lucienne had had a chance to question him. Before his own conscience had gotten the better of him.

Oh, yes, Julian Morrow understood his limits. He had drawn them often enough. He also understood how fragile those limits were. And the consequences of exceeding those limits. He had exceeded those limits with Colleen. And now he was doing the same with Romany. If he thought he was worth it, he could perhaps muster enough energy to despise himself. But thankfully there wasn't enough time. He had other matters to settle. Cardinal DeLario needed him in Rome.

The property registry basement was perversely depressing. All modern white tiles and primary colors, it was still windowless with row upon row of white fluorescent lights that beat down, artificial and merciless. After three and a half hours in a plastic chair, Marthe sat aching, staring blankly at the latest file in front of her.

For the first time since Helena Klimpt's visit, she was near to feeling despair. Today was not her first day of looking through properties. She had already been through the records for Rome in the fifties, when Friedrich von Hohenhofen was supposed to have arrived in the city. Now she had moved on to the outlying districts for those same years. If she came up with nothing, it would be back to Rome for the years immediately following. And so on and on.

She made herself look at the next page. It was hopeless if you thought too much. You had to narrow it down, think only about the file in front of you. Check the name against the page, and then move on to another. Only the name was the name of a Nazi, a name that surely he must have changed. If not before, at least at the time he had left South America.

She looked up at the clock. It was getting late. Bernardo would come back soon with her pills and bottled water, insisting that she stop. At least she would finish this one file. She could think again about how hopeless it all was tomorrow.

Only three pages later she found it. Not *the* name. An English name, Frederick Hightower. She wrote it down on her notepad to examine it. Frederick Hightower. The initials F.H. Frederick instead of Friedrich. And Hightower. She didn't know very much German, but *hohen,* she thought, meant high. And *hofen.* That could mean something like tower, couldn't it? She wished she could ask Theodor.

She looked for the date of the transfer. The year the property had changed hands. Nineteen fifty-three. Exactly right. The year that Helena had said he was supposed to have arrived in Rome.

She rested, breathless, slumped against the desk. The plastic chair curled behind her like a snail shell. There were tears never shed on her cheeks now, crushed out by the weight of the doubt that had now fallen away.

Black certainty filled her in its stead. In a moment she was all right again. And lifting her head, she began filling out the request form for a photocopy of the page.

David parked the rented car and got out across from the blank-faced government building. He'd been putting it off for days now, this wasted trip for the name of the owner of a building. Just the tying up of a last loose end that would mark the end of a lead. All those days tracking Anton Arendt for nothing.

He had gone up the stone stairs, was nearly to the glass doors when the woman coming out stumbled on the landing in front of him. His trained instinct was to step back. Middle-aged lady with cane was a perfect disguise for someone wanting to slip a three-inch spike between your vertebrae.

He knew in seconds she was only what she seemed, and moved to help. But another man, already at her side, was casting him poison glances.

He picked up her purse instead, handed it back. *"Scusi, Signora."*

"My fault," she said in American English. Smiled.

There was some quality in that brief expression that made him really look. But the big Italian who'd helped her stand was hustling her away.

". . . a hidden doorway in his room. I should have guessed it was that. He's always been so fond of his secrets." The voice of Metatron sounded hollow, an echo in the well of the confessional.

"The passageway leads out into the gardens," said the monk, "well beyond the Apostolic Palace. Of course, how the Cardinal got outside the gates . . . ?"

"He had help, my son," answered Metatron. "Be very sure of that. He has friends, does our dear Vittorio, who even now would not yet dare to cross him. They know his power and have not yet tasted ours. But they will, please God, they will."

"He did not take his car." The monk had returned to particulars.

"Little matter," Metatron said. "He is not, I think, wandering Rome on foot. Vittorio, I fear, has resources at which we can only begin to guess."

"Perhaps the CIA should be told of his escape?"

"No. Not yet."

"But perhaps with their help—"

"They cannot be told, Zuriel. They have given us time. We will take it. Andrew Douglas is a good man, I believe, a patient man, but he is not the top. If those above him should come to believe that we have lost control . . ." The voice slowed and stopped. The monk could feel the mind behind the wizened face working in the dark, the fingers moving like spiders counting invisible beads.

"We have not lost control, Zuriel." The voice came again. "And what could the Americans do better than we? They have no feeling, no instinct for our ancient games."

"And so, Metatron, Ambriel remains our last best hope?" He had spoken with an irony he thought the other would miss. He was wrong.

"You play games, Zuriel, but indeed, you have said it. Ambriel remains our hope."

CHAPTER 43

The Black Baron stared at the figure before him. Already the padding to bolster the naturally lean belly was sagging, and the greasepaint used to duplicate a Mediterranean complexion was a stinking ruin on the narrow, bony face. The black mustache cocked at a queer angle. The German had done a very poor job with his disguise, resembling only slightly some stock character from a very bad Italian opera. Not the worst of Arendt's flaws was his gross lack of imagination.

But Anton Arendt was the best Friedrich had. At this late stage, it seemed that the gods had seen fit to deal him an impossible hand.

"I trust you were not followed here," the Baron finally spoke, the "here" being the Palazzo Rozze.

"No, Herr Baron, or should I say Count—"

"That is not necessary." Friedrich cut the German short. He was not in good temper. Dealing with his own mortality was not something he'd yet mastered.

The German coughed self-consciously. "I think, Herr Baron, this disguise would fool anyone."

Friedrich reexamined the man's costume, and thought that the silly disguise would fool no one. He cursed the gods silently. Already he was beginning to regret his decision. "Yes, Anton, a very good disguise."

The little German smiled nakedly, puffed up his chest in obvious reaction to the Baron's compliment, his use of Arendt's Christian name. "I thought so, Herr Baron. I followed your orders as closely as possible. There is some urgency . . . ?"

The Baron walked away and stood by the glass doors leading out into the gardens. A fountain bubbled hotly in the Italian sunlight. "I think that summer is my least favorite season." The Baron spoke with his back still turned toward his visitor.

"It is very warm in Rome, Herr Baron. In our Germany the summers are milder."

Friedrich did not turn. "Yes, our Germany . . ."

Anton stood watching, the mustache at last peeling from one side of his mouth. He reached and tore it away, leaving a pasty white line of skin over his lip.

"Our operation is at an end." The Baron turned abruptly with his words.

"At an end . . . ?"

"Yes, Herr Arendt, that is precisely what I said. The forgery operation has been found out."

"How much do they know? Do they know—?"

"No, Herr Arendt, they do not know your identity." The little man was so predictable.

"What—?"

"They know that the art is being black-marketed through a middleman, and that some of the profits are going to support a new right-wing group in Germany."

"Right-wing?"

"I believe the exact phrase was neo-Nazi."

Arendt jerked at his collar as though it were a noose and gave out a single nasty curse.

For an instant Friedrich allowed himself to enjoy the little man's frustration. Then, "Now, now, Herr Arendt, our cause has done well. All things must end. And there is no real harm done."

"But what if—"

Friedrich raised a hand into the air. "Nothing will happen."

"How can you be so sure?"

The Baron smiled then, half closed the lizard lids of

his eyes. More than anything he wanted to dismiss this ignorant, pathetic man, banish him forever from his sight. But this he could not do. For Friedrich von Hohenhofen could not beat the gods at their own game. Not this time.

"I am sure." The words tasted like the finest wine in his mouth. "I am sure, Herr Arendt."

Friedrich moved to sit in a chair. He crossed his legs at the knees. "The Holy Mother Church is very powerful. Powerful in strange and beautiful ways." Friedrich ran his tongue over his lips. "That is why it will be all the more satisfying to see her beg like a cheap whore."

Arendt had not been offered a seat, and he stood across from the Baron, shifting the weight on his feet. His ugly features had at last begun to seep through the makeup.

"I know many things, Herr Arendt. Over the years I have had the privilege to keep many secrets. One especially has given me great pleasure."

"A secret, Herr Baron?"

"Yes, a secret." The Baron inhaled audibly, his nostrils flaring as though he breathed his own scent. "A secret that I shall at last share."

"With me, Herr Baron?" Anton's eyes opened wide.

"But, of course, you. We are true Germans."

"Yes, Herr Baron, yes." Anton stepped back, reached for the arm of the sofa, and sat.

The Black Baron gave him a sparkling smile. "I grow old. . . ."

"No, no. You are . . ."

He would have to tolerate much, but he would not be patronized by this little worm. "Please, Herr Arendt, do not be generous. I am old. I have few years left. And someone must take my secrets from me. Someone I can trust . . ."

"Herr Baron, you have always been able to trust me."

"Precisely, Anton, that is why you shall know the

secret that will keep the Holy Mother Church from ever bringing us harm."

Despite the heat of Roman midday, it was cool in the Temple of Aesculapius. Julian and the Cardinal stood facing one another, like two errant tourists, alone on the small island of the Giardino del Lago at the outer reaches of the vast Borghese Gardens.

"Where in the hell did you get this?" Julian was staring at the photographs. At the crisp photocopies of parched, fragmented text.

"An old friend has had it for years," said the Cardinal.

"Friend . . . ?" Julian looked up.

"A friend of Pius the Twelfth."

"You've lost me."

The Cardinal shook his head. "I would have thought you were a better student of history."

"Who?"

"A German."

Julian's eyes went back to the pages, scanning the black letters of ancient Aramaic. "Do you realize what this means for *Munificentissimus Deus?*"

"Of course, dear boy." The cherub smile spread. "Pius was warned at the time he made the pronouncement. By me, for one. He made it anyway. A huge mistake. Pinning papal infallibility on the skirts of a woman."

"So what message do you want me to give them?"

"Tell Niccolo that it would be wise to cooperate, if he doesn't want the world to see what you hold in your hands."

The words had sounded bitter, and Vittorio knew it. Perhaps a reaction to the hot fabric of the sport coat that made him want to scratch. Perhaps a real reluctance to have it come to this.

The Jesuit was silent, waiting for more.

"Tell His Holiness we'll stop the operation," Vittorio

said more easily. "Its time has passed. But the Church must not attempt to regain that which has already been sold."

"I understand."

"I, of course," the Cardinal continued, "shall remain in my position as Prefect of the Vatican Museum with all the benefits of that office."

"And I?"

"And you, dear boy, will take our dearly departed Monsignor Brisi's place as Curator. You will not want, my Jesuit friend."

"Thirty-three percent . . . gross," Julian reminded him.

"There is, of course, a most important condition." Vittorio had ignored the interruption. "Niccolo must give his promise that there will be no attempt, now or ever, to influence the course of German politics. Do you have that?"

"Yes. But what if they are not convinced? What if they believe these relics are fakes?"

The Cardinal's hand reached for the cross that wasn't there. "They will want to believe. They will grasp at their faith in their own power. But magisterium won't change the facts. Here." Vittorio reached into his pocket, and gave the Jesuit a small plastic bag. "Let them test this fragment of the papyrus. And this." He passed the priest a small object.

Sudden quiet made the temple a tomb. Lakewater lapped like tiny tongues sucking on the shore. A moment winked, and passed. Julian understood. The *rock* in his hand was an actual joint of ancient phalangeal bone.

"Are you sure this is the way?" Marthe looked out the backseat window of the car on what seemed unending countryside.

"I am sure, Signora Marthe. See, I have marked the place." Bernardo, his eyes on the twisting roadway ahead, lifted the map over his shoulder for her to inspect. "This is indeed the road that passes in front of the villa."

"It is very isolated."

"*Sì.* But there is a house there. Extremely old, according to the innkeeper."

"He knew of it?"

"Oh, *sì*, they all knew, though it took some time before I could get them to talk. I hope I did not leave you too long in the sun?"

"No, it was lovely out on the terrace. I sat beneath a laurel tree. And the food was good. . . . Tell me, Bernardo, what did you find out?"

"The house is still called the Villa Bassano, and the property did indeed change hands after the war. The village men all agreed on that."

"The owner . . . Hightower?"

"They have never seen the owner."

"Not in all these years?"

"No." Bernardo shook his head.

"Perhaps he is dead."

"I do not think so, Signora Marthe. The villagers never see him, but they do see members of his staff. All Germans."

"Germans, yes." Relief was in her voice.

"And the car," said Bernardo, "they see that. A large Mercedes. The model changes with the years, but it is always the same. Black, with the same chauffeur. It passes often, but usually late at night."

"Other cars, I wonder?"

"Not many, Signora. I asked them that. There are cars and small trucks used by the staff. But the Germans avoid the village, except when they come for wine or to the village market. And there are, of course, the delivery trucks from Rome. It is all very strange, Signora."

"What do the villagers say? There must be stories."

"What you'd expect from peasants. The devil lives there. Or vampires. They say it with a laugh but half believe it. The staff is German, so some say the Baron is really Hitler." Bernardo laughed. "He would have to be more than a hundred."

"The *baron?* They call him that?" said Marthe.

"Oh, *si*, though no one seems to remember when this began. Probably picked up from overhearing the Germans. . . . There was a young barmaid who claimed that her grandmother had once been inside the house. The others laughed."

"Laughed? Why?"

"It's a tale they've heard for nearly forty years. It seems the barmaid's mother was illegitimate. The villagers think the story was made up to explain why the grandmother's lover didn't marry her."

"What did she see there, this grandmother?"

"I was sure you'd want to know." Bernardo's smile lighted the rearview mirror. "I took the barmaid to the side before I left. She was pleased to tell me the story.

"Her grandmother's name is Philomena. She was, in her day, the most beautiful girl in the village. One of the Germans came often to buy the local wine, and fell in love with her. Although Wolfgang knew it was forbidden for the staff to mix with the villagers, he would sneak away from the villa every chance he got.

"Always when they lay together in her father's barn, Wolfgang would tell her fantastic stories about the things that went on in the Baron's house. Strange and perverse things, things that even now she will not repeat.

"Her lover's stories frightened her, but still she longed to see the house that Wolfgang said was very large and filled with treasures like a palace in a fairy story. She began to beg him to take her there, but always he answered that outsiders were forbidden, and to break the rule would mean his death.

"Philomena could not believe the punishment would be so harsh for just one look, and besides, they would be careful and not get caught. She continued to plead with him to take her there, and though Wolfgang grew angry every time she asked, Philomena was very beautiful, and he loved her, and so finally he did what she asked."

"And they were discovered?"

"Of course." Bernardo smiled. "Or else it would not be much of a story.

"Wolfgang brought her in one night very late. And Philomena vows the house was as beautiful as her lover had always described, with golden ceilings, and carved furniture, and paintings everywhere on the walls. She was to stay only a few moments, but it was all so wonderful with the moonlight flooding in through the great windows. Soon they were in each other's arms, and one thing led naturally to the other. The Baron himself found them."

"What happened?"

"The grandmother fainted."

"That's the end?"

"No, no. Philomena woke up in a field. Alone. A few weeks later she found out she was pregnant. But Wolfgang she never saw again. Killed by the Baron, she says. Run off to avoid a wedding, according to the villagers."

"How terrible."

"There are a few who say the child she bore was the Baron's."

"I think it's true."

"You think Philomena went inside the house?"

"I think the Baron killed Wolfgang and was the father of Philomena's child."

"This is the man you are looking for, this Baron?"

"Yes."

The humor died in Bernardo's eyes. "I do not ask for what you would not have me know, Signora Marthe, but this I do ask. Let me turn back the car."

"You are afraid, Bernardo?"

"*Sì,* I am afraid. For I see that this path is a dark one. There is no happiness for you in this."

"I am not looking for happiness, Bernardo. But peace."

"What will we do today, Signora Chase?"

"Only drive through the countryside today. Pass by the Villa Bassano."

"It is very beautiful land." His voice was normal. The guide again.

"Yes, I like the Alban Hills. I like the sound. Alban," she drew it out. "We drove to the Alban Hills today." She spoke the words as she would say them later to Theodor.

Colleen sat looking out her window to the river Sarine below, a bright silver sash threaded through the floor of the valley. A letter was in her lap, something written long ago by her Aunt Fiona, Sister Lucienne had said. Father Julian had left it, to be given to her when she was feeling better.

She was feeling better now. Her mind clearer every day. But things still seemed to frighten her. The past. The future. What she wanted most was to see her son, and that would happen only when the doctors said she was ready.

She picked up the letter. Happy memories came back. Aunt Fiona had been her refuge after her mother's death, had helped her go to college. She tore open the envelope and read:

My dear Colleen,

My heart always knew you'd be coming back. And so you have. Or you'd not be reading this letter. I only grieve that I'll not be there to greet you. My doctors, having no cure for me, go about mumbling now. So I know it will be soon. There's so much I want to tell you, so much you'll want to know. I only pray as I write this, that I can get it down in a way that won't be hurting. That will give you happiness, and some peace with all of this.

Your Da is gone, Colleen. Perhaps they'll have told you that. But not the way of it, I'm guessing. Your Da always was a man of extremes, God bless him. A bloody

bonfire of guns he built after you were hurt. They shot
him for it not three days gone, and you lying in the
hospital. He loved you, lass, and he saw your way of it in
the end.

And Father Julian you've already seen, I'm sure, or
again you'd not be reading this. Michael Casey, he was
to you. And if I'm not understanding all of what it was
that brought you two together in this way, I do know that
in his own sad heart he loves you. Whatever guilt he has,
I can bear him no ill. And I only hope the good Lord is
of a mind to do the same.

Be gentle with him, Colleen, for never have I seen
the spirit so wounded in a man. He might as well be
Irish, I tell him. And he smiles . . . but not his eyes.

It is Father Julian who has seen to you since you
were first brought to Belfast after your Da's passing. And
so many times in those first months, I'd come to find
him sitting at your bed, willing you back to us. In God's
own time, Father Julian, I'd say to him. Be grateful for
the healthy babe that's coming.

And, Lord, he does love his Patrick. Never doubt the
gift you've given him, lass. His eyes smiled that morning
his boy was born. Though it tears his heart the more that
he must have so little place in Patrick's life.

But a pure joy to me the boy has been. And though
it's late I've come to mothering, I shall have to say that
we've done you proud, both me and Patrick. He's a fine
wee man, though not yet three.

And now the saddest thing is knowing I must leave
him. It is not my way ever to question the Lord's will.
But it does seem harsh that a babe who must be without
father or mother shall now have to lose the only home
he's had.

And yet I know Patrick will not be wanting. Father
Julian has friends who will take the boy and love him
like their own. And I am as content as I can be with my
going.

Your son knows you, Colleen. His favorite stories are
the ones that I tell him about his mother. It is my one

wish, after I'm gone, that it be remembered you were someday coming back. That Patrick should not forget his mother.

Oh, how I wish I could be there with the two of you now. But truly I am in spirit. And I am saying to you, lass, hold no bitterness for the years you have lost. Be happy.

Your loving Aunt Fiona

CHAPTER 44

It was rather strange seeing Elliot dressed in jeans and a knit pullover. Elliot Peters, the ultimate coat-and-tie man. But it was Saturday, with little more than a skeleton crew working in the APP offices.

Elliot perched on top of her desk, and Romany thought in that exact moment he looked just like a teenager. "So we work out the Syrian mess, and what happens? The Vatican tells us His Eminence Cardinal Vittorio DeLario is 'indisposed,' and Father Julian Morrow is 'unavailable.' Just like the Church to use words like 'indisposed' and 'unavailable.' What in the hell's going on?"

"Beats me, Elliot. But it's not the first time Julian's pulled a disappearing act."

"What's Vance got to say?"

"You mean the Great Sphinx." Romany frowned. "The usual runaround. Morrow's due to return any day."

"God, you'd think the man would be a little more responsible. He *is* the papal liaison for this whole circus."

"Well, he's not." She reached for an opened can of Coke.

"I guess I could do a little snooping. Call Father Zitti."

"Elliot, you're entitled to call whoever the hell you want. Call Gregory, for chrissakes."

"I don't know, Rom, I hate to throw my weight around over there. Besides, the Vatican crowd doesn't take too kindly to strongarm tactics."

"Strongarm tactics! Hell, you're just trying to find out why the Vatican's handpicked boy hasn't shown up for work in days."

"If only Vance were a little more cooperative. Oh, I don't mean he isn't extremely efficient. But that's just the point. He does precisely what he's supposed to do and—"

"And not a damn thing more."

"Well, why don't you just go over and pay Father Vance a little visit? See what you can find out."

"Right now? Unannounced?"

Elliot nodded his head. The grin on his face was positively wicked. "Vance has been known to work Saturdays."

"Yeah . . ." She leaned back in her chair considering. Then she jumped up. "I'm off."

"Hey, wait a minute. I almost forgot. A messenger dropped this by earlier." He reached into the back pocket of his jeans and tossed a white envelope across Romany's desk.

"For me?"

There was just her name, all in caps, typed neatly on the front of the envelope. No return address. She slid a fingernail through the flap and pulled out a single sheet of typing paper.

"Anything important?"

"What? No, nothing important." She looked up and smiled.

"Well, I'm out of here. Fill me in on Monday if you get anything out of Vance."

She watched Elliot walk out of her office toward the elevator. She'd never noticed before, but for fifty-something, her boss had a really cute ass. She chuckled, then glanced back down at the note she held. Only seventeen words, but they told the whole story.

Patient's out of coma. Doing well. The kid belongs to lover-boy. Thought you'd like to know. S.

Richard Vance was a creature of habit. And a workaholic. He was in his office working. Romany could hear him through the closed outer door. He appeared to be talking on the telephone. She glanced at her watch. She would just wait it out for him to finish before she knocked.

She glanced down at her hand inches from the closed door. Slowly she reached out and grasped the knob. It twisted easily, noiselessly in her fist.

She'd been right. Vance was speaking on the telephone. The receiver clamped to his ear, his back toward her. Like Elliot he was out of uniform. Instead of the usual black clericals, he had on a short-sleeved checked shirt and jeans.

Luckily he wasn't aware of her presence, as she remained poised inside the half-opened door. He barely moved as he continued to speak into the phone.

"I don't think the earlier hour will present a problem." His voice was as static as his posture.

"Yes, of course, the house of Gemini will be occupied." For the first time Vance allowed just a trace of emotion to filter into his voice. Impatience.

A slight nod of the head. "Till tonight. Ten o'clock. The necropolis. . . . Yes, yes, His will be done."

She had enough time to close the door before he set the receiver back into its cradle and turned. Enough time, too, to disappear down the long corridor outside Julian Morrow's office, and to escape without Richard Vance ever having known she'd been there.

There could be no misunderstanding. The necropolis had to be *the* necropolis. The ancient catacombs that zigzagged beneath St. Peter's Basilica. A perfect location for what was obviously some sort of clandestine meeting. Everything about Vance's telephone conversation made that clear enough.

Romany knew that the necropolis was closed to the general public without special arrangement, and that even then there were certain passages that were completely off limits. She figured that Vatican insiders knew of special routes that made the subterranean labyrinth easily accessible. But she knew of only one way to gain admittance to the best burial ground in all of Rome. Through the Confessio inside the Basilica itself.

The Confessio was not difficult to locate even in St. Peter's. She had only to look for the ninety-five gilded lamps, hanging from the balustrades of the staircases. Descending one marble step after another, Romany watched bits and pieces of light land and skitter across her thighs.

From the Confessio down to the shrine of the crypt of St. Peter, down farther to the level overlaid by Constantine, then down deeper to the necropolis itself. Transported back in time, to the second century, into the dark belly of the earth, along paths more suitable to wily rats or lumpy moles.

Eyes watching, she made herself believe, as she had when she was a young girl and played her mystery games. Now, like then, there was the exhilarating fear of the unknown. But the eyes were in truth eyes no more, but dark hollows in empty skulls of bodies lying in repose in neatly shelved graves along the walls.

She switched on her flashlight, directing it first against the floor. Then slowly she raised her arm, carefully focusing the telltale beam. There was surely no margin for error. All she needed was for someone to spot her.

Glittering shards of glass immediately reflected back the light. And Romany recognized the bright mosaics that covered the pagans' tombs. The brilliant glass pictures were as fresh as yesterday.

For every five pagan crypts, there was one Christian tomb, decorated with happy childish drawings, a lively testament of an earlier faith. Her beam snared one particularly charming outline of Jonah and the whale. The certainty of death; the promise of resurrection.

Sound. In the distance. A kind of chanting. Actually more whine than song. But the acoustics could account for that. Then a surprising shift in octave. To something higher. Sweeter. A Gregorian Mass she'd once heard long ago came to mind. But this was different. Somehow less religious. Yet essentially spiritual.

She followed the sound, the beam of her flashlight focused low. The music was now almost an echo of something else. Something far less real. Then, as quickly as they'd come, the notes died on the air, became words. Human voices. Speaking. She stopped.

The sign ahead read No Admittance. Beyond the prohibition lay a narrow tunnel, far narrower than any passageway she'd been through so far. She moved behind the sign, directed her light forward to memorize the lay of the land. Then she switched off the light and began to move slowly forward. One foot carefully in front of the other, the fingers of one hand reading the wall like braille.

No tombs lined the interiors here. Just solid rock. Once when her hand snagged a jutting hard edge, she bit her lip to stifle a cry, thought the worst curse word she knew, then inched forward.

The tunnel really needed another infusion of light. She knew she'd already exceeded "familiar" territory by several hundred feet. But the voices were too close now; she could almost make out words. The flashlight was just too risky.

One foot in front of the other, one foot in front of the other . . . It became a kind of physical mantra. And it was some moments before she noticed that the passageway had grown brighter. She could actually make out her two feet, see her hand creep along the wall.

A light was coming from ahead, from what appeared to be a kind of wide-open space, totally out of architectural sync with the rest of the necropolis. She stopped.

The illumination was from candles, hundreds of candles, held in free-standing candelabras. And the voices . . . The voices now had bodies, if not faces. At least not faces that could be seen. For standing in a large circle were twelve robed and hooded men. Romany's instant impression was that of an order of medieval monks. The kind of order whose members wore camel's hair against their skin, who flagellated themselves as penance. Chaste, holy men. Spare, holy men.

A more deliberate impression, however, was of something else entirely. Something truly arcane. Omniscient. No abstinence here, but fulfillment. Abundance.

The candles guttered and flared, guttered and flared, and she caught a glimpse of bare feet on carpet. A carpet precisely woven to accommodate the circle of twelve. A carpet whose warp and weft met and fashioned itself into a perfect rendering of the twelve houses of the zodiac. *Of course, the house of Gemini will be occupied.* . . .

She counted: Aries, Taurus, Gemini. The house of Gemini was indeed occupied. As were all the others. Each house, one brown-robed, cowled monk. And at center a single figure. Unlike the others, fitted in a white robe, white hood. The leader?

"He has given me his assurances that there will be no interference." It was the white monk.

"But can the Americans be trusted?" The monk in Virgo.

"I believe we can trust this American." The monk in white again.

Then the monk who stood in Capricorn shook his head so that the point of the cowl wagged like a large brown horn. "But we are still left with the problem of the bones."

"Metatron, we have not accepted what DeLario has

presented us as the truth?" It was the monk who stood in the house of Taurus.

"Our faith tells us that it is a lie," the white monk replied.

"But what if it is not a lie?" It was the monk in Gemini.

"Then, Ambriel, we must pray," said the white monk. "Pray that the Paraclete guides us through this storm, as he has guided us many times before. For if the bones are real, we are . . ."

"Lost." The monk in Pisces.

"Do not speak it." The white monk's voice seemed to roar from beneath his cowl.

"There is testing to be done—testing of the papyrus, on the bone fragment itself." It was the monk in Libra.

"Yes, Zuriel, there is much testing to be done." The white monk again.

"But, Metatron, if our testing proves that what Vittorio has is authentic, should we not try to find the burial place ourselves? Surely it is a better course than to strike a bargain." It was the monk in Leo.

Metatron waved his hand in a kind of gentle gesture. "But of course, Verchiel, we should attempt to find the bones before they can do us harm. But where to look, my son, where to look?" Then the leader turned slightly to his left and said, "Read to me again, Ambriel, these fateful words that have come to us."

The monk in Gemini nodded, pulled a sheet of paper from inside the sleeve of his robe, and then, touching his cowl so as to move it a bit away from his eyes, began to read. . . .

"She came to live with us, this, the holiest of women. An outcast among her own people, His disciples too set upon the path He had made for them to care any longer for His mother. And He already gone back to His father. But she was resigned to her destiny. Her son had made her no promises, and long ago had she accustomed herself to the hurt He could bring.

"To live but a quiet life and die in peace was all she

asked. And this we did for her. Until the end of her eighty-second year she remained with us, free of the passions of the world, free of husband, free of sons and daughters.

"When she died, we buried her as we had buried so many of her sisters who had gone before. And for many years, each year, we paid homage, till the earth at last had reclaimed her flesh. Even after we came for a time, till there were but few of us left to pray over her sacred bones."

Romany walked in from the living room trailing her cast-off clothes. A man was standing by her bed, a dark silhouette against the grayer window. "David." The word came out whispered, barely aloud. But she knew as she said it that the figure, in fact, was Julian.

As she came toward him, he moved too. Meeting her somewhere near the end of the bed, clutching her. Arms, hands, mouth. Everywhere. As if he could not be close enough, physical enough.

Not in Switzerland, she thought, acknowledging three days of unspoken fear that she would never see him again. It was sick to love someone like Julian Morrow, she was telling herself. But she knew she didn't care. Not now. Not even with this morning's message from Sully.

He was pulling her onto the bed.

"Where have you been, Julian?" Ask him that.

He dragged her down against him, covered her. His mouth was on hers, smothering any will for questions.

He said her name. Not a whisper against her ear. But a prayer. A complaint.

He made love to her with a veiled explosiveness, a violence held back, like a giant in the dark who feared he was going to crush her. Was it for the last time? She tried to hold what was happening, but her images of what she felt kept dribbling away like rain. His eyes in the dark were only black pools above her.

The force of his coming drove her over the edge. *My God, my God . . . Julian.* Her own voice in her ears. A moment like unconsciousness, when he slipped from the bed. A shadow passing at the door.

Her hand emerged from beneath her mattress with her fingers locked on the gun. But there had never been the slightest chance she would really try to stop him.

CHAPTER 45

For a long moment Marthe simply stood watching the cab drive away. She hoped Bernardo had done as he'd promised and was spending the day with relatives away from Rome. And, God forgive her, she didn't want Theodor talking to him. She needed the time to do whatever it was she had come for.

The day was very beautiful, at odds with the sinister presence that she'd sensed all about her in the long and obvious approach of the taxi up the drive. It was probably foolish, this feeling of being watched, a figment of her own imagination. And yet it seemed not improbable that the Villa Bassano was protected by some sort of electronic surveillance.

She wondered suddenly how she appeared—the good cut of her simple flowered dress marred by the ugliness of the metal cane, the oversized sweater she wore because she was always cold. She had long ago ceased to be vain, even about her hair. Now, perversely, she wished she looked prettier than the frail, middle-aged woman that she was.

She gripped the cane's rubber handle, braced herself to reach the knocker. The door before her was huge. The house seemed to go on forever.

Minutes passed with no answer. She didn't move. The eyes, still watching, knew that she was there.

The door was opened by a silent liveried servant.

"Marthe Chase," she said. "I have come to see the Baron von Hohenhofen."

The man stared at her. "*Nicht verstehe!* There is no Baron von Hohenhofen." He spoke in German. "*Geh weg!*"

She understood the tone if not all the words. Held her ground. "The Baron," she said again. "I want to see him."

"What a pleasant surprise, Signora Chase." Another man had appeared behind the first. It was Count Sebastiano, the blue eyes doubly startling without the patch.

"I am the Baron Friedrich von Hohenhofen," he said. And he welcomed her in as the servant closed the door.

Romany walked over and stood in front of the old vanity that had come with the apartment. Her reflection in the mirror caused her to frown. The uniform of the day was a pair of ragged-out shorts and a cotton tee. No makeup, and hair that was about a day overdue for washing. Maybe lipstick would help. She opened one of the drawers in the vanity and found a tube of something called Orange Mocha. She pursed her lips and spread on a thick layer of color. She stepped back for another quick assessment. Ugh, nothing would help until her hair was shampooed.

She plopped back onto her bed. Another lost cause. It hadn't been made up in three days. And since last night . . . She sighed. How should she handle what she'd discovered?

Of course, she should go straight to Sully. Tell him about the secret meeting in the necropolis. Yet she had no more inclination to tell him about that than to tell him about seeing Julian last night. Besides, what in the hell was she supposed to say, anyway?

"Well, Sully, it's like this. I came home late last night after spying on a little get-together of some really far-out monk types and found Julian Morrow in my bedroom. I could have taken him, in fact I had my hand right on the gun, but things kind of got complicated. You see, he started making love to me, and I'm just not myself when Julian makes love to me. . . ."

Great, Sully will go for that in a big way. Hell, for all she knew, Sully knew that Julian was back from Switzerland and had tailed him last night to her apartment. But that didn't play. Sully would have contacted her by now. And the real truth was that it wasn't just her problem with Julian that kept her from phoning Sully. It was something else.

She rearranged the pillows at her back. Her reluctance to inform Sully had vaguely to do with ideas. More precisely, principles. There was something inside of her that wanted to give Holy Mother Church a break. A fighting chance to win whatever game it was playing. A chance to have a go at it alone, win or lose, without the Company's heavy-handed interference.

But who in the hell was the merry band of monks? The scene last night in the catacombs was right out of an Umberto Eco novel. Weird . . . that was the operative word. Yet familiar in a way too. For during the entire time she was underground, she felt a certain resonance in some of the voices.

And what about the bones? Whose bones? From the passage the monk read, she could make a pretty good educated guess. And so what? Why would their discovery be so devastating for the Church? She had no earthly idea, but this little Catholic girl was sure going to find out.

The ringing of the phone put a quick end to her rambling.

"*Pronto.*"

"Gypsy girl, it's Papa."

"Hi, Papa. I was going to call you and Mom later. . . ."

"She's not there with you?"

"Who? Mom?"

"Yes."

"No, is she supposed to be?"

"No, I just thought she might be." A heavy sigh.

"Where is she, Papa?"

"I don't know, Romany. I worked late last night. . . ."

"Those Etruscans."

His solid laugh came through the line. "Afraid so. Got to bed late. Overslept this morning. Marthe was gone before I got up."

"What about Bernardo?"

"I thought he had the day off, but I guess not. I wouldn't think your mom would take on Rome without Bernardo."

"Then there's nothing to worry about."

"No, no, I guess not. . . ."

"But . . . ?"

"I don't know for sure if she's with Bernardo, and . . . Do you think I should call someone, Romany?"

"The police? Of course not, Papa. Mom's just fine. She and Bernardo are probably walking in some ruins as we speak."

"Gypsy girl, I love you."

"I love you too, Papa. Etruscans and all. Give me a call when she comes in. *Ciao.*"

"Ciao, Rom."

Crossing for what seemed like the millionth time from the sofa to the window and back, Romany forced herself to stop pacing and collapsed in the corner of the couch. For ten seconds it felt good. It had been almost three hours since her father had called. Now she was really worried and wondering if she should call him back.

She got up and went to the kitchen. Considered having a Scotch, but instead poured herself a Coke. Cold and straight, no ice. It burned in her throat like acid, the way she liked it.

Walking back to the living room, she burrowed back

down in the sofa. What if something really was wrong with her mother?

"Romany . . ."

It was David. He'd come in as usual without knocking.

"What's the matter?" He walked toward her.

She didn't bother to comment on how easily he'd read her. "My father called a few hours ago," she said. "My mother seems to be missing."

"What do you mean 'missing'?"

"Well, she's been going out every day, sightseeing with her driver. But this is Sunday, and they're late. Mom tires easily." Nothing has happened, she told herself.

"This her?" David sat down on the sofa, picked up the photograph of her parents she'd left sitting on the table.

"Yes. It's my favorite photo. She's pretty, huh?"

"Yeah . . . does your mother walk with a cane?"

The question seemed immediately strange. She realized he was still holding the picture.

"Yes, she does. What is it, David?" She was watching his eyes, their expression, as if silent gears behind them were falling into place.

"I saw your mother," David said. "A few days ago at the Registry of Properties. I passed her as I was going in. *M. Chase* was the name before mine when I signed for a file. Your last name, so I noticed it."

"Registry of Properties . . . What was she doing there?"

He shook his head. "I'm not sure exactly, but . . . this is going to sound crazy, Romany, but I think I know where she is."

Cardinal Vittorio DeLario managed to mask his impatience well, accepting quite graciously the phone that Hans brought to the room and plugged in—telephones not being allowed as permanent fixtures in any of the villa's salons. He dialed with apparent unconcern the number that had gone unanswered for more than forty-eight hours, suppressing any sign of outward relief when finally Julian picked up the phone.

"Where have you been?" The question was calm.

"They said they wouldn't get back to me till some-time tonight. No sense in my just sitting."

"You might have shared that information with me, Father Morrow. . . . Have they called yet?"

"Yes. I spoke to His Holiness."

"To Niccolo himself? What did he say?"

"I *was* Gregory's protégé." The casualness in Mor-row's voice was, if possible, more irritating than usual.

"What did he say to you, Father Morrow?"

"You know, Vittorio, I haven't seen a cent."

"You will get your share of the money, Julian."

"If we pull this thing off."

"Is there any reason to doubt that?" Vittorio asked.

A moment of silence. "They want more time."

"Why?"

"They say they don't believe it's the genuine article. That it can't be."

An impatient grunt. "That's the official line. Friday, when you delivered the message, did you see Niccolo?"

"No. I called first, spoke to Antonini. I delivered the goods to him. . . . Why?"

"I just wish you had seen Niccolo's face."

"You mean, Vittorio, you wish you had."

More silence.

"How much time?" the Cardinal asked at last.

"Gregory didn't specify," said Julian. "They have to run their tests."

"Call them tomorrow. Tell them they have"—he looked across the room for confirmation—"one week."

"That isn't a lot of time."

"One week, Father Morrow. I thought you were anx-ious for your money." The Cardinal hung up.

"Well-done." The Baron had watched Vittorio re-place the receiver.

"Grazie. But I don't know." Vittorio allowed a frown. "Niccolo is stalling."

"A very natural reaction to blackmail. But we have him, as the saying goes, 'by the balls.'" The Baron walked over to a table near the door. The Becker picture hung behind him. "Wine?" he asked, turning back, an unconscious echo of his youthful stance in the portrait.

"Grazie, no." The Cardinal shook his head. Then, "Niccolo has surprised us before, Friedrich. He may do so again."

The Baron walked back with his wineglass. Sat down again in his formal way on the sofa beside the Cardinal.

"Have you forgotten how we met, Vittorio?" The Baron gave a short sigh, almost of impatience. "Surely," he said, "you are not suggesting that a pope would be willing to forfeit his own power, indeed the very power of the Church itself, even if it meant warning the world of a threat from Nazis."

There was the lizard smile, then a long, easy sip at the wine. The Baron put the glass down on the round-topped table beside the sofa. Sat erectly back. "What excuse does your Vatican give for stalling?"

"Faith," said Vittorio, shortly. "Faith tells them that what they have been given cannot, in fact, be that which we claim. They are running scientific analyses of the bone and the papyrus to prove it."

"A remarkable contradiction." The Baron remained smug. "Faith does not allow for analysis. You are silent, Vittorio. Do you doubt, yourself, that the bones are real? Or is it that in your heart of hearts you want them to be fake?"

"A *question?"* The Cardinal lifted his head.

"The game? . . . No. I had not meant it, Vittorio. But if you wish."

For a moment the Cardinal considered. There was indeed a question of his own he would like to ask the Baron. About the mystery guest, arrived this morning, but never seen. In the end he shook his head. "I am tired tonight, old friend."

"Then perhaps you will excuse me, Vittorio." The Baron stood. For a moment the smile widened into something almost genuine that warmed the cold eyes. "*Arrivederci*, Vittorio . . . until tomorrow, then."

"*Auf Wiedersehen*, Friedrich."

The Baron was gone.

Romany couldn't remember the last time she'd ridden in a car with David ben Haar. Was it all the way back in Geneva? She looked down at his brown hand on the stick shift. Strong, a network of veins running across its surface. She smiled, thinking how entirely masculine David's hands were, how secure they had always made her feel.

She turned as much as her seat belt would allow. "What I can't figure out, David, is why my mother would be at the Villa Bassano."

"Only connection I can make is that she was interested in the place for the same reason I was. Nazis."

"Nazis? What possible connection would my mother have with Nazis?"

He turned for a moment and looked at her. "Has your mother ever mentioned a woman by the name of Helena Klimpt?"

"No, never. Who is she?"

David's focus had already moved back to the road ahead. He twisted the steering wheel to take a sharp curve. "I guess you could say Klimpt herself was a Nazi of sorts. At least early on in the war. She bought into the system like so many of the young people then. A real idealist."

Romany stared at David as he spoke. Never in her life had she ever heard him make any kind of excuse for anyone in any way connected with what went on in Germany during the Third Reich.

"She was some type of researcher back then. A biogeneticist we'd call her today. Supposedly brilliant. That's why she was recruited by Mueller to assist him in his experiments at one of the camps."

"Mueller?"

"Yeah, Dr. Karl Mueller. One of Hitler's medical butchers. Was helping the Führer create the master race."

"Sounds like a real charming fellow."

"He was." David flashed her a completely nasty smile that somehow still managed to look sexy. "It wasn't too long before Klimpt became disillusioned. Wanted out. But in those days there was nowhere to go. Not without looking like a traitor."

"She stayed on at the camp?"

"Yeah. But she started doing little things to sabotage Mueller's experiments. Things like injecting water into the patients instead of Mueller's creative serums. The bottom line was that she was probably responsible for saving a lot of lives."

"Good girl. But what's this have to do with my mother?"

"Mueller's specialty was conducting fetal experiments. He worked on dozens of pregnant women, mostly Jewish girls."

"A left up ahead, David. Villa Bassano should be about ten or twelve miles after the turn if this map is right."

David nodded, downshifted, turned onto the side road.

"Lise Schulen was one of the women at the camp."

"Lise Schulen?"

"She was transferred to Mueller's camp when they found out she was pregnant."

David's voice had remained the same throughout his recitation. Yet Romany could now sense a subtle change. The muscles in his face seemed tauter, his dark brows threatened to frown. When she glanced down at his hand, he was squeezing the shift.

"The info I got from my contact said that Lise must

have been pretty special. I mean more so than most of Mueller's patients. It wasn't too long before Klimpt became attached to the woman, and then to her child."

"Her child?"

"A baby girl. Born with a bum leg. Probably something to do with one of Mueller's little experiments. Klimpt wasn't perfect. She couldn't always trip up the old doc."

"And the mother?"

"Lise lived until her daughter was about two and a half, three years old. Klimpt took over after that. Literally hid the girl from Mueller for almost a year. The camp was liberated by the Americans shortly after."

"What happened then?"

"Like many of the war orphans, the girl was adopted by an American family."

"Lise's daughter is in the United States?"

David nodded again, began to slow down as the imposing Villa Bassano came into view.

"David?"

He turned, his green eyes telling her something, something very important. Then he said it. "Lise Schulen's daughter is your mother, Romany."

They could have gone down into the tunnel to access Villa Bassano, but David thought an above-ground approach was safer. He wanted a car nearby just in case they needed to make a quick getaway. The problem now was entry.

They moved alongside the left wing. With any luck, one of the windows or doors would be open. Then they would have to take it a step at a time.

Romany followed David closely, thinking about not getting caught, but mostly about what David had just told her about her mother and Helena Klimpt. Her mother's decision to come to Rome must have been made right after Helena Klimpt's visit. That made the most sense.

From everything David had said, Klimpt was certainly an extraordinary woman. In her late seventies, Klimpt was still on the trail trying to locate Mueller's camp victims. Some called what she did her "atonement." A charitable mission joined to her thanksgiving for being spared punishment at Nuremberg.

"Romany, what're you waiting for?" David whispered impatiently, waiting for her to go first through the window.

"Sorry." She smiled, took his hand, and stepped into the Villa Bassano.

Inside, the villa was overwhelming and baroque in the density of form and detail. And vast, Romany realized, as they passed through room after room. She could sense the tiers above her, stone, plaster, wood, and gilt pressing down layer on layer, like a monstrous, mad cake. And the paintings and the sculpture, enough for ten museums. The Villa Bassano. Just one more shock among the many. A wonderment to which she was numb.

And numb was good, because any real feelings could only be paralyzing. As it was, she moved like an automaton, a creature programmed only to lift its feet and follow David ben Haar.

And David had got them this far.

The music they'd been hearing stopped again. David stopped too, turning to her with a signal to wait. They stood together, hugging the deepest shadows in the dark, empty ballroom. In a moment the piano began again somewhere still beyond, but the notes hammered, beaten out, as if the player were in a frenzy to finish the piece.

Her mother? she wondered. It didn't sound at all like her mother's playing, but it was their only clue to where Marthe might be in this whole huge pile. David touched her hand and they began to move again. Through double doors, and a paneled hall, then into a smaller passage. The music stopped midnote. A quavering, dull-thudded at its end. Something final in the silence . . .

He had switched to Mozart. Something bright and brisk. Marthe preferred it to the waltz he'd been playing. The waltz had been too sentimental, and there were few things she disliked more than excessive sentimentality.

She watched now as his long fingers plucked the keys in a rapid staccato motion, then as quickly slowed to a more moderate pace. Although she was no judge, she guessed that he would score high in technical merit and lose points in interpretation. The Baron's music was essentially passionless.

"You do not resemble her." His voice lifted above the level of his playing.

She glanced over his shoulder to the large, unfinished portrait that dominated the small room.

"Or look anything like your father." This time his smile was completely self-absorbed. "Except maybe for the hands."

She gazed down, examined her hands resting at the edge of the baby grand. Small, thin, too pale. She tucked them safely away inside the pockets of her sweater. They were *her* hands.

Immediately he'd assessed her agitation, rather seemed to enjoy her discomfort. His smile continued. "Perhaps there is the slightest facial similarity." He squinted his eyes as though he peered through the lens of a microscope. ". . . Just about the mouth." His brows arched. "Your mouth can be very cruel, Marthe."

He executed an elaborate run across the keys. "Mozart was her favorite, you know." Then a small chuckle. "But of course you wouldn't know, *Liebling.*"

The music flowed on for a while. Neither of them said anything. He, staring down at the keys. She, watching him at the piano. She wondered how old he was. His hair was silver-white, but his skin was the skin of a new-born. No trace of a beard. So unlike her Theodor, who was as woolly as a bear. She wondered if the Baron even shaved.

"I never knew she was pregnant," he said suddenly.

She stared into the blue, blue eyes and saw they had lost none of their composure. "Would it have made any difference?" she said simply.

His face went blank for an instant, the kind of blankness one saw only in the features of store mannequins. She imagined he was considering her question, fashioning a response. When his answer finally came, it was no more than another smile, which fitted itself perfectly to his mouth.

"Pour me some more wine, Marthe," he said casually, his attention once more focused on his play. He'd begun a new composition.

She placed the crystal stem within his grasp, and he reached for it with one hand, the other still making music. He sipped slowly. "A remarkable vintage," he said just beneath his breath. Then the free hand joined the other at the keyboard.

She didn't recognize this music as she had the Mozart. This was something tinny and high-pitched. The melody, if one could say there was melody, seemed more suited to some kind of reed instrument. A flute perhaps. Another sip of the red wine. More notes, more strange music. Then a final swallow, and his glass was empty.

She didn't know how long he played this particular selection, the sound winding upward and outward, then downward and in upon itself. But it seemed after a time that his fingers became less adept, and there were queer, unaccountable rests. Yet he struggled on, tearing at the keys, working as though he sucked blood from them. A small line of perspiration had formed above his upper lip, and she thought it was odd to see Friedrich von Hohenhofen sweat. Once when his eyes had found hers, the pupils had grown huge and black.

At the end his notes were fitful ones, his hands like claws upon the keys. When he looked up at the last, he wore a terrible question in his eyes. And this time, this, the final time, it was Marthe's smile that answered him.

A gun, the Ruger that had killed in Geneva, was now in David's hand. Romany followed him to the door at the end of the narrow corridor. He waved her to one side, took the point. Her own gun was ready too, but her fingers felt wooden on the grip. She took a deep breath, nodded. Watched David with a well-placed leap kick his way into the room.

She saw her mother first. Sitting, composed, her hands in her lap. She looked up only when Romany moved to her side. More strangely, no one spoke. And Romany watched David walk to the figure of a man slumped across the piano.

"Count Sebastiano!" Her words as David lifted the head, felt for the pulse point in the neck.

"Dead," said David. "Looks like a heart attack."

She barely heard. Her eyes had found the portrait. "It's me," she said. "A picture of me."

"No." Her mother's words, behind her. "No, Romany, it's your grandmother."

The Cardinal's second question had been, Why were the servants building a fire in the dead of summer, and scurrying around like an army of ants inside the Villa Bassano? A thousand more questions were to follow.

But the first had been, Why in the hell was Fritz banging on his door in the middle of the night? Had the man gone mad?

"Your Eminence, Cardinal DeLario. Please wake up. Please come."

He'd not even thrown on a robe before he opened the door to his suite. "What is the matter, Fritz? What has happened?"

The old man shook his head in a kind of deep sorrow. "Oh, Cardinal DeLario, it is awful. You must come. It is Baron von Hohenhofen."

Vittorio grabbed his dressing gown and followed the servant. Never had he seen the stolid Fritz lose his composure. Surely something terrible was wrong. Had he said something about Friedrich?

He moved quickly down the long dark corridor, the odor of charred wood in his nostrils. Was the villa on fire? But as soon as he passed the grand salon, that question was answered. Berthe was handing logs to Hans, who piled them inside the hearth as quickly as he could. But a fire in August?

Everywhere inside the house, the servants ran. Some carried, some dragged. But every one of them set on a mission.

"Hurry, Fritz." It was Greta who stood at the end of the dark hallway signaling to them. They followed her into a small room, set off to one side of a larger one. Vittorio realized he had never been in this particular section of the villa.

His first impression was of the portrait. The second was of the Baron slumped over the keyboard of a piano.

"What . . . ?" His tongue, thick inside his mouth, could not form the words. But already his heart knew.

"Please, Cardinal DeLario, the last rites." It was Greta's desperate voice.

Vittorio moved slowly, his legs stiff, reluctant. When at last he reached the body, his hand made a motion to touch the corpse. Cold, he flinched, the Baron was already cold. Then it seemed Greta bent down and angled the head in such a way that he finally glimpsed his old friend's face. Time at the last had been cruel to the old German. The Baron's face wore the lines of a thousand years. Already there seemed a stench.

He made the sign of the cross. Yet in his heart he believed what he did was nothing more than a futile, foolish act. If any man was destined for the fires of hell, it was surely Baron Friedrich von Hohenhofen. But he could do no less than administer the sacrament. He was after all a prince of the Holy Mother Church. He struggled to remember the new Roman rite of the Sacrament of Healing.

"Peace to this house and to all who live in it," he recalled the opening phrase. But already a greater battle ensued inside Cardinal Vittorio DeLario—how to leave the Villa Bassano as quickly as possible.

CHAPTER 46

Cocooned between the arms of the big bedroom chair, Romany woke . . . fought through the tangle of her cotton blanket. The dawning sun, filtered through her bedroom's gauzy sheers, was still enough to hurt her eyes, gritty with lack of sleep, as if the mellow travertine light actually were suffused with marble dust.

Last night, in the confusion, she had forgotten to pull the outer drapes, and the yellow haze of morning would soon give way to much stronger light. She could get up now, close the curtains. But the movement itself seemed more likely than the sun to disturb her mother, still sleeping in the bed. She stretched instead . . . carefully, wary of the kinks, and glanced across the room to where her father dozed, fully clothed, on the chaise.

Theodor had arrived very late. And with Marthe already asleep, had insisted that she remain undisturbed in the bed. He'd refused the living-room sofa, however, wanting to stay close should Marthe awake in the night.

Romany, too, had found a need to be here, had sat with her father in the silence lit only from the bulb left burning in the bathroom. She had intended at some point to move to the sofa. But despite the discomfort of trying to sleep in the chair, the moment had never come.

They had not talked yet, she and her father, not beyond the simplest, most superficial explanations. Last night had been a time too raw for questions, much less for answers. Her father, God bless him, had seen that.

And thank God too for David. For the fate that had put him at the property registry that day he'd seen her mother. Last evening, hustling them out of danger, David had driven her and Marthe to the city, then gone alone to make safe contact with his people, with Sully.

Her mother, in some sort of self-protective shock, had said virtually nothing after they'd left the villa. Romany had put her mother to bed as soon as they'd arrived at the apartment, able at last to phone her father with the news that Marthe was here and safe. The questions of "how" and "why" would have to be answered today.

"Theodor . . ."

Romany started at her mother's voice, realizing she had dozed. She opened her eyes, this time to see her father moving to the bed.

"How do you feel?" Theodor had reached down to help her mother sit, plumping the pillows behind her. He kissed her forehead.

"I feel good." Marthe said. "I slept so well. Where's Romany?"

"Here." She got up, walked around to where her mother could see her. "You look good, Mother." It was true. Her mother certainly seemed better rested than either of them. The hectic color was gone from her cheeks. She seemed at peace.

"Is it Sunday?" Marthe said.

"No, my love." Theodor was smiling. "You've lost a day. But it doesn't matter. Romany will fix us some coffee. Then we'll all crawl into bed just like it was a Sunday. . . . No funnies, I'm afraid." He smiled this time at Romany. "But you can tell us, Marthe, about what happened yesterday. Your daughter was very mysterious last night. All I got from her was that you were safe, and that the rest was something for you to tell me."

When Romany returned with cups of coffee on a bed tray, they both were waiting. Her father sitting with his arm around her mother in the bed. Sunday mornings had been a tradition, Theodor between his two girls with coffee and the paper, reading the cartoons. Making them more wonderful by taking all the parts. Changing his voice for Dagwood and Blondie. Lucy and Charlie Brown.

She passed the tray to her father. Let him settle it on his lap. Then this time she got into bed beside her mother. A simple thing. Her mother's eyes welcomed.

"Take your coffee, girls. Remember, I'm waiting to hear this story."

Obediently they took their cups. And Marthe began.

"A woman came to see me," she began softly. "Almost two months ago now. Her name was Helena Klimpt, a German woman. She told me something that I believe I'd always known. That I was adopted."

"Adopted, Marthe?"

"Yes. My parents . . . the people I had known as my parents were already dead when I found you, Theodor." Marthe had turned away from him, viewing some inner landscape. "They were wonderful people. I loved them, but I always knew that I didn't really belong."

Marthe's next words were intense, her vision still turned inward. "I remembered, you see. The feet. The sound of feet marching. And that other mother. The thin arms clutching at me. The lips . . ."

Silence, while Marthe found her breath. Romany sat very still. This was confirmation of everything that David had told her last night, but it was all new for her father.

"I was born in a concentration camp," Marthe said now. "My mother's name was Lise Schulen."

"My God." Theodor's arm had tightened around her. "And you remember the camp, Marthe?"

"Only what I said." She had turned to reassure him. "The feet and my mother holding me. I think I remember the night she died . . . being cold."

Her mother's voice was low, but even. Full of that peace that Romany had seen within her face. She felt tears, however, on her own cheeks. Wiped them quickly away.

"This is incredible," Theodor said. "Why didn't you tell me? Why didn't you tell me about the Klimpt woman?"

"There was something I had to do." Marthe stared forward. "I didn't want you to stop me."

He took her cheek, turned her face toward him.

Side to side, Romany sat touching her mother. But at this moment there were only two people occupying the universe that held Theodor and Marthe. This time it didn't hurt at all.

Her mother was speaking again. "Lise Schulen . . . my mother was from a wealthy family. The Schulens were Jewish, but no one knew. They were Germans, they felt like everyone else. And then they were betrayed."

"They were found out?"

"Yes, by Lise's fiancé. He was an aristocrat, an officer in the SS. He had the Schulens arrested."

The Count, thought Romany.

"The Baron Friedrich von Hohenhofen," Marthe said. "He was my father."

Romany felt the words hit. Actually hit. She caught her breath through a blank spot, as if the blow had actually been physical.

". . . Your father?" The question simultaneous, she and Theodor together.

"Lise was already pregnant with the Baron's child when she was arrested," Marthe said. "The Nazis sent her to a special camp. It was there she met Helena."

"What happened yesterday, Marthe?"

"I went to see him," said Marthe. "Count Sebastiano came to the door."

"The Count . . . ?"

"The Baron was Count Sebastiano, Theodor. I told him that I was Lise's daughter. And his."

"The Count Sebastiano," he repeated. "And he believed you?"

"Oh yes, because of Romany. She looks so much like Lise. There's a portrait." The words stopped again.

". . . He died," she said after a moment.

Concern was plain on her father's face. Romany saw that he had turned to look at her.

"A heart attack." She answered his silent question.

The words had seemed to put an end to something for her mother. Marthe squeezed her hand. "Romany came for me," she said to Theodor. "Romany and . . . her friend."

"You're tired, my love." It was Theodor taking charge. "I think maybe you should get a little more sleep while Romany and I see about breakfast. What d'ya say, Gypsy? You think we can get together a real 'Sunday' feast?"

"Sure." She pitched her voice at normal. "But you're in charge." She slid herself up from the bed. "You sleep some more now, Mom. Papa and I will take care of everything."

"You got that orange juice squeezed, Rom? Good, these two are ready." Theodor slid the second omelet out of the pan onto a plate. "I checked just a minute ago," he said, "and your mother was sleeping. I'll fix her something later. I don't want to wake her up yet. Here, hand me an orange juice and grab a plate. Let's move it to the table."

For a little while they sat not speaking. Her father's omelets as always were delicious, but Romany kept forgetting to eat. Her thoughts were moving in spirals, an awareness along the edges that her father was watching her. Finally he spoke.

"It's a miracle she got out alive. How did you find her, Romany?"

She laid down her fork, gave up the pretense of eating.

"David ben Haar." She took the plunge. "He's with the Mossad."

"And this David knew where your mother was?"

"It's a really long story, Papa. David found out about Helena Klimpt visiting Mom. And then he ran into her one day looking up the same piece of property he was. When I told him she was missing, he just guessed she was there. . . . It's weird. We were all looking for the same man."

"We? Meaning you too?"

"Me too, Papa. I've been working for Drew."

"Don't look so red-faced, Romany. I *had* guessed."

"Yes. Well, I thought you might."

"And don't worry"—he smiled at her now—"I'm not going to ask any more questions. Not about 'business.' "

"Thanks, Papa."

"What I want to know now is how you feel."

She took a deep breath. Shook her head. "I don't know." She looked up at him. "I don't think I feel anything yet."

"That's okay too, Rom. You didn't know about any of this . . . about the Count?"

"No. David only told me on the way yesterday about Helena Klimpt and Mom's being adopted out of the camps. I didn't know any of the rest of it till just now." She felt the prick of tears again, fought them back. "That monster was my grandfather."

Her father's hand moved to cover hers. "You're still the same, Rom. Still my gypsy."

"I have his genes."

Theodor lifted her chin, smiled. "Remember that *Star Trek* you liked? That old one where Captain Kirk splits into two. A good and a bad side. He finds out his strength comes from the dark . . . remember?"

"I remember, Papa." It was so corny, she had to smile back. "But my strength comes from you."

"Oh." He was suddenly serious. "And what about your mother? You think she's not strong?"

"No . . . you're right." She nodded.

He got up and took the seat next to hers. Made her come into his lap. Just like the old days, those far-ago Sundays.

"There's no more monster in you, Romany, than in any of us. It's hard to know what turns a man. What your grandfather did *was* monstrous, unforgivable even. But no one's all bad.

"I know." He felt her movement against his chest. "A cliché. But I believe it's true. Perhaps in the end it was remorse that killed the man . . . seeing your mother. He did, after all those years, still have that portrait."

"I wish you could have seen it, Papa. I thought it was me at first. Poor Lise." The tears came.

"My poor gypsy," he said, smoothing her hair. "The same, only wiser."

"Oh, Papa," she said. "I hope so."

"I always said it." David was pacing the thick carpet in what the Mossad had figured was Hohenhofen's former bedroom. "I knew in my gut that skinny Jew-hater, Anton Arendt, was the right one to follow."

Chaim Lieber watched the action from behind an antique desk. Emptied drawers with their useless debris sat around him on the floor. He had gained more weight since David had last seen him, and with his new thick black glasses, looked more than ever like Henry Kissinger. What he didn't have was the Dr. Strangelove accent. Chaim had immigrated from the United States, and still talked as if he lived in Queens.

"Yeah, yeah, David," Chaim said now, "you knew all right, except that last time I heard, you had this place figured for some kinda high-class sex club."

"So rub it in," David flashed back. "I should have busted this place weeks ago. I might have gotten records. Now, nothing." He kicked a drawer halfway across the room.

"That's your trouble, David. Always extremes." Admiring the plume of his Turkish cigarette, Chaim hadn't even blinked. "You did okay." He tipped back precariously in the delicate chair.

"Not my area of expertise," he said to David's back, "but some of the CIA boys running around here are having fits over all the shit in this place. Hohenhofen was the perfect broker."

"I should have gotten the Nazi bastard alive." David had turned again, was walking back toward him.

"What?" Chaim let the chair fall, pinned him with a look. "So he could deny everything and cost the state a trial? Die in prison before we ever shot him? Fucker must have been pushing ninety, though I hear he didn't look it. Count Klaus Sebastiano . . . in front of our noses for years. You are sure he was dead?"

"Trust me, Chaim. I know dead."

"Good. But we don't get a positive ID from what's left in that fireplace, and I can guarantee you we're gonna have rumors from here to Tel Aviv the bastard's still alive. Living in Buenos Aires, probably, with Hitler."

"Let me go after Arendt. He's the one with records."

Chaim's cigarette was down to an unfiltered nub. He took his time grinding it out in a bibelot on the desk. Then he looked up. "And what does that mean, David —'go after'?"

"Bring him in. Make him talk."

"Bring him in. You mean hijack him off the street. The man is not a skinhead, goddammit. Can you see the headlines? *Israelis Kidnap Prominent German Businessman Amid Wild Claims of Nazi Takeover Plot.* You know, they like that word . . . *amid.* And yeah, they'd really listen to us then."

"The Americans could back us up."

"With what? You talked to Sully? They have less proof than we do that this so-called neo-Nazi organization exists. I know it does. You know it. But we've got to have names named. A membership list that we can make stick."

"So what are you saying, Chaim? We found the middleman, but so what? This is as far as it goes?"

"Don't be a schmuck, David."

"Then tell me."

"Seems to me from what I hear, the Americans don't know from nothing because Andrew Douglas won't put the screws to his playmates here in the Vatican."

"So?" David waited.

"So . . ." Chaim leaned forward once more in his chair, pushed the thick glasses high on his nose. "So I think it's time that we fix that."

After she'd left her father, Romany had spent the whole morning scurrying around tracking down theology texts. About nine-thirty she'd called Gina and told her she didn't know when or if she'd make it into the office today. She'd give Elliot a call later.

When she finally made it back to her apartment, it was close to noon. A quick salad for lunch, and she settled in with the books. She needed a diversion after everything that had happened the last twenty-four hours. Although coming up with some kind of rationale for the "goings-on" in the necropolis Saturday night could hardly be considered a diversion.

The last ten minutes she had been rereading *Munificentissimus Deus,* the apostolic constitution that defined the dogma of the Blessed Virgin Mary's bodily assumption into heaven.

She slid the book off her lap and reexamined the equation she scribbled on a legal pad. The existence of the BVM's bones negates her Assumption; the negation of the Assumption undermines papal infallibility; papal infallibility is a primary cornerstone of the Roman Catholic Church. "Holy shit" seemed an appropriate expletive.

She read again. On November 1, 1950, Pope Pius XII wrote the final chapter of the centuries-long tradition of belief in the mystery of Mary's Assumption, by defining and proclaiming this event as a dogma of faith. As such, the Assumption, alongside Mary's Immaculate Conception, became a matter of binding and unconditional assent of all Catholics. In *Munificentissimus Deus,* Pius XII had spoken "ex cathedra," from the chair of Saint Peter, meaning that the dogma of the Assumption had been divinely revealed and therefore could not be in error.

You didn't have to be a theologian to figure this one out. If Mary's bones did in fact exist, it was certainly in the Church's interest to see to it that they stayed buried. Literally and figuratively.

When the telephone rang, Romany jumped. She watched it ring two more times before she picked up the receiver.

"Pronto."

"Romany?"

"Yes, this is Romany Chase."

"Romany, it's Andrew. You didn't sound like yourself."

"Hi, Drew. Sorry. Guess I'm a little tired."

"I can imagine. You okay?"

"Fine."

"And your mother?"

"Better. . . . Is it all right to talk?"

"The line's clear."

"I guess Sully filled you in."

"Yes. Although I still don't quite understand what Marthe was doing at the Villa Bassano."

"A long story."

"For later?"

"Please."

"Of course, Romany. Unfortunately, many other important questions are still left unanswered. Finding Hohenhofen turned out to be a dead end. The Villa

Bassano was clean. The Baron's servants were well trained."

"We are certain he was our middleman, aren't we?"

"As positive as we can be. The Baron Friedrich von Hohenhofen was a notorious Nazi, so it would seem only natural that he would be involved in an operation connected to an anticipated right-wing take-over in Germany."

"But nothing to tie him in directly."

"We have a couple of ideas. But as I said, without any hard information, we really can't do much. Although locating Hohenhofen was a real coup. At least what remains of him."

"What do you mean?"

"His servants gave the old boy a real Viking funeral."

"They burned the body?"

"Right in one of the fireplaces."

Romany felt something bitter rise up into her throat.

"Romany?"

"I'm okay, Andrew. The whole idea just doesn't seem very pleasant."

"Sorry, Romany, but none of this business is very pleasant. It never is."

"What about the Vatican? Have you told them what you found?"

"I've been in touch with Gregory. He's still keeping very quiet, though I'm sure he didn't know about Hohenhofen specifically. He knew DeLario had to have outside help, but I don't think the Vatican ever got as far as the Baron. I'm sure Gregory was very surprised to discover that Klaus Sebastiano and Friedrich von Hohenhofen were one and the same."

"Did Gregory say anything else?"

"Just what he always says. He needs more time to try to recover some of the stolen art."

"What about DeLario?"

"Nothing. I just wish our people had a chance to talk to him."

"Well, the Cardinal's very busy doing something. The story they've fed us over at APP is that he's 'indisposed.' "

"I hope 'indisposed' means they're working on getting some answers out of him like Gregory promised."

"You think they have him under some kind of house arrest?"

"Possibly. Who knows how the Vatican really operates?"

"Too true." A small pause. Then, "DeLario's a pretty smooth character. He could have his own separate agenda."

"What do you mean?"

"Oh, nothing specific. But to have pulled off what he's done all these years, I would imagine he wouldn't throw in the towel so easily."

"You're probably correct. I'd imagine His Eminence is a very creative thinker. Well, we can't know what we can't know."

"Very good, Drew."

He laughed. "I've got to make a couple more contacts. My love to Marthe."

"Always, Drew."

So the Pope was still playing it close to the vest with Andrew. And no wonder, in light of what she'd seen and heard the other night. DeLario had upped the ante.

Damn, why didn't she tell Drew what she knew? What was wrong with her? This was cheating. Yet her silence didn't feel like betrayal. More a combination of her feelings for Julian Morrow, and a kind of real sympathy for the Church.

She glanced over at the open text she'd been reviewing before Drew's call. She didn't have it in her to read another word. Everything that had been happening the last couple days was finally getting to her. And the strangest part was how so many of the events attached so intimately to her. Especially how the long-sought-after middleman had come to be at the heart of her own personal mystery. Count Klaus Sebastiano. Baron Friedrich von Hohenhofen. Nazi. Her grandfather.

She recalled the night she'd had dinner with him at the Palazzo Rozze. How he'd teased her, played his little games with her. Disappearing behind the secret panel into the secret room. And that strange painting of Mary. What had she seen when she'd squinted her eyes? Something about the pattern of lines in . . . She closed her eyes now and saw again the image of the Virgin.

Suddenly her eyes flew open. Yes! Yes, of course. The painting! That was it. The painting of the Madonna was the first and final clue.

Cardinal Vittorio DeLario stood in the bedroom of his Rome apartment, admiring his return to scarlet robes in the full-length mirror. The place was small but comfortable, a secret hideaway he had kept in the city since the long-ago days of his Orvieto widow. Still, as pleasant as it was, the apartment did not fit him like his more familiar rooms within the Apostolic Palace. Soon he would return to those rooms, he thought, and not through any secret passage. He smiled at his image in anticipation of his triumph. Gave his cross a friendly tug.

He was going to miss Friedrich, of course, perhaps even more than he now understood. But the Baron's death had cleared the way for a separate peace with Niccolo. For that he was grateful. As Niccolo would be grateful for the ending of this threat of the bones. He smiled, imagining himself delivering the news. His old friend had no real stomach for confrontation and could afford to be generous. Forgive and forget.

And if the deal required the return of the art? He could handle that. As for the Germans, he would gladly give to Niccolo what he had on them. Which was little or nothing. Let His Holiness play savior to the world. Love and fear of Friedrich was one thing, but what cared Vittorio for the rest of them?

When the knock came, he thought it was a trades-man. No one else knew anyone was here.

He walked through to the living room. Opened the door.

He had never met the man who smiled at him. But he recognized him at once from Friedrich's disparaging description. Anton Arendt in the dried-up flesh.

"Guten Tag." The man pushed past him. "I am Herr Anton Arendt, Your Eminence." The last was passable Italian, but the slit of a mouth had twisted on the honor-ific.

"Sì, I had guessed. You have been mentioned to me by the Baron."

"Sehr gut." The lapse into German. "I will not then have to say to you how saddened I am by the death of our dear friend." Arendt had settled himself without invitation in the room's most comfortable chair.

"A great tragedy," Vittorio agreed, taking another seat. Something had happened to change Friedrich's lit-tle skeleton into this strutting capon. The Cardinal felt a premonitory chill.

"What word then from the Vatican?" said the Ger-man.

"Word?" The chill had locked into ice.

"My country's elections are very close, Your Emi-nence. We cannot afford to have anything interfere with our success. We must have your pope's word, a written promise of silence. As he will have ours, of course. The Americans have an expression. You scratch our back, and we scratch yours."

"What are you talking about?"

"The bones, of course. The bones of the Virgin Mary, which can bring down your Church. *Ach so,* I begin to see. You thought, did you not, that our Herr Baron's death had ended this. *Nein, nein,* Mein Herr Cardinal, the rising spirit of a new Germany is beyond the life of one man." Arendt sat pitched at the edge of the chair. He looked across at Vittorio with bright, ma-niac eyes.

"Our dear Friedrich was a creature of the past," Arendt said now. "But wise enough, in spite of that, to see the future. He passed to me this secret of the bones. And I shall do whatever is necessary to insure that that vision which we shared shall indeed come to be."

Why had Germans always to make speeches? Vittorio wondered. It was tedious. An insult on top of the injury. He tried to smile. "I shall have to make further contacts," he said. "It all takes time with the Vatican."

Arendt's own mouth was little more successful. His smile was the ugly twist. *"Ein bisschen,"* he said. "A little time, mein Herr Cardinal. I am not, after all, a completely ungenerous man."

CHAPTER 47

"They're getting impatient." Cardinal Vittorio De-Lario spoke the words more urgently than he'd meant into the black receiver.

"So am I," said Julian. "This apartment you've stuck me in is a dump."

"Don't complain, Father Morrow. Have you any idea how hard it is on short notice to get an apartment in this city with a phone?"

"I bet it's nicer where you are. Why don't you let me bunk with you, Vittorio?"

"Listen to me, Julian, you must be serious. The players have changed slightly. They demand a written guarantee now that the Vatican will not expose them. Now, or ever. It's an actual document they want signed. You can pick it up at the post-office box we arranged."

"I see."

"And as thankless as the task seems, you must find a way to pressure Niccolo to sign it. Make him see there is no use at all in stalling for time. This new player is impossible. And relentless."

"I'll get my money, then? When Niccolo signs?"

"*Si, si.* Thirty-three percent of everything. I have said it."

He hung up, hating the Jesuit as much as Anton Arendt. And Friedrich . . . dying on him like that. Betraying him in the end to the Germans.

The Germans. If only he had the means to neutralize them. He had considered it, offering to join with Niccolo in exposing them to the world. But the truth was that he knew so very little that could be of any help. No names beyond that of Arendt. No proof of where the German part of the profits had actually gone. That end of things had always been handled by Friedrich.

He looked down at his nails that needed trimming. He longed for Basco. Pulling his dressing gown tighter around him, he resisted getting dressed, putting on the civilian clothes again. To go where?

Almost anywhere, was the unwelcome answer. His money was intact. He had been quick. His Swiss bank had amicably transferred his money to him in Rome. It rested now under a new alias, in a new location the Vatican hounds would never be able to find.

But what he wanted was his old life, the life that had again been almost in his grasp. Until Anton Arendt had walked through the door and destroyed it.

Elliot Peters was not the most instinctive man in the world. Nor was he a stone wall. For weeks now he'd been feeling a little off center. Of course, there were enough mysteries floating around to cause almost anyone to engage in some very interesting speculation. Mysteries like Brisi dying, Morrow evaporating into thin air, His Eminence Cardinal DeLario becoming suddenly "indisposed."

Yet it was the little things that nagged him most. Like Romany's not showing up for work Monday. True, she'd called. But still . . . And what about the conversation he'd just had with Theodor? Something was definitely going on. Of course, nothing Theodor had said should cause him to be suspicious. Maybe it was what he didn't say. Hell, he'd just spoken to his best friend, and he felt as if he'd just spoken to a stranger. Well, not quite. Theodor never made anyone feel like a stranger. Not even a stranger. But he was different. Remote. As if he had something on his mind.

He'd taken a chance and called Romany at her parents'. He hadn't even bothered to ring her at her own apartment. For some reason he figured she'd be visiting Marthe and Theodor. He was wrong. She wasn't there. Oh, she'd been there earlier and was expected back later. She just wasn't there now. He'd told Theodor not to worry; nothing was pressing. He'd get back to Romany later. It was just that he'd missed her call yesterday, and he hadn't seen her since Saturday. They needed to do some catch-up. Theodor said he would tell Rom he'd called.

Then he'd asked Theodor about Marthe.

"Marthe?" he asked.

"Yes, Theodor, your wife."

"Sorry, Elliot. Marthe's doing well."

"Enjoying Rome, I hope."

"Yes. Yes, she is enjoying Rome."

Damn, in all the years he'd known him, he'd never known Theodor Chase to be short on words. In fact, his friend was probably the most loquacious man he knew. But it had been like pulling eye-teeth getting anything out of Theodor.

Yes, Elliot decided, something was definitely wrong.

The monk could not say exactly why he did not like it here in the hidden library. Certainly he loved books, especially old books. He loved to explore their mysteries. But the Templar library, the depository of all that was left of the accumulated wisdom of his forebears, somehow made him uncomfortable. He inhaled shallowly, avoiding a sneeze. Perhaps, after all, it was nothing more sinister than dust.

Treading slowly, with the lantern held before him, he passed through the narrow corridors made by the shelves. At a desklike wooden table Metatron sat, ghostly in his white robes, his own lantern set beside a crumbling manuscript. The monk did not have to look to know it was the journal of Jacques de Beauvacque that the Thirteenth was reading.

"You think I am obsessed." Metatron, not even glancing up, had nevertheless seemed to guess his thoughts.

The monk placed himself across from the elder man at the table. "I think, Father, that you look for answers where there are none."

"Perhaps." The Thirteenth did at last look up. It seemed he had grown yet older in the time since they'd last met. But perhaps that was only an illusion of the oily shadows.

"You have read the text yourself, Zuriel," Metatron was saying. "What do you think, my son? Is it the Virgin's bones of which de Beauvacque speaks?"

"I don't know. You torture yourself with riddles."

Metatron smiled. In the lantern glow it made him look like a death's head. "Impatient as always, Zuriel. You are, indeed, no Roman."

"It is Germans with whom we deal, Father. And German time is short." He placed the agreement that was to be signed upon the desk. "I must return to Rome, where Ambriel is waiting," he said. "And there is something else."

"Speak." The voice was weary.

"We know the Americans have found the middleman. They may make other discoveries. What if circumstances force them to go forward despite their assurances to us? We will have done nothing, but the Germans might think we've betrayed them, and release what they have to the world."

"What are you saying? That we should tell the

Americans of this threat to us, Zuriel? That is most dangerous. Today the Americans wear the face of Andrew Douglas, but perhaps not tomorrow. No, my son, we must find where these relics lie hidden. We must claim them for ourselves."

To destroy them? was the question in Zuriel's mind. He did not voice it. His role was devil's advocate. He did not inflict a pain without a purpose.

"You are silent, my son."

"It feels wrong. Being in hock to these monsters." It was still more than he'd wanted to say.

Metatron sighed as if indeed the words had added to his burden. "Find the bones, and we can yet destroy these monsters."

"Find the bones, Father? How do we find them? Vittorio is a hedgehog, fat but quick. Too careful to let himself be followed. And what other route do we have to their location? These books? You have hunted them for two days now and found no mention except possibly for this." His hand came down, a fist at the side of the manuscript. "And of what use, even if they should be de Beauvacque's relics? They are no longer in Bezu."

"The tests . . . ?" It was the question that Metatron could no longer avoid.

"The bones seem to be of the correct age," Zuriel answered. "Within a wide range, of course. There are more accurate procedures, which take time. We are testing now for minerals, to see if the diet is consistent with what is known of the period."

"And the script?"

"A very small fragment. And very little text. The paper is definitely authentic, but such materials are not that difficult to acquire. The ink checks out so far. Carbon mostly. . . . You could say it doesn't look good."

"Oh ye of little faith . . ."

No answer for that.

Metatron too fell silent. Then, "Perhaps, Zuriel," he said, "we should call another meeting. These questions can again be put toward the whole of the Brotherhood.

Most readily I do confess I have no wish to make such decisions alone."

And once again he bent his head to the long-dead Templar's diary.

Romany could tell he was surprised to see her. And why shouldn't he be?

"I'm sorry to just show up like this. Not call or anything. But it couldn't wait."

"What couldn't wait, Romany?" Richard Vance asked.

She stared at him, suddenly deciding that he wasn't a half-bad-looking man. Then it sank in that he'd called her by her first name. Had he ever done that before?

"It's really difficult to explain. . . ." She paused, struggling. Trying to decide how to tell him what she knew without telling him everything.

"I'm listening." And this time he smiled. Richard Vance actually smiled. And yes, he was definitely cute.

"I don't even know why in the hell I'm here . . . sorry, I didn't mean to . . ."

"No problem. I've said worse, much worse."

She was really getting a fresh look at Vance. First he smiles, then admits he curses. Really curses.

"I just had this feeling that you were the one I should talk to. Don't ask me why."

"Womanly instinct." Another smile.

"Okay, I'll give you that one. At any rate, here I am. At your apartment. Eight o'clock at night."

"And?"

"I was in the necropolis. I know about the bones." Okay, there she'd said it.

He stared at her. She couldn't tell what he was thinking, or if he was thinking at all. Then, "What about the bones?" he finally asked.

"I know this whole situation is big trouble for the Church. Something about undermining papal infallibility. I've done a little reading. . . ." Her words drifted off. She certainly didn't want to sound as if she thought she was any kind of authority.

Vance nodded, and this time his smile looked more like a grin. She couldn't understand why he wasn't taking what she'd said more seriously.

"Father Vance," her voice was impatient, "I think I know where the bones are."

Bullseye! Vance's eyes suddenly widened, his brows rearing up in thick dark arches. Then he backed away, moved toward a closed door in the room. His right arm slipped behind him; his fingers groped for the knob. Slowly he inched open the door.

"I'm afraid you're speaking to the wrong person," he said rather loudly. Then he stepped away from the door, like some sort of stage magician about to dazzle his audience with a grand finale.

"There's someone out here to see you," Vance called out, directing his voice into the darkened room behind him.

Romany would always remember the Julian Morrow who appeared out of the shadows as the same Julian Morrow she'd seen that first time in the Apostolic Palace. That same boyishly handsome man, that same boyishly handsome smile.

Shell-shock. As good a name as any, Romany figured, for the way she felt, driving along in Vance's Fiat with Julian Morrow at the wheel. Burnout was more chic, but somehow didn't get it. *Inured.* Now there was a word with weight. Romany Chase, inured to any shock. The mental equivalent of the stage hypnotist's dupe you could stick pins in.

The traffic light turned red ahead of them, and Julian braked to a stop. *Julian Morrow.* Gregory's double agent. A good-guy Jesuit she didn't know, whose motives for sleeping with her she might be beginning to guess.

She remained staring ahead, but could easily sense

when he turned aside to watch her. They were close enough in the tiny car. Way too close for comfort.

"We need to talk," he said.

"The light," was her answer. It had rained a little earlier, and she could see reflected in the puddles on the street the amber glow from the opposite light already turning yellow.

Julian turned to put the car in motion. He was quiet for the moment, driving, but she could feel his mind working.

"Tell me more about the bones." She cut off the possibility of whatever he was planning to say. "I did some research, but it's not completely clear to me. The problem is that Mary's bones would blow infallibility? Right?"

"Right," Julian said. "If it can be proved that the Virgin was not assumed body and soul into heaven as Pius the Twelfth proclaimed, then the Pope is ipso facto not infallible. And the Catholic Church has no special pipeline to God."

"That's what I thought." She looked at him now, safer on impersonal territory. "I just wonder," she said. "Other people, non-Catholics . . . how much are they going to care? I mean, I see that this thing is bad for the Church. But is it *that* bad? Most don't accept the Pope's infallibility anyway."

She saw him smile. "On a certain level, Romany, what you say is true. Most non-Catholics don't accept it . . . rationally. But we're dealing with psychology, perception. We're talking about image. . . . Turn here?"

"Yes, turn here." She watched his profile as he focused on making the side street. He was really back at the start now—the complete Jesuit.

"What I'm saying"—he turned back to her briefly—"is that the Pope's authority comes from his own conviction in a belief system that projects outward. . . . Is this making any sense?"

"I think so . . . so far."

"The point is that it's not necessary for non-Catholics to actually buy into the Catholic worldview in order to feel its projected power. That's the secret of the Pope's influence in the world."

"Yes. I do see that," she said.

"But what if the belief system itself becomes damaged, impaired badly from within?"

"Like if the Pope is suddenly proved not to be infallible?"

"Exactly," he said. "Then the worldview collapses, and the power is gone. Like an old magic-lantern show when the candle at its heart is blown out."

The image was one her father might have chosen.

"I knew it all, I guess," was what she said to him. "Now I understand it." She saw him smile.

"If you're right about this painting, Romany"—he looked back toward the street—"you'll be the unsung hero of the Church. That ought to qualify you for sainthood some day. Though of course only a very few will know. St. Romany . . . a secret saint." She thought he might be laughing.

Makes two of us, she thought. Except that saints weren't usually priests with five-year-old sons. And not usually guilty of murder.

"I'm stopping here." Julian had slowed, was pulling to the curb. "This should be just a block away," he said. "I don't think we should even chance making a drive-by in the car."

"No," she agreed with him. "There's bound to be somebody watching the place."

It turned out not to be as difficult as she'd feared getting into the Palazzo Rozze unobserved. With just one man staked out in a car across the street, it was easy to make their way in through the terraced garden. The reason for the low-level security was immediately apparent once they'd gotten in. The place had been stripped to the walls.

Romany looked around, impressed, wondering if it was the same at the Villa Bassano. "Follow me," she said to Julian. "And pray they haven't stumbled across where the painting was hidden."

It was impossible to use flashlights except in interior rooms where the light wasn't detectable from the street. But the rain, luckily, had lifted. And the moon had climbed in the sky.

"Oh, damn . . ."

"What's wrong?"

"This *is* the right floor, Julian. I'm fairly sure of that, because I remember how it related to the terrace."

"But there's no furniture."

"Right. I think this is the dining room. It looks the correct size. I just can't be sure."

"So where to?" he asked her.

"Well, if this *is* right, there should be a smaller, squarish room through that door there. It was filled with paintings when I was here before."

". . . No paintings, but so far so good." Julian had gone on ahead of her, was playing his flashlight around. "Looks pretty 'squarish.' "

"I think this is it." She stepped in front of him. "I remember I couldn't believe what I was seeing . . . so many Old Masters."

She moved as she spoke, trying to get the original layout straight in her mind. Julian followed at her side.

"This wall." She had stopped again. "The panel's on this wall . . . somewhere not too far from the corner."

"Okay." Julian started tapping.

"There, that sounded kind of hollow."

"Maybe." He tried it again.

"The panel, I remember, is pretty thick. I think it's there."

"Did you see how to open it?"

"No. But it couldn't have been complicated. He did it so fast." Romany held her flashlight steady. "Try the molding."

"I can't find anything," Julian said. He began tapping farther over.

"That part doesn't sound as hollow," she said to

him. She knelt down. "Let me try here." She started pushing on the molding at the floor.

A black rectangle opened up, then quickly closed in front of her. "It's like a pedal," she said. "You're supposed to press it with your foot. Look."

Julian walked closer. The panel slid open as she depressed a section of molding. He caught and held it with his hand.

"I'm almost afraid to look." She stepped through. Lifted her flashlight. The small chamber was empty as before, except for the painting.

"God, it's really something." Julian's flashlight played with hers across the ornate surface. "Bigger than I thought." He moved past her, shoving his flashlight into his belt. He reached to take the painting from the wall.

"Help me hold it steady." He took out a knife and cut along the inside of the frame, then rolled the canvas up. "Let's get out of here," he said to her. "Richard's waiting."

CHAPTER 48

"... Three days," Chaim Lieber said in answer to Andrew Douglas's question.

Old friends and friendly rivals, they sat staring one another down across the small square table in the tiny trattoria near Chaim's less-than-elegant hotel. It was eight o'clock in the morning.

"Three days," Andrew repeated. "You can't be serious, Chaim?"

"I am." Chaim pushed away his coffee in favor of his burning cigarette. "This is from the top, Andrew . . . sorry."

"But Gregory's not the enemy." There was a defeated kind of anger in the way Andrew spoke. As if he knew the argument was already lost, and his emotion purely reactive. "The Pope did a good job heading off this latest feint from the Syrians," he said. "He just wants his paintings back, for chrissakes, not to protect the Nazis. . . . He only asked for time."

"Dammit, Andrew"—Chaim flicked ashes into his discarded mug—"can't you count in Washington? The German elections are in less than a year, and we know there are secret Nazis running in every party. What we've got to have is proof."

"I know that, Chaim."

"The Vatican is protecting DeLario, Andrew. You guys should have been heaping on the pressure. Making that bastard talk."

Andrew had no answer.

"The German government doesn't want to believe what we keep telling them." Chaim pressed his advantage. "And we can't force Bonn to put the screws to the people we suspect . . . prominent men like Arendt. But with the Vatican, we've got the goods. We've got leverage."

"So you've just unilaterally decided that leaking this story to the press will force Gregory's hand."

"Sure. He'll do whatever he must to save face. Name some names. But it's more than that, Andrew. When we go public that the Vatican's been forging its own art and sending profits to Nazis in Germany, it'll cause a stink so bad that Bonn will have to start investigating.

"Come on, Andrew." Chaim couldn't keep himself from a little bit of gloating. "Tell me it's not our best shot."

Vittorio was going home, and he had primped himself like a young girl getting ready for a suitor. He had adorned himself with all the trappings of his high office. Now he set the large Byzantine cross, the last of his ornaments, in place. He imagined that the gold chain had over the long years worn a deep indentation into the soft flesh around his neck.

He admired himself one last time in the full-length mirror, giving the heavy necklace a single strong tug. He made a slight adjustment to the links of the chain, and thought it was a dreadful irony that this morning the old relic should feel more like a noose than like the essential element that marked him a Prince of the Holy Roman Church.

How adept old Matterizzi was at disguising his emotions. That ancient face was stone as soon as Vittorio entered his offices, located just outside the papal apartments. Though all inside the Curia referred to the ancient monsignor as "the iron butterfly," to DeLario the man was no more than a persistent little gnat. What position Matterizzi actually held in the papal household was, however, a mystery. There had never been an official title. Yet all who knew the delicate protocol surrounding a Roman Catholic pope understood that "the iron butterfly" was the shield between Gregory XVII and the world.

"His Holiness will see you now, Your Eminence."

Vittorio turned at the sound of Matterizzi's surprisingly young voice. Polite, the old priest was always so fucking polite. Affording Vittorio all the dignity implied by his rank. It had always been a minor irritation not knowing what feelings really festered behind those blank dead eyes.

"Grazie, Monsignore Matterizzi, *grazie mille."* He beamed his most charming smile. The priest nodded humbly, moving to open the double doors leading into Gregory's apartments.

At first the two prelates merely stood facing one another, silent, appraising. Allowing, it seemed, the unspoken truth to have its own time. Then Vittorio walked forward.

"Your Holiness." He fluttered to the floor, a great red bird, reaching out for the ring of Peter. He kissed it. In a moment Gregory withdrew his hand, but made no move to bring Vittorio up to his feet. He stared down into the fat face. "I thought never to see you again, Vittorio. I imagined perhaps that you had defected to the Eastern rite. Or perhaps to the Episcopalians."

Vittorio waited, then he made a weak laugh. "You are a very humorous man, Your Holiness." He worked at flattery, though he still rested on the pads of his knees. "It is a pity the world knows so little of your sense of humor."

"The world need not know of my humor, Vittorio, only my sense of justice." The smile on the pontiff's face now appeared slightly worn. "Off your knees, Vittorio."

"Your Holiness." Vittorio kowtowed before he lumbered to his feet, his old joints rebelling. He imagined he presented Niccolo quite a sight struggling to gain his legs. The meeting was definitely not going as he'd planned.

"I know what it is I desire from you, Vittorio. But what is it exactly that you desire?"

DeLario shook his head. "I am a miserable man, Niccolo. . . ."

"*Basta*, Vittorio. I know you are a miserable man. Tell me what I do not know."

"I require your forgiveness, Niccolo."

Gregory glared at him. "I am not at this moment disposed to forgive you, Vittorio. Neither as a man, nor as an ordained priest of the Holy Mother Church."

Vittorio had prepared for a fight, but not for this. Not for this hardness. He swallowed the saliva pooling inside his mouth, then made to grasp his cross. His hand faltered. Alas, there was no comfort to be found anywhere. "I want to offer my services," he said softly.

"Your services?"

"*Sì*, I want to help His Holiness repair what damage I might have done."

The Pope refashioned his face into something startlingly ugly, repeated the words, ". . . might have done."

"I was not so important as you might think, Your Holiness."

"Where are the bones, Vittorio?" Anger, real anger.

"I . . . I do not know, Niccolo. I swear it. I am but a helpless instrument."

The Pope turned away, walked to a bookcase, snatched a book from a shelf. "Who is this who threatens the Church?"

"I do not know."

Vittorio heard the slap of the text hard against the shelf. "I am growing short of patience. Who, Vittorio?"

He paused a moment. "His name is Anton Arendt. He is a German. He was given . . ." Again he stopped, thinking how he'd been betrayed by Friedrich, how in all those years he'd never been told of the bones, how the secret now had been passed to the nasty little German. "Only Anton knows where the bones are," he said at last.

"Where is this German now?"

"I do not know, Your Holiness."

Niccolo picked up another volume, scanned a page of text. "I do not know why I should believe you, Vittorio, but I do." He returned the book to its place on the shelf.

"I can help get some of the art back, Niccolo." His voice was as sincere as he felt.

The ugly grin reappeared on Gregory's face. "Trust me, Vittorio, you will."

Then Gregory moved to his desk. Picked up a piece of stationery. Wrote down a few words. Set his pen down. "I hope this time you will not embarrass the Swiss guards."

At last Vittorio allowed himself to smile. "No, Your Holiness, no."

What Andrew liked best about Gregory was that he didn't have to tiptoe around the necessity of confidentiality. The old boy was good at discreetly clearing the

room of his high-level cronies without so much as ruffling a single feather. Of course, what happened after
their private meeting was something else entirely. But
he was at least allowed the momentary fiction of thinking that what passed between him and the Roman pope
would be strictly "entre nous."

Today he was especially grateful to face the pontiff
alone. He didn't even want to speculate what the scene
would have been if he had had to face an entire hierarchy of church clerics. The news he bore was decidedly
bad.

"There is some urgency, Mr. Douglas?"

He watched the Pope lift the fine china teacup to his
lips. Like the porcelain, Gregory was delicate but resil-
ient.

"I'm afraid the news is not good, Your Holiness."

Gregory nodded, as though he had already resigned
himself to whatever disaster was forthcoming.

"As we have previously discussed, this operation was
something of a joint venture."

"Between the United States and Israel."

"Yes. Mossad has from the beginning, however,
been most interested in the neo-Nazi link to the forgery
operation."

Another nod.

"Unfortunately, the progress in uncovering any direct evidence that ties the German right-wing group to
the black-marketing monies has been very poor. We had
hoped . . ."

"That His Eminence Cardinal DeLario would have
had some answers."

"Yes, Your Holiness."

"His Eminence claims he knows nothing about neo-
Nazis. I am forced at this time to accept his word."

"I understand." Andrew paused and looked down
into his empty cup. "Mossad is going to leak the story to
the press."

Gregory came alive. "Leak the story to the press?"

"Yes. They think if they break the story, they will be

able to arouse enough public interest to smoke out the neo-Nazis."

"But they cannot . . ."

"I am afraid that they can, Your Holiness."

"But do they not realize what harm will be done, how this will affect everything I am trying to do? What of Arte per Pace?"

"Mossad is not without compassion, Your Holiness," he lied. "But it is a matter of priorities."

"Sì, sì," the Pope's voice trailed off, "a matter of priorities."

"I am sorry, Your Holiness. I have, however, gotten them to agree not to mention Cardinal DeLario's name specifically."

The Pope smiled. He didn't seem grateful. "When, Mr. Douglas?"

"Three days. If DeLario cannot come up with anything concrete in three days, the Israelis go to the press."

"I see."

"Of course, my government is ready to support you in any way we can, Your Holiness. The State Department is prepared to issue a statement emphasizing papal cooperation. We will minimize Vatican involvement, confirm that the forgery operation was limited to a very small group of men in the Restoration Department."

Gregory made a weary wave of his hand, their private meeting at an end. "I am confident you will do your best, Andrew Douglas."

Niccolo was pouring a second cup of tea when his Secretary of State came into the room.

"What has happened, Niccolo?"

"The worst, Fabio. The world will soon know of Vittorio's indiscretions."

"How can this happen?"

"How can this happen?" Niccolo shook his head. "We live in an impatient world, a world that has little respect for secrets." He set his cup down. "Please sit. Keep me company for a while."

The secretary sat, poured himself tea.

"We will be spared, it seems, some indignity. At least for a time. DeLario's name will be withheld from the papers."

"I could almost wish that it would not."

"Shh, my friend. If one of us falls, we all fall. You know that."

"And what enemy is it this time?"

"Not really an enemy at all. But those who have old wounds that have yet to heal."

"I do not understand."

"The Israelis want the men who have used the money from the art sales."

"The neo-Nazis."

Niccolo nodded. "I cannot fault the Israelis' energies." He leaned back against his chair, sighed. "We have three days to make Vittorio talk, or they go to the newspapers."

"But Vittorio says he knows nothing of neo-Nazis."

"I know. But this German Arendt he speaks of, he may come again to Vittorio's apartment. We must see that it is watched."

"I will place it under surveillance immediately. Anything else, Your Holiness?"

"*Sì*, one more thing, Fabio. Should we tell Mr. Douglas about the bones?"

"No, Niccolo. We have already decided this is something we must keep to ourselves."

"Then pray, Fabio, that the bones can be found. Because if we cannot stop the Israelis, Anton Arendt will have his revenge, will tell all the world that Our Lord left his mother to rot inside a grave."

It was amusing, Romany thought, the way these priests all looked at her. It went beyond Sister Clemensia's more innocent disapproval of a short skirt and high heels, to a keen disapproval of her sex. A woman in the inner precincts was a heavy cross to bear. And after a whole night of having to tolerate both her presence and her participation in so sensitive a matter, Gregory's hand-assembled panel of curial experts seemed all to have been sucking on lemons.

"You are very sure, Signorina Chase," one of them addressed her now, "that this building in the background of the canvas is not the place that you call the Villa Bassano?"

It was the same question she had answered a dozen times throughout the night. "I'm as sure as I can be, Your Eminence." She tried not to show impatience. She was as tired as any of these men. More tired, she was sure. None of them had had to endure the tension of actually stealing the painting. They had only been summoned later from their beds for this futile attempt to decipher it.

"But you saw this Villa Bassano only once, and at night?" Another of the prelates had taken up the inquisition. "You admitted yourself, Signorina Chase, that your mind was on something other than architecture at the time."

"That is very true, Monsignor. But the structure seems somewhat fantastical, an invention of the artist, not meant to be any real place. . . . Don't you agree, Father Lazio?"

The priest looked pained. The lemon turned to bitters. Still, it was a matter of his expertise in art. "A fantastical building. Yes."

She sent him a smile, which clearly distressed him. He made much of straightening the folds of his black soutane.

"Besides," she said, "I don't think the Count, or the Baron von Hohenhofen if you wish, would have hidden the relics in the Villa. Practically, it makes sense—the place is so huge, and has caverns beneath it—but it just doesn't have the right feel psychologically. It's just too obvious. He liked more complicated games.

"And one other thing." She might as well pound it home while she had the floor. "You better hope the bones aren't hidden in the Villa Bassano, because I can guarantee that the place is still crawling with CIA and Mossad."

The door opened and Julian and Richard came in. She was more than glad to see them both. Vance, even more than Julian, had been her defender here, insisting from the beginning that she had every right to stay. Julian smiled at her now, seeing her. But a small smile, as if he wished to shield it from these men. She had felt him retreating almost from the moment they'd arrived at the Vatican.

The painting of the Madonna was stretched out on a table. Those closest to it parted, making way for Richard and Julian. All of them eager to hear of any news.

"The landscape does appear to be that around Bezu," Richard spoke first, "which removes any final doubt that the painting really is a key to the bones. The bad news is that identifying the landscape is no help in knowing where the relics are now."

"We've made the tests, and the painting is modern," Julian said. "The Count told Signorina Chase the truth about that." He looked at her.

"What about the person who painted the Madonna?" she asked him. "If the artist could be found, he, or she, might know something."

Richard was the one to answer. "We're getting to that," he said. "Trouble is, there are a lot of artists specializing in this kind of thing right now, painting 'Old Masters' for people who can afford it. We'll just have to work our way through the list."

"I'm afraid there will not be enough time for that." Pope Gregory had entered unnoticed behind them. Everyone turned toward him now.

"I have spoken with Andrew Douglas," he said. "It is not good news. In three days the press will have the story. The forgeries, the Nazis. All of it."

"But the Americans promised. . . ." An angry voice, followed by many murmurs.

"Signor Douglas has not betrayed us." Gregory held up a hand for quiet. "It is the Israelis who refuse to wait."

That brought silence.

Romany took a very deep breath. "Your Holiness," she said, conscious once again of hostile eyes upon her, "I hope you will not think me too presumptuous, but I have an offer to make."

Gregory smiled, his first since he'd entered the room. The frost around her lifted by degrees.

"Please, Signorina Chase," the pontiff said, "I am well aware that without you there would be no chance at all for us to salvage this situation. I would be grateful for anything further you might suggest."

"My father, Professor Theodor Chase, Your Holiness, is here in Rome. He serves as Chairman of the Georgetown University Language Department, but he is also an expert in cryptology." She pointed to the painting.

She could sense the resistance from the men around her. Saw the Pope wavering. "My father has helped Andrew Douglas with such things in the past . . . unofficially," she added.

The mention of Andrew had been a mistake. She knew that immediately. Despite what Gregory had said, the sentiment of these men was that Andrew had betrayed them. They had no choice but to trust her, but this needn't extend to her father.

"I thank you, Signorina Chase. I will not rule this out." Gregory softened his refusal. "But we do, after all, have our own experts." He cast a beneficent and diplomatic eye on those gathered in the room.

CHAPTER 49

The origin of the people of Etruria had been a hot debate even in classical times. The early Greeks and Romans believed the Etruscans were Lydians who had migrated to the Italian peninsula after colonizing in the Aegean. But the historian Dionysius, writing in the first century B.C., rejected any theory of migration, stating that the Etruscans themselves claimed descent from a native Italic people called the Rasenna.

Modern scholars still disagreed. The Etruscans, with their highly developed culture and fierce internecine wars, remained a contradiction and a mystery. Which was exactly why, Romany thought, her father so dearly loved them.

She stood in the shadow of the trees, watching as her father emerged from a dark cavity piercing the side of a hill.

"This is a nice surprise." Theodor walked up to her smiling. "Why didn't you let me know you were coming?" His face changed suddenly as the thought struck. "Is something wrong? Your mother . . . ?"

"Oh no, Mom's fine," she rushed in to reassure him. "I mean, I'm sure she is." She had realized as she spoke how long it had been since she'd talked to either of her parents. "I'm sorry, Papa, that I haven't phoned. It's complicated."

"It's okay." He smiled again. "I figured you were busy."

She knew he meant Drew.

"Come on in and see this." He was motioning her back toward the black opening. "It's unique for a tomb this close to Veii. More like the ones you'd expect nearer the coast. . . . What is wrong, Romany?" He was still searching her face.

"Nothing." She smiled to prove it. "Are there people in there?"

"Yes, of course . . . working."

"I'll have a look later then, if that's okay. I need to talk to you alone."

"No problem . . . come on." He put his arm around her shoulders, walked with her to another group of trees near some ruins. "A road was here that led out of Veii to Rome," he said looking back toward the city. "This foundation's all that's left from a villa of the late Augustan period.

"Here, this is good. . . ." They sat down together on a low wall of blocks. "Okay, Rom," he said to her, "shoot."

"Well, Papa, like I said, it's complicated. Some friends of mine need your help with a puzzle. A kind of picture puzzle . . . really tough. Just the kind you like, I said. I convinced them you could solve it."

"This sounds like a snow job, Gypsy. A puzzle? . . . Drew send you?"

"No, Papa . . . the Pope."

"The Pope"—he stared at her—"as in Gregory?"

"Yes." She stood up. "It's a long story, Papa, and I promise to explain. But I need you to come with me, right now if you can. We've got less than forty-eight hours left to save the Catholic Church."

David had beaten her to her apartment. He sat cross-legged on the couch leafing through a magazine.

"Reading in the dark?" She locked the door behind her.

"Just looking at the pictures." He set the magazine aside, did a lazy stretch against the back of the sofa. She thought he looked exactly like a panther.

She tossed her purse and keys. "What's the occasion?"

"Do I need an occasion?" He smiled, the white teeth whiter in the semidarkness of the living room. "Come here." He patted the cushion next to him. "You look tired."

"I am," she complained, kicking off her shoes as she walked over, then sat.

"You can do better than that." He frowned, noticing how she'd positioned her body exactly in the center of the cushion.

She slid over, snuggling in close, releasing her full weight against him. She felt his arms come around her.

"That's better." He kissed the top of her head, gave her a squeeze.

"How're things going over at the villa?" It was the wrong question.

"Like crap. We got nothing. And it's my fault. All my fault."

She pushed away, turned to look at him. "Your fault? How do you figure that?" Dumb question. She didn't need any specifics. When it came to his job, David was a perfectionist.

He gave her specifics. "I had the Nazi connection, fucking little bastard, right in my hand." She watched him make a tight fist. "But I was stupid, I let him get away."

"Come on, David. Everybody's batting average has been shitty."

"I'm not everybody." The green eyes got ugly.

"Excuse me. Maybe we better change the subject." She moved to get up, but he pulled her back down.

"Sorry." Then his mouth was on hers. Kissing her as though they'd been making love instead of arguing.

She drew back. His eyes had gotten friendly. "Well, that's certainly an improvement," she said.

He pinched her nose. "So what's happening on your end?"

"I thought we were finished with business." She gave him a look.

"So I'm curious. What'd you expect from the Mossad?"

She fitted herself back into his arms. "You know,

David—and don't get pissed off again—I really wish you could have gotten Anton Arendt."

"How'd you know his name? I never said . . . Sully, right?"

"Not exactly. But that's not important. What's important is that I'm going to tell you something that neither Drew nor Sully knows."

His face didn't change.

"I'm telling you because I believe you're the only person I can trust. The only one who can help." She stopped. "Okay? . . . Just between us?"

He glanced away. "You know I'm not supposed to make promises like that." He turned back.

"I know. But just this once. Just this one time for me?"

He groaned. "Romany . . ." He'd stretched out her name. Then, his eyes turning foxy, "Does this have anything to do with Morrow?"

"Sorta."

He jerked up from the sofa. "Fuck, I knew it."

"He's okay, David. He was on our side all along."

"What?" He was glaring down at her.

"He was a Vatican plant, out to trap DeLario."

"I'm listening."

"Arendt's blackmailing the Vatican."

"What? . . . How?"

"It seems before he died the Baron handed over a little bombshell to Arendt. The bones of the Blessed Virgin Mary."

"The what? I don't understand."

"I know. But the bottom line is that the existence of Mary's bones blows the Catholic Church right out of the water. You understand papal infallibility?"

"Enough. . . . So where does the blackmail come in?"

"Arendt says if his little gang of neo-Nazis is implicated in the art scandal, he goes to the press with the bones."

"Fuck."

"My sentiments exactly," she said.

"Chaim wants to unload on the papers right now."

"Yeah, I know."

"So what do you want me to do?"

"Find Anton Arendt."

They made love as if it were the first time. And the last. Her body sucking him inside of her. Deep. Deeper. And David, falling, falling as from a great distance. Into her. Then his explosion. All heat, and wetness. And words. Hebrew words. Words he'd never spoken to anyone but Becca.

Ahuva. And he licked the fine line of her eyebrow.

Yakar. And he kissed the lips between her thighs.

Malach. He was inside of her again.

He rested his head on her breasts after that second time. Sweat trickling down from his hair, mixing with her own. He swept his tongue over her skin, whispering against her nipple.

Yakeeratee. My darling.

"David?"

"Shhh . . ."

"Do you still love Rebecca?"

Silence. Then, "I will always love Becca."

She smiled to herself. It was the answer she'd wanted. "Good."

He looked up. "I love you too, Romany."

There. He'd said it. "And I love you too, David." It wasn't a lie. Could never be a lie.

He settled back down on her breast. Contented, a small baby boy nursing. She giggled.

"So you think this is funny?"

"You're tickling me." She pushed his head away, pulled the sheets up over her head.

"Romany . . . you know we're more alike than you realize. I mean . . ." He hesitated.

She came out from under the tent of sheets. "David, my finding out that my mother is Jewish doesn't change anything between us. It can't make me love you any more than I already do."

The set look in his eyes said he wasn't buying.

"Even if by some absurdity it did make a difference, I'm not Jewish, David. Not really." She gazed down at the fabric of the bedding, smoothing the fresh wrinkles. "Oh, technically I'm Jewish. But not on any level that really counts." She glanced over. His features hadn't changed; he was still waiting to be convinced. "Being Jewish is more than blood, David. It's years, it's a history. Neither of which I have."

"But you do have a history, Romany. All of us do. It's Dachau, and Auschwitz, and Buchenwald."

She didn't say anything for a moment. Thinking not of the camps. Not of the thousands of anonymous faces marching off to be gassed. But thinking of Lise, her grandmother. How she'd looked in that painting. And of Lise's parents. Of all the Schulens she'd never see. And thinking most of her mother. How she must have suffered. Still suffered. She brought her face close to his. There was no right, no wrong answer. No way to decide. She kissed him on the lips.

"You still have a gentile nose." He bit the tip.

"You . . ." She lifted the pillow and gave him a satisfying smack across his face.

But he was too quick. He grabbed her arms, pinned them over her head. Threw his thigh over her abdomen. "Say you're sorry, Chase." His green eyes glinted, pieces of mosaic in the tanned face.

"Okay . . . . okay. I'm sorry."

He loosened his hold, gave her a quick kiss. Then took the pillow, plumped it against his back. "I still think you should come to work for the Mossad after this mess is cleared up."

"God, David, who can think that far?"

He glanced over. "We'd make a good team."

"You've got to be kidding, David ben Haar. We'd fight all the time. And you know it."

"Maybe not." He turned away, began to massage the muscles in his thighs.

She watched him for a while, thinking how he would make the perfect artist's model. Then, "David, what're your chances of finding Anton Arendt?"

He gave her the famous smirk that passed for a smile. "I'm good, Romany. I'm damn good."

"Yeah, I know." She reached over and caressed his penis.

"You better stop that."

"Why?"

He wrapped his hand over hers. "That's why."

"Okay." She let go, leaned back against the headboard. "So you'll get Arendt?" She could feel him watching her.

"I'll get Arendt."

"Would you please stop looking at me like that?"

"Laazazel." He exclaimed the only curse word in the Hebrew language. "You're impossible." He took a deep breath, socking the pillow at his back a couple of times. Then after a few minutes, "Romany?"

"Yessss . . ."

"You know when we went to the Villa Bassano to get your mother?"

"Yes."

"That painting."

"Lise. My grandmother."

"What was Hohenhofen doing with it?"

The last of the mysteries. "He was my grandfather, David."

CHAPTER 50

It looked like an operating room. Everyone walking around the Restoration Department wore a lab coat, with an appropriately scientific expression on his face. The Vatican had certainly brushed off its must over the last decade or so. At least as far as the preservation and restoration of its artistic booty was concerned. Theodor Chase had made no such technological leap, and the sealed-off room that his daughter entered was certainly not his "scene."

A scholar from the ancient school, who still viewed computers with a healthy suspicion, Theodor Chase was a wizard who worked his magic intrinsically rather than extrinsically.

"Hi, Dad. Got your message. Came as soon as I could."

"Hi, gypsy girl," he said without looking up.

He'd been working all night and was clearing an area on one of the tables that seemed to have gotten out of hand. When he did glance up, his ear-to-ear grin said it all. He'd solved the puzzle. But she knew she'd have to wait. His style was never to go straight to the heart of the matter, but to dole out clues one by one, like a good mystery writer.

"The initial problem was that everyone kept seeking solutions in all the wrong places."

Romany smiled. The setup. "Yes, Dad."

"Of course, it was the obvious place to start. Match the landscape in the painting to a real location."

"Bezu," she filled in.

"Yes, but Bezu doesn't make any sense now," Theodor said.

"Then the villa seemed so much like Bassano." She kept him going.

"Yes, another error. The background had nothing to do with the burial place."

"We did eliminate the background eventually, Dad. Focused on the mantle."

"Oh, I know, gypsy girl, I'm not criticizing." He smiled his big woolly smile. "I was no better at the start myself. Stumbling around as I did." He pulled something out from under a stack of papers. "I wanted to believe the designs in the mantle were symbols of some sort. A kind of alphabet. Like Dee's Enochian Keys."

She smiled, waited for him to go on.

"I have a fault, gypsy girl. I always look for solutions in words." He winked. "Sometimes the answer is in a picture." He handed over the sheet of paper he'd been holding.

She stared at an ad for Absolut vodka torn from a magazine. She looked up.

"What do you see, Romany?"

"An ad for vodka, Dad."

He frowned. "What else?"

She looked again. "An aerial view of Manhattan?"

"Yes, an aerial photograph taken of the island of Manhattan."

"So?"

"So is the mantle thrown across the Madonna's lap."

"An aerial shot?"

"The artist's rendering of an aerial view, to be exact."

Romany glanced up from the glossy ad and looked across at the painting. "An aerial view of what, Dad?"

"The Roman Forum, gypsy girl, the Roman Forum."

It had once been the heart of the Empire. Now the Forum was little more than a lot full of rubble. Of course, that was the more cynical view. A more romantic posture saw the Roman Forum as an eerie landscape of sweeping arches and towering columns. A place of destiny, whose gaunt and craggy ruins held mystery and wonder.

Despite the rubber-soled shoes, Romany heard the soft crunch of her feet against gravel. She planted her next step on a patch of scruffy grass. The grass that grew everywhere in the Forum. Stubborn and relentless, growing up between, around, and over what was left.

She glanced over at Julian, crouched low, dressed in black from head to foot. The black catsuit she wore felt less like a second skin now that they were out in the open, hidden by the moonless dark. But when he'd picked her up earlier at her apartment, she'd stumbled over an explanation for the tight all-in-one. It was what she'd seen in his eyes that had done it. Caused her to stammer like a brainless school girl. Damn, the suit made perfectly good sense. But so did that look.

The soft crackle of Vance's signal.

"Yeah, Rich." Julian's answer.

"Round made. Green light." Richard's words let them know that the guard had made his scheduled circuit of the Forum. No problems. Everything was "a go."

"Are we on line with your father's calculations?" Julian whispered over his shoulder, clipping the receiver back onto his belt.

"Right on the money." She held a pinpoint of light against the small map she carried. "Another ten feet and we're home."

A rustle in the grass. Julian flinched. A low humping shadow skittered in the distance.

"A cat," Romany giggled. "The place is full of them."

"I don't like cats," Julian grumbled.

"Dog person, huh? I don't trust people who don't like cats."

Julian gave her a look.

"Just teasing."

Ten more feet and . . .

"Okay, this is 'mark one,' " he whispered, stopping in front of three white columns, thin fragile arms reaching out into the black Roman night. It was all that remained of the circular temple dedicated to the goddess Vesta, in whose honor vestal virgins had tended the sacred flame while living out their thirty-year vows of chastity.

" 'Mark two.' " Julian pointed dead ahead to the Church of Santa Maria Antiqua.

If the map had been drawn precisely to scale, and Theodor's best estimate was that it had been, then somewhere between the two monuments lay the bones of the Blessed Virgin Mary. The mother of the God-Man. Maternal bridge between the pagan world and the Christian.

It had not been so difficult to zero in on the exact location of the bones once Theodor had determined that the mantle in the Madonna's lap was really a map. It was merely a matter of finding the proverbial "x marks the spot." In this case the "x" was a single, small, and perfectly executed human skull.

Romany waited in front of the temple to Vesta, holding the round tape case as Julian stretched out the metal tape toward the Church of Santa Maria Antiqua. He stopped, wrote down the distance in feet, then divided by two. It was a crude process. They could be off by several feet, or miss the location of the bones by only inches. But it was the best they had. Given the circumstances. He let the tape snap back into the case and walked toward the temple.

"If I measured accurately, this is half the distance between 'mark one' and 'mark two.' " He held out a small piece of paper.

She stared down at the number he'd written. A number that under other circumstances might not mean so very much. The distance between a greenhouse and a swimming pool. Between a Laundromat and the corner grocery store. Between a house and a school bus stop. But tonight, this particular night, this particular number defined a great and serious distance. The distance between sacred truth and sacred lies.

Julian rubbed his foot a couple of times over the spot where he'd set his shovel. A kind of priestly blessing, it seemed, and she thought in that moment before he started to dig that he smiled at her. She held her breath as he reached in for that first shovelful of dirt, thinking what a great noise the end of the blade made against the earth. A sound so fierce, she imagined all of Rome, all of the world should hear it.

The expression was *dead tired,* and it fit Romany perfectly. Stressed out was another good one. How about on emotional overload? Yes, all of the above. God, she wanted to peel out of the tight catsuit and soak in a hot tub of water. Just one more little assignment, and she could call it quits for tonight.

She checked her watch. After eleven. She just might get lucky and reach David directly. If not, she'd just have to leave a message.

She dialed the number. One, two, three rings. After the fourth, the recording switched on. She listened patiently, waited for the beep.

"Friday. Eleven-ten P.M. I need to speak with you tonight. It's important. Call me as soon as you can. I don't care how late."

Romany set the receiver back in place. She had two hopes. One, that David would get back to her tonight. And two, that he had made good on his boast.

CHAPTER 51

Ringing . . . A telephone ringing. Somewhere a phone was ringing. She squinted open her eyes. It was still dark outside. Romany turned her face over on her pillow. The digital readout on the clock said 4:47. Damn, who was calling at this ungodly hour?

"Romany." Her name. She hadn't even said "hello."

"Elliot? Is that you?" If Elliot Peters was calling at this hour, the shit had hit the fan. "What's wrong, Elliot?" she asked.

"God, Romany, I can't believe it. The phone hasn't stopped ringing. Both continents and everywhere in between. You know the press."

"Slow down, Elliot."

"I'm sorry, Romany. Getting you up like this. Going on like a wild man."

"Stop apologizing, and just tell me what's happened."

"The newspapers are full of it, Romany. *Le Republica* has put out a special Saturday edition. So has *Le Monde*. Story made the front page of the *London Times*. The British tabloids will have a field day."

"I'm listening."

"Shit, where did this story come from? How could I have not known anything?"

"Elliot . . ."

"Okay, sorry."

She could hear him clear his throat as he began to read. " 'Vatican Forgery Ring Linked to Neo-Nazis.' Neo-Nazis! What the shit, Rom?"

"Just read, Elliot."

"Okay. This is the *Times.* 'Unnamed sources today made public claims that a high-ranking prelate of the Roman Catholic Church has been masterminding a forgery/black-marketing operation involving millions of dollars of Vatican art treasures. Insiders say that a major portion of the profits have been funneled to a secret right-wing group in Germany, a neo-Nazi type organization, whose secret members are front-running candidates in the upcoming elections.' "

"But no one in the Vatican is actually named?"

"No, but that doesn't mean anything. When it comes to shit like this, the Church bruises easily. God, I can't even think what this'll do to APP."

"I'll be right over. Let me grab a quick shower and throw on some clothes."

"But I haven't even read you the best part. The *Times* goes on to say that Count Klaus Sebastiano was believed to be the middleman between the Vatican and the neo-Nazi group. 'Sebastiano,'—I'm reading this— 'was, in reality, the infamous Black Baron, one of the Prussian aristocrats Hitler courted. Believed to have escaped to Argentina after the war, the Baron Friedrich von Hohenhofen, under the assumed identity of Count Klaus Sebastiano, settled in Rome in the early fifties. A member of Roman society and a patron of the arts, Sebastiano was always a man of mystery. Reports have been confirmed that the Count was found dead of unknown causes earlier this week.'

"Sebastiano a Nazi! It's unbelievable, Romany."

"Unbelievable. . . . I'll be there in thirty minutes, Elliot. Keep the press piranhas at bay."

She hung up the receiver. Suddenly she felt incredibly sorry for Elliot. She wished that somewhere along the line she could have said something, prepared him for this. But she knew there was nothing she could have done. The hand had to be played as it was dealt. Her only hope now was that David would come through. When he'd returned her call just after midnight, he said he'd picked up Arendt's trail. All that was left was to set the trap and pray that the rat took the bait.

Elliot Peters stood at Romany's office door. For the umpteenth time he was "checking in" in person. Nothing compared to the time they'd spent comparing notes on the interoffice phone. And the rest of the staff were drifting in now. The phones in every office buzzing off the hook. Not a three-ring circus anymore. But bedlam.

Romany laid down her pen. She'd been trying to compose a letter to all the APP countries, a backup for the phone calls she'd been making and receiving for the last five hours—an attempt to try to shore up a quickly sinking ship.

She looked up at Elliot.

"Where's Gina?" he asked her.

"It's weird. Natalie called her to come in this morning. The landlady finally answered her phone. She said that Gina had packed up lock, stock, and barrel. Something about leaving Rome."

"That's strange."

"Gina was strange."

Elliot sat down on the very edge of the chair in front of her desk—like if he leaned back any farther, he might not find the energy to get up. His hand went to the headlines of the papers that were strewn across her desk.

He looked grim. "You know we're going to get tarred with the same brush as Gregory. 'Vatican Art Scandal . . . Pope's Paintings Are Fakes,'" he quoted from the papers. "Can't get much worse than that."

"You talk to the Vatican yet?"

"You kidding, Romany? Switchboard just keeps saying that whatever office I ask for isn't available this morning."

"What's the latest word from New York?"

"Just what you'd think," he answered. "It's still the wee hours over there, but the dam has already broken. I've been on the phone the last thirty minutes with Gardner."

"And . . . ?"

"And he's talking shutdown. Cutting their losses before the damage spreads. You know how sensitive to scandal these corporations are."

"I'm not surprised. It's what I was afraid of. Elliot, you need to convince New York to hold off. Things might start looking a little better tomorrow."

"What makes you think that?"

"I just have this feeling that Gregory could still turn out looking like a good guy."

"I don't know." Elliot was skeptical. "If the Pope's

not guilty, they're going to say he's dumb—not knowing all this was happening right under his nose."

Oh God, here it was again. Another of those damned judgment calls about what she could say.

"Romany, if you know something. . . . No, wait." He'd seen the retreat in her eyes. "Let me back up. If you even suspect something . . ."

She took a breath. "What if Gregory did know about the forgeries and was secretly working to stop the Nazis? Get back the Vatican art? Would that make him a good guy?"

"Maybe."

"And what if our State Department confirmed he was a Boy Scout?"

"That ought to do it."

It was a minute before the smile appeared. Then slowly he shook his head. "Like father, like daughter . . ." He let the words trail away as he left.

Her telephone started buzzing.

The little restaurant was decades old and too squalid to be fashionable—crack-veined marble walls and counters, spotty mirrors limned with bare low-watt bulbs, dully lit even in the morning. In a back corner Anton Arendt perched on a wire-backed chair. A plate of pastries before him oozed yellow creme like pus.

Across the tiny table, David watched the German and his mirrored twins, one on either side, twitch over the pulling apart of one of the sugared rolls. For once little Anton seemed too nervous to actually eat.

"I want to know what you meant in your message, Severnos?" Arendt had given up on the mess in his plate, was looking at him now with a mix of suspicion and hope. "You hinted you had something that might help with this unfortunate business in the papers."

David lifted his coffee and, damning the stupid mustache, sipped slowly. He put down the cup and smiled. "Did I give that impression?" he asked.

"Scheiss!" The curse came out like a hiss beneath the German's breath. "I warn you, Severnos, do not play games with me." He had puffed up with the threat. "You knew enough to get me here. You know enough to fear me and those I represent."

It really was tempting, David thought, just to reach across the table, wrap his hands around the scrawny neck, and squeeze. Unfortunately there were practical problems with that. And besides, there was the message that he'd promised to deliver.

"This is for you," he said. He took the jar out of his jacket and pushed it across the table.

The German's anxiety betrayed him. He nearly jumped. "What is it?"

"Open it. See for yourself."

Arendt fumbled with the lid, his eyes darting between the jar itself and David watching. He stuck in a finger experimentally, rubbed the charred and crumbly bits of powder across his hand with his thumb. He lifted the blackened fingers to his nose and sniffed. "These are ashes." He looked perplexed.

"You might ask yourself whose?"

At the edges of irritation, fear had begun to show. A ring of white surrounded each brown iris. "Wh— whose . . . ?"

"I'll save you the stuttering, Anton." David leaned back. "You can forget about what was buried in the Forum. . . . That's right." He saw the comprehension dawn. "No more blackmail, Herr Arendt. You lose."

"Who are you?"

That had come out clear enough.

"Not the most likely messenger boy for the Vatican." David couldn't resist. Beneath the mustache, a smile had spread across his teeth. Not as good as a strangulation maybe, but he was enjoying this.

"Who . . . ?" Arendt insisted.

"A Jew." David shot forward in the chair. "What do you think of that, mein Herr Arendt, sitting here, drinking coffee with a Jew? So . . . civilized."

Like a plug being pulled, what color there was drained from Arendt's flesh. Fish-belly white, he stood, and ramrod straight flung the ashes at him.

David sat wiping the soot from his eyes with a napkin. He could see in the mirrors Arendt's stiff little figure disappearing at a clip through the door. And himself across the table . . . a green-eyed Jew with a fake mustache in blackface. He started to laugh, wishing he could be there when the German checked for himself an empty hole in the Forum.

" 'And yet was my sword left to me. Yet was I a Knight of the Temple of Solomon. And within my keeping the long leathern satchel with its holy treasure. I saw that in the east the moon had risen, its light steady now and pure in the late silver hours of its descent. To me it seemed a promise, a sign in the heavens that my journey would indeed be blessed, that in the secret depository near Bezu where tonight I rest, the sacred relics will again find peace. Till that far-off day when kings and popes might prove worthy of mysteries that in this age of barbarity and ignorance they would destroy.' " The monk looked up from the ancient book, across the lantern-lit table to where the white-robed figure sat with the jar and the vacuum-sealed bones of the Madonna.

"You need not quote the journal to me, Zuriel," the Thirteenth almost snapped. "I have read those same lines often enough these past days. The term, I believe, was 'obsessed.' "

Ambriel closed the tattered pages. "It is only that I fear, Father, that you intend to destroy these relics."

"It is the safest path."

"Shall the Knights of Solomon betray their trust? Shall they destroy what they have pledged to keep?"

"Be clear, Zuriel," said Metatron. "Do you draw the distinction between us? You are a Templar, I am the Pope. To be served to the death, to be sure, but only so long as I do not betray the sacred traditions."

"Please, Father, it is centuries since any such division marred our trust. My Brothers themselves stand equally divided on this question of the bones. It is now your decision alone to make. I speak only to insure that you consider well. That is my function."

"And what about you, Ambriel?" Metatron had turned to the monk standing alone in the shadows. "What do you say?"

"I am not sure I have the right to speak. You know that I am leaving the Brotherhood, Father."

"You have the right as much as any," Metatron said. "You have earned it."

"Then I wonder, Father, if we should not continue with the tests. Perhaps we hold nothing more here than old bones and a clever, if ancient, forgery."

Metatron shook his head. "It is faith that gives us absolutes, not science, as we discovered with the Shroud. There are techniques of medieval forgery of which we yet remain ignorant. The tests are not definitive."

"Someday they will be," said Zuriel. "Some day it will be possible to know if these are the bones of the Virgin. What pride is it that would destroy what may be holy to exalt and protect itself?"

Ambriel spoke into the harshness of the silence that followed. "I feel I must add this, Father," he said. "The papyrus, if authentic, would be of incalculable importance. We have nothing else beyond the gospels themselves that speaks so directly of the historical Christ. The Germans believe we have burned the relics. Surely they are safe now from misuse, hidden here with us."

"Safe?" Metatron repeated. "Is that not what de Beauvacque thought when he brought the bones to Bezu?" He shook his head wearily. "Leave me," he said to them. "I have heard your arguments. As Zuriel has said, I must make this decision alone."

When the two had gone, he spread before him the translation that had been made of the papyrus. Focused on the words that had struck him from the first. *But she*

was resigned to her destiny. Her son had made her no
promises, and long ago had she accustomed herself to the
hurt He could bring.

Not the Virgin's words, but those of an observer.
One who loved her, but perhaps had not understood the
truth of this calm resignation in a mother left behind.
Her son had made her no promises. No special prom-
ises, perhaps. None beyond what He had made to us all.
His Father's Kingdom, if we would but see, but open
our eyes to the eternal in every minute of this earth. *My*
Father's Kingdom is at hand.

Christ's message was simple. He had come to teach
us how to live. With purity and awareness, with love and
acceptance, like Mary marking her days in the desert.
Love one another. Simple, but so hard. Was that the
truth we would obscure with hierarchy and ritual? With
our demand for miracles and wonders?

To destroy the bones and their message was an act of
cowardice, a step backward into that ignorance and barbarity that Jacques de Beauvacque so hated in his own
time. Niccolo Fratelli was a weak man, but Gregory
XVII was Pope.

Thou art Peter, and upon this Rock I will build my
Church, and the gates of hell shall not prevail against it.
Another of Christ's promises. If he believed anything,
Niccolo Fratelli believed in that. For all its failures and
imperfections, the Church was the living embodiment of
the Kingdom. Were the bones real? Whatever the fact,
he must believe that the time would come when the
world and indeed the papacy itself would be ready to
bear such a truth.

He looked at the bones in the glassine case. At once
so awesome and vulnerable. The skull as tiny as a
child's.

Pope Gregory XVII made a leap of faith. The bones
and their message would abide.

CHAPTER 52

"... What are we doing drinking these things, David?" Romany picked up one of the glasses that the airport bar waitress had delivered to their table. Scotch and water for her, a double on the rocks for David.

"It's kind of early, isn't it?" she said. "I've got to go back to the office."

"And I've got to get on a plane." David was busy returning his change to his wallet.

It took half a second for the implication of his remark to sink in. "What . . . ?" She made her eyes wide. "David ben Haar is afraid to fly?"

"Not afraid." David's eyes avoided hers, shifting to his drink. "I fly all the time. I just don't like it much, that's all." He took a healthy swig.

"Uhn-uh." She wasn't about to let him off the hook. "I heard you right the first time." She grinned.

He tried not to grin back. "Romany Chase," his tone was half-mocking threat, "if this gets back to Chaim . . ."

"Not a word." She sipped at her drink.

"So how're things at work?" He'd changed the subject.

"Let's just say that you and Chaim have sure made my job interesting, David. Were you afraid I was going to get bored with you gone?"

He laughed. "Sorry. But it looks like the shock therapy worked. The German papers are full of the story this morning. And guess whose name came up."

"Our friend Anton Arendt's?"

"That's right. The little fucker's denying everything, of course. Calling it 'paranoid delusions.' But it's going to be a lot harder for him and his Nazi buddies to stay undercover now."

"And you'll keep the pressure on, of course."

"Whatever it takes to force the German government into a full-scale investigation." David knocked back the remainder of his drink. Lifted his hand for another.

"I wish I could have seen Arendt's face when you gave him the ashes."

"Yeah." David's lip curled. "But better you should have seen mine when he threw them back."

"Poor baby." She patted his hand.

"You need anything else?" he asked her. The girl had come with his drink.

"No, I'm fine."

She watched him pay, the waitress flirting outrageously.

"I should tell you again," she said, when the girl had gone, "how grateful Pope Gregory was that you could deliver so quickly. There was a real chance that Arendt might go public with the bones, believing that he still had them."

David shrugged. "He couldn't have proved anything by then."

"No, but more bad publicity is the last thing the Vatican needs right now."

"Morrow staying on with Arte per Pace?"

That had come out of left field. "That's the word," she said, "though I haven't talked to anyone but Richard Vance in days." She met David's eyes.

"My offer's still good," he said. "You can come to Tel Aviv any time you want. Learn a little Hebrew . . . some old army tricks." The green eyes could be very suggestive.

"Thanks, David. I'll remember."

". . . I gotta go." He was looking at his watch.

"Okay." She reached for her purse.

"No." He got up first. "Say good-bye here. It's better if I face the plane alone." He was smiling.

"I love you, David. I really do." She stood up, hugged him tight. *"Hizaher."* Take care, she said in Hebrew.

He kissed her once. Hard. *"Shalom,* Romany."

She watched him through the door. Could see him for a long last moment through the bar's plate-glass window as he walked with his light duffel down the crowded concourse.

She sat down and reached for her purse. The mezuzah that he'd given her in Geneva was inside. Some impulse had made her bring it from the office. She took it out now and, over her watered drink, read the now familiar Prayer for the Martyr.

The Swiss sun blazed through the uncurtained window of the hospital room, shone hotly against her hair so that it seemed not hair at all, but flame. The hair that was still an enchantment even after all these years.

"I love the name Patrick," she spoke timidly, tilting her head downward. The light still bounded in and out of her hair, played hide-and-seek in the thick waves.

"Thank you for everything . . . ," she said, looking up at him for a moment, then out to the rolling green lawn that stretched itself into dense dark forest.

"Colleen . . ." He stopped on her name. . . . What words? Oh God, what words to say?

"When I was a wee lass"—she hadn't heard him speak—"Da used to tell me that to keep the apple, you must sometimes give up the pear."

He smiled. "And which did you keep?"

"I wanted both." Her blue eyes danced.

He smiled again.

"Taken was never my favorite tale, but Da knew it was the story I most needed to hear."

"Tale?"

"An Irish folktale. With a lesson to teach. Did you never read fairy stories when you were a wee lad, Michael?"

Michael. She still called him Michael.

"Yes, of course."

"And did you learn anything?"

He shook his head. "I doubt that very much."

She laughed. It reminded him of quick water bubbling in a fountain.

"Da always hoped I'd learn. It was another kind of religion for him. The Church taught good and evil. Folktales taught a man how to really live."

"Da was smart."

"You remember Da, Michael?"

He nodded.

She nodded back. "There was once a man who had a beautiful wife whom he loved very much," she'd begun reciting Da's tale. "But one day the fairies in the liss came and took the wife away. The man was very, very sad. But after a time he became very lonely and took a second wife."

She turned a smile toward him, then gazed once more at the scene outside the window.

"The man was very happy with his second wife, as happy as he'd been with the first. In five years, there were three pretty children."

She paused. "Then one day the husband received a message from his first wife. She told him that she was in the liss with the fairies, and that he must come for her soon, or she should remain with the fairies forever. The husband felt very sorry for his first wife, but what was he to do? He had a second wife, and children. If the first wife was returned home, then the second and the children must be turned out."

Colleen's eyes glistened. She seemed to enjoy retelling Da's story.

"So the husband went to the priest for an answer to his terrible problem. The good priest thought and thought. It was a difficult choice. But at last the priest came to a decision. He said that the husband must choose the second wife and his children, and leave the first wife to the fairies in the liss. Better one broken heart than four."

"And . . . ?"

She smiled prettily. "The husband did as the priest said."

"That's a sad story, Colleen."

"Yes, it is. Da told me this tale many times." She stood, walked close to him. He felt her fingers slide across his palm.

He squeezed her hand.

"You break my heart, Michael," she whispered.

"Colleen . . ." His throat ached.

She shook her head. "Don't. You misunderstand."

"But Colleen, I hurt you. What I did was wrong. Wrong for me. Wrong for you. I deceived you. I had no right . . ."

She loosened his grip on her hand, pressed her fingers over his lips. "Did you love me, Michael? Did you love me then?"

"Yes."

"Then you didn't deceive me."

"Colleen, I was a priest."

She shook her head. "Never would I have asked you for more than you offered. Priest or not. I wanted nothing more than what you freely gave. Not then, not now."

She moved against him, pressed a little against his chest.

"For me, only a short while has passed. For you, it has been six years. We are no longer in the same place." She pushed away, searched his eyes. "We never were in the same place, Michael."

She brushed her lips against his cheek. Kissing him, he thought, much like a sister would kiss a brother. "Much of what happened to me in Ireland is still not clear. Maybe it will never be. Perhaps I should think of it as a blessing from God. But of one thing I am certain. I would not take back one moment of the love we shared." She smiled. "One of those moments gave us Patrick."

She moved out of his arms. "You have given me so much, Michael. Taken care of me . . ."

"Colleen, that was the least I could do. It was my responsibility."

"Oh God, Michael, please don't make me a responsibility."

"That's not what I meant. . . ."

"I know." She walked toward the window. "It is beautiful here. But I miss Ireland." She turned. "You will not hate me for taking Patrick away?"

"Hate you? My God, Colleen, I could never hate you. Patrick belongs with you. He belongs in Ireland."

She smiled. "I'm so glad you feel that way. You know, I made a vow once never to leave Ireland. It's a bad thing for an Irishman to break a vow."

"You haven't broken yours, Colleen."

"Will you visit us sometimes?"

He nodded, felt his throat tightening. "Of course."

"I'm glad. Patrick would miss his Uncle Julian."

He looked at her smiling face. So beautiful, so innocent . . . He had no choice. There had already been too many lies.

"Colleen, please, there is something else I must tell you."

"To think that Niccolo is angry. Angry, I tell you, Basco."

The masseur slapped hard the flanks of flesh.

Cardinal DeLario winced. "If I didn't know better, I would believe Niccolo put lira into your pocket to torture me." He half turned his bulk to check on the masseur's expression. As always, the wizened old face said nothing. Vittorio smiled, eased back down.

"*Si*, the world thinks I should be sent to prison. To prison, Basco." He gave a long, suffering sigh.

Basco's hands had begun working the bridge of muscle across the shoulders.

"And Niccolo, angry with me. Angry, because the world is angry with him for not putting Cardinal Vittorio DeLario away in some prison. Such a cruel life this is, Basco."

A warm drizzle slid down his spine.

He lumbered up on his elbows. "Oh, he threatened, Basco. Not to a prison, but to a monastery, he threatened to send me. A monastery!" Another deep sigh. "Our Pope is an unfeeling man. And to think, all these years, I did not know him."

The masseur had begun to move the oil in wide circles.

"But still I must do penance, Basco. *Mea culpa.* For Gregory." He wiggled a bit on the table, making a show of striking his breast. "His Holiness says he will not be satisfied until all of the Vatican's art is returned." A quick snap of the head. "What? Am I God, Basco?" He slumped down again. "I cannot get back all of what was sold. Some of it, *sì.* But all? No, Basco, no."

Basco's fists thumped against the padded spine.

"And I must pay compensation to the buyers. From my own pocket, Basco. Oh, that is the part that cuts the deepest. Retrieve the art is one thing, but to have to pay the buyers for their loss. The bastards are thieves themselves!"

The masseur forced the Cardinal's torso back against the mat.

"I will have precious little left in the Swiss accounts after this, Basco. Nothing left for my old age." Vittorio shook his head into the sheets, moaning like a little boy. Then slowly, very slowly, the moan transformed itself into a soft chuckle.

"Maybe I should let Niccolo prosecute me, Basco. I should be truly famous then. I could sell my story to all the papers. Write a book." The laugh had begun to infect his entire body.

"I should be a real celebrity. Nobody likes a good scandal like the Romans. Not so good perhaps as getting Sister Daniella pregnant." Now the laugh had become a roar, and Vittorio shook like a beached whale on the masseur's table. ". . . A bestseller, like the Americans say, my story could have been a bestseller, Basco."

. .   .

"That was Andrew on the phone." Theodor walked into the living room where Marthe lay with a book on the flowered sofa. "He's going through government channels to get that portrait for you when they finish with the house. He said to give you his love."

"I've always liked Andrew. He's been such a good friend to both of us." Marthe laid down her book. "Romany called today," she said. "She's going to try to drive out this weekend."

"Great." Theodor joined her on the sofa, pulling her into his arms. "Romany's been working too hard. You too, with this sudden interest in the Etruscans." He picked up her discarded book.

"Don't tease, Theodor." She took it back. "It's fascinating. And I want to come out to the site . . . see this tomb you're so proud of."

"In another week, my love. I want you to rest a little longer." He gave her shoulder a squeeze. "Remember now, you promised."

"But I feel so good. And Bernardo takes good care of me. . . . I'm not going to die yet, Theodor."

"Marthe"—he looked at her, frowning—"I didn't say you were."

"I know, but you spoke to Dr. Weissman."

"Yes . . ."

"I am going to die, Theodor. I didn't mean that. My heart is weak. I just think that it won't be so soon, now. . . . It's just a feeling."

He held her tightly. "I trust your feelings, Marthe. I always have."

"I'm not afraid of dying. . . ."

He could tell there was more. He waited.

". . . I killed him, Theodor."

The words made no kind of sense. Stunned him. It took him a moment to answer.

"You killed him?"

"Yes."

"Killed who, Marthe?"

"The Baron . . . my father."

He sat perfectly still. Her head was against his chest, rising and falling with his breath.

"That's impossible, Marthe," he said softly. "The man died of a heart attack." He looked down on the golden hair falling away in waves. The child's part, sharp and straight, showing white and vulnerable.

"I didn't know what I'd do when I got to the villa." Marthe spoke again. "But when he stared at my hands . . . like his hands, he said . . . and then I put them in my sweater."

Her words stopped. Seemed pointless. He knew better.

"My pills were there . . . in one of the pockets. My heart medicine, Theodor. When he asked me for more wine . . ." She looked up at him. No other words were necessary.

"He would never have let you leave alive, Marthe." He thanked God for the words that sprang to his lips, the control that kept anything but love from showing. There was a deep sadness in her own eyes. But she smiled, satisfied apparently. Her head sank again against his chest.

She was so light a thing against him. His *Mona Lisa.* This sad and gentle creature with her perfect trust in the unknown. It was impossible, what she had done. And yet his Marthe had done it. Walked in and out of the lion's den unscathed, physically . . . spiritually. Pure. The simple agent of fate.

Stay with me, Marthe, a little while longer, he prayed.

CHAPTER 53

Romany knew now what the cats felt when they screamed at night. Really knew. Viscerally. Inside her skin.

To hell with the air conditioner, which she'd finally turned off. To hell with the natural breezes of the mildest night in August. Nothing helped, nothing *had* helped since . . . since she'd had her last fix. Since the game had ended with Julian.

He had wanted to tell her that time in Vance's car that it was over between them. That he'd only slept with her for the greater glory of God. And hell, she had slept with him for good old Uncle Sam. Who was she to call the kettle black?

Still naked from her bath, she lay crosswise on the bed beneath the open window, aware of every smell and touch. The fresh starchiness of the sheet along her spine, the vague pressure of moonlight.

She wanted to scream like the cats. She wanted to cry.

Dammit, Romany, you can't really want this thing to go on. There're no excuses now. Just naked want. Love, if you have to name it that. But finally, an affair with a priest . . .

The knocking spared her an answer. It was Julian. She knew it. Here and now. And all bets were off.

She grabbed her terry robe.

"Who is it?"

"It's Julian, Romany."

She opened the door.

"Hi." He looked tired and a little rumpled. "May I come in?"

She stepped back, aware now that she'd still been blocking the door. "I'm not dressed. . . ." The words came out midway between apology and challenge.

"I should have called first." He walked toward her sofa. "But I just got in from Switzerland."

"You want some wine?"

"Yes, please."

Alone in the kitchen, she fell apart. *What was he doing here?* She reached for a fresh bottle, forced herself to take her time with the corkscrew, get out the wineglasses. She brought the bottle with her back to the living room.

While he poured for them, she arranged herself on the sofa. Her legs were tucked under, securing the robe. Her back to the arm, she faced him.

"This is good." He had taken a sip. He seemed about to set the glass down, but changed his mind. He held it instead, his fingers tight on the stem.

"There are some things we need to talk about, Romany." He set the glass down now. "How do you think Monsignor Brisi died?"

What was this? "I never believed it was a heart attack."

"I was supposed to kill him. DeLario's idea of an initiation rite."

"Did you?"

"The plan was to kidnap Umberto." He didn't answer her question. "Richard and I were going to keep him under wraps till this forgery mess got settled. Make him talk. DeLario would think I'd killed him, gotten rid of the body."

"But Brisi is dead, Julian. What happened?"

"He was dead when I got to his apartment. He'd killed himself."

"You're kidding? A suicide?"

He shook his head. "Accident . . . autoerotic strangulation."

"My God," she said.

"I guess he just lost consciousness too fast. I tried to bring him back, but it was too late."

"That's terrible." She was imagining the scene. "But what about the Cardinal?"

"I called him. Told him to go have a look at Umberto. He just figured I'd done it."

"But why the lie if what happened could pass for an accident?"

"Too kinky for the Curia."

So Julian hadn't killed Brisi. It was a relief.

Then abruptly, "I have a son." His blue eyes fixed on her.

She nodded. "Was his mother one of those . . . distractions, Julian?"

"Colleen was more than that. But it still wasn't right." He said it calmly, then smiled. "Things are better now, though."

"Why are you here, Julian?" She had decided just to ask him.

"I love you, Romany."

He seemed about to reach for her, and she stood up. Suddenly self-protective, aware more than ever of her nakedness beneath the robe. "I love you too, Julian," she said, almost laughing. "It's crazy. I don't even know you, but I love you."

She could still feel his eyes. He was waiting for her to go on. So was she.

She made herself look at him. "I want you, Julian, but I'm sick to death of lies. And an affair with a priest . . ."

Surprisingly, he smiled again. Patted the cushion. "Please, Romany, sit down. Just hear me out for a minute."

She felt stupid now, standing. "Okay." She sat, let him take her hand.

"It started with Jeremy's accident," he said. "I talked him into going out on the boat that day . . . and he died. I went into the priesthood because of that. But there were problems from the beginning. And after Colleen, it got worse."

His fingers were cool against her palm, but she could sense his tension, as near to the surface as hers.

"About two and a half years ago, I went into a

monastery. I had a breakdown. I was there for two years trying to pull myself together. Then this thing came up with the forgeries. The Pope asked for my help."

"And that's when you came to Rome?"

"Right, to work in public relations. But that was just a front. The Arte per Pace appointment seemed the best way to get the goods on DeLario."

He didn't say anything for a moment. Like a sudden vacuum in the room.

"But then you came along, Romany," he began again. "And I started feeling guilty about that. You made me feel too good. And then, having to lie about everything. Later, when things started getting heavy . . . I told myself you were only sleeping with me because you were CIA."

"But Julian, it was the same for me."

He brought her hands to his mouth, kissed them. "I want you to understand, Romany. You made me see how bad a lie my priesthood really was. Loving you makes me feel closer to God than I ever did as a priest. Now I know my decision was the right one."

"What decision, Julian?"

"My time in the monastery . . . I asked for a full dispensation from my vows. I haven't been a priest for more than two years."

She was stunned. *Not a priest.* What then had been really going on all these weeks? Did this make what had happened between them mean any more . . . or less?

"You said you wanted me. Do you? I'm no prize . . . Romany?"

Her name, wrung out of him by her silence, was a more open confession than his *I love you* had been.

She saw he was watching her face. Something in his eyes made her think of the way her father looked at her mother. More than love . . . appreciation. Total acceptance.

"We can take it real slow if you want. We can—"

"Julian . . ." His name had finally cut her free. She

was moving, crawling into his arms. He felt so good and
solid.

Then her robe had opened and he was kissing her,
laughing against her skin.

"Well"—and now she was laughing too—"maybe
not so slow."

EPILOGUE

As soon as the "fasten seat belt" light went out, he
wanted to crawl into her lap and look out the window.

"Are we close to heaven, Mommy?"

"Of course, we are, my love."

"Think we'll see an angel?"

Colleen laughed, squeezed her son closer. "I have
seen an angel."

"You have? You saw an angel and didn't show me?"

"Every time I look at Patrick Shaunessy, I see an
angel."

Patrick frowned. "Oh, Mom. I mean a real angel."

"You're real enough for me." She gave him another
hug, and a kiss on the hair that threatened to be every
bit as bright as her own. She leaned back into her seat,
easing him off her lap. He pushed in closer to the window.

When Julian had told her that afternoon in her hospital room that he was no longer a priest, there was a
single wild instant when she imagined them together
again. Together again in Ireland, loving each other like
before. In that one clear moment she wanted him forever, wanted him to be her husband, to be Patrick's father.

But the moment had passed. Passed even without his
sweet and gentle words. His words that wanted to make
everything all right. For her. For their son. She imagined
that it would have been a simple thing to make him "do

his duty," "face up to his responsibilities." But she loved him too much for that. And Julian's love for her was never Michael's love.

Julian's love belonged to Romany Chase. Oh, he hadn't wanted to say anything. At least not at first. But the more he talked, the more he kept getting closer to Romany. And then she had simply asked.

". . . I think I see an angel. Over there. On that great big cloud."

"Let me see, quick, let me see." She snuggled in close, pressing her face against the window next to his. "You know, I think you are right, my love. Playing a harp he is." She ruffled the red hair, thinking how very much his eyes were just like Michael's.

Oh yes, darling Da, she thought, 'tis true. You sometimes give up the pear to keep the apple.

About the Authors

Fate. That's how New Orleans authors DIANNE EDOUARD and SANDRA WARE explain the convoluted pathways that somehow ended in their writing novels as a team.

Both convent-educated, the two women met for the first time at college. Dianne, despite her passion for theater, graduated more practically with a degree in political science, having every good intention of attending law school. Sandra, always vacillating between art and science, began at LSU in physics, but later earned her degree in fine arts.

A lawyer and an artist. But the real world has a way of diverting dreams. Sandra found herself working as a research analyst to support her law-student husband. Dianne wound up in education. Both yearned for something more creative.

Inspiration came when Dianne was given a historical romance by a friend, and later told Sandra how much fun the book had been. Avid readers all their lives, they had occasionally talked about writing books themselves. Suddenly they were serious.

Two historical romances later, they made the jump to mainstream fiction with the contemporary thriller *Mortal Sins. Sacred Lies* is their second novel of intrigue and betrayal.

You have stirred the waters together before, a psychic once told them, speaking of partnership in past lives. Happily at work on the third novel of their "Church trilogy," Dianne and Sandra believe it.

If you loved SACRED LIES, don't miss

Mortal Sins
by
Dianne Edouard
and Sandra Ware

"The authors' style is vivid, the characters well developed and the plot totally contemporary and full of intrigue, betrayal, murder, and illicit sex....
Engrossing, thoughtful and entertaining."
—*Baton Rouge Morning Advocate*

Covering the power and privilege that rule the nation's capital, *Washington Post* Reporter Alexandra Venée was lucky to have her uncle's help in gaining access to the rich and the mighty. Cardinal Phillip Caméliève's name could open many doors...and did. But when the controversial leader began his crusade to liberate the Church from the rule of Rome—even, some said, to become the first American Pope—Alex knew it was the story she was born to write. But she never expected to be compromised by decades-old family secrets or to fall in love with her uncle's secret enemy—a handsome young priest torn three ways: between his devotion to the Church, his respect for the man he was sworn to discredit, and his passion for the beautiful young reporter who could destroy them all.

28929-2 $4.99/5.99 in Canada